The Mésalliance

Rockliffe Series Book 2

Stella Riley

Copyright © 2015 Stella Riley
All rights reserved.
ISBN-13: 978-1516834228
ISBN-10: 1516834224

Contents

	Page
Prologue	1
One	6
Two	14
Three	21
Four	32
Five	42
Six	54
Seven	63
Eight	74
Nine	90
Ten	102
Eleven	115
Twelve	126
Thirteen	139
Fourteen	153
Fifteen	166
Sixteen	178

	Page
Seventeen	193
Eighteen	207
Nineteen	220
Twenty	235
Twenty One	246
Twenty Two	262
Twenty Three	277
Author's Note	298

PROLOGUE

Northumberland, 1767

Despite the slowness of a pace dictated by unfamiliar country and the uselessness of his right arm, the solitary rider looked appreciatively across the wild splendour of Redesdale, shimmering beneath a cloudless July haze, and congratulated himself on finally eluding the bailiff.

For five days the fellow had shadowed his every step, reciting names and rents, acreages and tithes, leases and debts – until escape had become not only desirable but imperative. Not that the bailiff could be blamed; for since nothing was ever likely to make his noble employer forsake the delights of London in favour of his most distant and least favourite estate, it was only sensible to seize on the person of his noble employer's son and heir. But it was a great pity, thought the heir ruefully, that Mr Forne talked so much.

Grimacing slightly, he shifted his arm inside its sling in an attempt to ease the nagging discomfort of his shoulder and found, as usual, that it didn't help a great deal. But the heat of Northumberland was a good deal easier to bear than the heat of London and another week or two should see him fit enough to re-join his regiment. All in all – now that he was finally alone – it was possible to detect a mild stirring of content.

When he first saw the girl she had been gathering wild flowers and her arms were full of them, a riot of blazing colour against the faded pink of her gown and rendering her even more plain than she undoubtedly was. Flat as a board, angular and thin, she was all eyes and mouth and wildly disordered nut-brown hair. Startled and poised for flight, she regarded him out of dark-fringed cisterns of aquamarine, so that he said quickly, 'Don't be frightened. I'm quite harmless – as, no doubt, you can see.'

She appeared to absorb the glories of his immaculate full-skirted grey coat, and the black sling that supported his arm before saying simply, 'Yes. Does it hurt?'

Laughter gleamed in his eyes but he answered truthfully, 'A little.' And then, realising that the low, sweet voice was miraculously free of the local dialect, 'Do you live here?'

Nodding, she let fall some of the flowers to push back her hair and point across the fell. 'Over there.'

He looked but saw nothing and turned back to the wide, considering eyes below him. 'You've dropped your flowers. Allow me to -- '

But at his first movement, she took fright again and backed off saying breathlessly, 'It doesn't matter. I have to go. Goodbye.' And ran, graceful as a deer, away across the turf.

It was then that he noticed that her feet were bare.

He would almost certainly have forgotten her had he not seen her again the next day, sitting motionless on the far side of a beck. There were no flowers this time but the thin arms were curved round something else. A hare? He had to look twice to be sure and then, smiling, bowed to her from the saddle. She surveyed him solemnly and replied with a tiny inclination of her head. The hare, so far as he could see, did not even twitch.

He decided to put Mr Forne's knowledge to the test.

'That'd be old Mr Kendrick's grand-daughter, my lord. Her mother died when she were not more than two or three months old, poor lass. Aye ... I mind it well on account of the young mistress having seemed perfectly hale afore they set off on that visit to London-town – and then to have Mr Tom come home in black not six weeks later? Well, fair shocked us all, it did – and not even a nice funeral to go to, the young lady having been buried with her own kin in the south. Terrible! Then, after that, Mr Tom took to the drink and were killed in a tavern brawl over to Hexham-way only three years later.'

Mr Forne paused, shaking his head regretfully and, taking advantage of the opportunity to get a word in, his lordship said idly, 'And the girl is what – about twelve years old?'

'Bless you, no, sir. The young lady's more like sixteen, I reckon – but with only her grandpa and a couple of servants, it's no wonder she's grown up half gypsy. Seems hardly right when they say she's got a whole set of Quality relations on her mother's side. But there ... old Mr Kendrick's health ain't what it was and happen he's glad of the company. Took it hard he did when Mr Tom died ...'

Having already heard more than enough, his lordship allowed his attention to wander. Mr Forne continued to worry the subject for a further twenty minutes. His lordship sighed gently and reflected that it served him right for asking. Plain little Mistress Kendrick might have the indefinable promise of something that had nothing to do with beauty – but since he himself would never see it fulfilled, it really wasn't worth this amount of suffering.

After four days of paperwork accompanied by the bailiff's tireless tongue, his lordship was driven to rise a good two hours earlier than he liked in order to beat a strategic retreat. And when he came upon the Kendrick child at the foot of a tree, one hand upraised and her voice low and coaxing, it somehow failed to surprise him at all.

Half amused, half interested, he reined in some way behind her and quietly dismounted to approach on foot ... and had just enough time to see a squirrel accept the offering in her extended fingers before a twig snapped beneath his foot and the tableau dissolved. In a flash of red, the squirrel scampered back into its shelter of leaves and the girl whipped round to face him.

Expecting either alarm or justifiable exasperation, he flung up his hand in a gesture of surrender and said, 'I beg your pardon. I'm an oaf and quite obviously trespassing. Have I undone hours of patient work?'

The unkempt head tilted consideringly and then the wide mouth curved into a disconcertingly splendid smile. 'No. He'll come back – though not today for I've nothing else to give him. And I don't think you are an oaf.'

'That's generous of you,' he replied with careful gravity. 'But if not that – then what?'

She studied the long, blue-black hair neatly tied at his nape, the dark heavy-lidded eyes and the elegant blue coat with its deep, braided cuffs.

Concentration drew a single line between her brows and then she said seriously, 'It's difficult because I never met anyone like you before. But I suppose that you are a gentleman ... and I think that perhaps you are kind.'

'Thank you,' he said, distinctly taken-aback.

'For what?' The guileless eyes were puzzled.

And because he could not think of an answer and did not, in any case, know why he was conducting a conversation at some ungodly hour of the morning with an untidy child of incredible simplicity, he laughed at the absurdity of it all and wondered what his friends would say if they could see him.

Still eyeing him as if he were some rare and exotic species, the girl smiled doubtfully and said, 'You don't live here.'

'No,' he agreed, amusement still threaded through his lazy tones. 'And you don't wear shoes.'

'They're over there.' She moved for the first time, an unconsciously fluid gesture of vague disinterest. Then, 'What is your name?'

He smiled and opened his mouth to reply. But instead of supplying his title or even his army rank, he heard himself announcing his given name – which no one that he could recall ever used at all.

'Tracy. I should like you, if you will, to call me Tracy.'

EIGHT YEARS LATER

IN 1775 . . .

ONE

'Rosalind,' announced the Marquis of Amberley, pensively, 'will be distraught. I believe she had counted on serving you up in a garland of strawberry leaves to the Bishop's niece. Anything below a Viscount, you know, is quite below the lady's touch – so Rosalind thought that you might go down rather well. Or was it the other way about?'

His companion lifted one sardonic brow.

'Or was it that, having been married over a year, your eye has begun to wander and Rosalind – wise lady that she is – perceives the need to provide you with a rival?'

The Marquis regarded him with an air of mild hilarity.

'For the favours of the Bishop's niece, of course?'

'Of course. Have you something else in mind?' Dark eyes widening, the lazy voice became the epitome of shocked innocence. 'Has *Rosalind* something else in mind?'

There was a long silence as quizzical grey-green eyes met mocking black ones. Then Amberley said, 'Ask her. When you explain that you are leaving, for example. She might even tell you.'

'Tell him what?' enquired a musical voice from behind them. 'And what is this talk of leaving?'

The quizzical expression changed to something very different as Lord Amberley turned to look across at his wife. Rising, he said, 'Rock thinks you must, by now, be feeling the need to add spice to our failing relationship. And he's ready to offer his services.'

'With the result,' added the Duke of Rockliffe smoothly, 'that Dominic is throwing me out. He will tell you it is a matter of protecting his honour – but it's my belief that he is naturally reluctant to see my superior rank and charm cut him out with the Bishop's daughter.'

'Niece,' corrected the Marquis helpfully.

'Niece,' repeated Rockliffe. And smiled.

The Marchioness of Amberley gave a little rippling laugh and walked unerringly past him to her husband's side.

'How fortunate it is,' she remarked, 'that the two of you have each other. But I often wonder which one is pulling the strings.'

Amberley smiled down into the beautiful blind eyes and dropped a kiss into her palm. 'We take it in turns. Should you be standing there?'

'I look tired and frail? Thank you.' But she smiled and allowed him to hand her to the sofa, settling gracefully into the light circle of his arm.

Looking at them, his Grace of Rockliffe experienced a more than usually sharp twinge of envy. Never less than beautiful, Rosalind glowed now with the anticipation of meeting her first baby in three months' time; and Dominic, when he looked at her, did so with an expression that the Duke was discovering himself reluctant to witness. They were complete in each other and he was happy for them; but their joy had a growing ability to make him restless ... and the knowledge was disconcerting.

As if she sensed his withdrawal, Rosalind said, 'Rock? Are you really leaving us?'

'I am afraid that I must. Nell's term ends on Friday and so there arises the arduous necessity of removing her from Bath and keeping her safely under my eye until I can place her with either Lucilla or Aunt Augusta.' He sighed. 'You should thank God fasting, Dominic, that Eloise did not see fit to provide you with a trio of sisters. They are inevitably either tedious or fatiguing. And, as for my reckless little brother, I expect almost daily to hear of his demise in some hair-raising enterprise or other. However. My immediate problem is not Nicholas but Nell ... and I have the lowering feeling that it's going to be a very trying summer.'

'The last time I saw your Aunt Augusta,' said the Marquis reflectively, 'she vowed that nothing would induce her to take responsibility for Nell again.'

'Quite.' Rockliffe leaned back in apparent gloom. 'That was a year ago after the dear child let a frog loose in church and bludgeoned the under-footman into taking her to a race meeting. I live in hopes that Augusta may have got over it by now. Indeed, I am *praying* for it.'

'But there's always Lucilla,' Rosalind reminded him. And then, with a choke of laughter, 'Or is there?'

The Duke's gaze transferred itself to Lord Amberley.

'Forget the Bishop's niece,' he advised.

'Yes,' came the regretful reply. 'I suppose I'd better.'

He got Rosalind's elbow in his ribs for that but, before he could complain, she was inviting his Grace to tell them about Lucilla.

'Yes. *Do* tell us about Lucilla,' agreed Amberley cordially. 'And, after that, you can tell us about Nicholas ... and Kitty. We already know about Nell and Aunt Augusta.'

Rosalind frowned. 'Stop being facetious.'

'I'm not.' He grinned. 'I always liked Kitty.'

'If, by that, you mean you preferred her to Lucilla,' said Rockliffe languidly, 'I entirely agree with you. But then, I prefer almost everyone to Lucilla. Even Nell – which is saying a good deal.'

'No, it isn't,' objected Rosalind. 'Nell may be wilful but no one could help liking her.'

'Lucilla can. However, it is true to say that Lucilla doesn't actually like anyone. She merely approves or disapproves – usually the latter. For those who, like yourself, are fortunate enough to be unacquainted with her, she can be summed up by one simple fact. To the best of my knowledge, no one has ever called her Lucy. True, Dominic?'

'Well, *I* never did – but then I never called her anything if I could avoid it,' came the cheerful reply. 'Has she also banned Nell from entering her portals?'

'Not at all. Her Christian Duty would forbid it. She merely contents herself with pointing out that she has the moral welfare of her own children to consider and Nell constitutes a threat to it ... being, like myself, Addicted to Frivolous Pastimes and – also like me – Vulgarly Prone to forming Violent Attachments to Unsuitable Persons.' The Duke paused and, entirely without haste, helped himself to an infinitesimal pinch of snuff. 'In short, Lucilla believes that it is high time I fulfilled my dynastic obligations by choosing a wife so that I will be in a position to look after Nell myself.'

'And will you?' asked Rosalind casually.

'Between now and Friday? I doubt, my dear, that even *I* possess sufficient address.'

'Then you'd better bring Nell to us, hadn't you?'

There was a brief silence as Amberley and Rockliffe exchanged collaborative glances. Then, 'No,' said the Marquis firmly. 'It isn't that I don't like Nell, but --'

'But you prefer Kitty,' interposed his wife calmly. 'We know.'

' – but she's about as tranquil as a tidal wave and she'd wear you out inside a day. She'd wear *me* out inside a day.'

'That's silly,' objected Rosalind. 'I'm perfectly fit. And I like Nell. She makes me laugh.'

'No,' repeated her husband. His tone was as pleasant as ever but utterly final. 'After September, we'll see … but until then I'll not have you disturbed. And if we allow Rock to get a word in, I think you'll find that he agrees with me.'

'Completely,' drawled his Grace. 'But I thank you for the thought. And the problem, mercifully, is only temporary for I intend to present her this winter. If, that is, I can find anyone courageous enough to chaperone her.'

'Is she old enough?' asked Amberley. 'I thought she would spend another year at school.'

'She'll be eighteen in October – and, even if she were not, I doubt the school would have her back. The only reason they've kept her as long as this is because I have the inestimable advantage of a coronet,' explained Rockliffe caustically. 'No. It's a great pity that Kitty chose to marry a diplomat and is therefore scarcely ever in England for she could have saved me a good deal of effort. As it is, I shall simply have to hope to find a gentleman with a sense of humour and a partiality for tidal waves.'

'And what,' asked Rosalind, 'if Nell doesn't like him?'

'Given that his nose has an eye on either side, I expect she will,' came the careless reply. 'She's very susceptible – and, to date, her requirements haven't been what you could call exacting.'

She was not deceived. 'And yours?'

'Ah.' He smiled suddenly. 'Now that is a very different matter. Or are we still talking about Nell?'

'You know we are. Though I've no objection at all to changing the subject,' offered Rosalind kindly.

Having a shrewd idea of what was coming next, Amberley said quickly, 'But Rock might.'

'In which case he will simply describe his newest snuff-box to me in minute and excruciating detail,' said Rosalind, smiling in his Grace's direction. 'Won't you?'

'How well you know me.' The dark eyes gleamed appreciatively. 'But there is no need. In respect of Nell, I hope to see her married to a man who can make her happy - but would naturally draw the line at her dancing-master or the like. As for myself … you wish to ask if I have ever been in love and the answer is yes. A dozen times, at least – though not, it has to be admitted, very recently.'

'But – '

'Rosalind.' Amberley's light voice stopped her. 'Rock is being extremely patient – but any more of this and you'll earn a snub.'

'I only wanted to --'

'We know.' The Duke came slowly to his feet and a disquieting smile lit his face. 'And the answer this time is that none of them were in the least special – or even significantly different from each other. But then, it would be singularly profitless if any of them had been. For a girl so totally unlike her fellows would scarcely make a satisfactory duchess, would she?'

The blind eyes were troubled.

'And is that what you're looking for? A duchess?'

'Of course,' replied his Grace urbanely. 'What else?'

*

Later that night after Rosalind had retired, the two gentlemen sat down to a hand of picquet and a companiable glass of port. For a time, the conversation roamed desultorily over a number of different topics and then the Duke said, 'Have you made any progress in your search for a doctor who can help Rosalind?'

'No. Or, at least, nothing I'd care to rely on.' Amberley laid his cards face down on the table and sat back, eyeing his friend bleakly. 'You have no idea, Rock, just how many quacks, charlatans and tricksters there are in the world. They all claim to know a cure that can't fail to work but no two of them agree on what that cure is. All they really have in common is a desire to prise as much money out of me as possible.'

'That is not particularly surprising, is it?' His Grace also tossed his cards down, clearly abandoning the game. 'They must know you can afford it – and also what such a cure would be worth to you. You're their golden goose, Dominic.'

'You think I don't know it? And the truth is that I'd give the man who could restore Rosalind's sight every penny I have. But I won't be fleeced. Not because of the money – that's hardly important. But I can't have her living with false hope. Or myself, either, come to that.'

'She still doesn't know what you've been doing, then?'

'No – and she's not going to. Not unless I can be sure there's a point to it.'

Rockliffe toyed idly with his wine-glass for a moment and then said, 'There must be *some* honest doctors, surely?'

'There are. They're the ones who listen very carefully and absorb the fact that – aside from a blow to the head when she was nine years old – there is no discernible cause for Rosalind's blindness; no illness, no infection, no gradual loss of vision. And that's when they shake their heads regretfully and say that it's unlikely anything can be done to reverse it.' The Marquis paused and then said, 'There's a professor in Germany who might know something ... but I can't do anything about that now. Not until well after the baby is born, anyway.'

Something in Amberley's eyes told Rockliffe that here was a new source of torment. He said quietly, 'What is it, Dominic?'

For a moment, he did not think he was going to receive a reply. Then, running a distracted hand through his hair and speaking as thought the words were being wrenched out of him, Amberley said, 'She never mentions it and never complains or appears to worry. But she's going to have a child she'll never see and I don't know how she'll bear it. Christ – I don't know how *I'll* bear it. But I can't tell her that because, hearing it, would only make it harder for her and she hates being pitied. But this isn't pity, Rock. It's my personal bloody nightmare. And you are the only one I can talk to about it.'

Seconds ticked by in silence. Then, finally, the Duke said simply, 'I wish I could do more than listen. But, for that, I am entirely at your disposal whenever you feel the need.'

'I know – and I'm grateful.'

'Now you're being insulting. There is no question of gratitude between us.'

'I know that, too.' The Marquis managed a faintly crooked smile and then changed the subject. 'We'll be staying here at Amberley through the autumn – possibly even until Christmas. Failing Lucilla and Aunt Augusta, have you any idea what you're going to do about Nell?'

Rockliffe shrugged. 'I'll take her down to the Priors for the summer. As for her debut, if no other solution presents itself, I'll ask Serena Delahaye. She and Charles will be presenting their eldest – so having Nell in tow shouldn't be too much of an inconvenience.'

Amberley agreed that Lady Delahaye would be an ideal choice … and the conversation moved on to other shared acquaintances. The Duke asked whether Rosalind's brother and his new bride had yet visited them and the Marquis replied that they were to come for a week or two the following month.

'And how *is* Philip?' asked Rockliffe. 'No longer anxious to put a bullet through you, I assume?'

Amberley grinned. 'No. And he did apologise for that. Repeatedly.'

'Ah. Well, no doubt that completely made up for any discomfort.'

'Not entirely, perhaps – but you can't expect me to bear a grudge against my brother-in-law, can you?'

'Dominic … I don't expect you to bear a grudge against *anyone*,' sighed Rockliffe. 'Speaking of which … what did Philip do with *his* tedious brother-in-law?'

'He bought him a commission.'

'In which unfortunate regiment?'

Amusement brimmed in the grey-green eyes. 'The 22nd Foot.'

'An *infantry* regiment? Dear me!' Rockliffe smiled slowly and then added meditatively, 'Of course the 22nd has a long and distinguished history.'

'It did have. Sadly, it now also has Robert Dacre. And a posting to the war in America.'

Their laughter woke the occupant of the large gilt cage in the corner who opened one beady eye and said clearly, 'Sod it.'

'I see that bird's manners haven't improved,' remarked Rockliffe lazily.

'No.' Amberley grinned and, rising, strolled across to the parrot. 'Sleep, Broody.'

'Bugger!' said Broody crossly. 'Buggrit, buggrit, *buggrit!*'

'Sleep,' repeated the Marquis firmly, throwing a cloth over the cage.

'Buggrit,' repeated Broody. And then, in slightly more muffled tones, '*Merde.*'

Rockliffe sat up. 'Did he – ?'

'Yes.'

'Who taught him ... or no. Of course. Your mother?'

'Unfortunately, yes,' sighed Amberley. 'Who else?'

And watched as the Duke dissolved into rare, helpless laughter.

TWO

All his very considerable charm having failed to placate Aunt Augusta, Rockliffe set foot in Bath still with no practical plan for the disposal of his sister. A lesser man might have allowed this, combined with the catalogue of misdemeanours that greeted him in Queen's Square, to dismay him; the Duke, having expected both, was able to accept them philosophically and with no diminution of his customary *sang-froid*. He merely smiled languidly upon the head-mistress, bestowed a hefty donation upon the school and removed his sister with impressive speed and efficiency.

It was not until the chaise set forth again that any real conversation passed between them. And then, casting her demure bonnet triumphantly into the corner, Lady Elinor Wynstanton said forcefully, 'Well! I never thought you'd come for me yourself.'

'I beg your pardon.' His Grace achieved a mocking bow. 'And who should I have sent? Who do you suppose there is left who would come?'

'Hercules? Christian? St George?' Dark eyes, very like his own encompassed him unabashed. 'But – truly, dearest Rock – if I wasn't perfectly awful, would I ever see you at all?'

'Dear me! Do I take it that I only have myself to blame? How very flattering. I had no notion that I was worth so much effort to anyone.'

Nell grinned. 'It's no effort, I assure you. But it *is* true that, for some reason I can't fathom, I like you best of all our horrid family.'

'Thank you. I am suitably honoured. Tell me ... did you indeed burn off one of the Honourable Cecily Garfield's lustrous tresses with the curling irons?'

'Well, yes. But I didn't do it on purpose. And it wasn't lustrous. It was thin and straggly and mud-coloured. You aren't upset about *that*, are you?'

His Grace shaded his eyes with one shapely white hand.

'Oh no,' he said valiantly. 'Not at all. Her brother Lewis and I were never on more than what you might describe as nodding terms.'

'That's what I thought,' responded Nell, cheerfully. 'Cecily says he thinks *all* we Wynstantons are essentially frivolous. I told her that, if he thinks that, he can't have met Lucilla.' She stopped and sat rather still. 'And, speaking of Lucilla ... where are we going?'

Withdrawing a Sèvres snuff-box from his pocket, the Duke inspected it with gentle admiration. 'Where do you think?'

'How should I know? I didn't think either Aunt Augusta or Lucilla would have me again – but Lucilla is a great one for duty and you're more than capable of talking her round if you set your mind to it.' She eyed him forebodingly. '*Have* you set your mind to it?'

'And if I have?'

'Then all I can say is that it would do you a lot of good to be obliged to live with her yourself for a week or two!'

'I seem to recall ... er ... living with her ... for rather longer than that.'

'Oh – when you were young. That doesn't count. And you avoid her like the plague now – you know you do! Then, when you can't, you smile that obnoxious smile you keep for people who bore you and start discussing snuff-boxes.' The mulish look dissolved into a ripple of laughter. 'Yes, you abominable creature – *just* that smile. Only I won't be diverted, so you might as well confess. Where are we going?'

His Grace sighed. 'London.'

Nell's eyes widened. 'Rock! Do you mean it?'

'With reluctance, yes.' He surveyed her with lurking amusement. 'But before you become carried away with the prospect of unbridled gaiety, you had best accept the fact that I don't intend you to make your debut just yet.'

With a gesture that set her dusky curls dancing, Nell shrugged this aside.

'But I'll be able to get some clothes made – and you can have no idea how I long for some pretty hats instead of these dreadful things.' She gave the inoffensive straw bonnet a savage poke. 'I want you to take me to the most exclusive milliners and modistes in London.'

'And just what,' enquired her brother gently, 'makes you suppose that I'm likely to know which they are?'

'Well, if half what's said of you is true, you must do.'

'Indeed?'

'Yes. Several of the girls at school have older sisters and it seems you're generally held to be a charming but dangerous flirt,' responded Nell placidly and not without a note of satisfaction. 'And Cecily Garfield is convinced you're a rake.'

'Lewis says?' asked the Duke, not noticeably perturbed.

'Yes.' She examined him with an air of faintly nonplussed curiosity. 'It seems very odd to think of you having dozens of – of ... well, you know.'

'It must do,' he agreed, a vagrant smile tugging at the corners of his mouth. 'But, much though it pains me to disillusion you, honesty compels me to admit that the word 'dozens' is a slight exaggeration.'

Nell sat back, plainly considering this.

'Does that mean you *don't* know a good milliner?'

And, finally admitting defeat, his Grace gave way to unwilling laughter. 'No, it doesn't. Not at all.'

*

With an equanimity that surprised him, Rockliffe not only escorted his sister through the discreet portals of Madame Tissot's expensive hat-shop in Bond Street but also to the equally chic Maison Phanie, London's leading modiste. And when, with the exception of a scarlet silk ball gown more suited to a courtesan, it became apparent that Nell did not intend to weary him with demands for totally unsuitable attire, he even found a certain pleasure in the exercise.

It could not be denied that she certainly paid for dressing and he was not particularly surprised at the degree of attention she provoked when he took her driving a few days later. The buttercup dimity carriage dress showed off both her colouring and diminutive figure to advantage and the natural straw with its cream roses and trailing yellow ribbons sat saucily on her curly head. She looked, decided the Duke resignedly, a pretty enough picture to turn any young man's head.

It was, of course, too much to expect that Nell should be oblivious to the admiration surrounding her but her reaction to it was less predictable.

'I suppose,' she said thoughtfully, one evening as they were finishing dinner, 'that, when you present me, it will be with the purpose of finding me a husband.'

'That is certainly the usual result,' agreed his Grace, warily. 'Are you against marriage?'

'No. I just wanted to warn you not to set your heart on a brilliant match for me.'

Sudden laughter lit his eyes.

'My dear, I wouldn't presume! If you make one that is merely respectable, I think that's as much as we can reasonably hope for. Don't you?'

'No – I'm serious, Rock. Lucilla is a Viscountess and Kitty's husband is related to all the best families and promises to be a Great Man himself one day. And, since I can't help knowing I'm not exactly ugly, you could expect to do just as well for me.'

'Possibly. But let us not overlook the fact that Lucilla was ... well-behaved ... and Kitty was generally held to be irresistible. However, we can rule out Viscounts and the cream of the diplomatic service, if you prefer.' He rose languidly. 'Is that all you wished to say on the subject?'

'No, it isn't,' said Nell flatly. 'What I wished to say was that I won't be shuffled off into marriage just to suit everybody's convenience.'

'Meaning mine?'

'Well – yes.' She picked up her fork and began to draw patterns on the table-cloth. 'I realise that having to look after me disrupts your life and makes things ... difficult for you. But you can't really expect me to marry the first man who offers just to – to --'

'But I don't expect it,' said Rockliffe gently.

'Oh. You don't?' She looked up, searching his face. Apart from a trace of unaccustomed grimness, it looked much as usual. 'Really?'

He said, 'No. In fact, I would much prefer you *not* to do so. And neither do I intend to steer you into the arms of some noble, wealthy or influential gentleman for no better reason than that he is what the world calls an eligible *parti*. In fact, unless you choose someone completely unsuitable, you'll probably find that I won't interfere with the matter at all.'

Nell's mouth quivered. 'Oh, *Rock*!'

'I know,' he smiled. 'Quite the nicest of our horrid family.'

He was rewarded with a husky laugh. Then she said slowly, 'Actually you know – I think *you* are the one who should be married. I don't suppose you've anyone in mind?'

'No. Why? Did you wish to make a suggestion?'

'No-o. Not that exactly. But I *do* think you ought to set about it fairly soon. You must be nearly forty, after all.'

'Thirty-six. But I hope you won't tell anyone.'

'You're being flippant again. Don't. Just admit that it's high time you had a wife. Someone pretty and charming and intelligent.'

'You don't think,' murmured Rockliffe, 'that perhaps I'd better just settle for one of those qualities? After all, when one is approaching forty – with an habitually flippant manner and rakish propensities – one shouldn't expect too much.'

Nell grinned, decided that it was entirely unnecessary to pander to his vanity and said kindly, 'Oh I don't know. But it's probably just as well that you're a Duke.'

*

At some time between retiring to his bed that night and rising from it next morning, his Grace lost at least an hour of sleep in a manner quite foreign to him. It had never before occurred to him that his sister might conceivably feel herself to be a nuisance but it did so now and aroused a faint feeling of guilt. When their mother had died, Nell had been thirteen and he thirty-two – a large enough margin, it would seem, to enable him to care for her without indulging in pass-the-parcel with Lucilla. Something, he decided wryly, as sleep overcame him, would have to be done.

The letter lay amongst others beside his plate on the breakfast table and, by the time Nell put in an appearance, he had not only read it but also drawn certain noble if vaguely depressing conclusions. He therefore watched her heap her plate with scrambled egg and kidneys and then said lightly, 'Who – or what – is Dianthea? It sounds like a stomach disorder.'

Nell deposited her plate on the table to stretch out a hand for the sheet of pink note-paper he was scrutinising dispassionately at arm's length.

'Di and Thea. Diana and Althea – the Franklin twins. If that is for me, may I have it please?'

'With pleasure.' He passed it to her and dusted his fingers with his napkin. 'I have never liked Eau de Chypre ... but one should always be wary of making rash judgements. They may be charming girls.'

'They are.' Nell looked up, flushed and expectant. 'They say their mama has written to you.'

'She has.' He picked up a second, closely-written sheet. 'She asks – at some length, you will notice – that I permit you to make one of the small house party she holds each summer.'

'I know. Di promised me she would. What do you think?'

'That my lady's literary style leaves a lot to be desired.'

Nell impaled a kidney on her fork with unnecessary force.

'Yes, yes – but can I go? Di and Thea are my very dearest friends. They look almost exactly alike, you know.'

Rockliffe's expression remained sceptical.

'What perfume do they use?'

'Oh Rock – stop being trivial!'

'I am never trivial. I am trying to establish a very vital point. Not for anything will I commit myself to spending two weeks in a house reeking of chypre.' He paused and met her open-mouthed stare with lifted brows. 'If you intend to eat that shrivelled piece of offal, I wish you would do so.'

Nell laid her fork carefully back on her plate.

'*You* won't spend two weeks ...?'

'Ah. Did I neglect to mention that I am invited as well?'

'Yes. You did.'

'My lamentable memory. Well?'

Nell swallowed. 'Di uses gillyflower essence and Thea likes lavender. Can – do you mean that I can go?'

'I mean that I am prepared to take you.' He fixed her with a deceptively lazy stare. 'Omitting your dearest friends for a moment, what — briefly! — do you know of their family?'

She grinned and ticked off points, reciting.

'One: that their parents are Sir Roland and Lady Franklin. Two: that they have two brothers — Andrew, the elder and Tom, the younger. Three: that the household includes her ladyship's brother and an indigent female cousin of uncertain age. Four: that the party will include other neighbouring families and — '

'Enough.' Shuddering slightly, his Grace set down his cup and rose from the table. 'I see it all. Informal balls, *al fresco* luncheons, playing cards for sixpenny points and endless, insipid conversation. A nightmare.'

'Don't be so superior. And there's nothing insipid about Diana. She's ravishingly beautiful and you'll probably fall hopelessly in love with her.'

Rockliffe looked down with saturnine mockery and gave her ample time to regret this remark. Then he said sweetly, 'Well, of course. I thought that was why I've been asked.'

THREE

It was, reflected Rockliffe as he moved easily with the motion of the chaise, not entirely unpleasant to play the martyr for once. He was deriving a certain amount of quiet amusement from Nell's evident appreciation of his sacrifice; and, if he had to pay for this with a fortnight's tedium ... well, it was rapidly beginning to seem that this might be preferable to the storm-clouds that were about to burst over his life in London.

Although never destined for operatic renown, Carlotta Felucci was possessed of an outstanding degree of beauty and, at the start of their liaison, her occasional bouts of Neapolitan temperament had been amusing. But that had been seven months ago and, now that the novelty had worn off, the only amusing thing about Carlotta was her undoubted talent between the sheets. Unfortunately, this - unique as it was - no longer outweighed her jealousy, her rapaciousness or her tantrums. Had he been less lethargic of late, he would probably have terminated their relationship several weeks ago. As it was, he had simply allowed his visits to become less frequent and thus been put in the inconceivable position of having Carlotta accost him on the street while Nell was on his arm. The mere thought of it still made him shudder and he had wasted no time in sending the lady a sapphire bracelet and her *congé*. But he was glad he would be out of range for a time. He abhorred scenes and Carlotta liked throwing things.

He watched Nell gazing eagerly through the window. Really, apart from escaping unattended to buy some ribbons she'd previously forgotten she needed, she had given no trouble and had even, if one were honest, contrived to brighten an otherwise increasingly empty existence. Perhaps Rosalind and the rest of them were right, he thought unenthusiastically. Perhaps it *was* time he married. The trouble was that, although it was not difficult to call to mind some half-dozen young ladies who might suit Nell as a sister-in-law and chaperone, it was impossible to think of even one with whom he felt in the least inclined to share the rest of his life.

Sighing faintly, he attempted to approach the problem logically. When you were thirty-six years old and head of your house, it was probably time to forget the foolish notion that had kept you single and remember what you owed to your name. For if, in all this time, you had not found what you sought, it was probably because it did not exist. Therefore, it would be only sensible to choose between the merits of the various alternatives available; and if Louisa Rushton's laugh was irritating or Mistress Grantham's tongue only capable of endorsing the opinions of others, they were at least born of your world and generally held by it to be beautiful. They and three or four others, all of whom you regarded with equal indifference.

The question was a depressing one and he finally followed his usual habit of postponing a decision. There was, after all, nothing to be done in the immediate future and therefore the matter could wait until next month or next season or next year. The only pity was that it could not wait forever.

'Rock?' Nell's voice cut across his thoughts. 'Rock – we're here. Look!'

He looked. Brick-built in the compact Dutch style of the previous century, the Franklin home held an appearance of unostentatious comfort that immediately banished at least one of his Grace's private fears. At the foot of the shallow flight of steps which led to the door, a liveried footman waited to let down the carriage steps while, in front of the door itself, the butler stood ready to welcome them. And then the picture changed as a pair of identically-gowned, identical blondes emerged quickly through the portal to skim, hand-in-hand, down to the chaise.

'Gemini!' murmured the Duke softly. 'It's the stomach disorder.'

Fortunately, Nell did not hear him. Almost before the steps were down she tumbled laughing and talking into the twins' arms, leaving Rockliffe to follow with a languor bordering on reluctance.

'Oh Di – Thea - it's so good to see you. It's been *weeks* and I've so much to tell you! Truly, I thought we'd never get here – for nothing will persuade Rock to be jolted about in the chaise and – oh, this *is* Rock, by the way!' She turned, drawing him forward and continued buoyantly, 'It'll be days before you can tell them apart, of course. However ... this is Diana and this is Althea – my very dearest friends.'

His Grace smiled lazily into two pairs of wide, blue eyes and made his bow.

'How pleasant to discover that not quite all of Nell's descriptions spring from her imagination.'

Rising from her curtsy, Diana Franklin dimpled and said archly, 'Oh? And how is that, sir?'

'Merely,' came the adroit reply, 'that it will indeed be a challenge to tell you apart.'

Diana, annoyingly aware that the expected compliment had somehow eluded her, took immediate steps to mend matters. Laying one hand lightly on the Duke's sleeve and catching Nell's fingers affectionately in the other, she drew them towards the house, talking all the time.

'But how foolish to be standing here! Do please come in – Mama will be wondering what can be keeping us. Thea – run in and tell them that we'll be with them directly. Nell, dearest – where did you get that hat? It's quite ravishing and I'm green with envy for I've nothing one half so elegant.' And then, with a slanting smile up at the Duke, 'I suppose it was shockingly expensive?'

'Shockingly,' agreed Rockliffe. 'As were the other dozen. Also, the gowns and cloaks, ribbons, laces and feathers. Not to mention the sh --'

'I think,' Nell choked, 'that Di has the general idea.'

'Shoes,' he finished mildly. 'What did you think I was going to say?'

The salon into which Diana ushered them appeared to be full of people and, surprisingly, the Duke recognised one of them as a friend. However, he acknowledged this unexpected pleasure with no more than a lifted brow and gave his attention to his hostess. Lady Franklin, cool of manner and still bearing traces of the golden beauty she had bequeathed to her daughters, chided Diana for causing their guests to make so informal an entry – but was plainly not displeased by it. Ambitious, thought his Grace as he bowed and uttered suave commonplaces; ambitious and calculating. Sir Roland, by contrast, was the complete epitome of a country squire, being rotund, determinedly affable and somehow a trifle out of place. Rockliffe was not without sympathy. He felt somewhat out of place himself.

'And this,' announced Lady Franklin complacently, 'is my first-born, Andrew.'

Andrew, tall, loose-limbed and sulky, achieved a graceless bow and then found himself cornered by Nell's smile.

'How do you do? I'm so pleased to meet you at last for I understand you've a pure-bred Arab mare that you've trained to do all manner of clever things. It is true she can dance the minuet?'

The sulkiness evaporated into a reluctant grin.

'You've been talking to Althea,' he said. And then, 'Yes, it's true enough.'

'You'll have to put Rozalea through her paces for Lady Elinor,' instructed his mother, pleasantly, 'I'm sure that she would find it most entertaining. But you will have to wait a little longer before putting your heads together – as I've no doubt you are both eager to do – until she has met your uncle and Lord Harry.'

Nell blinked, somewhat taken aback by this assumption. His Grace, who understood it perfectly, hid a smile and moved on to exchange courtesies with the over-dressed, foppish gentleman, complete with rouge and patches, who it appeared was her ladyship's brother. Then, without waiting for an introduction, he turned to that gentlemen's nearest companion and said, 'Well, Harry ... and how was Paris?'

Lord Harry Caversham grinned cheerfully.

'So-so. It all depends on whether one likes rushing from one engagement to the next like a demented ferret and braving the crush at Versailles to get the merest glimpse of Marie Antoinette. For myself, the best I can say of it is that the company was fair and the wine better.' He turned to Nell and bowed with mischievous formality over her hand. 'Hello, Nell. Have you forgiven me yet for removing you from the Overbury masquerade last Christmas?'

Her colour deepened but she said with creditable aplomb, 'I'd forgotten all about it. But, since you ask, I still don't see what business it is of yours *what* parties I attend.'

'None at all, of course,' he replied promptly. 'It's just that it's usual to have an invitation.'

At least two people laughed. One of them was Diana.

'*Pique, repique* and *capot*,' drawled Rockliffe. 'And you, Nell, would do well to hold your peace before Lady Franklin realises just how undesirable is the company her daughters are keeping.'

This time the laughter was more general and, into it, her ladyship remarked that, reprehensible though it undoubtedly was, such pranks were merely the result of girlish high-spirits and did no lasting harm.

The Duke, who knew they could do a great deal of harm, said dryly, 'That is a matter of opinion. But I should have realised that we could rely on your ladyship giving poor Nell the benefit of the doubt.'

Effectively silenced, her ladyship smiled uncertainly and Harry Caversham found himself obliged to study the richly patterned carpet beneath his feet. The stage was therefore left free for Diana who surged gaily forward with the observation that, excepting only her little brother, Tom – who had had gone off goodness only knew where as usual and would doubtless reappear in his own good time – his Grace and Nell had now met everyone.

'They haven't, Di,' came Althea's timid whisper. 'There's still Addie. She's over there.'

Diana drew an impatient breath and glanced irritably at her twin. Then, gesturing carelessly to the slight, motionless figure waiting in the shadows, she said, 'Oh yes. Of course. How could I possibly have forgotten that? Your Grace, Nell dearest ... allow me to present Mama's companion – our cousin, Adeline.'

The indigent female of uncertain age, deduced Rockliffe; plain, middle-aged and down-trodden. And, largely because he was beginning to feel that Mistress Diana needed a lesson in manners, he smiled pleasantly into the gloom and executed the same bow he would have accorded a countess.

It was only then, as he straightened, that the figure moved unhurriedly out into the light and, in a cool, husky voice that stopped his breath, said, 'We've met. But your Grace wouldn't remember that, I daresay.'

Meeting long-lashed aquamarine eyes filled with detached irony and set beneath narrow, winged brows, his first thought was that she was changed beyond recognition ... and his second, that he would have known her anywhere. The eyes and the voice were the same; it was only the suggestion of frosted bitterness that was new. And if the dark brown hair was now neatly — if unbecomingly — arranged, the wide mouth was instantly familiar; too generous for so fine-boned a face and too vulnerable for the new poise she had apparently acquired.

He became aware that the air was alive with curiosity and said carefully, 'Then you malign me, Mistress Kendrick. And flatter me, too — for it must be all of seven years ago and you were little more than a child, as I recall.'

'Eight,' she corrected. 'And I was sixteen.'

Frowning, Lady Franklin said coldly, 'I was not aware of this, Adeline. Why did you not mention it?'

'Because I didn't think it important,' came the laconic reply. And then, with the merest hint of malicious amusement, 'But if I was mistaken, I beg your pardon.'

The discreetly-veiled jibe found its mark.

'That will do, Miss! I find your secrecy incomprehensible and your timing lacking in taste. For the rest, do not over-rate yourself.'

The blue-green eyes opened guilelessly wide.

'I don't, Aunt. That's what I said.'

Her extraordinary self-possession contrasted sharply with Rockliffe's own sense of shock and he resented it. She must, of course, have known that he was coming — but that was neither a satisfactory explanation nor a balm; and it was already more than enough that she should manage to set him at a disadvantage like this without the addition of her unnecessarily ingenuous remarks.

He smiled at her with what at least two persons present recognised as dangerous benevolence and said gently, 'Perhaps you did indeed have just cause for doubting my ability to place you. After all, I'm compelled to acknowledge that I find you considerably changed.' He paused and conducted a leisurely head to foot appraisal. 'You appear, for example, to have discovered the benefits of wearing shoes – an achievement on which I can only congratulate you.'

And watched her pallor vanish beneath a tide of colour as the silence dissolved into a light ripple of laughter.

*

Later, while his valet helped him into the claret velvet coat he had selected to wear for dinner, he wondered why having to explain that he'd once spent an enforced furlough in Northumberland should cause the past to close up like a telescope when there was so little to recall. He had stayed in Redesdale for roughly two weeks and had met Adeline Kendrick no more than half a dozen times – always seemingly by accident. That was all there was to it; a handful of random, almost other-worldly conversations. And now the simple truth was that the feelings he'd been unable to understand eight years ago and rarely thought of since, were no more than dust. His memories had been of a wild creature ... unspoilt, sensitive and fragile. All that remained was a cold-eyed woman with a barbed tongue – a fact that left him feeling faintly cheated until he remembered that painful flush, swiftly followed by flight. And then resentment gave way, unwillingly, to shame; and anger with himself for being betrayed into a lack of manners.

There was a tap at the door, succeeded almost immediately by a rustling vision in rose taffeta. Rockliffe sighed, dismissed his valet and gave his attention to the serious business of choosing a snuff-box from the impressive array in front of him.

'Rock?' said Nell, realising the need to distract him from this occupation. 'You don't mind if I come in?'

'The question seems a trifle redundant, don't you think?' he murmured, frowning with a dissatisfied air at the enamelled box in his hand. 'How provoking. I ordered this coat in the belief that it was a perfect match for this box, but it isn't. In fact, it clashes quite horribly. I must be slipping.'

'Take the silver one, then,' she said carelessly.

He eyed her incredulously. 'With gold lacing? I hardly think so.'

'Then change your coat. I don't know why you have to go through this performance all the time. You don't even *take* snuff – you just pretend.'

A flicker of humour appeared.

'You must allow me my little affectations, Nell. No one might notice me otherwise.'

Nell narrowly avoided pointing out that no one – particularly females - could *help* noticing him. Even she, his sister, had to admit that he was exceptionally good-looking. His height, his bearing … the long, thickly-powdered hair, tonight tied back with black ribands … his dark, often mocking, eyes and the tailored planes of his face … well, she wouldn't have been surprised to learn that London was littered with girls who dreamed of him at night. But it would never, never do to say so; and *those* girls, of course, had no idea of how utterly infuriating he could be when he chose.

Attempting to fulfil her purpose in seeking him out in private, she said, 'I didn't come to talk about snuff-boxes. I came to see what you think of - of the family.'

'My dear, I can scarcely admit to having thought of them at all.' Rockliffe laid the box down and picked up another. 'I suppose it will have to be this one … but I've never been entirely happy with the tracery. A little too florid, don't you think?'

'No.' She sat down on a rosewood chair, her expression determined. 'I expect you were glad to find Ha – Lord Harry here, weren't you?'

'More so than you, I imagine.'

'Yes. Well … I think he's insufferably rude and interfering but I don't intend to let him annoy me,' she said handsomely. And then, 'Fancy you knowing Di's cousin – and recognising her, too. They're all agog with curiosity.'

'Are they?' His eyes rose briefly to encompass her. 'Then I fear they are doomed to disappointment.'

'Oh – not about you. It's her – the cousin. Di can't understand why she didn't say that she knew you when she first heard we were coming.' She paused, irritatingly aware that his attention had wandered again. 'I must say, it does seem very odd. But then, according to Di, she *is* odd. I gather, when she first came to live here, Lady Franklin had to resort to quite strong measures to stop her wandering off for hours on end and then coming back with her hair like a hayrick and her shoes in her hand.'

Rockliffe continued to scrutinise the gold box through his quizzing-glass.

'Strong measures?'

'Mm. Thea was about to tell me only Di began talking of something else so the chance was lost.' Another pause and then, casually, 'Which reminds me ... what do you think of Diana?'

'Diana?' He lowered the glass and examined the box at arm's length. 'Ah yes. A pretty child and possessed of a certain ... vivacity. I believe I must disagree with you, my dear. It is most definitely florid.'

Not without difficulty, Nell ignored this diversion and said flatly, 'Pretty? Is that the best you can do?'

'Isn't it enough?' He turned to her, a gleam of lazy amusement lurking in his eyes. 'You appear put out, Nell.'

'That's not surprising, is it?' She came abruptly to her feet. 'You're being as provoking as you know how.'

'Oh no,' he said softly. 'Not quite. Not at all, in fact.'

For perhaps half a minute, she fixed him with a fulminating stare before sweeping wordlessly to the door and shutting it behind her with a distinct snap.

The Duke smiled. He dropped the snuff-box into his pocket, picked up a fine, cambric handkerchief and prepared, without haste, to follow in her wake.

*

Dinner was a gargantuan affair and lasted far longer than Rockliffe thought necessary. He had been placed, as expected, beside Mistress Diana – whose conversation consisted almost solely of attempts to lure him into juvenile flirtation. He declined to play but with such adroit ambiguity that she could not be sure of it and, in between parries, he surveyed the company with an increasingly jaundiced eye.

Nell had been awarded the heir of the house but was receiving scant attention from him. The Duke smiled to himself. Young Mr Franklin had plainly been given his instructions and either found them unpalatable or was simply digging his heels in. But he need not worry. No matter how pretty Lady Franklin's planning, Nell could – and almost certainly would – wreck it in a moment.

Opposite himself and Diana, Harry Caversham engaged Althea in stilted and rather desperate conversation. Really, taken all in all, her ladyship deserved credit for trying. His Grace caught Harry's eye and lifted one sardonic brow. Harry choked over his wine.

At the other end of the table, Sir Roland expounded on field drainage to a palpably bored Mr Horton. The younger son still remained notable only by his absence and Cousin Adeline was not present either – which was, of course, hardly to be wondered at. Rockliffe's boredom deepened.

It was not until the ladies retired that he was finally free to speak to Harry Caversham and then that gentleman's first words were exactly what he'd expected.

'Ye gods! I hope I don't have to go through that too often.'

Black eyes encompassed him with sympathetic mockery.

'Hard work, Harry?'

'Exhausting. And it makes me somewhat resentful of the fact that, when Dick asked me up here, he didn't say anything about ducal competition.'

'No? But you might have had my place for the asking, you know.'

'Aha!' grinned Harry. 'Got other interests, have you? And how *is* the fair Carlotta?'

'Open to offers, I imagine. Interested?'

'Not me. I like a quiet life.'

'Do you? Well, I'm sure it's here for the asking.'

'I said quiet – not silent!' His lordship reached for the decanter and delivered a casual riposte. 'It must be that little witch of a cousin, then. I suspected as much. No beauty, of course ... but she has a damnably seductive mouth – as I'm sure you've noticed.'

The Duke sighed. 'Don't be vulgar, Harry.'

'Me? Never!' came the laughing response. And then, 'Tell me all about Northumberland.'

'You would be disappointed. I have the most shocking memory.'

'You mean you've a very convenient one.'

'The privilege of age, my dear,' replied Rockliffe blandly, continuing to smile. 'And now, if it's not too much trouble, do you think I might have the port?'

FOUR

A stray shaft of sunlight creeping mischievously under his lids pricked the Duke into wakefulness and caused him to look sleepily across at the chink in the curtains that was its source. The silence and the absence of his valet told him all he needed to know about the hour and, with a muffled groan, he turned over and resolutely closed his eyes. From outside came the plaintive call of a peacock; then again and again. Rockliffe settled deeper into his pillow and thought longingly of sleep ... but it was too late. He was wide awake and filled, moreover, with a strange restlessness that could only have one result. He flung back the covers and got up.

Despite his air of fashionable laziness, there was little Perkins habitually did for him that he could not do for himself when the need arose and an hour later he was dressed, shaved – albeit in cold water – and about to pull on his coat when a tap at the door heralded his valet.

'Your Grace!' said Perkins, plainly aghast. 'Why did you not ring?'

'I suppose because I am not entirely helpless,' came the calm response. And then, not without amusement, 'Why so appalled, John? I'm fairly sure I fastened my breeches.'

Perkins smothered a grin and said severely, 'But your Grace's hair!'

'Ah. Yes.' Despite a thorough brushing, traces of last night's powder still clung to it and he had drawn the line at washing it in cold water. 'That is a problem, I grant you.'

The valet reached for the powder box, shook out the cape that would protect his noble employer's clothes and said, 'If your Grace will sit down – it is but the work of a moment. And you must understand, sir, that a man has his reputation to consider.'

'That is indisputably true,' sighed Rockliffe. He had wanted to simply walk outside and take a breath of early morning air - but Perkins' reputation was not the only one that would be at stake should he be unlucky enough to meet anyone. He sat.

His hair once more adequately powdered and neatly tied, he left his room behind him, descended the stairs and found his way into the garden.

It was cool yet and quiet and the dew was still heavy on the grass as he strolled unhurriedly through the arbour to the tiny pavilion he had glimpsed from his window. The early sun dappled its shallow steps and endowed the roses that curtained its trellised walls with flamboyant splendour. Rockliffe disposed himself negligently on the stone bench within and watched idly as a small bird winged its way into some hidden retreat behind the crimson blossoms. Somewhere close at hand, the gurgling sound of water was punctuated by the spasmodic croaking of frogs and all around was the tranquil whisper of leaves. And then, without warning, Adeline was there before him.

He realised that he had known she would come. For a long moment he merely looked at her and then, rising slowly, said the only thing that seemed relevant.

'You have changed.'

The narrow brows arched.

'So you said. So have you.' She surveyed his powdered head with an air of mild enquiry. 'You are going grey, perhaps?'

'Alas,' came the equally gentle retort, 'you will never know.'

'You think I care?' Her smile was brittle.

'Enough, at least, to comment on it.'

She shrugged. 'It makes you look older.'

'I *am* older. And so, my dear, are you. Old enough, shall we say, to know better than make clever little remarks in the bosom of your family.'

'We can't always choose our weapons,' she said, in a tone which suggested that he should have known it. 'But I'll admit I hadn't expected you to be embarrassed.'

'Is that an apology?'

'For what?' The aquamarine gaze remained perfectly impervious. 'It is not my fault that you allowed yourself to be betrayed into a lack of finesse.'

Since this was a fairly accurate echo of his own thoughts, it was unreasonable to be annoyed. His drawl became a fraction more pronounced and he said, 'Is it not? It could not, I suppose, be that the improvement in your appearance is exactly proportional to the deterioration in your manners?'

This time her smile was faintly compassionate.

'But the one is a direct result of the other. Isn't it obvious?'

'Ah. I see. Neatly brushed hair and a fresh gown are but outward signs of a relentless campaign of persecution that has naturally left you with no alternative but to fight back with your tongue. How foolish of me not to have guessed it.'

She stared consideringly at him and, for a brief instant, he had the feeling she was about to say something that might matter. Then it was gone as she moved away from him to touch one swaying bloom with long, delicate fingers.

'One does what one can,' she said. 'I haven't any excuses.'

'Have you not?'

'No. Or none that you would understand.'

His hostility evaporated again.

'You used not to be so insular. Try me.'

Silence stretched between them for a long moment before the dark brown head moved in a slight gesture of denial.

'To what end? These people you call my family are of your world ... and they are like you in attitude, if nothing else.'

'You make a lot of assumptions.'

'I don't think so. There is a basic truth you haven't yet accepted. It is that, in the only senses that matter, you and I are total strangers.'

He found himself noticing that the skin which used to be lightly golden was now pale, like that of one kept too much indoors; and then the air became curiously charged. Though no longer angular, she was still very slender and the wide, passionate mouth, coupled with the fluid grace of her every movement, combined to fulfil and exceed the promise he had seen in her eight years ago. What she had now in abundance was a rare quality he could only describe as allure; rare and dangerously heightened by the remoteness in her eyes.

His next thought was no more than a logical progression but the unexpectedness of it produced an instinctive recoil that caused him to say abruptly, 'How long have you been here?'

'Since grandfather died. It was the spring following your visit. There was no money and they said I was too young to live alone so they wrote to my aunt.'

Seven years, then. He received a hazy impression of what it might have meant to be uprooted and brought to a place where everything she did was suddenly and bewilderingly wrong. He said slowly, 'It was hard, no doubt. But it can't have been entirely without its advantages.'

'Of course not,' came the ironic reply. 'It saved me from a barbaric existence in equally barbaric Redesdale and I am now a different person. Let the bells ring out.'

Once again her bitterness grated. Very well; so life had not dealt particularly kindly with her – but neither had she apparently made any effort to come to terms with it. She was twenty-four years old, unpleasantly barbed and no more than passably good-looking ... and she made him want to both kiss and shake her. It wasn't a sensation he relished.

Brusquely, he said, 'Why so ungrateful? What is it you lack? A husband?' And saw, with some relief, the first crack in her composure.

It was short-lived, however. For an instant the blue-green eyes reflected something he could not put a name to and then she had recovered herself well enough to say coldly, 'That is a singularly stupid suggestion. I am far too useful to my aunt to be married. And who is there, do you think, who would have me? The curate? The schoolmaster? You?' She paused and favoured him with a mocking smile. 'Or no. I forgot. They want you for Diana.'

'Your powers of observation astound me,' he said caustically. 'Do pray continue.'

'What else is there to say?' She turned away, as if losing interest. And then, 'Of course, she's extraordinarily pretty.'

'As you say,' he agreed, watching her carefully in an attempt to decide if there really had been a trace of wistfulness in her voice. 'But beauty, as they say, is only skin deep.'

'Or in the eye of the beholder? Yes, I know. Does that complete the platitudes for today?'

'Not quite.' He wondered why he was persevering when she was so obviously determined to be difficult. 'It's also in the possession of an extensive wardrobe.'

The slim shoulders stiffened. 'If that remark was designed to console me, I'd like to point out that it was neither necessary nor accurate. I have two gowns that once belonged to Thea and I look attractive in neither of them. Diana, on the other hand, could be wrapped in a sack and still be beautiful. Couldn't she?'

'Perhaps. It's not a question to which I've given any thought.'

'No?' She turned her head and there was a wholly astonishing gleam of laughter in her eyes. 'Poor Diana ... and she so very set on becoming a duchess.'

'That,' complained Rockliffe gently, 'is not very flattering.'

'True. But I daresay you're accustomed to it and I doubt it causes you to lose any sleep. Everything has to be paid for, you know.'

'Is that what you think?'

'Of course. Don't you?' Her smile gathered a note of provocative indulgence. 'But I'll give you some free advice, if you like – and that is to point out that a wise man would take Thea instead. She's just as pretty and much less trouble.'

And, before he could open his mouth to reply, she was gone.

It was not until much later that he realised that their prior acquaintance had not featured in the conversation at all.

*

Leaving the garden behind her, Adeline made her way unhurriedly towards the stables. She considered – without probing the question too deeply – that she'd handled the interview tolerably well. He had not, after all, said a tithe of the things he might have said; and, more importantly, neither had she. Under the circumstances, it was probably the best one could hope for and ought to render any future meetings between them substantially less hazardous than they might otherwise have been.

The stable-yard was deserted. Adeline crossed it like a wraith and entered the dim, straw-strewn abode of the horses.

'You're late,' said Tom Franklin, tersely. 'He's fidgety.'

'Yes.' She pulled an apple from her pocket and held it out to the great black stallion who ate it as though conferring a favour on her and then nuzzled her ear. 'He needs some proper exercise.'

'He won't get it. Ever since he nearly broke Andrew's neck they've all been terrified of him. There's only you and me who'd dare ride him – and we're not let,' came the bitter reply. 'They'll sell him. You see if they don't.'

'I know.'

Tom directed a speculative fourteen-year-old stare at her.

'But then again, maybe they mightn't. Not if Father were to see how docile he is with you.'

Adeline rested her head against the velvety neck for a moment and then, lifting it again to meet his eyes, said, 'It wouldn't make any difference. Who takes any notice of me? And I don't even ride.'

'No. Thanks to Mother, you don't. Probably because she knows that, if you did, you'd soon take the shine out of Di and Thea.' He brooded on this for a few seconds and then added, with a grin, 'Not that it'd be difficult. Thea's mouse-scared and Di's cow-handed.'

Adeline said nothing. This was a mistake because it allowed Tom's thoughts to progress to what he plainly thought was a vital point.

'You know, I do think you might have told *me* that you knew this precious Duke of theirs.'

She gave the slight shrug that was so peculiarly her own.

'I didn't tell anyone.'

'No. I see that, of course. But you could've told me,' he insisted. 'I'm not a blabbermouth.'

'I know you're not.' She paused briefly and then said, 'I'm sorry, Tom. When I met him years ago his father was still alive and he hadn't inherited the title so I didn't …' She hesitated again and then said flatly, 'It wasn't until Diana referred to his sister as Lady Elinor Wynstanton that I guessed – and, even then, I couldn't be absolutely sure until I saw him, so it seemed best not to say anything. Who told you, anyway?'

'Who didn't? Diana's pretty well miffed over it – though I can't see why. It doesn't make any difference to her, does it?'

'None at all.'

'That's what I told her. But, if you ask me, she's dotty. She must be – or she wouldn't be dead set on marrying some old man she's never met and scarcely even *seen* before ... let alone telling everybody she's going to be a duchess before Christmas.'

Adeline looked at him consideringly and then chose to answer the least contentious part of his speech. 'Is that what she's doing?'

'Yes. Well, Thea says she told Cecily Garfield – and that's the same as putting it in the *Morning Chronicle*.' He searched his pockets and finally produced some fluff-encrusted titbit that the black horse consumed with relish. 'They're coming today – Cecily and her brother. I can't think why Mother always asks them because nobody really likes either of them.'

Adeline's brows rose and she smiled suddenly. It was a singularly beautiful smile that only Tom was ever privileged to see.

'Dear Tom,' she said. 'Have you ever seen a plainer girl than Cecily Garfield?'

'No,' came the prompt reply. Then, with a grin, 'Oh, I see. No competition.'

'Quite.'

Tom restored his attention to the stallion.

'So what's he like then, this Duke?'

Adeline allowed her gaze to wander back to the horse while a dozen confused thoughts jostled in her head. Foremost amongst them was the fact that, when she had told Rockliffe that he had changed it had been a lie in all but one particular. Eight years ago, he had left his hair in its natural state and it had been thick and glossy and so black it sometimes glinted blue in the sun. She remembered wanting, more than anything, to touch it – but, of course, she never had. And now he chose to wear it powdered ... and, stupidly, illogically, she had felt disappointed.

Realising that Tom was still waiting for an answer, she said distantly, 'He's clever. He's probably also the only one amongst your mother's motley crew of guests who could not only appreciate The Trojan but also ride him.'

*

She spent the rest of the day – as, indeed, she spent every day – at the beck and call of her aunt. The only difference was that today the weekly task of untangling and sorting the embroidery silks was performed to an accompanying lecture. Adeline answered with economy when required and allowed the tide to flow over her. It was the first art she had learned in this house and still the most useful.

In the early days, bewildered by change, she had tried to go on as before, escaping from time to time in order to walk barefoot on the grass again and imagine herself far, far away from the cage that now possessed her. At first, her aunt had done no more than rap her knuckles and scold; then she took to confining her in her chamber for a day or two. And finally, when all else failed and Adeline – aided by a young and impressionable stable-hand – was caught trying to run away, her ladyship had ordered a beating.

A part of the older Adeline was able to appreciate the inevitability of what had happened – but not the manner of it. For, Sir Roland having felt unequal to the task, it had been her Uncle Richard who had taken his riding-crop to her back ... and who had, quite unmistakeably, enjoyed it. She had spat in his face, ruining his *maquillage* and it had felt like a victory. But not for long. Not once she found herself shut in the dark, cut off from every sight and sound of freedom.

That week had taught her to conform and marked the beginning of her metamorphosis. For having begun by simply erecting invisible defensive barriers about herself, she had swiftly progressed to the discovery that it was also possible to fight back in small ways – if one was subtle. And the result was a now flawless technique for combining apparent docility with an under-current of clever, hard to combat acidity. Self-protection and self-destruction inextricably woven into one; and she knew it.

These days, her aunt was rarely unkind and Adeline had come to recognise that what she had at first taken for personal dislike was in reality more a mixture of indifference and resentment. Indifference because a dowerless niece was useless in the marriage market and resentment at having the child of her dead sister – a sister, moreover, whom she had plainly despised – foisted upon her. The truth, of course, was that Lady Franklin was an ambitious, unfeeling woman whose small store of affection was centred on Andrew and Diana – and, to a lesser extent, on young Tom. Althea, existing perpetually in the shadows, was the recipient only of duty and a good deal of impatience; and Sir Roland, except in his role as provider, appeared barely to impinge on his wife's consciousness at all.

All things considered, it was an ill-assorted and not especially happy household. Andrew - loathing the role of delicate, dutiful son in which his mother had cast him but too spineless to repudiate it - grew daily more irritable and sulky. Diana, self-absorbed and brought up to place too high a value on her beauty, was capable of creating utter havoc when crossed. And Richard Horton ... sly, sadistic and too idle to fend for himself, all-too-frequently used his brother-in-law's house as a refuge from his creditors.

Nor, as Adeline had intimated to Tom, were Lady Franklin's regular guests much improvement. Lewis Garfield had money but few graces and his sister, the face and voice of a shrew. The Osborne's were intent on finding an *entrée* to polite society and Sir Oswald Pickering and his daughter Lizzie cared for little save the hunting field. About Lord Harry Caversham, Adeline as yet knew very little. He was apparently her Uncle Richard's newest friend; but, aside from that rather damning fact, he seemed a pleasant enough young man – and also appeared to be on very easy terms with Tracy Wynstanton and his sister.

Tracy Wynstanton? A mistake, that. He was the Duke of Rockliffe now – and it was something she would do well to remember. But she could not help wondering how he was going to enjoy two weeks of the kind of company to be found in this house. Very little, she suspected sardonically. It was almost a pity that she would not, from her position in the background, be privileged to see it. Almost a pity; almost – but not quite. For she was very well aware that if she didn't want her hard-won resignation to be damaged by useless recollections of that other, unrestricted life, then the background was the only place to be.

It worked for two days and would have gone on doing so had not his Grace of Rockliffe – sophisticated, clever and possessed of a streak of pure devilment – decided to set the cat amongst the pigeons.

FIVE

After forty-eight hours of being openly pursued by Diana, fawned on by Jane Osborne and bored to death by Sir Oswald, Rockliffe came to the conclusion that, if he was to survive the fortnight, something would have to be done to preserve his sanity.

It was not, he felt, that he was particularly hard to please. On the contrary. All he required was a modicum of amusing conversation, a little riding perhaps and the occasional, stimulating hand of cards. But the conversation was banal in the extreme; the rides – when taken between neck-or-nothing Lizzie Pickering and a coquettish chit with probably the worst hands in four counties – were a nightmare; and the one game of macao he'd played with Richard Horton had resulted in a mood of dire foreboding and a few very private words with Harry Caversham.

'May I ask if Mr Horton is a particularly close friend of yours, Harry?'

Mobile brows soared over startled blue eyes.

'Dick? Lord, no! I haven't known the fellow above a month or two. Met him at Devane's – or that discreet little place off Bruton Street, I think. One of them, anyway. Why do you ask?'

The Duke gazed thoughtfully down at his snuff-box and ignored the question.

'I see. Do you often play in such … do you know, I really think I am forced to call them hells?'

'And so they are,' came the cordial reply. Then, 'No. I don't frequent them and I don't intend to start. Devil take it, Rock – you know I'm not a gamester!'

'I do, of course. But neither, my dear, did I suppose you a flat.'

His lordship's habitual levity evaporated.

'What are you saying precisely?'

His Grace sighed.

'I am saying – and I do beg that you will not feel impelled to repeat it just yet – that your dear friend Richard fuzzes the cards.' He paused and met Harry's astounded gaze with one of indulgent mockery. 'I really am surprised you hadn't noticed.'

It was not a good start; nor, with Nell growing daily more flirtatious, was there any promise of improvement. Rockliffe found that he did not care to see his sister acquiring the same unfortunate manners and techniques employed by Mistress Diana and he was determined, at the end of this horrendous visit, to break the association. But in the meantime he was most definitely not enjoying himself. Indeed, the only light relief so far had been provided by young Tom Franklin, who seemed to have more sense than the rest of his family put together and who had introduced him to the best bit of horse-flesh he'd seen in months. But the prospect of persuading Tom's father to part with The Trojan was little consolation for having to spend another twelve days in purgatory; and it was thus that, when he experienced the first stirrings of his own particular devil, Rockliffe did nothing to silence them.

He began by encouraging Diana to go her length – a process which, in a well brought-up girl, would have required a lot more than merely alternating his very real indifference with a few ambiguous and faintly indulgent compliments. And then, without any prior planning whatsoever and purely because he couldn't resist the opportunity, he went on to hoist Diana's mama with her own petard.

It occurred on the third evening that the extended company sat down to dine and Lady Franklin bemoaned, at some length, the unexpected departure of Sir Oswald's wife.

'I fear that I must crave your indulgence, your Grace,' she began, 'for the fact that we shall be but fifteen to dinner. Poor Mary has been called to the side of her eldest girl who is about to give Frensham an heir. And though of course one understands completely, it is rather regrettable. Quite vexing, in fact – since it means we are a lady short. I can only hope, however, that you will appreciate the suddenness of it all and not judge us too harshly. You may believe that I am not so poor a hostess that I could not have remedied the situation had I been granted a modicum of warning. Sadly, I was not.'

If Rockliffe found the tenor of this speech in any way remarkable, he did not show it but merely said smoothly, 'It is very unfortunate, of course. But these small inconveniences, so they say, are sent by the Almighty to try us.'

'Quite possibly.' Her ladyship's tone suggested that, if this were the case, the Almighty would presently receive her views on the subject. 'Certainly it seems that there is nothing to be done. I only wish there were for, of all things, I particularly dislike an unequal party.'

'Indeed,' murmured his Grace. A glint that any of his close friends would have instantly recognised appeared in his eyes. 'Indeed. But I would have thought that a very obvious remedy is already at hand.'

'Oh? And what, pray, is that?'

'Why... simply to have your niece join the party,' came the bland reply. 'It seems, if you will permit me to say so, perfectly proper that she should do so – and, under the circumstances, it would appear to be the only possible solution.'

He smiled lazily and Lady Franklin stared at him, for once in her life bereft of speech. Finally, she said stiffly, 'Adeline has no taste for society.'

'My sister has no taste for rational conversation,' responded Rockliffe lightly. 'It is a fault, however, that I hope to correct.'

Her gaze sharpened and, for the second time, she sought a suitably quelling reply. Then, failing to find it, she said lamely, 'You may be right. I will consider the matter. It is quite impossible, of course, to change the arrangements for this evening.'

'Perish the thought! But – with no less than five young ladies to be adequately chaperoned – you will also, I feel sure, consider both the propriety and the advantages of enlisting Mistress Kendrick's assistance with the task,' he observed sweetly. 'Beginning, perhaps, tomorrow?'

He had, of course, no way of knowing exactly what he'd started.

*

'I won't have it!' cried Diana petulantly. 'She's no notion at all how to behave in polite company and I don't want her there spoiling my chances and making her nasty little remarks. It's the most stupid idea I ever heard!'

'Possibly it is,' snapped her mother. 'But if you have been attending to what I've just said, you'll realise that the Duke has left me little choice.'

'I don't see why. It's none of his business.'

'No. And I'd as soon he was given no excuse to make it so,' came the exasperated reply. 'Have you no conception of what we are dealing with here? Rockliffe has a reputation as a wit and a raconteur. They say he misses nothing. He also has the power to make or break aspiring debutantes – or else turn them into a laughing-stock. Is that what you want?'

'He wouldn't. He *couldn't*! Not to me.'

'I'm glad you're so sure. Unfortunately, we can't afford the risk.'

There was a long silence and then, for the first time, Diana's bright gaze moved to rest squarely on her cousin's still figure.

'All right,' she said, with suppressed violence. 'All right. But if you ever get in my way ... if you ever dare to presume on the fact that you've met the Duke before, I'll make sure you regret it. Is that understood?'

'Perfectly,' replied Adeline dryly. 'With you, what else would I expect?'

Furious cornflower eyes met aquamarine ones filled with detached irony and, for a brief instant, the years rolled back to the day when, catching Diana taking a heavy stick to her pony, Adeline had dealt her own summary justice. Then it was gone and Diana was saying savagely, 'Mind your manners – and try to remember that you're only here out of charity.'

'How could I ever forget?'

'That will do,' said Lady Franklin. 'Adeline – I have told you many times that I consider your tone unsuitably sarcastic. Diana – I am grieved to say that your conduct this morning has been somewhat unbecoming and that you must strive to master your temper. Now ... I wish to hear no more such squabbling. Adeline will dine with us this evening – and you need not concern yourself in any way, Diana. She knows exactly what is required of her, do you not, Adeline?'

'Oh yes. To the letter.'

'Good. Then the matter is settled ... except, that is, for the question of what you will wear.'

'Well, it's no use asking *me* to give her anything because I shan't!' stated Diana. 'Let her come as she is. I don't care!'

'Then you should or we shall all be made ridiculous,' replied her mother tartly, her eyes turning back to encompass her niece. 'Althea gave you her straw-coloured taffeta, I believe. That will have to do for this evening since you have presumably already altered it to fit. For the future, we must contrive something. Let me think. Yes. You may have my mulberry brocade. It is a trifle behind the mode but that is of little consequence. There is also a grey-striped polonaise which I have never cared for and not worn above twice. And you, Diana, will produce that green tiffany which turned out to be not at all the shade we thought and which does not become you in the least. And that,' she concluded, 'should be more than sufficient. Diana, you may re-join our guests – and remember to be careful what you say in front of Cecily Garfield. Adeline – come with me. You may collect the gowns now so that Thérèse can help you to alter them.'

And, so saying, she sailed majestically to the door.

*

A brief but distinct hush fell across the drawing-room when Adeline entered it that evening, but she had expected that. What she had not expected, but perhaps should have done, was that it would be broken by Cecily Garfield saying clearly, 'My goodness, Di – I thought you were joking. How perfectly frightful!'

Diana, under the admonitory gaze of her mother and therefore unable to reply as she would have liked, contented herself with a speaking glance and immediately resumed her conversation with Nell. Althea, miserably embarrassed but too nervous to move, welcomed her cousin as best she could with a tense smile; and Harry Caversham's blue eyes travelled from face to face with growing surprise and distaste. No one else seemed inclined to acknowledge Adeline's presence at all.

No one, that is, except for his Grace of Rockliffe who strolled urbanely into the centre of the stage, made Mistress Kendrick the bow for which he was famous and said with a smile, 'Good evening. I am delighted your aunt was able to persuade you to join us for I'd begun to fear my ill-timed pleasantry of the other day had driven you to avoid me. Dare I hope that I'm forgiven and that we may now talk over old times?'

It sounded, on the face of it, like a graceful apology. Adeline, seeing the glint in his eyes, knew better.

'Devil,' she thought. And said, 'Certainly – if that is your wish. But there is nothing to forgive. The truth, so far as I'm aware, never hurt anyone.'

'Your mistake, then.' He was at her side now and able to lower his voice. 'The truth can be the sharpest weapon of all ... if, of course, one wields it correctly.'

'As you do, you mean?' she asked. And then, suddenly unable to stop herself, *'Why did you do it?'*

His smile gathered an element of provocation and he went on as if she hadn't spoken.

'Take, for example, that gown you are wearing. It is, I presume, one of those donated to you by Mistress Althea?'

'Yes. Can't you see that I've no desire to be part of this farce?'

'Just so. Now ... candour would compel me to own that you were quite right. It doesn't suit you in the least and, in fact, looks quite appalling.'

'Thank you.'

'You see? A perfect example of truth. But if I add a grain or two more ... that the gown itself is an over-trimmed disaster and that your cousin – being a blonde – probably looked worse in it than you do ... well, then the matter becomes rather different.' Calmly, he flicked open his snuff-box and appeared to help himself from it. 'I, myself,' he finished reflectively, 'would dress you in pale blue silk and silver tissue.'

'You won't be granted the opportunity,' she returned coldly. 'I suppose you realise the trouble you're causing? Yes – of course you do. It's the only reason I'm here, isn't it? To dilute the monotony for you by forcing everybody to associate with the poor relation who ought, by rights, to be kept decently out of sight.'

'In part, yes. But you are overlooking something.'

'Which is?'

'That you possess the inestimable advantage of being neither dull nor vulgar.'

The air in her lungs evaporated and she silently damned him for it.

'Dear me,' she said satirically. 'You can't conceive how flattered I am.'

Rockliffe laughed, causing Lord Harry's brows to fly up and Diana to clench unladylike fists. Nearer to hand and equally unladylike, Adeline experienced a strong desire to box his ears.

'Don't be,' he said. 'Everything is relative, after all. And try not to look so murderous. Your aunt is about to descend. I wonder who ... ah. Yes. The so-cultivated and charming Mr Garfield. You have my sympathy. He will not, I think, amuse you.'

'Well of course he won't,' came the waspish, low-voiced reply. 'He's so aware of his own consequence, he's unlikely even to *speak* to me.'

'No, no. For where I lead – how can he fail to follow?' murmured the Duke wickedly. And turned, smiling, to face Lady Franklin.

He was, as it transpired, quite right. For though Lewis Garfield was by no means pleased to be seated by a Poor Relation, he knew that it would not do for him to appear higher in the instep than Rockliffe himself. He therefore condescended to address Mistress Kendrick from time to time – and, in doing so, discovered her an admirable audience. It was not, obviously, as satisfactory as being placed beside the Lady Elinor; but Adeline's contemplative gaze and monosyllabic answers were a vast improvement on Lizzie Pickering's forceful tones and wandering attention. And she had, he suddenly noticed, a remarkably beautiful neck.

A poor head for claret combined with the very natural assumption that dowerless females past their first blush cannot afford to be choosy, caused him to lay his hand on her thigh. Instantly, the blue-green eyes impaled him with something not quite a smile.

'Remove it,' said Adeline quietly. 'Now.'

He did so and felt his colour rise.

The cutting-edge vanished as swiftly as it had come and she said, 'Merely a misapprehension, I am sure ... and one soon forgotten, sir.

Now ... you were delighting me with a description of your Venetian mirrors, were you not?'

And Mr Garfield found himself following her lead with a good deal less than his usual assurance whilst wondering just how positively he had been repudiated. Or indeed, by the time several glasses of port had joined the claret, whether he had been repudiated at all.

Back in the drawing-room, meanwhile, talk amongst the younger ladies had naturally gravitated to the forthcoming ball – now only five days distant and thus looming large on their horizons. Cecily informed the interested that she intended to dazzle the company with her mother's rubies; Nell admitted a desperate desire to have her hair powdered for the occasion – something Rockliffe had previously always vetoed; and Diana regaled them all with a detailed description of her ball-gown – newly arrived from the mantua-makers and made of ivory satin, looped up over a petticoat of gold lace.

'Such stuff!' Having prowled restlessly about the room throughout most of this, Lizzie Pickering came eventually to roost beside Adeline. 'All this fuss over a dozen or so couples standing up in the blue salon after the furniture's been pushed back. I've no patience with it – and nor have you, I shouldn't think.'

Adeline looked at her consideringly. So far as she could recall, it was the first time they had ever spoken. She said, 'Perhaps not. But it's rather different for me, isn't it?'

'Yes – but that's not what I meant,' came the blunt reply. 'Andrew told me you once mended his spaniel's leg after it got caught in snare. Is that true?'

'Yes.'

'Well *they* wouldn't dirty their hands. All Diana and Cecily care for is which of them will catch a husband first. Di thinks she'll win because she's beautiful – and Cecy things *she* will because she's an heiress. It's a race. Have you ever heard anything so silly?' She grinned suddenly. 'It's a wonder they're not laying bets on it.'

'And if they were?'

'I'd put my money on Diana. I never met anyone so selfish or stubborn in my life. Not that I think she'll get Rockliffe. From what I've seen of him, he's got more sense. Did you know he's offered to buy that temperamental black from Sir Roland? It's almost enough to persuade me to make a push for him myself.'

'Rockliffe,' asked Adeline, with a hint of humour, 'or The Trojan?'

'Both.' Without warning, Lizzie arose again and stood frowning at the small portrait adorning the wall above Adeline's head. 'I've a blue satin gown that my sister Amelia had made for me but I prefer my old green taffeta because it's more comfortable and doesn't make me look quite so freckled. I thought ... it occurred to me that the blue might look well on you and that perhaps you'd care to borrow it. For the ball, I mean.' She turned as if to go and then added abruptly, 'It's new or I wouldn't suggest it – so I hope you're not offended.' And stalked back across the room to sit beside Althea.

Adeline was still trying to account for this surprising behaviour when the door opened to admit the gentlemen ... and her Uncle Richard was before her.

'You're either a fool,' he said softly, 'or a great deal brighter than I had previously supposed. I wonder which it is?'

'Why the latter, of course,' she replied carelessly. 'Which means, I suppose, that it's you who are the fool, Uncle.'

His eyes narrowed and, for a second, she felt a prickle of something akin to fear. Then she took hold of herself and it was gone. Ridiculous to fear this absurdly-dressed mammet with his powder and patches and scent. One might as well be frightened of a tailor's dummy.

Richard Horton toyed delicately with an elegant *brisé* fan. He said, 'You are insolent, Adeline. It is a mistake ... and a pity. But for that, I believe I might be able to help you.'

'Really? In what way?'

'To advance yourself. What else?' A sneering smile touched his mouth. 'It is beginning to seem possible that you have certain marketable qualities. You look surprised. I do not blame you. I am surprised myself. But it becomes apparent that Mr Garfield sees something in you – and so, unless I am mistaken, does our fastidious friend, Rockliffe.' He paused and the cat-like smile grew. 'I don't admire their taste. But I might – if it suited me – be prepared to assist you to exploit it.'

'If it profited you, you mean,' said Adeline dryly. 'The duns must be after you with a vengeance. I thought you were committed to advancing Diana?'

'I am. But one may hedge one's bets, you know. And Diana is set on Rockliffe – while you, whether by accident or design, have made an excellent start with the extremely rich Mr Garfield.'

'Have I?'

'Oh yes. That little scene at dinner ... really, I am forced to congratulate you.' He opened the fan and plied it gently. 'Of course, marriage – though not entirely impossible – is probably a little too much to hope for. But an *affaire* can pay just as well and, if carefully managed, last almost as long.'

'Can it really? You fascinate me.'

'Yes. I thought I would. But you will need me, Adeline – or you won't clear the first ditch.'

'I see. And you, in return, would need to be sure of my continuing gratitude?'

'Precisely. I am delighted to find you so direct.'

'Are you?' She rose, her honey-sweet tone contrasting oddly with the hardness in her eyes. 'That's nice. It enables me to tell you two things. Firstly – that I'd sooner beg from door to door than accept anything from you; and secondly, that – if and when I decide to prostitute myself – I'll do it without the aid of a pander.'

She gathered up the despised straw-coloured skirts and moved to step past him but was detained by his fingers closing painfully around her wrist.

'That was unnecessarily stupid,' he hissed. 'And you'll regret it. Believe me.'

'Tell you what, Dick,' said Harry Caversham, blithely splintering the tension, 'you ought to be doing your duty by Lizzie Pickering or the Garfield chit – not monopolising your own niece. It's a scurvy trick, so it is!'

By degrees, the nasty glint faded from Mr Horton's eyes and his hand left Adeline's arm. Then, flourishing his fan, he said airily, 'You wish me to remove myself? Consider it done. I feel sure Lady Elinor will commiserate with me.' And he trod mincingly across the carpet to Nell's side.

Adeline watched him go and then turned back to Lord Harry. His eyes were resting upon the finger-marks about her wrist and some of the customary good-humour was missing from his face. Then he smiled at her and said simply, 'Your cousins are about to delight us with some music. Unfortunately, I have a problem.'

She found herself smiling back, mainly because it didn't seem possible to do anything else. 'Oh? And what is that?'

'I've no ear for music. Absolutely none. So I thought you might keep me company and tell me what expressions of pleasure I may best employ when it's over.'

'Aside from "Thank God!" you mean?'

Harry laughed. 'That's it exactly. You see, the thing is that I'd like to escape the inevitable jokes at my expense.'

Adeline gave him an oblique glance. 'From his Grace of Rockliffe, I presume?'

'Rock? God, no!' came the startled response. And then shrewdly, 'You don't know him very well, do you?'

'Scarcely at all.'

'I thought not. Rock might – and probably would – torment me in private. But in public? Never. No. It's Nell I'm worried about,' he confided apologetically. 'I'm rather against giving her the satisfaction of calling me a philistine – or of watching your aunt look down her nose at me. I'm suffering enough as it is.'

'Are you indeed?'

'Lord, yes! No effort too great, no opportunity neglected,' said Harry cheerfully. 'She's trying to put me in my place, you see.'

'I can't help wondering why. However … what precisely are *you* doing?'

'Turning the tables.' His grin was the epitome of winsome innocence. 'I knew you'd understand. After all, you take a similar line yourself, don't you?'

SIX

'I wish,' said Nell in somewhat nettled accents, 'that I could see what's so fascinating about Diana's cousin. It's not as though she's anything above the ordinary, after all ... and that dreadful mulberry brocade she wore last night made her look at least forty.'

Rockliffe raised his eyes from the book he'd been reading and surveyed his sister without noticeable pleasure. It was the day before the ball and, in deference to the fine weather – not to mention the amount of work still to be accomplished inside the house – Lady Franklin had decreed that her guests should enjoy an *al fresco* luncheon in the park. Shuddering inwardly, his Grace had immediately escaped to Sir Roland's book-room for a brief period of restorative peace – to which Nell, charmingly attired in pale pink tiffany and with time on her hands, had presently followed him. She had thought to make use of a few minutes of rare privacy ... but, meeting the coolness in his gaze, she wondered if she had not perhaps made a mistake.

'Well?' she demanded when he still did not speak. 'Haven't you anything to say?'

'*Yes. You sound like Diana,*' he thought. And then, closing his book, 'Several, in fact. And I'll begin by observing that you are fast becoming a mannerless and ill-natured coquette. Also, I have heard you use that particular tone with Harry and can only marvel at his forbearance. You will not, however, be well advised to use it with me.'

Colour flooded Nell's cheeks and she said protestingly, 'Wh-what do you mean? I'm not a coquette – and I wasn't r-rude!'

'No? I am beginning to wonder if you still have the ability to discriminate.'

'That's not fair!'

'Unfortunately,' said Rockliffe, coming smoothly to his feet, 'it is. Your behaviour over the last few days has been both arrogant and vain. And I have not, I regret to say, been proud of you.'

The fact that he had never before – no matter what scrapes she had got into – spoken to her like that gave Nell pause. Looking stricken, she said, 'Do you really mean it?'

'Yes. I do. As for your unnecessary remark about Mistress Kendrick's gown – it must be plain to an even meaner intelligence than your own that she is wearing cast-offs. And if you, my dear, had ever been forced to wear Lucilla's or Aunt Augusta's mistakes, you might perhaps be a little more tolerant.'

There was a long silence while Nell stared down at the beribboned straw hat in her hands. Finally, she said, 'You're right, of course. I hadn't thought.'

'Obviously not.'

'And I'm sorry. For all of it. But all I really meant,' she went on, 'is that I don't understand why Mr Garfield is suddenly so taken with her and why even Ha- Lord Harry has started seeking her out. It doesn't make sense.'

'Jealous, Nell?'

'Certainly not! As far as I'm concerned, they're both equally obnoxious.'

'Ah.'

She eyed him suspiciously for a moment and then decided that the best method of defence was attack. 'And it's not just them, is it? I've seen you talking to her yourself.'

'Have you?'

'You know I have. Are you in love with her?'

His brows soared. 'My dear! Is it likely?'

'No,' said Nell frankly. 'What's likely is that you're either doing it out of devilment or to make Diana jealous.'

'And which does your instinct suggest?'

'I don't know.' She hesitated and then said abruptly, 'The truth is that I'd hoped you might consider marrying Diana.'

'I think I might be said to be tolerably aware of that fact.'

'Oh. So will you?'

'Will I what?'

Nell resisted a temptation to stamp her foot.

'Think about marrying Diana. I know she's not especially well-connected but her birth is respectable enough – even for Lucilla. And she has to be the most ravishingly beautiful girl you've ever seen. Also, although I really oughtn't to say this ... she'd head over ears in love with you.'

'Dear me!' drawled Rockliffe. 'Is she indeed? I really had no idea.'

'Perhaps not. But now I've told you ... well, you must know that you could do a lot worse.'

A faintly crooked smile touched his mouth but he refrained from saying that he doubted it. Instead, he said mildly, 'Correct me if I'm mistaken ... but what you are really saying is that the match would please *you*.'

'Yes. I think it would be perfect.'

'That is honest, at least. But you will, I am sure, appreciate my difficulty.'

'What difficulty?'

'Simply that – while you are determined to choose your own husband – I am equally set on choosing my own wife.'

It was, as he very well knew, unanswerable ... and, to her credit, Nell did not even try.

'I suppose,' she sighed, 'that I should have expected that. Shall I apologise again?'

'No.' He tucked her hand through his arm and let her to the door. 'Just try to be a little more civil to Harry. And who knows? Once you have become used to the idea, you may even find him less ... er ... obnoxious than you first thought.'

*

'And that,' confided Nell later to her dearest friend, 'made me darkly suspicious, I can tell you. It would suit Rock admirably to have me safely betrothed – and to someone as eligible as Harry.'

'But I thought he'd promised not to force you?' objected Diana.

'He did – and he won't. But he's quite capable of arranging matters so I'll *think* I've pleased myself, when all the time I'll really be doing exactly what he always intended that I should. You simply wouldn't believe how sneaky he can be.'

Diana looked across the grass to where Rockliffe formed one of a group with Althea, Andrew, Lizzie and his lordship, in the shade of a large beech tree. She said inconsequently, 'Do you know, I'm sure poor Lizzie gets more freckled every time I see her.' And then, 'Lord Harry is extremely attractive, though ... at least, I suspect that Thea finds him so.'

'Oh?' Nell sniffed disparagingly. 'Then she'd better be warned – for he's also odiously interfering.'

'I doubt she'd mind that. Not, of course, that she has the smallest hope of gaining his affections. She's too much of a mouse, poor dear.' She paused and then added wistfully, 'I suppose ... I suppose your brother hasn't said anything about *me*?'

'No – no.' Nell took the tactful rather than the truthful path and had the grace to blush a little. 'No – not a word. But you mustn't give up hope. It's just that Rock isn't ... well, one can never tell what he's truly thinking. But you know I'll do what I can.'

'Dearest!' Diana clasped her friend's hand. 'I know you will. And you can't imagine what a comfort it is to me.'

Nell smiled weakly. And then, in order to extricate herself from the awkwardness of the moment, said, 'I see Mr Garfield has attached himself to your cousin again. What *do* you suppose he finds to say to her?'

'Who knows?' shrugged Diana. 'He's probably boring on about his stupid house or telling her exactly what he paid for some thing or other. After all, he's hardly likely to consider marrying her, is he? And I can't see him giving her a slip on the shoulder either. She's not nearly pretty enough.'

Nell's eyes widened a little at the vulgarity of the expression but she saw no reason to quarrel with its meaning. In this she was wrong for Mr Garfield was, at that very moment, working his way round to offering Mistress Kendrick a *carte blanche* – and finding it a good deal more difficult than he'd anticipated.

He realised, of course, that these things probably grew easier with practice and that he, having arrived at the age of twenty-eight with only one recognised liaison to his credit, was somewhat lacking in this respect. But he did not recall needing to tread quite so carefully with Betty – whom he had set up as his mistress more as a matter of form than anything else; and he'd certainly never had the peculiar sensation that she was more in control of his words than he was himself. Under Adeline's dispassionate gaze, he knew both; and, unnerving though this was, it also increased his ardour.

He looked at her now, cool and restrained, the nut-brown hair demurely arranged and her neck rising slender and white above the dove-coloured gown. The blood rose to his head and he said baldly, 'I'll give you a house in London and a carriage of your own and as many gowns and furbelows as you like. I'll even take you to Paris - or Rome, if you'd prefer it. Anything you want. All you need do is to name it.'

The narrow brows rose and Adeline examined him meditatively. At length, she said, 'Dear me, Mr Garfield. Can it be that you are asking me to become your wife?'

His jaw dropped. '*Wife?*'

'Yes.' She smiled sweetly upon him. 'What else could you possibly mean?'

Lewis stared at her aghast.

'Well, in truth,' he began weakly, 'I ... er ...'

'You were wondering if it is not a little too soon to ask?' she suggested helpfully. 'Of course. I understand completely. Indeed, I am honoured that you should consider me ... and very, very tempted.'

An unpleasant, sinking feeling was taking place in the pit of Mr Garfield's stomach and he knew that he had better speak now – and swiftly – or forever hold his peace.

'However,' continued Adeline smoothly, 'I fear I must decline your extremely flattering offer ... at least until we get to know each other a little better. And that day, I feel sure, cannot be far distant.'

Lewis Garfield was not a man whose mind moved quickly but, on this occasion, he surpassed himself. The implications of Mistress Kendrick's words were only too horribly clear and, since it did not now seem possible to correct her misconception without finding himself in very deep water indeed, he grasped the reprieve with both hands. Far, far better to nip his infatuation in the bud than to risk further embarrassment of this kind – or worse.

Suddenly a man of decision, he surged to his feet, mumbled some tangled excuses and vanished, without more ado, into the shrubbery.

'*Exit, pursued by a bear,*' said a reflective voice beside her. 'What *can* you have said to him?'

'Guess,' said Adeline. And then, meeting Rockliffe's eyes, 'Or no. On second thoughts – don't.'

'No,' he agreed, resting one elegantly-shod foot on the fallen tree-trunk where she sat and producing the inevitable snuff-box from his pocket whilst enjoying the honey-coloured glints the sun found in her hair. 'One cannot but wonder, however, why it is that you don't appear to feel insulted.'

'In general terms, because he won't trouble me again.' She surveyed him with faint, amusement. 'You did not enjoy your luncheon.'

'I dislike indulging in a balancing act with my plate whilst removing various species of insect from the syllabub. A sign, if you like, of my declining years.'

Adeline's expression did not waver by so much as a hairsbreadth but, behind her grey-striped bodice came a tug of something she neither wanted nor was prepared for. She said, 'Tom tells me you've finally persuaded my uncle to sell you The Trojan.'

'Did you think I wouldn't?'

'On the contrary. I was sure you would.' She paused, tilting her head consideringly. 'Hardly the horse for anyone's declining years, I would have thought.'

His Grace smiled. 'Oh – quite. But it is hard, you understand, to relinquish one's image.'

'Yes. It must be. And easier by far to hazard one's neck.'

'You're concerned for my safety? I'm touched.' He watched as she rose and shook out her skirts – absorbing, as always, her innate grace. 'You're going?'

'Retreating,' replied Adeline pleasantly. 'And leaving the field to Diana.'

Rockliffe cast a brief glance over his shoulder and then prepared to utter a sardonic rejoinder – but too late. Mistress Kendrick was already several paces distant and he was left with no alternative but to turn and smile on her cousin.

Determinedly hiding her chagrin that he had paid her almost no attention all day and then added insult to injury by blatantly seeking out Adeline instead, Diana summoned her most brilliant smile and said, 'I wanted to consult you on a matter of taste, your Grace. Mama has said that I may powder my hair for the ball tomorrow and I wanted to know if you feel that it will suit me.'

Rockliffe regarded her enigmatically. Although he invariably wore his own hair powdered these days, he was generally known to uphold the view that very young ladies appeared to greater advantage without it. It was something, he had always felt, to do with freshness and innocence; which was why he replied suavely, 'Admirably, I should imagine.'

'Oh – do you think so, indeed?' she cooed. 'Then I shan't hesitate. It's simply that Nell says you do not permit *her* to do so.'

'Ah. But Nell, you see, is an entirely different matter.'

'I'm glad,' she said daringly, 'that you think so.'

'How could I not?' His tone was as bland as butter but, beneath their heavy lids, his eyes gleamed. 'In your case, my dear, I am convinced that they broke the mould.'

It did not occur to Diana to remark – as Adeline might have done – that no doubt he considered this fortunate. It did not even occur to her to point out that she had a twin. She merely dimpled complacently, dropped a mock curtsy and thanked him. Rockliffe felt boredom stirring and toyed restlessly with his snuff-box. He had spent the past week blowing hot and cold on Mistress Di but today the game had suddenly ceased to amuse him ... and, because it had, he terminated it.

The result was that, on the night before the one on which she fully intended to eclipse every other lady, Diana was deprived of her beauty sleep. Something, she sensed, was going horribly wrong. For Rockliffe – who ought, by now, to be eating out of the palm of her hand – was growing increasingly elusive; and every time she felt she had him in her grasp, he seemed to melt through her fingers. He had accorded her no more than a bare five minutes that evening and had not paid a single compliment worth repeating to Cecily. Worse still, he had not yet asked her to dance with him at the ball. Diana buffeted her pillow and turned over, frowning. It wasn't fair. She was beautiful and she'd done everything in her power to charm him – so why did he show no sign of wanting her? *Why?*

Rockliffe, staring thoughtfully from his window into the darkened garden, could have told her. What he had *not* done, until this moment, mainly because it had seemed too ludicrous to be worth the trouble, was to analyse the knowledge for himself. Now, however, with this feeling that he had not sought and did not want threatening to challenge his reason, he recognised the need to enumerate the facts. And the facts, of course, were remarkably simple.

He was in the market for a wife who would occupy her position with well-bred grace and curb Nell's excesses but who would not bore him to distraction. There were, he knew, a number of ladies who could fulfil the first two; and there was Diana Franklin – who did not qualify in any respect at all. Unfortunately, in an already insoluble situation, there was also Adeline.

It was not, he reflected clinically, that he loved her. Not at all. It was merely that she never failed to surprise and intrigue him. She was cold and sharp as a razor, no beauty and utterly infuriating; and he wanted her.

It was impossible, of course. He had never been in the habit of seducing respectable females and didn't intend to start now ... and, as a prospective bride, Adeline was out of the question. She was badly-connected and not of his world. It wasn't that he cared a jot what that world might say, but he was aware that he owed something to his name. He also had a decided aversion to acquiring Richard Horton and Diana as relatives; so even if he had wanted to marry Adeline – which he didn't – it was quite out of the question.

The sensible course, therefore, was to resist the attraction ... but that was beginning to prove difficult. He should never, he now realised, have coerced Lady Franklin into putting Adeline in his way – but there was little point in bemoaning that fact. All he could do was appreciate the irony of it. He had baited his own trap and must live with the consequences. But only for four more days and then he would be free. It was a calming thought ... and one on which to retire.

SEVEN

The day of the ball dawned without a cloud in the sky. Cecily Garfield wasted no time at all in putting one there.

'You won't get him, you know,' she informed Diana pityingly. 'It's a shame, too – after all the trouble you've gone to.'

'What trouble?' snapped Diana, her nerves already stretched. 'I haven't even begun yet.'

'No? Then I suggest you do, dearest. Because, so far, I don't think he'd notice if you disappeared in a puff of smoke.'

'Which only goes to show how much *you* know about it!'

'Well, you would say that, wouldn't you?' Cecily smiled maddeningly. 'But the proof of the pudding, you know ... and he hasn't exactly taken to dogging your footsteps, has he? I'll wager he hasn't even asked you to dance with him this evening.'

'He will,' replied Diana, tossing her head. 'He will.'

'Oh – no doubt. But I daresay he'll dance with Thea, too – and Lizzie and me. In such a small party, it would look very odd if he didn't. But it takes more than courtesy to promote an offer of marriage ... and although I'm sure he thinks you're very pretty, I suspect you don't attract him in the least.'

Two bright spots of colour burned in Diana's cheeks and her palm itched to banish the sympathetic smile from Mistress Cecy's face. She said tightly, 'You'd better wait and see, then. I've told you I'll be Duchess of Rockliffe before the year's out – and I will.'

'I'm sorry to say it, Di, but I doubt it. I really do,' sighed Cecily. 'And I honestly think it would be ever so much better if you were to face the facts. For even if he were madly in love with you – which he obviously isn't – I doubt he'd offer for you. The thing is, dearest, that he's not just a Duke. He's a Wynstanton.'

'Meaning what, precisely?'

'Well, I don't want to offend you or suggest that your family isn't perfectly respectable or anything. But it has to be said that the

Wynstantons don't marry just *anybody*. Rockliffe's mother, for instance, was sister to the Earl of Leominster and his sister, Lucilla, is Viscountess Grassmere. So I really don't see him settling for the daughter of a mere baronet. Do you?'

Diana rose and shook out her pale pink taffeta skirt with hands that weren't quite steady. Then, fixing Cecily with a glittering blue stare, she said unevenly, 'You're very smug, aren't you? But if the Gunning girls could do it, then so can I. And, unlike you, I don't have to rely on my money to catch a husband. I'm beautiful – everyone says so – and I'm good enough to marry anyone I choose.'

'So you say. But I'll believe it,' yawned Cecily, 'on the day that it happens.'

The flush faded, leaving Diana's face white with temper.

'Watch me, then. And get ready to eat your words ... because I'll be betrothed to Rockliffe before he leaves here next week. And that's a promise.'

On which Parthian shot, she stalked away to her bedchamber to relieve her feelings by smashing a crystal rose-bowl in the hearth.

*

While the rest of the party spent a lazy day in preparation for a night's unbridled gaiety, Adeline arranged flowers, relayed her aunt's orders to the servants and dissuaded the head cook from suicide over a belated request for turbot. Of the ball itself, she thought very little – and, when she did think of it, was more than half-inclined to absent herself from it altogether. She did not dance and, since dinner was to be replaced by a buffet supper, she was unlikely to be missed. All in all, the only thing against spending the evening in her room with a book was a very natural reluctance to please Diana – who had made her wishes known with all her usual *éclat*.

'Stay out of the way tonight,' she'd said, without preamble, having met Adeline by chance on the stairs. 'No one will care whether you're there or not – and I don't want you.'

'Of course you don't,' Adeline had replied kindly. 'But cheer up. If Rockliffe asks me to dance, I'll tell him that you're my official substitute.' And shaking free of Diana's restraining hand, had continued on her way.

After that, she didn't think of the matter again until she entered her bedchamber in the early part of the evening and checked on the threshold at the sight of the gown reposing on her bed. Then, carefully closing the door behind her, she crossed the room to investigate.

It was the colour of bluebells and simply designed, its only ornamentation the white, quilted petticoat embroidered with blue and silver thread – and it was beautiful. Adeline looked at it thoughtfully for a long time. Two things surprised her; first, that Lizzie had apparently neither forgotten nor changed her mind – and, second, the strength of her own desire to at least try the gown on. Visions of appearing to advantage, for just once in her life, hovered on the edges of her mind. And though she apostrophised herself for a fool and told herself that a borrowed gown was unlikely to fit and could not be altered, still the temptation persisted.

By the time she yielded to it there were sounds from below betokening further arrivals but Adeline did not hurry. She removed her clothes and washed in cold water from the jug before unpinning her hair and brushing it with slow, deliberate strokes. Then, with unaccustomed care, she set about piling it up on her head and perfecting the two glossy ringlets that were to lie demurely on one shoulder. And finally – half-terrified, half-elated – she stepped into the gown.

It was a trifle loose but nothing that could not be corrected by tighter lacing – a tricky manoeuvre, but one which she eventually accomplished to her satisfaction. Then, as though it were the only thing that mattered, she took a long, long look at herself in the glass … and wondered what she had done.

*

Adeline entered the blue salon, transformed for the evening into a ballroom, as unobtrusively as possible and with only one purpose in mind – that of thanking Mistress Pickering. But this, since Lizzie was just about to take to the floor with Andrew and was not, in any case, desirous of being thanked, was not easy. Adeline found herself able to utter no more than a half-sentence before her benefactress cut in with a laconic, 'It suits you. I thought it would.' And dragged Mr Franklin willy-nilly into the gavotte.

Perplexed but conscious of a tug of admiration for the girl's style, Adeline watched her go. Then Althea was beside her, looking worried.

'Addie ... you look beautiful,' she said breathlessly but with sincerity. And then, 'I think Di's planning something dreadful – and I don't know what to do.'

Adeline, who knew as well as anyone the extremes of which Diana was capable, regarded her cousin with attention. 'Tell me.'

'She says I'm to go to the book-room on the stroke of nine and be sure to have Cecy with me. I don't know how she managed it – but I th-think she's in there with the Duke. What *can* she be doing?'

'At a guess, something exceedingly stupid.' Adeline scanned the room for Rockliffe's unmistakable presence and failed to find it. Inexplicably, her heart sank. 'I take it you've said nothing to Cecily?'

'No. But what shall I do? It's almost nine now.'

'Leave it to me. Diana's expecting an audience – and it would be a shame to disappoint her, wouldn't it?'

The hour chimed as she crossed the hall and a sardonic gleam entered Adeline's eye. It did not take a genius to imagine what Diana might be hoping to achieve and it would be a pleasure to put a spoke in her wheel. Without any hesitation, she swung open the book-room door and went in.

For the space of a heart-beat she was granted the sight of Diana apparently languishing inert in his Grace's arms before one of her hands moved to rest lovingly against his cheek and she stood on tiptoe to press her mouth to his. Rockliffe's head jerked back and his arms dropped away from Diana as if scalded. She, however, continued to cling until he spoke.

'Unless you're a party to this little charade,' he said bitingly, his gaze locked with Adeline's, 'I'd be grateful if you would shut the damned door.'

An unsuspected weight fell from Adeline's shoulders and she immediately did as he asked – while, at precisely the same moment,

Diana uncoiled herself from him, crying, 'Oh my God – Cecy! I never dreamed --' And stopped dead as she realised her mistake.

Rockliffe's mouth twitched and he raised one brow in silent enquiry.

'She was expecting Cecily Garfield,' explained Adeline, 'on whose indiscretion one may always rely. You can close your mouth, Diana. I'm not a figment of your imagination.'

Diana took an abrupt step forward and then stopped, as if poised for attack. Beneath the skilfully applied cosmetics, her face was white with temper and she said jerkily, 'I haven't the faintest idea what you're talking about. I wasn't expecting anyone. And you have no business here.'

'On the contrary. I'm here to preserve your reputation and stop you making a complete fool of yourself. If you had any sense, you'd be grateful.'

'Perfectly true.' Rockliffe's tone was grim. 'I am not so easily trapped, believe me. And young ladies who depend on these little schemes are apt to acquire a certain type of reputation.'

'It's not true!' Diana's control was slipping and her voice rose accordingly. 'She's a lying cat! I was faint and – just for a second – I thought it was Cecily who'd just come in. She's always following me about. And I don't need *any* kind of schemes in order to be married. I'm beau--'

'Beautiful,' drawled Rockliffe. 'Yes. We know.'

Diana stared at him out of dangerously narrowed eyes and her hands clenched on her satin skirts. Then, sweeping round to Adeline, she said furiously, 'This is your doing! You've been saying things, haven't you? Things to poison him against me.'

'I think,' observed Adeline, 'that it might be as well if we permitted his Grace to return to the ballroom so that you can lose your temper in private.' And to Rockliffe, 'Your absence will be noticed. And I can deal with this.'

He directed a swift, measuring glance at Diana and then said, 'You're sure?'

'Yes. She's going to make a complete exhibition of herself. It's what she does. So it's best that you go.'

Acknowledging the sense of this, he said, 'Very well. But first I think I must take this opportunity of clarifying a few matters for Mistress Diana.' He paused, waiting for the girl to meet his eyes and then continued blandly, 'During the course of our brief acquaintance, you have successively pursued me, coquetted with me, thrown yourself at my head and attempted to compromise me. I have responded to none of these and, indeed, have come only to deplore your upbringing. You are – as you are only too well-aware – an uncommonly beautiful girl but you are also spoiled, selfish and rude. Consequently, the chances of you receiving an offer of marriage from me – regardless of any circumstances you may have contrived – are, and always were, completely non-existent. I trust that makes the position plain?' And without waiting for a reply, he strolled unhurriedly to the door, delaying only to say urbanely, 'My compliments on your appearance, Mistress Kendrick. You look both elegant and charming.'

*

Back in the ballroom, Rockliffe did his duty by Lizzie Pickering, watched young Mr Franklin imbibing vast quantities of wine and exchanged a few words with Harry Caversham on the subject of Nell's sudden switch to chill formality. And, throughout it all, his mind was almost wholly taken up with a picture of Adeline standing framed against the dark wood of the book-room door. He gave himself a mental shake and decided that the week he'd spent in this house had damaged his sanity. There was no other explanation.

It was while he was soliciting Cecily Garfield's hand for the next minuet that he saw Diana come back. She was flushed and there was the merest suggestion of dishevelment about her person. But it was her face that drew the Duke's attention. She looked, he thought, like a cat who had just killed one bird and was already stalking another. Of Adeline, there was no sign at all.

He told himself that there could be no harm in satisfying what was really no more than idle curiosity. Then, excusing himself from Cecily, he retraced his steps once more to the book-room. He did not notice that Richard Horton was watching him whilst simultaneously preparing to cross-examine his niece. There was, after all, no reason why he should.

He found Adeline standing as if carved from stone, her head bent and her hands resting on the edge of Sir Roland's desk. Her hair, once so carefully arranged, was falling loose about her face and the blue gown bore every appearance of having been so savagely torn that one sleeve was completely adrift. Rockliffe, who was rarely angry, experienced a gust of pure temper and, shutting the door with a snap, exorcised it in a manner equally rare. He swore.

Pushing back her hair, Adeline raised her head and managed a crooked smile. 'Just what I was thinking myself. It's Lizzie's dress, you see.'

'Is it? Then Lizzie goes up in my estimation.' He crossed the room and, taking her shoulders, turned her to face him. It was the closest he had ever been to her and he was aware of a faint, almost indiscernible scent of something he didn't recognise. Doing his best to ignore it, he said, 'I need not ask, of course, how this happened. You'd better get those scratches attended to. The claws of a wild animal are frequently venomous, I believe.'

She raised her hands to the torn bodice and discovered that they were shaking.

'It's nothing. I'm perfectly all right. It's just the gown. I don't know what to tell Lizzie.'

'The truth?'

'I can't.'

'No? Then allow me to do it for you.' He drew a long breath and, releasing his clasp on her shoulders, perched himself on a corner of the desk. Sternly forbidding himself to dwell on the interesting view provided by the ruined dress, he regarded her out of hooded eyes and said, 'I suppose you know that your cousin is a candidate for Bedlam?'

'She – she's always had an awful temper but I've never seen her quite so wild. She was beside herself.'

'That, my dear, is glaringly obvious. The question is – why?'

'Who knows? Something I said – something you said – possibly even something Cecily Garfield said.' The trembling was no longer confined to her hands and she said irritably, 'If you want to help, I'd be glad if you stopped asking pointless questions and tried to find some pins. I need to get back to my room and I can't cross the hall looking like this.'

'No?' He awarded her a swift, audacious smile. And then, 'No. Perhaps not. It wouldn't do for poor Lewis to see what he's missed, would it?' And, rising, he began a systematic search through the drawers of Sir Roland's desk.

Adeline watched in silence and tried to re-assemble her composure. She was more shaken by Diana's attack than she was prepared to admit and it did not help that Rockliffe was being so kind. She looked at him now – magnificent in black brocade heavily laced with silver, his hair thickly powdered and confined at the nape by narrow velvet ribands. He was the epitome of sophistication ... assured, worldly and far too attractive for her peace of mind. He was also easily bored, prone to mischievous whims and often deliberately provoking. And yet, though she knew all the arguments for keeping him safely at arm's length, they apparently were not enough to prevent her trusting him. She wished she knew why.

'I make your uncle my compliments,' said Rockliffe, producing a small box. 'I fear my own escritoire is less well equipped. However ... if you will stand still, I shall attempt the necessary repairs.'

Her brows rose. '*You?*'

'Why not? You can scarcely to it yourself, after all ... and my skill may surprise you. I am not entirely lacking in versatility, you see.'

Adeline saw. 'Or practice, it seems.'

His mouth curled.

'Or practice,' he agreed imperturbably. And then, continuing his task of pinning her sleeve back in position, 'May I at least ask why Diana was permitted to emerge unscathed?'

'What would *you* have done? I was intent only on self-preservation and not alerting the whole house. I doubt, though, that she'll do much dancing tonight.'

'Oh?'

'No.' She met his eyes and her face was suddenly transformed by a wickedly slanting smile. 'I'm afraid I stamped on her foot. Hard.'

Rockliffe stood very still, his fingers resting against the satin skin of her shoulder and a coil of her hair brushing his wrist. Again, that enticing, indefinable scent reached him, sending a clear signal to every nerve in his body; a signal that, this time, he found himself unable to completely resist. He said, with commendable restraint, 'Did you? My congratulations.' And then broke all his sterling resolutions to drop a light, fleeting kiss on her lips.

Adeline drew a sharp, startled breath. But before either of them could speak, a purring voice from the door said, 'Well, well - one knows not whether to be touched or shocked. The only certainty, my dear Mistress Garfield, is that we intrude.'

It was Richard Horton, a satisfied smile on his painted face and, beside him, Cecily Garfield with her eyes on stalks.

'Hell,' murmured his Grace softly, 'and damnation. *Twice in one evening*?' And gave way, reluctantly, to ironic amusement.

Able to see the funny side but unable, as yet, to appreciate it, Adeline had no more colour to lose.

'Stop it,' she said flatly, 'and tell him to shut the door.'

'The *damned* door,' corrected Rockliffe. He had stopped laughing but it seemed to her that little devils danced in his eyes. 'No. I rather suspect that – this time – that horse has bolted.'

'Look!' crowed Cecily gleefully and with volume over the encroaching strains of a minuet. 'Her dress is all torn. What *do* you suppose has been happening?'

'Something which I not only refuse to sully your ears with,' replied Mr Horton smoothly, 'but which, I must confess, astounds me.'

'How awful! I can't *imagine* what Di's going to say.'

'Oh – I think you probably can,' said Rockliffe sardonically, his mind busy with the various possibilities. Richard Horton cheated at cards and could be silenced. But no power on earth was going to silence Lewis Garfield's sallow-faced sister; she was enjoying herself too much. On the other hand, the ramblings of an over-excited schoolgirl did not particularly concern him. He said, 'Tell me something, Mr Horton. Did Diana send you here?'

'Diana? No. Though it is true that the poor child seems somewhat ... upset.' Richard paused artistically. 'But no. I came, one might say, purely by chance as escort to Mistress Garfield – with whom your Grace was engaged to dance.'

It sounded plausible enough but Rockliffe didn't believe a word of it.

'He knows,' said Adeline tonelessly. 'He's spoken to Diana and he knows exactly what happened. But, for reasons of his own, he's going to encourage Cecily to think exactly what she's thinking. Aren't you, Uncle?'

'Whas goin' on?' demanded the slurred accents of Andrew Franklin. He had arrived to lean heavily against the door-jamb behind Cecily. 'Why's everyone in here 'stead of the ballroom?'

Rockliffe re-seated himself on the desk and folded his arms.

'What a pity that fellow Sheridan isn't here,' he drawled. 'He could make a play out of this.'

'It's not funny!' snapped Adeline. 'Why don't you *do* something? Tell Cecily the truth before this whole farce gets completely out of hand.'

'Too late, my dear. Here is your aunt ... ah – and Diana. Almost the whole cast, in fact.'

'I'm glad you can be so philosophical. Don't you care?'

'You mean am I panic-stricken. And the answer to that is no.'

Lady Franklin had sailed into the centre of the room and came to an abrupt halt, her gaze fixed on Adeline.

'What,' she asked glacially, 'is the meaning of this?'

'I hardly dare say, my lady,' volunteered Cecily, without noticeable hesitation. 'But you can see the state of Adeline's hair and gown for yourself. And when Mr Horton and I came in, she and the Duke were *kissing*!'

There was a long, fragile silence during which his Grace reviewed his options. There were three. What he *could* do; what he probably *should* do; and what he *wanted* to do. He was still reviewing them when her ladyship said carefully, 'Am I to understand that your Grace is responsible for – for my niece's present reprehensible appearance?'

'Well that would depend on whom you ask,' he replied reflectively. 'You might, for example, try asking Mistress Diana. But I, personally, would be extremely surprised if she told you.'

The cold gaze swivelled to Diana, standing transfixed beside Cecily in the doorway.

'Well?'

For a moment, Diana appeared to be at a loss. Then she said chokingly, 'I don't know what he's talking about. It – it's perfectly obvious what's been going on between them. And I, for one, think it's disgusting!' And, pushing both her brother and Mistress Garfield aside, she fled.

His balance already precarious, Andrew slithered slowly down the wall and sat on the floor. No one paid the remotest attention.

'I am waiting,' announced Lady Franklin, 'for an explanation.'

'Yes. I daresay you are.' Rockliffe came collectedly to his feet and faced Adeline. He was in the grip of a mood of dangerous exhilaration and it showed. He said, 'I think it's time we put an end to this. Don't you?'

'By all means,' came the acidulous reply. 'It's what I've been suggesting for the past ten minutes. But I don't see, now, how you expect to achieve it.'

'Don't you?' He trapped her eyes with his own and his smile was one she had never seen before. He said, 'It's really very simple. I'm going to marry you.'

EIGHT

The silence that followed this announcement was of cataclysmic proportions. Then several things happened at once.

Andrew began to sing a particularly bawdy song but was summarily cut off as Cecily tripped over him in her haste to break the news to Diana; Lady Franklin and her brother both began talking at the same time; and Adeline disgraced herself still further by dissolving into helpless laughter.

This had the immediate effect of silencing her ladyship and Mr Horton as they stared at Rockliffe, searching for signs of affront. There were none. His Grace merely studied his snuff-box with a thoughtful air – and waited.

Finally, when Adeline's paroxysm had dwindled to the odd gasping sob, he said, 'Not quite the usual response ... but one sees your point, of course.'

'Wh-what did you expect?' she asked, with some difficulty. 'I might have said *"My lord Duke – this is so s-sudden!"* But then you'd have thought I believed you m-meant it.'

'I see.' The dark eyes gleamed. 'And don't you?'

Adeline drew a long, steadying breath and pulled herself together. Beneath the laughter was a tiny core of pain but that was for later. She would not think of it now. She said, 'In a word – no. I could, however, list half a dozen reasons why you said it – but, just now, that would be a trifle tactless, wouldn't it?'

'Perhaps ... but that need no longer concern you.'

'I cannot,' declaimed Lady Franklin, annoyed at being so long ignored, 'understand any of this. I demand to know what has taken place in this room and whether your Grace can seriously be intending to marry my niece – though a more ludicrous suggestion I have never heard. I wish also to --'

'Presently,' said Rockliffe, quietly but with utter finality. 'I will discuss the matter with you in detail presently. In fact, I look forward to doing so. In the meantime, however, I wish to address your niece.' He paused briefly. Out in the hall, Andrew was singing again. 'Mr Horton ... perhaps you will now do me the favour of closing the door? I do not, you will notice, ask you to remain outside it.'

'How very wise,' said Richard, calmly shutting out Andrew's ditty, 'since I have no intention of doing so.'

'Quite.' The Duke turned back to Adeline. 'And now, my dear, let us explode a few misconceptions. You think I suffer from a sometimes questionable and frequently misplaced sense of humour – and you are right. But do you also take me for a fool?'

'No.' An arrested expression crept into the aquamarine eyes. 'No. What are you saying?'

'I am saying that I have just announced, before witnesses, my intention to make you my wife ... and, even as we speak, Mistress Garfield is busy spreading the glad tidings to all and sundry. So if I spoke out of levity, my folly is well-served, is it not?' He smiled at her. '*He that diggeth a pit* – and so on. There are no loop-holes. None. Nor am I looking for any.'

It was a long time before Adeline spoke and, when she did, her voice seemed to come from a long way off. 'I still can't believe you mean it.'

'Neither can I!' snapped her ladyship. 'I can only say that, if his Grace has *indeed* trifled with you --'

'The word,' interposed Richard Horton sweetly, 'is compromised.'

'Very well – compromised, then. *If* he has done so – though I can by no means accept the fact --'

'Accept it,' advised her brother again. 'Look at her. How else do you think she came to look like that?'

'I was set upon by a wildcat,' snapped Adeline tartly, 'and you know it perfectly well. His Grace didn't touch me. It was Diana.'

'*What?*' repeated Richard, his tone a nice blend of incredulity and amusement. 'You will have to do better than that, I fear. And as for the question of whether or not his Grace has touched you ... Mistress Garfield has already testified to the truth of that, has she not? No, dear Adeline, I'm afraid it will not do. It will not do at all.'

'I wish you will be quiet!' said his sister, her annoyance getting the better of her. 'There is no need for any of this. Adeline is not a schoolgirl and, if she has behaved foolishly, she has only herself to blame. As for your Grace's generous offer – it does you credit. But I cannot permit you to make such a sacrifice.'

'Your ladyship is too kind,' remarked Rockliffe dryly.

And then, before he could continue, the door burst open again to admit Nell with Harry Caversham hard on her heels.

'Is it true?' Nell demanded hotly. 'Cecily is telling everyone you're going to marry Mistress Kendrick because – oh God!' She stopped abruptly, staring at Adeline. 'Oh God –it's true, isn't it?'

'Yes,' said his Grace, his gaze resting with lightly-veiled mockery on Lady Franklin. 'It's true. And now, if we have established that fact to everyone's satisfaction, I suggest that you all return to the ballroom and attempt to enjoy yourselves.'

'That is all very well,' objected her ladyship irritably, 'but unfortunately --'

'Lady Franklin – you have other guests,' drawled Rockliffe. 'You should go and attend to them. Furthermore, your son is too drunk to stand and ought, I fancy, be removed from the hall. Mr Horton – who, I suspect, would very much like a private word with you - will doubtless be happy to assist.'

'Just so. Ecstatic, in fact,' said Richard, boundless satisfaction informing every syllable. And, taking his sister's arm, he led her firmly from the room.

'Why did you do it?' asked Nell, her eyes suspiciously bright. 'How can *you*, of all people, have been so *stupid*?'

'Go away, Nell. Console yourself with the thought that, if I am married, you won't have to stay with Lucilla ... and try to mind what you say this evening – particularly within the hearing of Mistress Garfield. None of this is what it seems and it's by no means the tragedy you appear to think. No – don't argue. We'll talk later ... but not now. Just go.'

Rockliffe waited while she made a slow and very reluctant exit. For a second, he considered asking Harry to leave as well and then, deciding against it, said, 'Adeline. Sufficient unto the day, my dear. I'd like you to allow Harry to escort you to your door and then forget everything except the simple fact that I know what I'm doing. Will you do that?'

'I don't know.' She both sounded and looked exceptionally tired. 'I don't know. But there's no need to trouble Lord Harry.'

'It's no trouble,' his lordship assured her. 'None at all.'

'Thank you. But I'd prefer, if you don't mind, to be alone.' She hesitated, looking at his Grace and the ghost of her customary irony flickered in her eyes. 'It's been quite an evening, hasn't it? But I think you know, without being told, that – though I appreciate you making the gesture – it will be for nothing.'

He silenced her with a faint shake of his head and his eyes still smiled.

'Don't turn me down tonight. Tomorrow, if you must ... but not tonight.' Then, taking her hand, he lightly kissed her fingers. 'Goodnight, Adeline. Try to get some sleep.'

Something tore at her throat and she fled before it could take possession of her.

Rockliffe watched her go and then said resignedly, 'Well, Harry?'

His lordship was looking uncharacteristically grim.

'The Garfield chit is going around telling everyone that you compromised Mistress Kendrick.'

'Is that a piece of information ... or are you asking a question?'

'Of course it's not a bloody question! Do you think I don't know you better than that? And I saw the state of her. Only a complete idiot could suppose you had anything to do with it.'

'Harry ... you overwhelm me.' His Grace flicked an imaginary speck from one immaculate cuff. 'But sadly, people are very much inclined to see what they wish to see.'

'And you're going to let them?'

'In this particular instance, yes. Why not?'

Harry gave a sudden crack of laughter.

'You're incorrigible, Rock. Are you really going to marry her?'

'Yes. I rather think I am. Do I take it that you disapprove?'

'Much you'd care if I did. But no,' said Harry thoughtfully. 'No. As it happens, I don't. I like her. And you could do a lot worse – little Miss

Look-at-me-I'm-Beautiful, for example. But you must know as well as I do that there won't be any shortage of critics.'

'You are saying that I'll be held to have made a *mésalliance*,' said Rockliffe placidly. 'Yes. But I'm sure you'll agree that is no one's business but my own.'

'Then I wish you the best of good fortune,' shrugged his lordship. 'But tell me one thing, will you? Who *did* try ripping your future duchess to shreds?'

The Duke was engaged in shaking out his ruffles and thus took his time about replying. But finally he said, with caustic humour, 'Think about it, Harry. I'm sure you'll work it out.'

*

As early as possible on the following morning, Lady Franklin summoned her husband and brother to a private conference in her boudoir. She was not in the best of moods. Her cherished ball had been an unmitigated disaster; Diana was still indulging in pointless hysterics; and before retiring for the night, Rockliffe had found time to address her in terms which she suspected were vaguely threatening. It was enough to make a lesser woman take to her bed ... but my lady, fortunately, was made of sterner stuff.

'I have called you here to discuss the consequences of last night,' she began briskly. 'Obviously, Rockliffe can't be allowed to marry Adeline.'

'Can't he?' enquired her husband blankly. 'Why not?'

'Don't be stupid, Roland. It's absolutely out of the question. I wish – just occasionally – that you would *think*.'

'I *am* thinking, he objected mildly. 'Seems to me it'd be a good thing. It would stop Adeline getting on your nerves. And the fellow's old enough to know his own mind, ain't he?'

'You are missing the point,' said Mr Horton maliciously. 'Miriam wanted Rockliffe for Diana. What she assuredly does *not* want is for Adeline to get him instead. I, on the other hand, am strongly of the opinion that any duchess in the family is better than no duchess at all. And if Miriam has spoken to his Grace she must have discovered that Diana has put herself quite beyond the pale.'

There was an ominous silence before her ladyship said sharply, 'Are you saying there's some truth in Adeline's monstrous allegation?'

'Well, of course. Didn't Rockliffe tell you?'

'No. He merely said that, under the circumstances, the precise truth of the matter could serve little purpose. Then he told me that, if she would accept him, he intended to marry Adeline and that it would be wise of me to accept it with a good grace.'

'How very diplomatic!' marvelled Richard. 'Really, you know, it's almost enough to make one wonder if he doesn't *want* to marry her.'

'Don't see why he shouldn't,' remarked Sir Roland. 'Always thought her quite a taking little thing, myself.'

'You,' said his wife witheringly, 'are not Rockliffe. The idea's preposterous.'

'Is it?' mused Richard. 'Then why didn't he tell you that it was Diana who lured him into the book-room in order to try and force his hand? I don't suppose it was Adeline who was supposed to witness what ensued – though Diana was naturally reticent on that point. But she did admit laying hands on her cousin ... which is why I followed Rockliffe back there.' He smiled reminiscently. 'It seemed a pity, you see, that Di should have gone to so much trouble for nothing. But it's small wonder she is still overwrought. It must be galling to know that she's been instrumental in making Adeline a duchess.'

Lady Franklin stared at him with slowly gathering wrath and it was a long time before she said unsteadily, 'Do you know ... have you the remotest idea what you've done?'

'Yes. Since Diana's fences are past mending, I've used her folly to its best advantage. And, if you were less of a fool, Miriam, you'd see it for yourself.'

A tide of apoplectic colour rose to her cheeks and, seeing it, Sir Roland tried to make a strategic exit. 'If you don't need me, I think I'll just go and --'

'Sit down and be quiet!' snapped his wife. And then, to Richard, 'It's you who are the fool. Adeline can't possible marry Rockliffe and you know it.'

'Ah. You're thinking of our dear sister, Joanna.'

'Well, of course I'm thinking of Joanna! I, for one, haven't concealed the truth all these years only to have it come out now.'

'There's no reason why it should,' sighed Richard. 'You were not, I imagine, planning on telling Rockliffe that – far from being decently dead, as everyone believes – his future mama-in-law might at any time walk into his house with her paramour?'

'Naturally not. But --'

'I'm glad to hear it. Because, for all we know, she may actually *be* dead by now. And if she's not – what matter? It's not very likely that, after a silence of nearly twenty-four years, Joanna is going to reappear now.' He stopped, raising enquiring brows at his brother-in-law. 'Yes, Roland? You have something to say?'

'No,' muttered the baronet unhappily. 'Nothing.'

'Good. Then I'm sure you'll both agree that it's quite unnecessary to tell Rockliffe anything.'

'I've no intention of doing so,' said her ladyship. 'Do you think I want Joanna's disgrace casting its shadow over all of us? But I *do* intend telling Adeline the truth at last.'

'And what good will that do?'

'Isn't it obvious? She won't want it made public any more than we do – so she'll refuse Rockliffe.'

'But he need never know.' Richard was fast losing patience. 'Look. Tom Kendrick's dead and, outside the three of us, no one else knows – so how can Rockliffe find out? Moreover, why should he even try?'

'Because he'll want to know about Adeline's background,' came the brittle reply, 'and he's capable of raking through the ashes till he knows everything. The only safe way now is to tell Adeline. I should have done it years ago.'

'So you should,' nodded Sir Roland, unexpectedly. 'Always said she had a right to know. Rockliffe too, if he marries her.'

'Wonderful,' drawled Richard with sudden, deadly sarcasm. 'Absolutely wonderful. Why do we not also set a notice in the newspaper?'

'There's no need to be facetious,' said his sister coldly.

'Isn't there? Let us suppose for a moment that you *do* tell Adeline. What guarantee do we have of her discretion? How do we know she won't tell Rockliffe the whole story – or start digging things up for herself in an effort to trace her mother? Why should she feel,' he finished venomously, 'that, if she can't marry Rockliffe, she has anything further to lose?'

Lady Franklin opened her mouth to speak and then closed it again as if struck by doubt. Richard saw it and pressed his advantage.

'As for Rockliffe himself, the likelihood is that he'll marry her first and ask questions later – if, indeed, he asks them at all. And if he learns the truth once Adeline is his wife, he'll be as eager to keep the secret as we are.'

'I suppose,' came the grudging response, 'that may be true.'

'We progress at last. It is also true that Rockliffe knows enough about our dear Diana to effectively ruin her.'

Some of her ladyship's colour left her. She said, 'I hadn't thought of that.'

'Obviously not. But, once again, Adeline is our safeguard. Rockliffe won't gossip about his wife's cousin.' He paused, his smile once more bland as milk. 'You really have very little choice but to keep your mouth shut and make the best of it, you know.'

She fought with herself and then said sourly, 'You may be right. The most important thing is that Diana should have her chance.'

Richard laughed derisively.

'If Diana had an ounce of intelligence, we would not be having this conversation,' he observed. 'However. Is it agreed that we encourage Rockliffe's suit and say nothing about our unfortunate sister?'

'I suppose so. If we must.'

'I don't like it,' said Sir Roland gloomily. 'Adeline ought to know. It's not right to keep it from her. Not right to keep it from Rockliffe, either.'

There was a brief space while his wife and brother-in-law stared at him. Then, her temper finally getting the better of her, Lady Franklin said, 'Oh – get back to your sheep and your tenants! I don't know why I asked you to join us in the first place – for you've no more social sense than a fly. And if Diana hadn't inherited your brain, it's she who'd be

Duchess of Rockliffe instead of Joanna's aggravating child – who, for all any of us know to the contrary, may even be a bastard!'

*

Whilst his fate was under discussion above stairs, Rockliffe entered the breakfast parlour to find it inhabited only by Harry and Mistress Pickering. His brows rose and, scanning the empty places, he said languidly, 'Dear me! Last night's ball must have been a greater success than I realised.'

Lizzie's grin was unexpectedly spectacular.

'It was. I never thought an evening in this house could be half so amusing. To begin with there was Diana, all powdered and patched and bobbing in and out of the ballroom like a bird with twigs in its beak – and getting sulkier with every trip; and then Cecily disappeared and came rushing back looking as though she was going to burst.' Lizzie paused, apparently savouring the memory. 'She told Diana first, of course.'

'Of course,' agreed Rockliffe, placidly helping himself to coffee. 'And then?'

'Well, for one glorious moment, I thought Di was either going to box Cecily's ears or lie on the floor and have a fit. But she didn't.'

Harry looked up from his plate. 'You sound disappointed.'

'I was – but not for long. She dragged poor Thea on to the terrace where she thought no one could see and boxed *her* ears instead. Then she turned round, stormed right through the middle of a gavotte and didn't come back.'

'While Cecily,' suggested Rockliffe, 'continued spreading the good news?'

'With gusto.' Lizzie rose to help herself to more scrambled eggs from the sideboard. Then, standing plate in hand, she looked him in the eye and said bluntly, 'I know better than believe most of what Cecy Garfield says. But if it's true that you're going to marry Adeline, I'd like to wish you both happy.'

'Bravo!' applauded Harry. 'Well said indeed.'

Rockliffe smiled at her.

'Thank you. That, considering the fate of your dress, is generous of you.'

'Oh – that.' Lizzie sat down again in the manner of one who feels there is no more to be said.

The Duke and Lord Harry exchanged an amused glance. Then the door opened and Adeline came in looking decidedly underslept.

'Good morning,' she said. 'Or, then again, is it?'

'Only time will tell.' His Grace came unhurriedly to his feet and pulled out the chair next to his own. 'May I serve you with something?'

'Just coffee, if you please.' She took her seat with slightly heightened colour. 'Lizzie ... I don't know how to begin to apologise. You've heard, of course?'

'Yes. Don't worry about it. I don't suppose it was your fault, anyway.'

'Perhaps not. But it – I'm afraid your gown is entirely beyond repair. And I'm concerned about how you'll explain it to your mother.'

'Oh – that's easy.' Lizzie reached for another slice of bread-and-butter. 'I'll tell her the truth.'

'Which is?' asked Rockliffe gently.

'Not what Cecily thinks, obviously,' she replied. 'Myself, I rather suspect Diana. I always said she was capable of anything.'

'This young lady,' remarked Harry to no one in particular, 'is plainly destined to go far.'

'I thought as much,' said Lizzie, with satisfaction. And then, to Adeline, 'How *is* Diana this morning?'

'Still in hysterics, I believe.'

'And the rest of our illustrious party?' asked Harry.

'Well, I can't speak for them all ... but Lady Elinor is Comforting The Afflicted, Althea is in hiding and Andrew is still doubtless nursing his head. As for my aunt ...' Adeline turned a perfectly expressionless gaze on the Duke. 'Rumour has it that she's in enclave with Uncle Richard and Sir Roland.'

'Ah. Then, since you and I have not been invited, perhaps we should form our own.'

It was no surprise but this did not prevent her nerves vibrating like plucked wires. She said, 'There really isn't any need.'

'On the contrary. There is every need,' responded Rockliffe calmly. And then, 'Harry?'

'I'm going – I'm going!' His lordship rose, grinning. 'Never let it be said that I don't know when I'm not wanted.'

'Thank you. And could you also oblige me by ... seeing that we're not disturbed?'

'I might manage that.'

'I'll help.' Having demolished the last of her egg, Lizzie also quitted her chair and looked meaningfully at Adeline. 'If you want my advice, you'll think of The Trojan and not quibble,' she said. And walked to the door, bearing Harry with her.

For a moment after they had gone, there was silence. Then Rockliffe leaned back, folded his arms and said, 'Well?'

Adeline eyed him with what she personally considered to be justifiable irritation.

'Aside from the fact that this is probably the most ridiculous situation anyone was ever in, what do you expect me to say?'

His mouth curled in a singularly charming smile.

'I expect you to say "*Yes, Tracy. I'll marry you*".'

That, she felt, was distinctly underhand. Her stomach was in knots. She said, 'Why? You can't possibly want to marry me. And you're supposed to be the clever one - so you must be able to find a way out of this.'

'You're forgetting Cecily Garfield,' he reproved. 'My reputation will be in tatters and my name in the dust. Society will turn a cold shoulder and doors will be slammed in my face. I look to you to spare me all that.'

'Fiddlesticks! If Lord Harry is any indication, the people who know you won't believe a word Cecily says – and your rank and wealth are such that the Polite World will get over its shock fast enough.'

'I know.'

Not unnaturally, it was several seconds before she felt able to reply to this and, during them, she realised something she should have known all along.

'You're enjoying this,' she said slowly. 'God alone knows why – but you are actually *enjoying* it.'

'Well, yes,' he admitted, mock-ruefully. 'I'm afraid I am. But you must not judge me too harshly, you know. I get so little pleasure.'

She suffered a sudden wave of temper, oddly mixed with an impulse to laugh and, unable to trust herself, rose from her chair to put herself on the far side of the table. Only then did she turn and say carefully, 'All right. Play your little game with the rest of them, if you will – but stop playing it with me.'

Rockliffe looked at her thoughtfully for a moment and much of the mischief left his eyes.

'You want the truth?'

'If it isn't too much to ask – yes.'

'Very well.' Rising to face her, he laid his fingers against the rim of the table and, when he spoke, there was no levity in his voice. 'In plain terms, then ... I am thirty-six years old, head of my family and possessed of a seventeen-year-old sister. I am therefore under some pressure to enter into the bonds of holy matrimony. My difficulty has been that, among all the young ladies of birth, breeding and beauty, I cannot find one who wouldn't bore me to death in a week – and that, as you know, is the one thing I can't tolerate. You, on the other hand, don't bore me at all; moreover ... if you will pardon the indelicacy ... I find myself experiencing an increasing desire to take you to bed.' He paused to enjoy the expression on her face, which was less shocked than incredulous. Then he finished simply, 'In short, my dear, I think we might deal very well together ... and am inclined to hope that you may think so too.'

Discovering that her knees were malfunctioning, Adeline slid weakly into Harry's vacated chair. The battle that had raged in her head and heart through the long hours of the night re-surfaced with a vengeance. It was hard when the man who had intrigued and dazzled you at the age of sixteen and whose image had remained, untarnished, in all the years since, offered you marriage. It was even harder when he did it out of a mixture of devilment, clinical logic and, quite unbelievably, lust. And when you added the fact that you wanted to say yes more than you had wanted anything in a very long time, it became downright impossible. So she sat and looked at her hands and finally acknowledged a truth that could no longer be avoided. *'This is dangerous. I could easily – so very easily – love you.'*

In the remotest tone she could manage, she said, 'It is not, then, because of what happened last night?'

'In the sense that you mean it, no. Harry's discretion is to be trusted, Lizzie has plainly drawn her own conclusions and my sister will do as she's told. Aside from yourself, there is no one else in this house whose opinion matters a jot to me ... and neither am I feeble enough to be coerced. On the other hand, when Nemesis speaks, I listen.'

'I see. And you are proposing, in effect, a marriage of convenience?'

'Something of the sort. Yes. I believe you might call it that – at least, for the time being.' He continued to regard her enigmatically. 'I do not, you will notice, expound on what I can offer you.'

'No.' *Pale blue silk and silver tissue*, she thought wildly. 'No. It's self-evident, isn't it? You can take me away from this house. That, as I imagine you probably know, is a greater gift than I ever expected to have.'

He replied with the merest inclination of his head and waited. Silence yawned about them and, finally, when she still did not speak, he said courteously, 'I am sorry to be importunate ... but I really would like an answer. Would it help if I went down on one knee?'

She shook her head, incapable of either humour or her usual astringency.

'Well, then,' said Rockliffe. 'If you could see your way clear to putting me out of my misery, I would be more than grateful. I was rather hoping, you see, that we might leave this place today.'

The aquamarine eyes flew to meet his. *'Today?'*

'Yes. I see no reason to linger. Quite the reverse, in fact. And my valet is already packing.'

'Oh.' Her hands tightened on one another till the knuckles glowed white and she made one last attempt to combat temptation. 'Marriage to me will relate you to Diana. You can't want that.'

He sighed but a glint of humour re-appeared in his face. He said, 'I don't. But, unless you are planning to make a bosom friend of her, I believe I can resign myself to it.'

A faint answering smile touched her mouth.

'Does nothing at all about this worry you?'

'No.' He circumnavigated the table to her side. Then, taking her hands, he drew her to her feet and said, 'We've talked enough for now, I think. Look at me ... and, if you feel you can't live with me, say so now.'

'You – that is unfair.'

'*Do it.*' His tone was still soft but unmistakeably magisterial.

Slowly, very slowly, she looked up at him and drew a long, unsteady breath. Then, smiling crookedly, she said, 'I can't, of course. It would be a lie.'

'So you'll marry me?'

She swallowed hard and nodded.

'Do you think you could say it?'

She hesitated, but only for a second. 'Yes. If you truly wish it, I'll marry you.'

For perhaps the space of a heart-beat, he continued to look at her with an expression she was unable to interpret. Then, 'Thank you. We may now attend to the practicalities. But before we do ...' And, without any warning whatsoever, he slid one hand around her waist and used the other to lift her chin. Then his mouth found hers.

This time it was no fleeting brush of the lips. This time, he took what he had been wanting to take for a week; and Adeline, stunned as much by the suddenness of it as by the feel of his body against hers, found herself powerless to resist. As her hands crept up to grip his shoulders, Rockliffe gathered her even closer and slid his fingers into her hair. Her mouth was indescribably sweet and her response little short of intoxicating; and it was that which made him forget – since it was unlikely she'd ever been kissed before – that he had meant to keep this first time lightly experimental and, instead, deepen the kiss beyond the bounds of either sense or good intentions. He had known he wanted her. Until this moment, he had not known how much.

Drowning in sensations that flooded her body with inexplicable heat, her pulse pounding erratically and her breathing hopelessly disrupted, Adeline simply dissolved against him. His kiss both enticed and demanded, filling her senses to the exclusion of all else and shrinking the world to the compass of his arms. The moment lasted forever and ended too soon.

Slowly releasing her, Rockliffe looked into eyes that were no longer coolly composed but startled, confused and a little shy. Eyes that belonged less to the woman she was now than to the girl she had been eight years ago. '*Ah,*' he thought. '*Yes. There you are.*' And said lightly, 'My apologies. That ... went a little further than I had intended. I will try, for a time at least, not to make a habit of it.'

She looked back at him, noticing the faint hint of colour touching his cheekbones and the odd expression in his eyes. She supposed she ought to say something but she didn't know what. As if he understood, Rockliffe raised one hand to gently caress her cheek with the back of his curved fingers. Then, stepping away from her and becoming unusually brisk, he said, 'Pack only what you need for tonight – and bring the remains of Lizzie's dress. Then make your goodbyes.'

'Is that all?' she managed to ask. 'Shouldn't – shouldn't I go and speak with my aunt?'

'No. That pleasure,' he replied with a sudden, sardonic smile, 'will be all mine.'

*

Having ejected Mr Horton from the room and shut the door in his face, Rockliffe's interview with Lady Franklin was brief and to the point. He said, 'Your niece has done me the honour to accept my hand in marriage. We will return to London today and I shall arrange for the wedding to take place as soon as possible. Since there will be no need for you to put yourself to the inconvenience of attending the ceremony, you may offer Adeline and myself your good wishes before we leave.'

Her ladyship's expression indicated that she had numerous wishes she'd like to offer but none of them were good. She said stiffly, 'This is all very sudden. I hope your Grace does not come to regret it.'

'Your concern is appreciated,' came the smooth reply. Then, 'I imagine that you will be bringing your daughters to town for the season?'

'I – yes. That is certainly my intention.'

'Of course. Then perhaps you will accept a word of advice? As I imagine you are already fully aware, it would be ... inadvisable ... to gossip about the events of last evening since, if the true facts were to become known, Mistress Diana is the one who would suffer most from it.'

Lady Franklin's colour rose. 'I doubt that very much.'

'Your mistake, then. I regret to say it – but your daughter's behaviour reflects very poorly on her upbringing and if she cannot learn to govern her temper, her prospects are bleak. Also, neither you nor she should rely on my sister's continuing friendship since I would prefer Nell not to acquire any of Diana's other unfortunate habits. I trust I make myself clear?'

'You are insulting, sir.'

'That is not my intention – though, in Diana's case, one would have to admit that it is hardly possible,' he returned calmly. 'There is just one final thing. I shall expect my wife to be accorded the courtesy that is her due. Anything less than that and I fear I may be a trifle ... annoyed.'

The threat was veiled but it was there nonetheless. Left with nothing she could usefully say, her ladyship merely inclined her head glacially.

'I rejoice that we understand each other,' murmured Rockliffe. 'All that remains, then, is for me to thank you for your hospitality. I believe I may truthfully say that my sojourn in your house has been one I shall never forget.'

NINE

Adeline was never to know what took place that day between Rockliffe and her aunt. He did not tell her and neither did she ask. Her own leave-taking was discreet in the extreme and had about it a curious feeling of unreality. She did not see Diana; Lady Franklin was frigidly polite and only Tom seemed to mind her going. Aside from that, her sole and abiding recollection of the event was contained in Richard Horton's strangely satisfied smile.

Then they were in the carriage, she and Nell and the Duke ... and the unreality persisted. Nell, who strongly objected both to her brother's decision to wed and her own enforced early departure, stared darkly through the window and declined to talk. Adeline tried to think of something to say that might help matters but eventually concluded that her wits were still too scrambled to be relied upon and abandoned the notion.

It should have been a relief, therefore, when they arrived in St James' Square – but somehow it wasn't. Adeline took one look, first at the majestic porticoed entrance and then, past his Grace's dignified butler, at the exquisitely appointed hall beyond, and her nerve failed.

'*My God!*' she thought feebly. '*What have I done?*'

Rockliffe drew her hand through his arm.

'Welcome,' he drawled, not without a hint of humour, 'to Wynstanton House. Something of a mausoleum, of course ... but one does one's poor best.'

'Yes. I can see that,' she responded, with as much acerbity as she could muster, before somehow finding herself inside.

Nell had already vanished – which could not be considered a hardship – so when the Duke decreed that she herself should have dinner in her room and go early to bed, it seemed a lot easier to acquiesce than to point out the unlikelihood of her sleeping. So she did as he asked, dined in solitary state on duck and green peas, climbed into the vast splendour of the red silk bed ... and knew nothing more until morning.

The maid who opened her curtains and brought the hot water offered to help her dress. Adeline, accustomed to helping herself, sent her away. Half an hour later, having asked for and received directions, she found his Grace at breakfast with a round-faced young man whom he introduced as Matthew Bennett, his secretary.

'Matthew,' he told her, 'is entrusted with the matter of arranging our wedding. An onerous task but one which will not, I hope, tax him unduly.'

Mr Bennett grinned and rose, clutching a fistful of papers.

'Much obliged, sir! I'll try not to let it. And may I just say that I wish you both every happiness?'

'You may – and we thank you,' replied Rockliffe lazily. And then, to Adeline, 'Will the day after tomorrow suit you?'

Having resolved to retain her composure at all costs, she kept her expression at its most impervious and said, 'Yes. Perfectly.'

'You hear, Matthew?'

'Indeed, sir. With your Grace's permission, I'll put things in train immediately.'

'By all means. Ah – and just one thing more. On my bureau, you will find two letters. The one to Lord Amberley, I require him to receive today; the other, to Mr Ingram, will need to be with him by noon tomorrow at the latest. You might, perhaps, send Fletcher with them. And … er … Matthew?'

This, as Mr Bennett showed visible signs of wishing to be gone.

'Yes, your Grace?'

'I'll need the carriage at the door in half an hour,' said Rockliffe.

The young man left the room laughing.

'You're going somewhere?' asked Adeline.

'Not I, my dear. We,' he corrected. 'Yes. I'm taking you shopping.'

'Oh.' A tiny frisson of excitement crept down her spine but she hid it, saying, 'What about Lady Elinor?'

'Nell is still abed. I think we shall not disturb her.' He rose from his chair. 'And now I must leave you for a few minutes. So little time and so much to do, you know. Ring the bell if you need anything - and I will see you presently. Ah …' He turned back, smiling faintly. 'Have Lizzie's dress put in a box and brought downstairs, would you? We will need to take it with us.' And was gone.

Adeline indulged in a number of very natural reflections and summoned her fortitude over two cups of coffee. Then she prepared to accompany his Grace.

He took her first to the Maison Phanie where Madame la Directrice was discreetly informed that she was to have the honour of providing a complete wardrobe for the future Duchess of Rockliffe. Madame refrained from rubbing her hands together and, instead, adopted a mood of brisk elation. Then, having scrutinised Adeline from head to toe, she announced that – since Mademoiselle's figure and deportment were possessed of a certain elegance – it would be a pleasure to create for her A Style.

Having agreed that this was certainly desirable, Rockliffe then proceeded to take a hand in the matter, approving some gowns, vetoing others and suggesting alterations in style or fabric to yet more. Far from being annoyed by this, Madame considered each of his remarks with pursed lips before, more often than not, agreeing that his Grace was perfectly right.

At the end of two hours, Adeline had lost track of precisely how many gowns had been ordered and in what materials; at the end of three, all she remembered with any clarity was that Lizzie Pickering would presently receive a copy of her ruined gown in bronze-green watered silk. She herself had been parted from Lady Franklin's grey polonaise and arrayed in a pink and cream striped gown, hot from Madame's work-room. The carriage already held boxes containing garments of every description – whose purpose, it appeared, was merely to equip her suitably for the next few days; and a complete trousseau, including the *pièce de resistance* which would be her bridal gown, was to follow in due course. Adeline contemplated the probable cost of it all and felt faint. Rockliffe waved her qualms aside and bore her off to buy some hats.

They returned to St James' Square in the late afternoon, heavily laden with spoils. Nell, who had spent a very tedious day and felt decidedly hard done by, greeted them reproachfully. His Grace replied with provocative levity and Adeline, seeing a storm approaching, retreated to her room on the excuse of exploring her new wardrobe and stayed there until it was time for dinner.

When, with unaccustomed self-consciousness because of her new gown, she took her seat at the table, there did not seem to have been any appreciable improvement in the atmosphere. Rockliffe complimented her on the embroidered blue taffeta he himself had chosen and maintained his deliberately light manner, while Nell continued to address both of them with chilly politeness and as rarely as possible. Adeline talked composedly of generalities, swallowed her food without enjoyment and wondered how long it was going to last. And then, when the sweetmeats had been brought in and the servants withdrew for the last time, his Grace brought matters to a head.

'I have to tell you, Nell, that Adeline and I are to be married on Wednesday – with or without your blessing. It would be better for us all, therefore, if you could accept the fact with some semblance of grace. If, on the other hand, you wish to continue sulking, I shall be forced to arrange for you to do so beneath Lucilla's roof rather than mine.'

Nell's cheeks grew very pink.

'Lucilla,' she said crossly, 'won't approve of this any more than I do.'

'In which case, the two of you should deal extremely together,' came the gentle reply. 'Please sit down, Adeline. If Nell has something to say, you have as much right as anyone to hear it.' He waited while she sank reluctantly back into her seat and then turned back to his sister. 'You have our undivided attention. Speak now or not at all.'

'All right!' said Nell. 'I can't understand how it can have happened and I can't bear the thought of what everyone will say. Also, I think I've a right to hear the truth.'

'Well there,' remarked Adeline, 'I have to agree with you.'

Nell looked faintly nonplussed.

'Thank you.' And to her brother, 'Well?'

Rockliffe sighed and made a gesture of surrender.

'It seems that I am out-voted, doesn't it? Tell her, Adeline. She won't believe it, of course … but there's no harm in trying.'

The narrow brows rose but she turned calmly to Nell and, in as few words as possible, told her exactly what had occurred in the book-room on the night of the Franklin ball.

When she had finished, Nell said hotly, 'I – I don't believe it! Di couldn't!'

'Unfortunately, she both could and did,' replied Adeline. 'I'm afraid you don't know Diana nearly as well as you think.'

'A fact,' drawled his Grace, 'on which you are to be congratulated.'

'You're horrid!' cried Nell, surging to her feet. 'I think you've just made it all up.'

'Why?' Adeline's voice was suddenly stripped of all tolerance. 'Because it's easier to believe your brother a clumsy and unprincipled lecher than your friend a selfish and monumentally spiteful cat?'

Nell stared at her and lost most of her rosy glow. Then she made a small strangled sound and fled.

Completely unperturbed, the Duke rested a companionable gaze on Adeline.

'Far be it from me to say I told you so.'

She met his eyes irritably. 'I suppose you realise that there are times when you're not an enormous help?'

Laughter stirred.

'Naturally. But I strongly suspect that, of all women, you are the one least likely to be defeated by it.'

*

With the best will in the world, it was impossible to simply dismiss this remark and Adeline was still considering its implications on the following morning whilst under the ministering hands of the hairdresser. Then there was a tap on the door and Nell's face appeared anxiously around it.

'May I come in?'

'Please do,' invited Adeline. 'You may be able to help me convince Signor Leonardo here that I don't want my hair standing on end as though I've had a fright.'

Nell surprised herself by giggling. The signor sniffed and brandished his scissors.

'Eet eez zee *moda*,' he said severely. 'I am harteest! 'Ow I create eef youno leesten what I say? You wanna look like meelkmide, hah?'

There was a pregnant pause.

'Meelkmide?' Adeline asked of Nell.

'*Si* – meelkmide! *Meelkmide*!' He was almost hopping with excitement. 'I, Leonardo, no do eet! Eet ruin me! I do for you nice 'edge'og, no?'

'No,' responded Adeline, cheerfully but with finality. 'You do for me exactly what I asked. And, if I look like a milkmaid, I'll promise not to tell anyone who did it. And now,' she said, turning to Nell, 'tell me what I may do for you.'

'Nothing.' Nell advanced and the laughter faded from her eyes. 'I came to apologise for behaving so stupidly. I don't know why – but I seem to have done nothing but make a fool of myself recently.'

'Diana,' said Adeline carefully, 'has a variety of ways of bringing out the worst in people. I should know. She's been doing it to me for years.'

Dark eyes, so like Rockliffe's, searched her face.

'Thank you. It's very confusing. I – I liked her so much, you see.'

'Actually, I *don't* see. But that's because I've had several years of watching and sometimes experiencing a side of her nature that she seems to have managed to conceal from you.' There was a pause, and then, 'What made you change your mind?'

'It was what you said about Rock. I hadn't really thought ... but of course he couldn't ever have done what Diana said. He isn't unprincipled or clumsy or... or that other thing.'

'No. He isn't.' A tiny tremor flickered through her as she remembered the kiss – which had been far from clumsy and for which he had apologised. 'Not at all.'

'So, if you really *are* to marry him – though that still seems very strange – I hope that we can become friends. It would be dreadful if we couldn't – for he is my very favourite brother, you know.'

'Yes.' Adeline smiled a little. 'I can see that he would be. And I too would wish us to be friends.'

'Considering how awful I've been, that's generous of you,' acknowledged Nell. And then, 'For someone who's to be married tomorrow, you're extremely calm, aren't you?'

'I *look* extremely calm,' came the dry response. 'Underneath, I'm panicking. What seems strange to you, is to me entirely incomprehensible.'

Nell thought about this.

'Yes. I suppose it must be. Do you -- ?' She checked herself, realising that not only was it too soon for personal questions but that Signor Leonardo was probably absorbing every word. 'You were quite right not to have the Hedgehog, you know. It's become fearfully common-place. Oh – is that a carriage?' She ran to the window. 'I wonder who ... why, it's Lord Amberley! How nice!'

'Lord Amberley?' Adeline rose and allowed the signor to remove the cape she had donned to protect her gown.

'The most attractive man in London – next to Rock, perhaps – and the one with the nicest wife. He's Rock's closest friend. They've known each other forever and --' She turned back to Adeline and stopped. 'But that's charming! And not in the least like a milkmaid. Do you not think so, Signor Leonardo?'

'Eez elegant,' he admitted, critically surveying Adeline's loosely-piled curls and the three thick ringlets lying against one shoulder. 'On *you* eez elegant. On other lady, no.'

'Thank you,' murmured Adeline. 'It sounds like a compliment of no mean order.'

'*Si.*' He laid the tools of his trade neatly away and prepared to depart. 'Eef you ask, I come again to you. But I 'ope you no set *moda* – or I be making many, many meelkmide. *Arriverderci, madonna.*' And, with a quick, flourishing bow, he was gone.

Nell shook her head laughingly.

'What an odd little man he is, to be sure. But he's quite right – you *do* look elegant. It's just the moment to come and meet Amberley.'

Adeline looked dubious.

'You don't think we should just wait for a little while? After all, he and your brother must have things to discuss.'

'Well, of course. He'll have come to stand up for Rock at the wedding – and he's probably dying to meet the bride.' Nell seized her hand, impulsively. 'Oh, *do* come. You'll have to meet him some time, you know.'

Which, though it was true, thought Adeline as she accompanied Nell down the stairs, did nothing to reduce the amount of courage she needed to meet the man who was her betrothed's best friend.

In the parlour, Rockliffe poured wine for his guest and, before the conversation could be monopolised by his own affairs, asked after Rosalind.

'She's in perfect health and glowing, I thank you.'

'And you?'

The Marquis shrugged. 'Less frayed than when we last met. It's a strange thing, Rock – but there's a tranquillity to her these days. Even that bloody bird seems to sense it. He sits on the back of her chair, almost cooing and leans his head against her cheek. It's bizarre – not to mention downright unnerving.'

'Yes. It must be. I take it he doesn't ... coo ... at you?'

'Not so far. He doesn't sit on my chair either. I wouldn't trust him not to take a piece out of my ear. Or, worse still, leave a -- '

He stopped as the door opened and Nell came in followed by a slender, brown-haired lady in palest turquoise. His first thought was that she was not at all what he would have expected; his second, something more puzzling still.

As for Adeline herself, it quickly became apparent that she need not have been nervous about meeting the Marquis. Apart from a slightly thoughtful expression in his grey-green eyes, he greeted her with complete equanimity and charm. He delivered the good wishes of his lady wife along with the small, heart-shaped gold brooch that Rosalind had sent as a bridal gift ... and gave no sign of any inner concern.

But the truth was that Adeline's cool detachment bothered him – as did Rockliffe's more than usually enigmatic gaze. And there was that other thing that nagged at the back of his mind but would not quite come into focus.

Dinner passed more pleasantly than on the previous evening, with Rockliffe and Amberley indulging in their usual sporadic banter and Nell asking endless questions about Rosalind and the coming baby and Broody. Since, with regard to the last of these, Adeline had no idea what they were talking about, Broody had then to be explained, as politely as was possible, given his usual propensities ... and thus leaving Adeline still partially in the dark until Nell leaned across and whispered something in her ear which startled her into laughter. At this point, Lord Amberley noticed that she had a surprisingly lovely smile. His Grace of Rockliffe noticed something else altogether and, as soon as they rose from the table, he drew Adeline to one side and said, 'You appear to have won Nell over. How did that come about?'

'She thought about it properly and realised she was doing you a serious injustice,' she replied evasively. 'She's very sorry. And I think you'll find she'll tell you so, if you just give her time.'

'Instead of locking her in her room on bread and water? I think I might manage that. And, for what you said last night, I thank you.'

Adeline flushed a little. 'She would have worked it out on her own, eventually.'

'Perhaps. But in the meantime, she would have sulked and argued. Her present demeanour is a great deal more pleasant and means I can let her attend our wedding without having to worry if she'll try to enforce the 'just cause and impediment' clause.'

It was not until much later that night that Lord Amberley was finally granted the opportunity of exchanging a private word with the Duke. And even then, he took his time about coming to what he personally regarded as the crux of the matter.

'It's not a criticism ... but I can't help noticing that she's not your usual style, Rock.'

'No. She isn't, is she?'

'And this is all very sudden.'

'Very.' Sighing, Rockliffe paused in the act of pouring two glasses of port and said, 'I suppose you want chapter and verse.'

'Since I'm going to stand up for you tomorrow at your wedding, I'd certainly like to hear more than that you accompanied Nell to what turned out to be the house-party from hell and came back with a bride.'

'Actually, I came back with more than a bride.' He placed a glass before Amberley and sat down on the other side of the hearth. 'I've also acquired a particularly fine horse.'

'Stable the horse for the time being. Just tell me about Adeline.'

'Very well. If I must.'

Since he'd never spoken of it before and, in any case, felt that its relevance could be misconstrued, Rockliffe neglected to mention Northumberland. In fact, he neglected to mention a number of things – choosing to concentrate on Diana's unrelenting pursuit of himself, her unfortunate influence on Nell and the fact that Adeline's presence had been virtually the only saving grace in the whole sorry week. He did, however, describe the night of the ball in some detail and with a dry humour that made the Marquis laugh ... until, that was, he arrived at the point in the tale where he had announced his intention to marry Adeline.

No longer remotely amused, Amberley stared at him and said, 'Had you been drinking?'

'No.'

'Then what possessed you? Or no. Don't tell me. It had turned into farce and you couldn't resist playing along with it. But did you *have* to do something so – so final?'

'Possibly not. But it wasn't completely irrevocable, you know. No one believed that I meant it.'

'Adeline clearly did.'

'No. She laughed ... rather more than was warranted, I thought ... and then she turned me down.'

'She did?' Amberley frowned a little. 'Given her circumstances, that is not just surprising but actually rather remarkable.'

'I'm glad you can see that,' said Rockliffe idly. 'She was still making commendable efforts to make me withdraw my proposal the next morning ... and when I alluded to what I could offer her, she basically said that getting her away from that house would be more than enough.'

'Ah.' Seconds stretched out in silence as Amberley considered the implications of this. Then he said, 'Obviously you overcame her resistance eventually.'

'Yes. It took a little persuasion ... but yes.'

The Marquis hesitated again and then asked the question that had been in his mind all along. 'Are you in love with her?'

His Grace leaned back in his chair and stared remotely into the burgundy brightness of his glass.

'I don't believe so. You will find that peculiar, I daresay ... but it's the only answer I can give. She intrigues me and infuriates me and occasionally arouses a protective instinct I didn't know I had ... all of which is a far cry from my usual indifference. But I've not yet been tempted to lay my heart at her feet – even though, throughout every other emotion she inspires in me, there is inevitably present one that is stronger than any of them.'

'And that is?'

Rockliffe shrugged and a wry smile touched the corners of his mouth.

'For your ears only, Dominic?'

'Naturally.'

'Then ... it's very simple and distressingly basic. I want her.'

Startled by receiving such an honest reply, Amberley drew a long breath and eyed his friend thoughtfully. 'That can't be new, surely?'

'In itself, no ... in its degree, yes.' The smile deepened a little. 'A rakish reputation, you see, rests solely on one's ability to regard lovemaking as no more than a delightful game.'

'And you're saying you've lost that ability?'

'No. Merely that, with Adeline, it doesn't seem to exist. And that, also, is new.'

Searching the hooded, dark eyes, the Marquis said, 'I see. And may one ask how she feels?'

'Unless I'm mistaken, she's panicking over the prospect of becoming a duchess,' replied Rockliffe with languid amusement. 'But about me? I doubt she knows. I am still entirely removed from her experience and

I've a feeling that she hasn't yet decided whether I'm to be taken seriously or not. I believe she suspects me of laughing at her. On the other hand, my touch confuses her ... and that is encouraging.'

'Only you could think so,' retorted his lordship before adding more thoughtfully, 'However. Despite all this, she seems to trust you.'

'Ah. Yes.' Rockliffe again fell to contemplating his wine. 'It does appear so, doesn't it?'

This was not the answer Amberley had anticipated. He said, 'You don't think it might be advisable to wait?'

'Since I am marrying her tomorrow – obviously not,' came the mildly caustic reply. Then, sighing a little, 'Dominic ... I am as aware as you could possibly wish that I need to know her better. But things being as they are, I shall have to marry her in order to do it.'

An ironic gleam lit the grey-green eyes.

'I suppose you realise that, at this point, anyone else would be smugly understanding?'

'Which is why – had I been speaking to anyone else – I would have phrased it differently. Or not at all.'

Amberley acknowledged the point with a faint inclination of his head but it was a long time before he said, 'Will you allow me to observe that you hardly appear to have a sound basis for matrimony?'

Rockliffe set down his glass and came unhurriedly to his feet.

'But I already know that,' he said gently.

TEN

The wedding of Tracy Giles Wynstanton, fourth Duke of Rockliffe and Mistress Adeline Mary Kendrick was celebrated very privately at St George's, Hanover Square and went off without a hitch. The groom, resplendent in pearl-grey brocade with diamonds in his cravat and on the buckles of his shoes, was accompanied by the most noble Marquis of Amberley and exuded an air of lazy amusement throughout. The bride, wearing an exquisitely-cut gown of ice-blue watered silk, lavishly trimmed with pearls, was attended by Lady Elinor Wynstanton and looked pale enough to satisfy the most exacting of critics. And the Honourable Jack Ingram – arriving from deepest Sussex, breathless, but in time to give the bride away – thought her the chilliest creature he had ever met and wondered what could have ailed his discriminating friend; until, that was, she turned and smiled at him.

Back in St James' Square, Adeline awoke to the fact that she had a ring on her finger and that the servants were suddenly addressing her as 'your Grace'. It was, she felt, the most unnerving experience of her life. She looked at the cold collation that had been laid out in their absence as a wedding breakfast and decided that she felt sick.

'If you've changed your mind and would like to be rescued,' murmured Rockliffe helpfully, 'Jack's your man. Or would be, did he not suspect that I might run him through.'

She looked at him blankly.

'And would you?'

'But of course! What self-respecting bridegroom of less than an hour could do less? Have some buttered crab.'

As a lover-like overture or a move of predatory intent, this left something to be desired. Adeline felt her tension ebb slightly and said, '*You* have some. I'm going to keep Nell away from the port.'

On the far side of the room a pair of grey eyes watched them thoughtfully. Like Rockliffe and Amberley, Jack Ingram was also in his middle thirties but cast in a less flamboyant mould. Brown-haired and of medium height, his face was pleasant rather than handsome and his taste in dress more for neatness than ostentation. But his friendship with the other two was of many years standing and, just now, he was concerned.

'Why is he doing this?' he asked of Amberley. 'Oh – it's not that there's anything wrong with her! But she's not exactly his usual type, is she? And, more to the point, who *is* she? I can't remember ever hearing of any Kendricks ... and the only thing Rock's told me is that it's a Northumberland family. *Northumberland*! I ask you!'

The Marquis smiled apologetically.

'Absolve me, Jack. I don't know anything about Northumberland. It's true Rock has estates in the north – but to my knowledge he hasn't visited them in years. And the idea that he's been nourishing a *tendre* all this time is stretching credulity too far. Also, from the little he's told me, it would appear that he met the lady quite recently.'

'But why the hurry?' asked Jack, absently accepting another glass of Chambertin. 'Why couldn't he wait and have a proper wedding? Where are her relatives? It stands to reason that she must have some. And if she hasn't – Rock has. Hundreds of them! Where, for example, is Lady Grassmere?'

'Presumably in a state of blissful ignorance.'

'And you don't find that peculiar?'

'No. I wouldn't have wanted Lucilla at my wedding either,' came the unhelpful reply. And then, 'Why so agitated, Jack? Can you remember a time when Rock didn't know what he was doing?'

'Well, no. But one can't help wondering -- '

His words petered out as the Duke himself crossed to join them, his smile mocking but not unfriendly. 'Well, Jack? Have you come to any conclusions?'

'No,' retorted Mr Ingram. 'I don't know what the devil's going on and Dominic won't tell me – though he seems to think there may be method in your madness.'

'How comforting.' Rockliffe looked at Amberley. 'So what is causing that expression of puzzled concentration?'

The Marquis grinned and withdrew his gaze from Adeline.

'If you must know, I'm plagued by a sensation of having seen your bride – or someone very like her – before.'

His Grace surveyed him imperturbably and reached for his snuff-box.

'Have you ever visited the home of Sir Roland Franklin in Oxfordshire?'

'Franklin? No. I've never met the man.'

'Then you have never seen Adeline before. But you will both of you soon have the ... pleasure ... of meeting Sir Roland's daughters. They are – or were - Nell's dearest friends. They are also Adeline's cousins.'

Light dawned on Mr Ingram. 'So that's how you met her? Through Nell?'

'It is indeed. But I don't think I shall weary you with the full story just now – and, it would, in any case, be a pity to steal Harry Caversham's thunder. Ah.' He paused, looking at Amberley. 'Did I neglect to mention that he was also one of the party?'

'You know you did. Who else did you forget to mention?'

Rockliffe sighed. 'Lewis Garfield and his appalling sister. Cecily.'

'That,' said his lordship, recalling that the name Cecily had featured in the story of the ball, 'is unfortunate.'

'Isn't it?'

'She'll talk. Or Lewis will. Either way, you won't avoid some gossip.'

'Gossip?' asked Mr Ingram. 'About what? This sudden rush to the altar?'

'Amongst other things.' The Duke smiled. 'All will become clear to you in the fullness of time, Jack – and I feel sure I may count on your support, should the need arise. As sure, shall we say, as I am that you will both do me the inestimable kindness of escorting Nell to the play this evening.'

Mr Ingram and the Marquis exchanged glances.

'He wants a favour,' said Amberley. 'We could force him to tell us everything.'

'We could,' agreed Jack regretfully, 'except that a man's entitled to his wedding-night.'

'Dear Jack,' murmured his Grace. 'I knew I might rely on you.'

*

Adeline did not know whether to be glad or sorry when she finally found herself alone with her husband – for the constraint of having to mind her tongue with his friends was immediately replaced by apprehension of a different kind.

It was not, she told herself, that she was ignorant of - or frightened by - what marriage entailed. How could she be? She was twenty-four years old and, she hoped, not a prude. No. What disturbed her was the thought that, after tonight, her safe shores might forever be removed from reach, leaving her out of her depth and with no straw to cling to. She neither wanted nor was ready to love Rockliffe; but, knowing what a mere kiss had done to her, she did not know if she would still have a choice once she had lain in his arms. And that was the crux of the matter.

'Shall I change my gown?' she asked, as soon as the others had gone.

'Why? You look beautiful – and I doubt you will ever wear it again,' replied Rockliffe. 'Or perhaps you were hoping to escape for a little while.'

'Not at all,' she lied coolly. 'Why should I?'

'I can't imagine. But if you are not poised for flight, it would please me if you felt able to sit down and take a glass of wine with me.'

There was not, under the circumstances, any very satisfactory answer to this. Adeline seated herself on a small sofa, accepted the glass he offered and said politely, 'Was there something you wanted to say to me?'

He did not sit beside her and it was a long time before he spoke. Finally, he said slowly, 'Yes. Why is it you never use my name?'

This was unexpected. To gain time, she said, 'Does anyone?'

'That, my dear, is immaterial. I asked why *you* do not.'

She shrugged. 'Who am I to be different? Does it matter?'

'Yes. I rather think it does ... but we won't labour the point. Suffice it to say that, though I'm aware it's the fashion for wives to address their spouses by their title, it's not a fashion I care for.' He leaned negligently against the mantelpiece and continued to regard her enigmatically. 'On a more practical note, you will be pleased to learn that Matthew has discovered a suitable maid for you and has therefore instructed her to present herself for your approval before we leave in the morning.'

'*Leave?*' echoed Adeline, jolted out of her *sangfroid*. 'But we've only just got here!'

'Quite. And tomorrow we leave for Kent and Wynstanton Priors. Nothing, I am afraid, could induce me to remain in town through August.'

For a moment or two, she eyed him with misgiving. Then, setting down her glass untouched, she stood up and said, 'I see. In that case, I should go and attend to some packing.'

Rockliffe smiled but refrained from pointing out that she need never again perform such tasks with her own hands.

'I think you will find that everything has been properly taken care of – including, one hopes, the removal of your things to the suite of rooms traditionally occupied by the duchess.'

'You've had my clothes moved from one room to another just for *one night*?' she asked incredulously. 'Why? Or do you just like making extra work for the servants?'

'My servants, since you ask, are well-paid, well-treated and, in general, not exactly over-worked,' he replied carelessly. 'As for why ... there are three rooms known as the Duchess's Suite – which now belong to you. They also, of course, adjoin my own rooms.' Beneath their heavy lids, the dark eyes gleamed and he held out his hand to her. 'I imagine you'd like to see them. Come, I'll show you.'

'Now?' she asked weakly.

'Why not? There's no time like the present, you know.'

The suite of rooms – bedroom, dressing-room and sitting-room - to which he took her were hung with lilac silk and furnished in mahogany from the hand of Mr Chippendale; there were pale Aubusson carpets, huge gilt-framed mirrors and bowls of fragrant white roses. Adeline, however, was conscious only that the curtains were drawn, the candles lit and an elegant supper for two was laid out in the boudoir.

Rockliffe surveyed the room more critically and said, 'My mother had a fondness for mauve. I have never been sure why. If you wish to change it, please feel free to do so.'

On top of everything else, the suggestion that she might like to re-decorate was a little too much. She swallowed and said, more abruptly than she had intended, 'I'm not sure I can cope with all this. You realise that I don't know the first thing about being a duchess?'

'I realise you *think* you don't – but the truth is that the only trick is in being a lady; and that, my dear, you already are.'

'But there are so many things I don't know!'

'I am aware of that, too. But it's nothing that can't be remedied.' He paused. 'It hadn't, I suppose, occurred to you that I might help?'

She flushed a little and looked down at her hands, saying nothing.

'Obviously not,' he continued dryly. 'But you may believe that I'm not entirely insensitive. I know that you need time to adjust ... and that there are things which you must learn. It is probably the main reason we are going to the Priors. Yes – I know I said I won't stay in London during August and that is true. But it will be easier for you to settle into your new life in Kent with just Nell and myself than it would be here with the vulgarly curious coming to call.'

'Would they?'

'Without doubt. There will be a notice of our marriage in tomorrow's *Morning Chronicle* - a necessary precaution if we are to avoid the appearance of furtiveness.' He smiled down on her bent head. 'So – as I was saying. You will have time to acquire some of the skills you think you lack. But make no mistake. I am not Pygmalion looking for my Galatea ... and I neither expect nor want you to change.'

The blue-green gaze rose slowly to his.

'You don't?'

'Odd as it may seem – no. I do, however, wish to give you this.' He gestured to the flat leather box reposing on the small table between them. 'Open it.'

Her nerves snarled again. With careful reluctance, she did as he asked ... and yet was still unprepared either for what she saw or what it did to her.

'A bridal gift,' said Rockliffe at length. 'You don't like it?'

'I – yes. Yes.' Her throat was paralysed. *Oh God – don't let me cry.* 'How could I not? It's exquisite. But you shouldn't – I can't -- '

'Quite.' His fingers were at her nape, calmly removing the single strand of pearls she'd borrowed from Nell and causing strange sensations to ripple down her spine. Then the glittering necklace of aquamarines and diamonds slid coldly around her throat and she was being turned to face him.

'Yes,' he said. 'Just as I thought. Look.'

Once more she obeyed the pressure of his hands to view herself in the mirror. He was still behind her ... tall, undeniably magnificent and so close that she could feel his warmth against her back. She said unevenly, 'It's beautiful. Thank you. But you – you ought not to have done it. You've given me so much already.'

'My dear, no. I have merely provided a few necessities. This – dare I say it? - is different. There is also, you may have noticed, a bracelet.'

Without moving away, he lifted it from the box and, reaching both arms round her, fastened the pretty thing on her wrist. He felt, rather than heard, her breath catch; and, with his fingers still against her wrist, knew also that her pulse leapt. He was distantly aware that he ought to let her go ... but there was something in the wide aquamarine gaze that he couldn't quite interpret, so he didn't.

His eyes, dangerously mesmeric, met hers in the glass and held them. That and the fact of being so close to him made Adeline feel faintly dizzy. Her senses were wholly disordered and she knew a sudden over-powering urge to lean against him and stop fighting. But her fear of where it would lead was stronger and it jerked her mind awake again. *'It's too soon,'* she told herself. *'Much too soon. Take hold of yourself and use your brain. Now.'*

With the best smile she could manage, she twisted smoothly away from him towards the supper table. A bottle of wine caught her eye and, unable to think of anything else, she said a trifle breathlessly, 'Your generosity is a little overwhelming. I think, if you don't mind, I should like that wine now.'

'With pleasure.' His tone remained perfectly bland but, just for an instant as he attended to the bottle, his eyes were shadowed by something akin to disappointment. 'As you can see, I took the liberty of ordering supper – in the hope that you might now feel inclined to eat.'

She had done no more than toy with the various delicacies of their wedding breakfast. It surprised her that he had noticed.

She said, 'And you? Are you hungry?'

He raised his head and gave her the sudden, uncluttered smile that was beginning to have the effect of turning her bones to water.

'That, dearest Adeline, is a question probably best left unanswered,' he replied audaciously. And then, 'Tell me; would it cast you into a fever of apprehension if I removed my coat?'

'Not at all,' she managed carelessly. 'It's only when the shoes come off that I'm prone to panic.'

'Oh? I must remember to bear that in mind.' He shed the pearl brocade coat, followed it up with his embroidered vest and then handed her a glass of wine before raising his own. 'To us ... and a long, harmonious life.'

Adeline drank gratefully, half-inclined to think that it wouldn't matter which of them got drunk so long as one of them did. It was manifestly unfair, she thought, that shirt-sleeves should suit him so well for she had enough problems already.

Rockliffe remained where he was for a moment, looking at her and recognising that, for possibly the first time in his life, his feelings defied logic. He had known all along that he wanted her but found himself shaken, again, by the force of it. And what utterly astounded him was the fact that it suddenly seemed ridiculously important that *she* should also want *him*. He had intended, this first time, to use all his arts to seduce her ... and he knew that he could still do so. What he did *not* know was whether it might, after all, be better to make the ultimate sacrifice and wait.

He was torn ... and, that, in itself was a novelty. The only trouble was that he was growing impatient to sample that wide, inviting mouth again; and if he did that, he suspected he would be even more reluctant than he already was to spend his wedding-night alone. On the other hand, it was possible that a little patience and temperance at this point might eventually yield rewards of unimaginable sweetness ... for he did not think she was entirely indifferent to him even now. It was a gamble. The question was whether or not he wished to take it.

He sat down and, for the next hour over supper, allowed her to direct the conversation. This she did by pursuing strictly impersonal topics and maintaining her brightest, most impervious manner. Rockliffe had no difficulty at all in ascribing this to nerves and an attempt to keep him at bay with her tongue. In one sense, it was perfectly understandable; in another, he felt vaguely insulted that she didn't seem to credit him with any self-control. He also started to notice the way she appeared to be seeking refuge in her wine-glass. He felt a twinge of something he didn't immediately recognise ... and, from there, it was a short step to irritation.

'Are you merely trying to dull your senses or aiming at complete unconsciousness?' he asked caustically, at length. 'If it's the latter, we'd better ring for another bottle.'

Adeline blinked, startled both by the unexpectedness of his attack and its accuracy.

'N-neither.'

'Don't lie. If the prospect of sleeping with me strikes you as a fate worse than death, I'd prefer you to do me the courtesy of saying so.'

'If it were true, I probably would,' she replied. 'As it is, I'm trying quite hard to come to terms with the fact that, married or not, we scarcely know each other.'

'Indeed?' He leaned back and folded his arms. 'And how long do you suppose it will take to remedy that? Another eight years?'

'That is both stupid and unfair! Eight years ago we met on a handful of occasions – and have hardly exceeded that score in the last ten days. Yet here we are, married. And if you were as sensitive as you think you are, you'd realise ...' She stopped.

'I'd realise what? That you'd like me to keep my distance?'

She flushed. 'I wasn't going to say that.'

'No? Well, then ...perhaps you were going to observe that, since I'm clearly *in*sensitive, I'm sitting here with every intention of presently ravishing my reluctant bride. Is that it?'

'You tell me,' she snapped. 'Or am I mistaken and this intimate little scene isn't leading to the Grand Seduction at all.'

'That, madam, would naturally depend on exactly how reluctant you are,' he drawled. 'Which, my intuition suggests, is less than you'd have me believe.'

This was too close for comfort. Adeline raised her brows and said inimically, 'You would think that, of course. Anything else would be an affront to your vanity, wouldn't it?'

She was given ample time, before he spoke again, to regret this remark. Then, in a tone of dangerous sweetness, he said, 'For someone who admits to hardly knowing me, you are extremely free with your judgements. It is a mistake.'

She was already miserably aware of this but was careful not to let it show.

'I suppose you're going to tell me why.'

He looked at her out of implacable dark eyes for a moment and then came collectedly to his feet. 'Dear me. *What* a lot of traps you're springing for yourself this evening.'

'Meaning?'

'That it is not my custom to justify myself – particularly when it would, in any case, be a waste of breath.' An odd smile invested his mouth. 'I'm sorry if it disappoints you, my dear – but I can actually manage to keep my hands off you. And that being so, I shall do myself the honour of bidding you goodnight.'

It should have been a relief but somehow it wasn't. She watched him retrieve his coat and said tonelessly, 'You're going? Just like that?'

'I'm going – just like that,' he agreed. And making her a slight but very formal bow, he headed for the door which led to his own rooms.

Suddenly ashamed of herself, Adeline rose quickly from her chair. The years rushed back at her and, aware of nothing but the importance of making peace with him, she said, 'Tracy – please wait!'

He stopped dead but did not turn. And Adeline, seeing only his unyielding back, had no way of knowing that he was holding his breath whilst waiting to see what she would say.

She said, 'I'm sorry. This – this is all my fault. It seems I've grown so used to waging my own war of cutting remarks that I'm unable to stop.'

There was a pause and then he said remotely, 'A war requires an adversary. Do you see one in me?'

'No.'

'No?' He turned then and a vestige of humour reappeared in his eyes. 'I am relieved to hear it. What makes you think it was your fault?'

'You know why. The reason you - one of the reasons you married me was because you wanted ... you said you wanted ...'

'To make love to you,' said Rockliffe helpfully. 'Yes. Did you believe me?'

'I don't know,' came the truthful reply. 'But you were quite clear about it so I knew the bargain I was making. Only here I am now, behaving as if - oh, as if you've just abducted me by force, when I know perfectly well that there's no need for it because all I ever had to do was ask you to wait for a little while. And you would have done.'

'I'm glad,' he said simply, 'that you realise it. I was beginning to think you didn't. For the rest, of course ... the fault was probably mine.'

Adeline stared at him.

'My sense of guilt,' she remarked wryly, 'is already thriving. You don't need to tend it.'

'My dear, you malign me. I am merely admitting that, originally, it was indeed to have been the seduction scene. Or so I hoped. But you need not fear another ... or not, at least, until you give me reason to suppose that it will be welcome. Does that,' he finished amicably, 'go some way towards restoring me to grace?'

Since she had neither hoped for nor expected such an offer, it went much further. It also taught her that, in some perverse way, it was probably the last thing she wanted. She said helplessly, 'You are more generous than I deserve.'

'And shall doubtless, in due course, be rewarded.' Smiling faintly, he returned to possess himself of her hands. Then, dropping a light kiss on each slender wrist, he said, 'Once more – and in better understanding – goodnight, Adeline. Sleep well.'

And was gone.

*

Alone in his room with a book he did not read and a glass of wine he did not drink, Rockliffe spent an hour in serious thought. It was the first time, he realised, that he had actually addressed the reality of the situation facing him and the problems that might arise from it. He had been too busy ensuring Adeline's comfort, equipping her suitably and, of course, getting married. What he had *not* done was to consider properly the things that might be going on in her head – so the fact that he was spending his wedding-night in solitary state was, rather annoyingly, his own fault.

It had been naïve of him to suppose that merely removing Adeline from the Franklin's house and showering her with clothes and jewels would be enough to mend the damage of the last seven years. Years in which, layer by layer and brick by brick, she had built a defensive wall that nothing could penetrate. And which he, stupidly, had expected to crumble in the space of five days.

He thought about the Franklin household and her life within it. Lady Franklin, who plainly disliked her, had treated her as a sort of upper servant; Richard Horton was extremely unpleasant – if not something worse; and Diana was an ill-natured brat. Sir Roland was a cipher, Althea a ghost and Andrew a sulky youth ... leaving fourteen-year-old Tom as Adeline's only possible friend. Rockliffe's mouth tightened as he tried to imagine what that had been like and how lonely she must have been. All in all, it was not a pretty picture.

His own behaviour, too, had been less than perfect. Thinking about it now, it was hard to understand how he could have recognised that she needed time to become accustomed to her new position but not that she also needed time to become comfortable with himself. The hope that she might immediately fall into his arms for no better reason than that it was what he wanted, was as selfish as it was asinine; as for allowing his disappointment to get the better of him for a moment ... that had been downright crass and he was damned if he would let it happen again.

He re-examined the thought that had occurred to him much earlier in the evening. The tantalising notion that, if he only employed a little patience, there might come a time when the desire was not his alone -

but hers also. And for that, he suddenly knew, he was prepared to wait as long as was necessary ... because the rewards would undoubtedly be worth it.

ELEVEN

The maid Matthew had chosen was a neat, capable-looking young woman who admitted to having been born Martha Jane Potter but begged to be known to the household as Jeanne. It was not until later that Adeline discovered that this, being a matter of status and fashion, was perfectly right and proper; and by then, Martha Jane was following her to Kent along with Nell's maid and his Grace's valet.

Their cavalcade – which set forth not much more than an hour later than Rockliffe had intended - arrived at Wynstanton Priors in the early evening just as the sinking sun gilded mullioned windows and warmed the pale stone walls. The house thus appeared inviting rather than impressive and was not as vast as Adeline had feared. Her rooms, moreover, overlooked rolling parkland and the tree-fringed shores of the lake – a view which would undoubtedly have delighted her had her mind not been almost wholly taken up with other matters. But the truth was that, every time she felt she had her new husband's measure, he did something totally unexpected ... and she, with misgiving, was left wondering what he would do next.

The following morning, Jeanne woke her with a cup of chocolate and then proceeded to lay out a blue dimity gown that Adeline couldn't remember having seen before. When she said so, Jeanne replied that his Grace had arranged for a wardrobe suitable for a sojourn in the country to be delivered directly to the estate.

'*More* clothes? Really?' asked Adeline, watching the maid deftly twist her hair up into a simple knot and secure it with a couple of silver pins. 'What's wrong with the ones I already have?'

'Nothing, my lady – or not in London. But here in the country, you don't have to dress so formally. And with the weather being so warm, I expect his Grace thought you'd like to have something cooler to wear.'

'His Grace,' muttered Adeline beneath her breath, 'must have more money than sense.'

'Beg pardon, my lady?'

'Nothing.' She eyed her reflection thoughtfully, surprised at how well she looked and, rising, said 'Thank you, Jeanne. That's lovely. How clever of you.'

The girl flushed with gratification and dropped a curtsy. 'It's a pleasure, my lady.'

Adeline did not fully realise the implications of what her maid had said about country fashions until she neared the foot of the staircase and Rockliffe emerged from the breakfast-room. His coat was of plain black cloth and, beneath it, his shirt was open at the neck and worn without cravat or vest. But it wasn't his clothes that stopped her mid-step and made her forget to breathe. His hair, apparently freshly washed, was unpowdered ... and black as a raven's wing. The air froze in her lungs, something lurched behind her blue dimity bodice and she thought foolishly, *'Oh. There you are.'*

Catching sight of her, his Grace started to say good morning and then, absorbing the expression on her face, said instead, 'What is it?'

She shook her head and a strange, almost hesitant smile quivered into being.

Rockliffe crossed to the foot of the stairs and looked up at her.

'Adeline? What's the matter?'

'Nothing,' she said huskily. 'Nothing at all.'

'Then why are you staring at me as if you'd never seen me before.'

'Because, for a long time, I haven't,' she replied. And then, simply, 'Your hair. I'd started to forget.'

Amusement stirred, oddly mingled with faint bewilderment.

'Forget what?'

'How it really looks.' She paused. 'Why on earth do you powder it?'

'I don't when I'm here. But in London? Out of habit, I suppose. I gather you don't like it.'

'No.' Another pause and then, as if she suddenly realised what she'd been saying, her colour rose a little and she moved down to the foot of the stairs. 'I'm so sorry. That was rude of me.'

'No – merely truthful. And you are entitled to your opinion.' He put an arm about her waist and swept her to the door. 'You never know. I might even take notice of it.' Then, continuing out on to the porch, 'Look. And old friend of yours – or so young Tom told me.'

And there, irritably pawing the gravel and threatening to run away with the groom who was holding him, was The Trojan.

*

On the following morning, the Duke found his wife in the stables. The Trojan, who had nearly succeeded in depositing him in a ditch on the previous day, nudged Adeline playfully while she fed him bits of apple. Rockliffe watched for a minute or two and then walked towards her saying, 'Tom told me about this. But after the hellish time that horse gave me yesterday, I came to the conclusion he'd made it up just so that I'd buy him.'

She turned, smiling. 'No. I used to take him an apple every morning. No one else – aside from Tom, of course – ever went near him if they could avoid it. That's why he's so … difficult.'

'My dear, the word difficult really doesn't cover it. He has the strength of the devil – as my shoulders and wrists can testify.' He took the last piece of apple from her and held it out to the horse. The Trojan eyed it disdainfully for a moment and then decided to be won over. 'I'm relieved. I rather thought he might take my hand as well.'

'I'm sure,' said Adeline, 'that you'll improve his manners. In time.'

'One would certainly hope so.' Rockliffe tucked her hand in his arm, led her out into the sunlight and strolled on in the direction of the walled garden. 'If you would like to learn to ride, I'll teach you.'

'You will?' She encompassed him in a wide, beautiful smile. 'Really?'

'Really,' he agreed. 'And now, having done something to please you, I hope you'll forgive what I'm about to say. I should begin by pointing out that, for myself, I have no strong feelings either way … but I'm bound to mention the matter.'

'What matter?'

'Yesterday I believe you went down to the kitchens to ask that some water be sent up for a bath. The results of this simple request appear to have been legion. The kitchen-maid you spoke to locked herself in the scullery for an hour having hysterics on account of her Grace, the Duchess having appeared without warning; your maid was reprimanded for not being available when you required her; and someone was sent to your room to make sure that the bell was working correctly. I trust you are with me so far?'

'I think so.' There was a tremor of something that might have been laughter in her voice. 'Who told you all this?'

'My valet.' He did not add that Perkins, though he had maintained a perfectly straight face, had clearly not been blind to the funny side. 'This, of course, meant that I then had to have a word with Bolton – since it is the province of the butler rather than that of my valet, to apprise me of any malfunction within the household – and Bolton respectfully requested that I lay the matter before you. Which, I hope, I have now done.' He looked down at her with perfect urbanity. 'And the moral of this tale is?'

'Being helpful isn't helpful? Or, next time, pull the bell?'

'Exactly,' said Rockliffe. 'I couldn't have put it better myself.'

*

In the days that followed, Rockliffe spent nearly as much time with his bailiff as he did with his bride ... but still managed to extend her education. He devoted an hour every morning to teaching her to ride on a placid little mare which was plainly reluctant to move beyond a trot. Even so, Adeline found it a difficult skill to acquire until one day, like a bolt from the blue, the knack of controlling the horse from a side-saddle suddenly came to her. Rockliffe then produced a rather more lively mount for her to practice on but, when she asked him if he thought that, one day, she might be able to ride The Trojan, he said flatly, 'Over my dead body. Or, if you were foolish enough to try it, over yours.'

In the evenings, after dinner, he taught her to dance – and this, being naturally graceful, came easily to her. While Nell played gavottes and minuets on the spinet, Adeline held her husband's hand and trod sedate measures up and down the long gallery ... and was happier than she had ever been in her life.

Her afternoons were usually spent with Nell learning to play cards, acquiring a little French or hearing about some of the people she might expect to meet on their return to London. Occasionally, Nell – who was plainly wondering about the precise nature of Adeline's relationship with her brother – asked questions which Adeline found difficult to answer. It would, of course, never do to let her inquisitive and indiscreet sister-in-law discover that her emotions were in a state of near-chaos. Especially when she couldn't, with the best will in the world, account for it even to herself.

Despite this, however, the first weeks slid pleasantly by and Adeline began to settle into her new position. Then, like a hawk descending on sparrows, Lady Grassmere arrived.

She entered unannounced, to find her sister laughingly expounding to Adeline upon the so-called 'language of the fan' – a fact in no wise calculated to improve her mood. And, advancing purposefully into the abrupt silence of her own creating, she said frostily, 'Nell. I have come, as you may imagine, to see Rockliffe. Where is he?'

Nell rose slowly, her face settling into lines of unconcealed resignation.

'Hello, Lucilla. What took you so long?'

'I said,' repeated her ladyship with ominous patience, *'where is Rockliffe?'*

'How should I know? He went out with Wilson to see one of the tenants and will no doubt be back presently. In the meantime, you can meet our new sister – since I suppose that's the other reason why you're here.'

For the first time, the grey eyes turned to rest squarely on Adeline. Then, drawing a long breath, Lucilla said sharply, 'It's true, then. He's married you?'

'Yes.' Adeline's voice was cool and non-committal.

'Why?'

'That, surely, is a question you had best ask your brother, don't you think?'

'I *shall* ask him.' Her ladyship sat down, spread out her moss-green taffeta and subjected Adeline to a critical head-to-toe appraisal. 'Your name, as I understand it, is Kendrick?'

'It was,' came the honeyed reply. 'It is now Wynstanton.'

Nell stifled a giggle and watched a hint of angry colour stain her sister's cheeks.

'Quite. You have done very well for yourself, have you not? From provincial nobody to Duchess of Rockliffe in one move. I only wish I felt able to congratulate you on it.'

'Oh no,' smiled Adeline. 'I wouldn't want you to put yourself out.'

The silence, this time, was positively cataclysmic. Then, 'Despite his deplorable tendency towards levity,' remarked Lucilla glacially, 'my brother has previously always known what was due to his name. Since he has now apparently disregarded this, I can only deduce that it is because you have some hold over him. Am I right?'

Nell opened her mouth and then thought better of it. It did not seem possible that, once Diana and Cecily came to London for the season, the events of Lady Franklin's disastrous ball could long remain a secret; but she herself had promised Rock not to speak of them and she would not.

'You don't,' remarked Adeline dryly, 'appear to have a very high regard either for your brother's intelligence or for his strength of character.'

'How else is one to account for it?' came the reply. 'If you were a beauty, I might understand it better. As it is, I see nothing to explain why – after years of resisting every lure – Rockliffe should suddenly hurl himself into matrimony with such clandestine and unseemly haste.' She paused for a moment and then said baldly, 'You're not breeding, are you?'

Nell clamped her fingers over her mouth. Adeline merely stared, torn between amusement and sheer vexation. Then, before she could answer, Rockliffe's voice said smoothly, 'No, Lucilla, she is not. And I would be obliged if you refrained from repeating that suggestion ... otherwise I am very much afraid that we shall fall out.'

Lucilla came to her feet, slightly discomposed but with enough presence of mind to say tartly, 'Outside these walls, I am not likely to say it. I think you can't deny that *I*, at least, have a care for the reputation of our family.'

'No,' sighed the Duke. He closed the door and crossed to Adeline's side. 'I don't deny it. I could wish, however, that you were a trifle less rigid. You might also, just occasionally, look on the bright side. You wanted me to marry and I've done so. You ought to be pleased.'

'*Pleased*? That you – who could have had Salisbury's girl for the asking – have instead made what can only be considered a *mésalliance*? You must be mad. You make yourself a target for speculation of the most sordid kind; you elevate a person of neither breeding nor consequence into the place our dear mother occupied with such distinction -- '

'*What?*' gasped Nell. 'You always used to say that mama was the most tactless and unpredictable woman in the world and the greatest mortification to you. Even *I* remember that!'

The ribbons on Lucilla's hat quivered with affront.

'I will not,' she said, ignoring Nell, 'be deflected. I am still waiting for an explanation.'

'But I never explain myself,' Rockliffe replied gently. 'Surely you know that.'

'But what am I going to say to people?'

'Why should you need to say anything?'

'Oh – don't be so provoking! It's obvious, isn't it? Everyone will want to know who she is and they'll ask me. It will look every bit as peculiar as it *is* if I'm forced to admit that I don't know.'

Rockliffe contemplated her for a moment and then shrugged.

'Very well. You may say that the Kendricks are an old and respected Northumbrian family and that, on the distaff side, Adeline is related to Sir Roland Franklin – in whose house we met. Will that do?'

'Her parents are dead?'

'Quite.'

'Well, I suppose that's something.' She paused, frowning. 'Do you expect to get away with this without becoming the subject of gossip?'

'I really don't care whether I do or not,' he drawled. 'And now, if you please, we will end this entirely pointless discussion. Adeline is my wife. There is nothing you can do to change it ... and, indeed, if I am satisfied, who are you to cavil?' He paused, allowing his words and tone to have their effect. Then, 'The only question remaining, therefore, is how long we are to enjoy your company?'

'Only until tomorrow,' responded Lucilla waspishly. 'You may be sure I've better uses for my time than to be trailing about after you, trying to find sense where there plainly is none.'

The heavy lids rose and his Grace inspected her with mocking interest.

'Really? Then it's a pity you didn't think of that before you came, isn't it?'

*

Lucilla took her leave without in any sense coming to terms with her brother's marriage – a fact which disturbed Rockliffe not at all but which sent Adeline to the solitude of the lakeside for the purpose of examining a few vital implications.

Since the day her grandfather had died, she had never had to consider anyone but herself. The knowledge that this was no longer so, therefore, was simultaneously both alarming and sweet. One grew used to being alone and, in some ways, it made life simpler. One could say what one wished, for example, and hang the consequences. But all that was changed now – for, in allying himself with her, Tracy had placed his name where mud could be thrown at it. And the more people she antagonised, the more mud would be thrown.

Stooping, she cast a stone into the water and watched the ripples spreading. He had given her a life beyond anything she had ever dreamed ... and had still not expected her to come to him for that alone. If gratitude were all, she thought ... but it wasn't. Far from it. And, for him, she would learn the new skills that were the only means she had of minimising the damage and protecting him from any hurt that might touch him because of her.

His approach behind her made no sound and yet, even before he spoke, she knew he was there. It came to her suddenly that she would always know.

He said, 'Your concern is needless, you know. Lucilla was bound to disapprove of you on principle ... but it really isn't anything to worry about. I should know. She's disapproved of me for years.'

Adeline rose slowly and turned, laughter stirring in her eyes.

'I see,' she said, 'that you have no difficulty in living with it.'

'No. These things tend to be mutual, don't you find? If I dislike you, can you like me? I doubt it. And Lucilla, unfortunately, disapproves of almost everyone. Also, her taste is poor.'

'Obviously.'

'Yes.' His smile was inviting. His words caught her unprepared. 'Tell me about your parents.'

'I can't.' She made the required effort and kept her voice level. 'I don't remember them. My mother died when I was just over two months old and my father, three years later. Aside from that, I know virtually nothing.'

'Did you never ask?'

'Oh yes,' she replied bitterly. 'I asked. Repeatedly. And then learned not to do so. Grandfather would tell me nothing, you see. It was from the servants I found out that my mother had succumbed to a fever and my father to brandy.' She paused and lifted her chin. 'He was killed, I believe, in a drunken brawl.'

Strangely, his Grace did not appear in the least discomposed.

'At Hexham,' he nodded. 'Yes.'

Adeline stared at him. 'You *knew*?'

'I was told. Eight years ago, in fact. I had no way of knowing if it was true.'

'Well, now you do.'

'You sound defensive.'

'Is that so surprising?' she asked. 'How did *your* father die?'

'In bed.'

'Exactly!'

'Not quite,' said Rockliffe, unexpected hilarity sweeping across his face. 'He *was* in bed ... but what killed him was the exertion involved in pleasing a young and particularly demanding actress. His mistress, at the time.'

There was a long silence. Then she said uncertainly, 'You *are* joking?'

'Ask Lucilla. You may find you've something in common after all.'

'Oh God!' Having been lured into laughter, Adeline found it quite difficult to stop. 'So much for respectability.'

He waited for her to recover herself and then said, 'Respectability is all about sweeping the dust under the carpet and keeping the skeletons securely in the closet – something that families with titles or money or both are extremely good at. So ... having established that point, may we now talk about your mother?'

'If you wish. But it's the same story over again,' she shrugged. 'It always seemed to me that there was no love lost between my aunt and my mother. At any rate, Aunt Miriam would say little beyond the fact that my mother was dead and buried – and, she intimated, best forgotten.' Plucking a spray of leaves from the branch drooping beside her, she twirled it thoughtfully in her fingers. 'I remember once asking if I might be taken to visit my mother's grave. A reasonable enough request, wouldn't you say?'

'Eminently so. And?'

'She refused point blank. And when I persisted, she ... lost her temper. I never asked again.'

'I see.' A faint frown touched Rockliffe's eyes. 'And what of Sir Roland ... and your estimable uncle?'

'Richard?' She smiled derisively. 'He told me nothing – for no better reason than that I wanted to know. It is his way. It is also his way to drop little innuendos. For example, I tried to run away once and ... and was stopped. *"Like mother, like daughter,"* said Uncle Richard. I didn't ask what he meant. It wasn't worth it. I wouldn't have believed anything that he said anyway.' She drew a long breath and concentrated on the leaves between her hands. 'Sir Roland was a different matter. I had the feeling he'd have liked to talk to me but didn't dare cross my aunt. As it was, he only ever said two things that mattered. He said that my mother had loved me; and that, if I wanted to know how she looked, I should consult my mirror. *"You are her image,"* he said.' The aquamarine eyes rose expressionlessly to meet his. 'And that, I suppose, explains more or less everything.'

*

The conversation lingered in Rockliffe's mind ... more, he decided, on account of the things she had left unsaid than anything else. His opinion of Lady Franklin, never very high, plummeted to several points below zero and he wondered what it was about Richard Horton that Adeline was not telling him.

I tried to run away once ...

With nowhere to go, that had been brave. Brave or desperate. Had it been worse for her, then, than he could guess?

... and was stopped.

So much and no more. Just three short words to cover – what? Something, he felt sure. She had schooled her voice but not, for a brief, telling second, her eyes. And what he had seen in them was enough to stop him enquiring further.

He pondered it for several days before he finally began to realise where his care of her was leading him; and still, when he had the answer, could not quite believe it.

TWELVE

'Well,' said Adeline, turning slowly from the mirror, 'it seems I'm as ready as I'll ever be. What do you think?'

During the six weeks they had spent in the country before returning to St James' Square, Jeanne had come to know her mistress quite well and to like her. In her opinion, the duchess was easy to serve and – though she demanded no great formality – a born lady. She was also, thankfully, a pleasure to dress.

It was therefore with no small degree of satisfaction that Jeanne now took in the dark, loosely-piled curls scattered with diamonds, the aquamarine necklace encircling the alabaster throat and, finally, the arresting gown of pale blue silk and silver tissue – the significance of which she was completely unaware. Then she said hopefully, 'A hint of rouge, perhaps? And just one small patch?'

'Neither. I've told you. I'll hide behind cosmetics when I have to and not before. In the meantime, you'll just have to possess your soul in patience.'

'It's not my soul that bothers me, my lady,' sighed the maid, unsuccessfully smothering a grin. 'But if you really want to know, you look a treat.'

And, of course, she did.

Rockliffe had chosen the gown – just as he had elected to present his bride to the Polite World by holding a vast, extravagant ball at Wynstanton House. Adeline, contemplating the first of these decisions, hoped that the second would prove equally felicitous.

She descended the great, curved staircase with care, aware of nothing save the fact that he was waiting for her below. Since their return to town, he had taken to wearing his hair powdered again – but not tonight. Tonight, save that it was fastened with a jewelled buckle rather than ribbon, it was innocent of anything except the elusive blue sheen provided by the candlelight. His coat was of sapphire velvet extravagantly laced with gold, over a gold embroidered vest and sapphires winked in his cravat. More than any of that, his gaze turned her bones to water. She hesitated on the last step and said lightly, 'Well? Is the effect all you'd hoped?'

The strange smile in his eyes deepened and he continued to look at her for what seemed a very long time. Then, taking her hands, he drew her towards him and, in one smooth unhurried movement, dropped a brief kiss in each palm – followed with a third on her lips.

'All and more, my dear. You are beautiful.'

Fire licked her skin and she stopped breathing for a second. His face was only inches from her own and his mouth beckoned. Re-inflating her lungs, she reached one tentative hand up to touch his hair and said shyly, 'Thank you.'

'If you are pleased, that is thanks enough.' Her other hand was still in his and his fingers tangled seductively with hers. 'It also has the advantage of giving the dowagers something else to whisper about behind their fans.'

'And the young ladies something to sigh over behind theirs,' she replied without stopping to think.

The dark eyes widened and held hers with sudden intensity for a moment, before travelling to her mouth. She thought, for one dizzying instant, that he was going to kiss her. Then, for good or ill, the mood was shattered as Nell came skimming down the stairs.

'Good heavens – there's no time for that sort of thing! They're starting to arrive. I heard a carriage. How do I look?'

With apparently unimpaired urbanity, Rockliffe released Adeline and stepped back. There was a hint of rare colour along his cheekbones but fortunately, Nell was too preoccupied to notice it.

'Well?' she demanded, executing a neat pirouette. 'Will I break hearts, do you think?'

The Duke raised his glass and scrutinised her at length. Her hair was dressed *à la capricieuse*, a tiny black silk patch adorned one corner of her mouth and the rose satin gown sported ribbons *à l'attention*.

'Quite possibly,' he drawled. 'At any event, you certainly take the eye.'

She giggled. 'I do, don't I?'

The bell pealed, servants sprang into position and the door was thrown wide.

'But you will, I trust, exhibit a little discretion? This is not a *bourgoise* country party and I pray you to remember it,' warned her brother pleasantly. Then, offering Adeline his arm, 'The world awaits, my dear – but all you need do is to be yourself. Ah ... and comfortable shoes help. But perhaps I should have mentioned that earlier?'

And was rewarded with a tiny gurgle of laughter.

At the end of an hour, the house was full of people and Adeline's head, none too clear at the beginning of the proceedings, was positively reeling. She had sustained introductions to Horace Walpole, Lord Sandwich and the Earl of March, and had her first amazing glimpse of the extreme fashions favoured by the Macaroni Club when Mr Fox came in arm in arm with Lord Carlisle. She had met eagle-eyed dowagers, confidently sophisticated young matrons and a stream of blushing debutantes – not one of whom she could with any certainty put a name to. There were only two familiar faces in the entire company. Jack Ingram, who had greeted her with his usual unaffected friendliness; and Harry Caversham, who had given her a wicked grin, demanded a kiss "for old times' sake" and engaged her hand for the reel.

'Old times' sake, indeed!' muttered Nell, having herself received no more than a charmingly polite acknowledgement and not best pleased by it. 'Anyone would think he'd known Adeline for years.'

'I expect,' said Rockliffe blandly, 'he feels that he has.'

'Really? Well, I only hope you're sure he can be trusted not to tell anyone what happened in Oxfordshire.'

The dark eyes rested on her kindly.

'I can. The question is – can *you*?' And, without waiting for her to reply, he turned to meet the next arrivals. 'Isabel, my dear – and Philip. How very well you both look. Marriage must agree with you.'

Tall and good-looking, Lord Philip shook hands with his Grace and smiled pleasantly at Adeline. 'Well enough. I'd planned to recommend it to you – but can now see why you took us all by surprise.'

'You weren't,' said his gentle, brown-eyed wife patiently, 'supposed to say that.'

'Why not? It wasn't a criticism. And Rock knows as well as you that I'm forever putting my foot in it.'

'Always with the best of intentions, however,' murmured Rockliffe. 'But I am remiss. Adeline ... I would like you to meet Lord Philip and Lady Isabel Vernon. His lordship's sister is married to Lord Amberley. Philip, Isabel ... allow me to present my wife.'

Isabel wondered why the note of pride should surprise her and decided that it was probably because Adeline was not at all what she had expected. She smiled and said, 'We knew of you from Rosalind, of course. She wrote and told us that Amberley had dashed to town for your wedding – and how sorry she was to have missed it. She has a particular kindness for Rock, you see – mostly because he was such a help in the days when Philip and Lord Amberley didn't quite see eye to eye.'

'Oh?' Adeline raised an innocently enquiring gaze to her husband's face. 'Pouring oil instead of making waves? I'm intrigued.'

'Are you?' He smiled at her. 'But then – after less than two months of matrimony – so you should be, don't you think? Upon which happy note, we will go and open the dancing.'

She had known that they would have to take the floor alone to formally begin the ball. She had not anticipated having to do so with her wits in urgent need of re-assembly. Taking her place under the battery of eyes, she said with low-voiced resentment, 'You know, I hope, that if you go on the way you've begun, I shall most likely end the evening with a nervous twitch?'

He raised one amused dark brow.

'If I thought that, my dear, it is improbable that I would have married you. As it is, I know you to be fully capable of coping with my little ... vagaries. Furthermore, if you could only relax a little, I suspect you might become the latest toast before morning.' The music began and his mouth curled as he bowed over her hand. 'You are supposed to curtsy, you know. And a smile would be nice.'

It was fortunate that, along with Adeline's own natural grace, Rockliffe had proved a good teacher. Even so, the minutes before Nell and Lord March joined in behind them seemed interminable and it was not until the floor became suitably populated that she lost the desire to sink through it.

From the periphery, Philip Vernon and Mr Ingram watched with interest.

'Why do you think he's stopped powdering his hair?' asked Philip who, seeing how it suited the Duke, was considering forsaking the fashion himself.

'I have no idea. Probably his latest whim. You know what he's like,' Jack replied. And then, 'What do you think of the bride?'

'I've barely exchanged two words with her so far. Not his usual type though, is she? I mean, the one thing you've always been able to say for Rock is that he has extremely high standards. Mundane, perhaps – but high. And I'm still trying to decide whether or not she's pretty.'

'She's not,' said a pleasant voice from behind them. 'But she's damnably seductive. And sometimes … just sometimes … beautiful.'

'Harry,' breathed Jack, with satisfaction.

And, 'God. Why didn't I notice all that?' grinned Philip.

'Because you're a good and dutiful husband,' responded Harry Caversham promptly. And then, meeting Mr Ingram's expectant gaze with one of brimming hilarity, 'Well, Jack? Our naughty, naughty friend told you half a story, has he?'

'Not even that. He said, as I recall it, something about not stealing your thunder.'

'Mighty nice of him, I'm sure. And I suppose you've been waiting for the chance to pounce on me ever since.'

'Something like that. Well?'

'Wait a minute.' Philip stared at the man who was, in reality, his closest friend. 'Are you saying that you know more of this sudden marriage than we do?'

'Yes,' said Harry simply. And then, 'What it is to be in a position of power.'

'What it is,' retorted Philip, folding his arms, 'to be in a position of having your jaw broken. Come on. Tell.'

'Devil a word, Phil – devil a word.' His lordship's face was alight with palpable enjoyment. 'But I'll give the pair of you a word of advice, if you like.'

'And that is?' asked Jack.

'Not to believe everything you hear,' replied Harry airily. And sauntered off to claim his dance with Adeline.

On the other side of the ballroom, his Grace appeared to take snuff in the languid manner so peculiarly his own and looked pensively at the outrageously-clad person of his friend, Mr Fox.

'Instinct warns me that you are about to insult my wig,' said that gentleman calmly. 'Don't.'

'*Is* it a wig?' Rockliffe eyed the enormous ladder-toupé with mild disbelief. 'But you malign me. I was simply wondering if you felt a trifle bilious ... or whether it is merely the lavender powder that makes you *appear* so.'

'You know, my dear,' sighed Mr Fox, 'there are times when I am forced to seriously consider dropping you. Particularly,' with a wave at his Grace's unpowdered head, 'if you are about to adopt country fashions.'

The Duke's brows rose over eyes full of amusement.

'But where would you be then, Charles? You must know that your greatest social advantage is being noticed by me. It is just a tremendous pity that I have never succeeded in teaching you how to dress.'

An answering gleam lit Mr Fox's sallow countenance and he said, 'It is as well you are amusing, Rock. Otherwise I fear your conceit would be unbearable. And you have pupils enough, surely? Why even now, I'll wager you're busy devising a style for your bride.' He paused and, flicking open his chicken-skin fan, plied it gently. 'She is a very striking woman, by the way. Very striking. I congratulate you.'

'Thank you.'

'But what I would give a great deal to know,' continued Mr Fox meditatively, 'is why she is the image of a lady I met some years ago in Paris.'

There was a tiny, arrested pause. Then Rockliffe said idly, 'Dear me. Is she?'

'Oh yes. The resemblance is quite uncanny. The lady, as I recall, was married to a military gentleman.' Mr Fox matched his smile with a faintly deprecating gesture of his fan. 'I daresay I should have forgotten her but for the fact that she lodged with the particularly inviting little widow I was pursuing at the time.'

'Dear Charles,' sighed the Duke. 'How very like you.'

'Quite.' Mr Fox eyed him with gentle expectation and then, when nothing was forthcoming, said, 'One cannot but wonder if the lady I met is perhaps a relation?'

Again, the briefest of hesitations. Then, smiling urbanely, Rockliffe said, 'Unlikely, I should think. And they do say, do they not, that every one of us has a double?'

'Ah yes. So they do. A singularly tedious thought ... and therefore, perhaps, not worth bothering about?'

'Certainly not worth bothering about.'

For a long moment, Mr Fox's speculative stare met Rockliffe's bland one. Then, holding out his snuff-box, the Duke said smoothly, 'Silver-gilt and decorated in the Florentine style. I considerate it rather unusual. What is your opinion?'

While Adeline fell into the clutches of the dowagers and tried, in fulfilment of the promise she had made to herself, to answer their questions with submissive patience, Nell found herself face to face with Harry Caversham in the library.

'Oh,' she said disdainfully. 'It's you.'

'Profound,' grinned his lordship, 'and beyond dispute. But best tell me quickly; are you merely in hiding – or have I stumbled on a tryst?'

'Neither. I came in here to repair a torn flounce. What's your excuse?'

'Oh – I'm avoiding Jack,' he replied carelessly. And then, 'What happened, Nell? One of your admirers get carried away by your charms, did he?'

'No! And I'll thank you to stop making such – such vulgar insinuations,' she snapped. 'If you must know, I caught my heel in my petticoat – not that it's any business of yours! And why, exactly, are you avoiding Jack?'

Harry laughed. 'Isn't it obvious? He knows that I know but doesn't know *what* I know. And he wishes he did.'

Nell frowned. 'I suppose that means you let something slip.'

'Yes. Well, you *would* suppose that, wouldn't you?' he returned with unabashed good-humour. And then, 'I don't suppose you'd care to come and dance with me?'

'Unfortunately,' she mourned with relish, 'I am fully engaged for the entire evening.'

'Yes,' said Harry ambiguously. 'I thought you would be.'

And, turning on his heel, left her to grind her teeth at his retreating back.

It was the Earl of March who unwittingly released Adeline from her ordeal of interrogation by soliciting her hand for the gavotte.

'Insipid,' remarked Lady Fitzroy disparagingly, as soon as they were out of earshot. 'Insipid, provincial and rather plain. One wonders what Rockliffe can have seen in her.'

'Indeed,' agreed her friend, Mrs Lowerby. 'One cannot also help but wonder what dear Lucilla thinks of it all.'

Dolly Cavendish regarded them with mildly exasperated amusement.

'Since dear Lucilla has been persistently trying to thrust Rock into the arms of Salisbury's daughter, I imagine what she thinks is fairly obvious,' she said dryly. 'And don't be too quick to dismiss our little Duchess. There is more to her, I feel sure, than meets the eye … for Rock's taste, as we know, is never less than impeccable.'

Lord March, meanwhile, was finding his companion far from insipid and it was with open reluctance that he relinquished her at length to Mr Ingram.

'It seems you've made a conquest,' said Jack lightly. And then, with what – for him – was quite remarkable cunning, 'Another one.'

Adeline looked at him with perfectly-concealed wariness and a good deal of enquiry.

'I was referring to Harry Caversham,' he explained. 'He admires you a good deal.'

'Does he?' she asked blankly. 'Good heavens!'

This was not quite what Jack had expected and neither was it a help. It was also ill-timed since at that moment they were separated by the movement of the dance and he had to wait before adding casually, 'Of course, Harry has the advantage of knowing you better than the rest of us.'

The aquamarine eyes gathered sudden brilliance and her mouth curved into a disconcertingly splendid smile.

'But for which – like the rest of you – he'd naturally admire me much less?'

Belatedly aware of his *faux pas*, Jack coloured and lost himself in a tangle of apologies.

Adeline laughed.

'Mr Ingram – please! I know exactly what you meant and also what you hoped to achieve by it, so I'm afraid I couldn't help teasing you a little. And if you really want to question me, you'd do much better to go about it directly, you know. It would come more naturally to you – and I'd respond better.'

Jack stared at her, temporarily bewitched by those luminous dark-fringed eyes. Then, slowly and ruefully, he smiled.

'You're right, of course. And I'm sorry.'

'Don't be.' She pivoted gracefully under his arm and sank down before him in a deep, final curtsy. Then, rising, she said bluntly, 'The position is very simple. I'm not going to tell you exactly how my marriage came about because I don't know you well enough. Yet. And Tracy won't tell you because he's having fun watching you guess.'

'Point taken,' said Jack, his smile broadening. And then, 'You understand him rather well, don't you?'

'I'm learning,' came the candid reply. 'But I can always use help.'

Something in her tone touched him and she had his allegiance from that moment. In token of it, he kissed her hand and said, 'Then – as an old family friend – do you think you might get used to calling me Jack?'

Never so far away that he could not intervene should the need arise, Rockliffe had kept a proprietorial eye on his wife all evening. He had seen her dance with Harry, Jack, Philip and countless others; he'd watched her laugh at something Charles Fox said, blush at something

Lord March said and enjoy quite a long conversation with Isabel Vernon. And at around midnight, seeing her about to bestow her hand on Lord Harry for the second time, he decided that enough was enough.

Emerging beside them and looking down into Adeline's eyes, he said, 'My dance, I think.'

'Your mistake, then,' said Harry promptly. 'Her Grace is promised to me.'

Rockliffe recognised the provocation and responded to it.

'Perhaps. But I have a husband's prerogative. You'll forgive me, I'm sure.'

'And if I won't?'

'In that case ... I might have no choice but to call out that pretty small-sword of yours.'

Harry laughed. 'Not a chance! If you challenge me, it'll be pistols at dawn. Amberley says you're a lousy shot.'

'Dominic,' sighed the Duke, 'thinks virtually *everyone* a lousy shot.' He paused, smiling faintly, 'Well, Harry? The music is starting, you know.'

His lordship grinned and then made Adeline a flourishing bow, 'He's a pirate, of course. But my mother always told me to defer to my elders – so I concede.' And stepped smartly away before Rockliffe could respond.

Her eyes brilliant and brimming with laughter, Adeline let his Grace take her hand and lead her into the dance. She said, 'Your friends have all been so kind.'

'Yes. I've noticed. What did March say to you?'

'Lord March?' she asked, surprised. 'I've talked with so many people, it's hard to recall. Why?'

'No particular reason.' His gaze, no longer smiling and curiously intent, travelled to her mouth and stayed there.

A wave of heat washed through her and she felt her colour rise.

'Ah,' said Rockliffe. And then, obscurely, 'That's comforting.'

Watching from the edge of the floor, Dolly Cavendish drew a long breath.

'Well,' she said, in satisfied tones. 'At last.'

Gently plying his fan, Mr Fox raised languid brows. 'What is?'

'Nothing.' She smiled. 'I think I must pay the new Duchess a morning-call.'

It was not until after three in the morning that the last of the carriages rolled away and Rockliffe was left alone with his wife and sister. He looked at Nell, collapsed in a state of happy exhaustion ... and smiled at Adeline, whose first instinct had been to take off her shoes. Then, pouring two glasses of wine, he handed her one of them and said, 'A very successful evening, I think. Did you enjoy it?'

Adeline gazed speechlessly back at him. She had been put on show like a prize heifer and forced to frame tactful answers to impertinent questions. Her nerves, through much of the evening, had been stretched like violin strings and her husband – who had, from time to time, been at his most provoking – was now calmly asking if she had enjoyed it.

'Yes,' she heard herself say. 'Yes. I did.'

'Surprising, isn't it?' He smiled. 'But no surprise at all, I hope, to learn that I was extraordinarily proud of you.'

'Were you?' asked Adeline, flushing a little. 'Thank you.'

Rockliffe shook his head very slightly and continued to look at her with an expression she could not interpret. Then, turning his gaze to his sister, he said, 'If you are going to sleep, Nell, I suggest you do it in bed.'

'Mm.' She yawned, swung her feet to the floor and sat up. 'I'm trying to summon up the energy to move.'

'I'm not surprised,' remarked Adeline. 'You weren't exactly lacking in partners, were you?'

'No.' Nell beamed. 'And you wouldn't *believe* how many gentlemen I had to refuse.'

'Really?' queried her brother. 'Then it is a great pity that Jasper Brierley couldn't have been one of them.'

'Why?' Nell was suddenly wide awake. 'He's vastly elegant and very amusing.'

'He is also twice your age, a hardened gamester and something of a rake,' replied Rockliffe dryly. 'I should prefer, therefore, that you did not encourage him.'

For a moment, Nell's expression grew mutinous. Then her face cleared again and, laughing, she rose to plant a kiss on his cheek.

'Dear Rock. Are you worried I'll fall victim to Sir Jasper's fatal charm? You needn't be, you know. Cassie Delahaye says he's hanging out for a rich wife and I think it's very likely true so I wouldn't dream of taking him seriously.'

'I rejoice to hear it.'

'But, on the other hand, he *is* very distinguished and it will improve my consequence no end if he is seen to admire me. So, if you don't mind, I shan't discourage him just yet because I think one has to make the most of one's opportunities.' Nell's smile became a yawn and she moved towards the door. 'I'm going to bed. It was a lovely evening – and you were splendid, Adeline. Cassie says you're the most elegant creature she's ever seen and she wishes she were only *half* as graceful. Isn't that nice? Goodnight, darlings.' And she was gone.

'Cassie says,' remarked Rockliffe lazily. 'The new *leitmotif*, do you think?'

'Probably. The question is, which one was Cassie?'

'The brown-haired child in apple-green satin. Her father is a friend of mine and her mother has both humour and a good deal of sense.' He smiled. 'I think we may safely approve of Cassie. Her influence should not be a problem.'

'Speaking of which,' said Adeline obliquely, 'what happens when my aunt brings dear Diana to town?'

His brows rose.

'Why, nothing. Your aunt will not gossip for fear that I may retaliate in kind and thus ruin Diana. It is really very simple, you see – and need in no way concern you.'

'That's nice. And what about Cecily Garfield?'

'Ah. Now she, of course, is less easy to silence. But without corroboration, who is going to believe her?'

'I see,' said Adeline, acidly-admiring, 'that you've got it all worked out.'

'Naturally. Confident to the last. Would you expect anything less?'

*

Later, when he could not go to sleep, he wished the words had been true. But a sense of unease nagged ominously at the back of his mind and would not be ignored.

The root of it was contained in a handful of apparently random facts. Amberley had been plagued by a feeling of having seen Adeline before; Adeline herself, amid an inexplicable wall of silence, had been told only that she was the image of her dead mother; and Charles Fox had been struck by the remarkable likeness Adeline bore to a woman he'd met years ago in Paris. If one was inclined towards a belief in coincidence, one would simply dismiss it. If not, it pointed towards a suspicion so bizarre that one would have to investigate it further.

'And I,' thought Rockliffe, with a sigh, *am of a suspicious turn of mind. Damn.*'

But what if he made enquiries and found himself proved right? It might, he reflected, be better not to know; except that it was generally the things you didn't know about that tended to drop on you from a great height. And if that happened, it was not he who would be crushed by it – but Adeline.

Adeline. He had begun their marriage simply wanting to make love to her – and that was still true. Since the day at the lake, however, he had become increasingly aware that that, in itself, was no longer enough ... that what he wanted now was a good deal more complex and difficult to attain. Recalling, all too vividly, her response to his proposal of marriage, baring his soul to her wasn't a risk he was prepared to take just yet. Consequently, it seemed that his only viable course was to set aside the fact that she was his wife and court her as he had never courted a woman in his life. Unfortunately, however, after his conversation with Charles Fox, it also appeared that his first and most important task was going to be finding out if her mother wasn't dead after all.

'Hell,' he enunciated delicately, 'and damnation. I hope ... I really hope I'm wrong and the whole thing *is* just a coincidence. Because if it's not, I'm going to have to do something about it. And the obvious question is – what?'

THIRTEEN

The polite world accepted Adeline with mixed feelings whilst marvelling at Rockliffe's sustained attentiveness. Some maintained that this was obviously due to a desire to see his bride securely established in society; others said, with amusement, that he had lost his heart at last. The gentlemen argued lightly over the precise nature of the indefinable quality so many of them found attractive in the new duchess; the ladies, by and large, voted her insipid.

Having paid her promised morning-call and found herself in the company of Mr Fox, Lord March and Serena Delahaye, Dolly Cavendish did not get a chance to speak to her Grace of Rockliffe privately until the evening of Lady Hervey's *soirée*. Then, finding herself temporarily alone with Adeline, she said pleasantly, 'Do you mind if I give you a word of advice?'

'Not at all,' came the equally pleasant reply. 'As long as you won't mind if I choose not to take it.'

'There! That's exactly the point I was about to make.'

'I don't think I follow.'

Her ladyship sighed. 'My dear, you just answered me like the person of character I suspected you to be. I merely wanted to suggest that you do it more often.'

The aquamarine eyes remained perfectly expressionless.

'Meaning that, at present, I'm hiding my teeth?'

'Aren't you? Why else – after ample provocation – haven't you put the likes of Maria Fitzroy firmly in their places?'

'Perhaps because I'm reluctant to sink to their level.'

'Or perhaps because you've an over-developed awareness of the vulnerability of your position,' returned Dolly calmly. 'It's up to you, of course. I know a soft answer is supposed to turn away wrath – but, in my experience, you can't beat a clever one for quelling patronising impertinence. And if it's Rock you're worrying about rather than yourself – don't. He'd flatten them with a look if he heard how they speak to you. Think about it.' And she drifted away to claim the attention of Lord Carlisle.

Thoughtfully, Adeline watched her go. There was no need, with Dolly, to ponder the question of possible malice ... and therefore the only thing worth considering was whether her advice was sound.

'You look,' said a voice beside her, 'as though you're addressing deeply moral questions. You must've been listening to Horry Walpole's essays.'

'And what have you been listening to?' she retorted. 'The tenor with a posy of violets or Mistress Lichfield's harp?'

Harry Caversham winced, laughter crinkling his eyes.

'Is it likely?'

'No. So perhaps you've come for the poetry. Never say that you're consumed of an ode!'

'You'd look no-how if I said I was, wouldn't you?'

'Less so than you by the time you've been asked to read it.'

'Fiend!' said Harry amicably. 'All right. I'll admit I don't usually attend *soirées* and that I'd have given this one the go-by too, except that I – I hadn't an invitation I liked better. And, of course, I counted on seeing you here.'

Adeline surveyed him clinically.

'If I were the credulous type, I daresay I'd be flattered. As it is, I'll simply tell you that Nell's gone to the Pantheon in Lady Delahaye's party.'

There was a short silence. Then Harry said, 'Do you do that to everyone?'

'No – but I think I'm about to start. And then we'll see, won't we, if I'm still considered insipid?'

'Ah.' He nodded. 'And you won't be. Not before time, either. Your Uncle Richard has written announcing his imminent arrival in town – along with your aunt and cousins.'

Adeline's mouth curled and her tone grew noticeably mellow.

'A family reunion, in fact. How delightful. All we need is Lewis and dear Cecily and it will be just like old times.'

'Quite. Is Rock worried?'

'*Worried*? Don't be silly. He's looking forward to it.'

'God,' grinned Harry. 'Now that really *is* all we need.'

'We?'

'Well, of course. It's my secret too, you know.'

An acidulous glint lit Adeline's eyes but, before she could reply, Isabel Vernon joined them looking radiant with pleasure.

'Just the people I've been looking for. I have wonderful news. I am an aunt!'

'Rosalind?' asked Harry.

'Yes. A little boy, born the day before yesterday – and both doing well. Isn't that splendid?'

'Absolutely splendid,' he agreed. And then, diffidently, 'And the baby is ... healthy?'

'Perfectly. Oh – you mean can he see?' said Isabel, light dawning. 'Well, of course it's rather too early to tell – but there's no reason why he should not. After all, Rosalind wasn't born blind, was she? Ah - there's Jack. Do excuse me.'

When she had left them, Adeline looked with careful restraint into his lordship's blue eyes.

'The Marchioness of Amberley is blind?' she asked.

'Yes. Didn't you know?'

'No. I didn't. Why, do you suppose, no one thought fit to mention it?'

'Probably,' remarked Rockliffe from behind her, 'because it is less important than you might think. Well, Harry? Have you forsaken the card table in favour of more cultured pursuits?'

'No,' said his lordship flatly. 'And what's more, I'm not going to let myself be roasted twice in one evening. In short, I'm going.' And went.

The Duke turned a lazy regard on his wife.

'Now what, I wonder, brought Harry to break the pattern of a lifetime?'

Adeline opened her mouth to tell him and then, struck by the novelty of knowing something he did not, changed her mind. She said, 'My uncle has written to say that the family are on their way to town. Harry thought we'd like to know.'

'Ah. Yes. That would naturally explain it.'

His tone held a trace of something oddly disquieting and she eyed him suspiciously for a moment before saying, 'Lord and Lady Amberley have a son. Did you know?'

'Philip told me. It seems that he and Isabel are to stand sponsors to the child and, being Philip, it's a responsibility he is taking very seriously.' A gleam of humour appeared in his eyes. 'Since Dominic apparently said that he also plans to ask me, Philip was anxious to seek my advice. It's a habit with him. I believe he regards me somewhat in the light of parent – but it is not a question I care to probe too deeply.'

She smiled. 'No. I can see why you wouldn't.'

'You comfort me. And now, my dear, I thought we might go and listen to my friend Mr Fox. He has a certain reputation for wit ... largely undeserved, of course – but it would never do to say so.'

*

On the following afternoon whilst Adeline and Nell were taking tea with Dolly Cavendish, Rockliffe's man of law – having been charged with certain enquiries – came to St James' Square to report his findings.

'Your Grace, I have visited the parish of Evesham in the Cotswolds from whence the Horton family originate and likewise the parish adjacent to Sir Roland Franklin's property in Oxfordshire,' announced Mr Osborne primly. 'At Evesham, I found the graves of numerous Hortons but neither there nor in Oxfordshire could I locate a grave bearing the name of Joanna Kendrick. Nor is there any mention of her in the Parish Records.'

'I see.' The Duke surveyed his hands. 'No private chapels?'

'None, your Grace.'

'No. I thought not.' He sighed faintly. 'How very inefficient of them. It surely cannot be so very difficult to bury a weighted casket?'

Mr Osborne stiffened.

'I am afraid I cannot say, your Grace. It is not a matter I have ever had occasion to contemplate.'

'Nor I, Mr Osborne – nor I. But you do see my dilemma, don't you? The absence of a grave suggests the lack of a body ... and that naturally leads me to suppose that my original suspicion was correct and my mother-in-law is still very much alive. Only think, my dear fellow – she could walk into my life even as we speak.'

A haunted expressed crossed the desiccated face and then was gone.

'But why, your Grace, should the lady's family wish the world to believe her dead?'

'Now that,' said Rockliffe, 'is probably the crux of the matter. And I can only think of one reason.'

'Scandal, your Grace?'

'Scandal, Mr Osborne.'

The lawyer shuddered.

'Then how does your Grace suggest we proceed? Without further information, our hands are tied.'

'Quite. But a chain, so they say, is only as strong as its weakest link.' The Duke came unhurriedly to his feet. 'I propose, therefore, to exploit that link.'

Mr Osborne looked dubious.

'It is a very delicate matter.'

The dark eyes mocked him.

'Do you doubt my powers of diplomacy?'

'No, no. Not at all. But does your Grace not think that it might perhaps be best to leave well alone? After all, a secret preserved so carefully and for so many years by the lady's family is unlikely to come out now.'

'On the contrary,' responded Rockliffe dryly. 'Now is precisely when it *would* come out. And forewarned is most definitely forearmed. But be of good cheer, Mr Osborne. I will take the matter into my own hands for a time and see what comes of it. If and when I have further instructions for you, I will notify you of them in due course. Meanwhile I rely, as always, on your complete discretion.'

Mr Osborne bowed.

'Your Grace may safely do so.'

'A thought,' remarked his Grace, winsomely, 'which is a constant comfort to me.'

*

Two evenings later and for only the second time in his marriage, Rockliffe walked unceremoniously through the communicating door leading to his wife's boudoir.

Seated at her mirror, with only a pink silk wrapper covering her under-dress while Jeanne put the finishing touches to her hair, Adeline saw him through the glass and froze. Then, summoning her resources, she said lightly, 'If I'm late, I beg your pardon. But it took me quite twenty minutes to convince Nell that, however dashing she may think her new coquelicot stripe, it is *not* the thing for Bedford House.'

'Certainly not,' he agreed placidly. 'In fact, unless she cares to attend a masquerade disguised as a travelling show-booth, it is out of place anywhere. And you are not late.'

'Oh.' Since he must obviously have had some special reason for breaking his own embargo, this was confusing. Trickier still was the question of whether or not etiquette demanded that, when one's husband came to call, one should dismiss one's maid.

In the seconds that she hesitated, Jeanne solved the dilemma for her by murmuring that, with her Grace's permission, she would retire to the dressing-closet to lay out her Grace's cloak. And almost before Adeline knew it, she was alone with the Duke.

'You wished to speak to me?' she asked. His eyes were tracing the line of her throat, causing odd sensations to take place in the pit of her stomach and making her absurdly shy.

'Ah, yes. I believe I did.' Without any sign of haste, his gaze travelled back to her face. 'I came to tell you that my lords March and Carlisle presented themselves a short time ago in the hope that you might grant them the honour of admitting them to your *toilette*.'

Adeline stared at him.

'In the hope that I'd *what*?'

'It is, of course, quite proper for you to do so once the under-dress is on,' he explained. 'They will advise you on the placing of your patches --'

'I don't *wear* patches. I should think everyone knows that by now.'

' – and on the selection of your perfume and jewels,' he finished urbanely. 'I'm afraid, however, that I took the liberty of having these helpful gentlemen denied.'

'Good,' said Adeline. And then, as an afterthought, 'Why?'

Still smiling a little, he advanced to stand beside her.

'Well, it seemed to me,' he replied softly, 'that I could advise you on all these matters myself. If, of course, you will permit me?'

She found that it was necessary to take her time about replying. Finally, she said, 'Gladly ... on one condition.'

'And that is?'

'That you resign yourself to the fact that I've no intention of painting my face.'

His brows rose.

'My dear, I've not the slightest desire to have you do so. Your instinct is entirely correct – and I can name at least three ladies who have recently chosen to follow your example.'

A slow and faintly incredulous smile dawned.

'You mean I'm setting a fashion? Really?'

'Really,' he agreed. 'You are becoming known as one of the most stylish women in London. And I'd hazard a guess that, by the end of the Season, you will be in the delightful position of being able to start any trend which may amuse you.'

'Dandelions in my hair?' she teased, only half believing him. 'A gown embroidered with strawberry leaves over a petticoat emblazoned from waist to hem with your Coat of Arms?'

'Why not?' he laughed. 'In the meantime, however, we must establish your influence. You are wearing the oyster satin this evening?'

She nodded.

'Excellent. Then you will require the sapphire set.'

He unlatched the chest containing the family jewels and perused it for a moment.

'I appear to have neglected to furnish you with the Wynstanton diamonds,' he observed idly. 'For reasons best known to herself, my mother stored them at the bank. I'll have Matthew retrieve them for you tomorrow.'

Then, selecting the case containing the sapphires and, extracting the necklace, he proceeded to fasten it around her throat. Adeline's breath stopped and she sat very still as his fingers completed their task and slid down to rest lightly on her shoulders. His eyes met hers in the mirror and then, the merest hint of a question in his smile, he bent to lay his mouth against her neck.

The door opened.

'Aren't you ready yet, Adeline? We're going to be dreadfully late,' said Nell. And then, staring at her brother, 'Oh. Am I interrupting?'

'No,' said Adeline, arising decidedly pink.

'Yes,' said Rockliffe with rare irascibility. 'Don't you ever knock?'

'I didn't,' replied Nell affrontedly, 'expect you to be here. How could I? You don't usually attend Adeline's *toilette*. But I beg your pardon, I'm sure!' And she swept out of the room again, shutting the door behind her with a distinct snap.

For a moment or two after she had gone, Rockliffe communed silently with the ceiling. Then he said simply, 'If I didn't know better, I'd begin to think that her quite deplorable timing was deliberate. As it is, I'm bound to own the justice of her remarks.' He smiled suddenly. 'It's something, however, that can be mended.'

Adeline spotted the ambiguity but declined – on the suspicion that it was intentional – to query it. Instead, she said mildly, 'She was right about the time, too. I ought to finish dressing.'

'Ought you?' he asked. Then, regretfully, 'Yes. I suppose you ought. A pity. But I'm sure you'll say that it wouldn't do to disappoint Nell.'

'N-no,' she agreed weakly, wondering what else he had in mind.

'No. I thought not.' He picked up the sapphire bracelet and clasped it around her wrist. Then, toying abstractedly with her fingers, he said gently, 'I have given you time, Adeline – and shall continue to do so. I am also, you may have noticed, trying to rectify earlier omissions by courting you. I don't ask you to meet me half-way ... but I would be grateful if you could retreat a trifle less swiftly.'

Her throat closed and she had to avert her gaze before he could read it.

'I'm sorry. It isn't intentional.'

'No.' His hand tightened on hers. 'Tell me something. Do you trust me?'

She looked at him then, her eyes wide and candid.

'Of course.'

'Good.' He dropped a light kiss on her fingers and released them. 'Remember it.' And turned to go, leaving her prey to a whole battery of mixed emotions.

*

The first person she set eyes on inside Bedford House was her cousin Diana, dancing with Jack Ingram.

'Armageddon,' murmured Adeline to her husband. 'The next time you imply that you'd welcome an evening at home, I promise I'll listen.'

'And I shall hold you to it.' Rockliffe awarded her a flicker of ironic amusement and raised his glass to survey the company.

'Are we,' demanded Nell, 'supposed to appear enthusiastic?'

'No,' replied her brother placidly. 'Just beautifully civil. Lady Franklin is sitting with Alice Morton. I suggest we take the initiative and pay our respects. Adeline?'

'Why not?' Her smile was brittle. 'We may as well get it over with. But I'd advise against looking her in the eye.'

'The basilisk stare? I don't think we need fear it. Or not until she is finally convinced that we're not going to help her stalk a title for Diana. And by then, my loved ones, it will not matter one whit.'

It was Rockliffe whom Lady Franklin saw first. She stiffened and, ignoring Nell, stared inimically at the strikingly elegant woman on his arm. For a moment the oyster satin and sapphires produced a sense of unreality; then she met long-lashed aquamarine eyes filled with all-too-familiar mockery and, with a word of excuse to Lady Morton, rose to meet her niece.

'Adeline ... how very well you look.'

'I *am* well, Aunt.' Adeline allowed her smooth cheek to brush my lady's powdered one and took the opportunity to smile at Althea, standing nervously in her mother's shadow. 'I have, after all, every reason to be.'

'Quite.' Lady Franklin extended her hand to receive Rockliffe's languid salute. 'How pleasant to see you again, your Grace. And Lady Elinor, too … Diana will be so pleased.'

'Will she?' Nell arose from her curtsy and looked thoughtfully at Diana's twin. Then, as if making up her mind, she said, 'Is this your first party, Thea?'

'Yes.' Althea's fingers twisted on her fan. 'It is so very crowded, is it not?'

'And destined to become more so, I fear,' replied Rockliffe with suitable gravity, having himself considered the rooms a little thin of company. 'But you will enjoy it all so much better when you know a few people. Nell … I see the Delahayes are here. Why do you not present Mistress Althea to Cassie and some of the other young ladies? Lady Franklin, I feel sure, will have no objection.'

'None at all,' said her ladyship, thawing visibly. And then, as the girls moved away, 'Poor Thea is so timid, I sometimes despair of her. I only wish she could acquire just a fraction of dear Diana's confidence.'

'I am sure you must do,' agreed Rockliffe sympathetically. 'And *vice versa*.'

Adeline smothered a choke of laughter. 'Has Sir Roland also come to town?'

'No.' Lady Franklin continued to gaze up at the Duke with faintly baffled suspicion for a moment and then gave it up. 'No. He felt disinclined to leave the estate at this time. Fortunately, however, I am able to depend on the company and support of my dear brother.'

'Ah yes.' Adeline smiled. 'My estimable Uncle Richard. How happy you must be to have him.'

Able, as always, to recognise but not quite comprehend Adeline's barbs, her ladyship mourned the fact that it was no longer possible to quell them as she would wish. Then, with mixed feelings, she noted the approach of her favourite child.

She immediately perceived that there was a stormy glint in the beautiful eyes and prayed that Diana would at least have the sense to be civil. Goodness only knew, she'd been told often enough. Regrettably, however, it did not always make a difference.

'Well!' said Diana, staring hard at Adeline. 'Fine feathers certainly make fine birds, don't they?'

A step behind her, Jack Ingram's somewhat forced smile withered completely and it was several seconds before he remembered to close his mouth.

'And manners,' responded Adeline sweetly, 'maketh man. Whether or not they also maketh woman is plainly something upon which we can only speculate.' And then, cryptically, 'Never mind, Jack. The things we look forward to seldom live up to expectation.'

Not being possessed either of a devious nature or any marked histrionic talent, Mr Ingram had to expend quite a lot of concentration in order to look as if he didn't know what she meant. He did not, as a consequence, come up with a suitable reply and it was left to the Duke, his eyes agleam, to say understandingly, 'I take it Harry is here?'

'Yes,' replied Jack baldly. 'And, if you'll excuse me, I'm rather anxious to have a word with him. Lady Franklin ... Adeline.' And, with an uncharacteristically curt bow, he set off in the direction of the card room.

'Dear me. Was that an exit – or an escape?' murmured his Grace softly. Then, smiling provokingly at Diana, 'Still ... I'm sure you will be able to take his defection philosophically.'

Diana, who had never in her life accepted anything philosophically, achieved a small, brittle smile. 'Naturally. Though I'm at a loss to know why you should think so.'

'Are you?' His brows rose in mild reproof. 'You can't have asked the right questions, then.'

'He is ineligible?' asked Lady Franklin coldly.

'It would depend, I imagine, on your criteria,' came the maddening reply. Then, 'Adeline, my dear ... I see Dolly Cavendish is trying to attract our attention. And Lord March. Again. Ah well ... needs must, I suppose.' And with practised grace, he brought the confrontation to an end.

Diana watched them go, her face stony.

'He's every bit as foul as she is,' she muttered savagely. 'But I'll teach them to poke fun at me!'

'It seems,' replied her mother tartly, 'that you've already done so. And I'll tell you something else, my girl. If you don't learn to hide your temper, you'll probably live to see Althea married before you.'

The mutinous look vanished. Diana laughed.

Adeline, meanwhile, was looking appreciatively up at her husband.

'I thought we were to be civil.'

'And weren't we?'

'Not entirely. Unless, of course, I was imagining insinuations where really there were none?'

His smile was swift and magnetic.

'Oh no. You imagined nothing. And I am never rude by accident.'

Harry Caversham was not finding the evening one of unmixed pleasure. On the one hand, he was deriving a great deal of amusement out of making it difficult for Jack to speak privately with him ... but, on the other, no amusement at all from watching Nell flirt with Sir Jasper Brierley. Finally, in continuance of the one and an attempt to halt the other, he invited the Duchess of Rockliffe to dance and said bluntly, 'Do *you* know what Nell sees in that fellow?'

'No.' Adeline spread her skirts and moved gracefully towards him. 'She says he adds to her consequence. Personally, I can't see it but I suppose there's no accounting for taste.'

'But he's a fortune-hunter and everybody knows it. Why doesn't Rock do something?'

'I expect he will in time. And meanwhile – since you're so worried – why don't *you* do something?'

'Such as what? She avoids me like the plague. Oh damn.' This as the movement of the dance brought them face to face with Mr Ingram and Cassandra Delahaye.

'One of these days,' remarked Jack grimly, 'someone will wring your neck.'

'What did *I* do?' The angelic blue eyes danced. 'You wanted to meet Adeline's cousins and I introduced you. What's wrong with that?'

'Nothing – if you'd left it there and not interfered.'

'Oh dear. Got the wrong one, did you?' sympathised his lordship. 'Never mind. Better luck next time.' And he moved Adeline dextrously on.

'What *did* you do?' she asked.

'Me? Not a thing. I just saw him looking at Mistress Thea and thought he'd appreciate her all the more for having a taste of Mistress Di first. If you were determined to be uncharitable, you might say that I sort of ... manoeuvred him. That's all.'

The evening was well-advanced before Richard Horton, who had been charting his niece's progress with interest, finally achieved his objective and caught her alone.

'Well, my dear. You seem to suit your new life admirably.'

Adeline started and wheeled to face him. Then, controlling her nerves, 'You are surprised?' she said.

'Very. But no doubt Rockliffe is an excellent tutor.'

'Exceptional,' she sighed, smiling. 'And now, if you will excuse me --'

'Not so fast, Adeline. Not so fast.' His hand trapped her arm and held it with seeming affection. 'You owe me a little something, you know.'

'I don't think so.'

'Certainly you do. But for me you would not be standing here now in satin and sapphires.' He paused, examining her necklace through his glass. 'Such very *fine* sapphires, too.'

'Jealous, Uncle? Don't be. They wouldn't suit you.'

He sighed and the pressure of his fingers increased.

'You are still very sharp, are you not? You ought to be careful. You may cut yourself.'

'Unlikely.' The blue-green eyes were perfectly inimical. 'Let go of me and tell me what you want.'

Slowly and with reluctance, he released her.

'You may not be aware of it but Miriam wished to prevent your marriage.'

'So?' shrugged Adeline. 'She could not have done so.'

'On the contrary. She could. I, however, persuaded her to change her mind.'

'But how noble of you!' she said scathingly. 'And now, of course, I am supposed to repay you. But with what, precisely?'

'For the moment,' replied Mr Horton, delicately smoothing a crease from one rose-tinted sleeve, 'all I require is a small favour. Later ... well, later we shall see.'

Adeline's brows soared. 'Shall we indeed?'

'We shall. But at present I merely wish you to exert your influence a little.'

'Over whom?'

'Over your husband. Who else?' came the silky reply. 'I want to become a member of White's and Rockliffe could arrange it. Persuade him for me.'

Adeline was fully aware that White's was the most exclusive club in London and that Rockliffe was one of its most respected members. A strange calm took hold of her and her mouth curled in a slow, honeyed smile.

'No,' she said.

Some of Mr Horton's suavity left him.

'You will not, if you are wise, put me to the trouble of coercing you.'

'Dear me. You think you could?'

'I know I could. But let us avoid unpleasantness while we may. I ask you again, Adeline. Speak to your husband.'

Quite deliberately, she made him wait. Then, 'Speak to him yourself,' she said.

And left him.

FOURTEEN

Next morning over breakfast, she told Rockliffe.

She had not, in fairness, intended to do so; but when she stretched out her hand for the coffee-pot and the lace at her elbow fell back to reveal her forearm, she found she had little choice.

'*Who in Hades did that*?' The Duke's eyes were riveted on the shadowy marks lying stark on her skin and for the first time, the temper in his eyes was echoed in his voice.

As calmly as she was able, Adeline withdrew her hand to her lap.

'It's nothing,' she said. 'I bruise easily.'

'Don't prevaricate. I can recognise finger-prints when I see them. Whose are they?'

She looked at him for a moment and then, sighing, lowered her gaze.

'My uncle's.'

'Richard Horton?'

'Yes.'

There was a long silence.

'Then I promise you that he'll regret it.' Rockliffe's tone had regained its usual smoothness but was none the less dangerous for that. 'One presumes that he was not merely mauling you for fun but that he had a reason. What was it?'

Adeline knew better than anyone that Mr Horton was by no means devoid of sadistic tendencies. She also knew that, if she said so, his Grace would demand details.

'He wants to become a member of White's. The general idea was that I should coax you into arranging it.'

'And you refused?'

'Well, of course.'

'And his reaction was to man-handle you and leave you with bruises.'

This time, she said nothing. Since he was clearly still angry, there didn't seem to be anything she *could* say that would be helpful.

Rockliffe was more than just angry – he was inwardly seething and was aware of a distressingly crude impulse that would have boded ill for Mr Horton, had he been within reach. However, since relieving his feelings in that particular manner was out of the question, the Duke battened down his temper in order to consider other options. But first he said flatly, 'If anything of this kind occurs again, you will tell me of it immediately. Is that understood?'

'Yes.'

'I mean it, Adeline.'

She looked up at him and met an implacable black gaze. 'Yes. I know you do.'

'Good.' Rockliffe thought for a moment and then said slowly, 'Since Mr Horton clearly feels he can't get into White's without assistance of some kind, one must assume he's already tried in the usual way and been refused.'

'He didn't say. But yes – I suppose that must be true.'

'Interesting.' He considered her attentively and then, the merest hint of humour creeping back into his voice, he said, 'At the risk of sinking myself below reproach, I am constrained to admit that sponsoring your uncle at the Club is the one thing I will never do. Not even for you.'

'Obviously. I knew that.'

'Ah. But did you know why?'

'I assumed ... because of dislike both for Richard and for having your hand forced. Is that not all?'

'Not quite. You see, my dear, I have known for some time that the so-charming Mr Horton attempts to earn the odd crust by means of his expertise at the card-table. And when his expertise isn't enough ... he cheats.'

Adeline's gaze grew utterly blank and it was a long time before she spoke. Then she said, 'I was about to ask if you're sure ... but of course you are.'

'Yes. I played cards with him in Oxfordshire – but only once. He's quite good at it ... one would have to say, well-practised – but not undetectable to anyone watching closely.'

'I see. What a delightful family I have. It makes you wonder what we'll discover next, doesn't it?'

Rockliffe, who for very good reasons, knew exactly what they might expect to discover next, kept his expression carefully neutral.

'You should not,' he observed, 'allow it to concern you. No one, as they say, can choose their relatives. And nothing they do is any reflection on you.'

'It's kind of you to say so,' came the bitter reply, 'but you must forgive me if I find it hard to accept.' She paused and drew a long, steadying breath. 'Can you make sure that Richard most assuredly does *not* gain membership of White's?'

'Oh yes.' He gave the ghost of a laugh. 'And what is more, it will be my pleasure to ensure that he knows it.'

*

For reasons not entirely easy to identify, Nell was conscious of a faint dissatisfaction with life in general. It could not, of course, be put down to boredom for her days were crammed with engagements – from Venetian breakfasts to masked balls; and neither, since Rock had already received two offers for her hand and her rooms were daily bedecked with floral tributes from her various admirers, had she any cause to worry that she was not a Success. Her closets overflowed with expensive gowns and elegant fripperies, no one plagued her to practise her embroidery or read dull books and she had dearest Cassie to share her confidences. In short, life ought to be perfect ... but somehow it wasn't.

She rather suspected – though she'd have died sooner than admit it even to Cassie – that her vague sense of unease was partly connected to her friendship with Sir Jasper Brierley. It was not that he was ever anything less than correct ... well, not *much* less anyway; and at least he treated her as a grown woman – which was more than could be said of some people. But she had begun, from time to time, to feel ever so slightly out of her depth and she did not know what she should do about it.

The safe, sensible course was to do what everyone wanted and cut the connection. And, despite the fact that she still found Sir Jasper fascinating and was learning from him every nuance of sophisticated flirtation, she might even have considered doing so ... but for Harry Caversham.

'You're playing with fire, Nell,' he'd said. 'Haven't you *any* sense?'

'More,' she had retorted, 'than you give me credit for. And I can take care of myself, thank you.'

'You may think you can. But the fact is that men like Jasper Brierley eat little girls like you for breakfast.'

He had realised as soon as he'd said it that it had been a mistake.

'*Little girl*?' snapped Nell. 'Is *that* what you think? Then let me tell you, my lord, that others see me differently!'

'I'm aware of it. But perhaps they have less interest in your well-being.'

'Or are less in the habit of interfering with what is none of their concern!'

She remembered afterwards how he'd looked at her for a long time, his normally laughing eyes shuttered and opaque.

'Then I'd better stop it immediately, hadn't I?' he had said at length. And gone off to dance with Diana Franklin.

In retrospect, it occurred to Nell that she could have put up with anything but that. No matter how hard she tried to shrug it off, the picture of him smiling down on that exquisite, deceitful face refused to be quite banished. Indeed, in the days that followed, it seemed to become a recurring theme – for wherever she went, there was Lord Harry paying light-hearted court to Mistress Di, and Mistress Di thoroughly enjoying it.

Sir Jasper's attentions therefore came as a welcome balm – particularly as he showed no inclination to join the little *côterie* of gentlemen who regularly besieged Diana. And his opinion, when she casually sought it, was more comforting still.

'*Farouche*,' he said simply. 'Pretty ... but destined, I fear, to appeal only to unsophisticated palates. Unlike – dare I say it? – yourself.'

Nell's smile regained some of its usual sparkle.

'I think, sir, that you flatter me.'

'Not only is that not possible – but I have too much respect for your intelligence.'

It was precisely what she wanted to hear – but he could not have known that. Flushing with pleasure, she said naively, 'That is the nicest compliment anyone has ever paid me.'

Sir Jasper smiled upon her.

'I find that hard to believe. Surely all the young gentlemen who surround you cannot be so unappreciative?'

'No-o. But they all say pretty much the same things, you know.' She gave a tiny chuckle. 'Some even write poetry. And though you'll probably think it quite horrid of me, most of it usually just makes me laugh.'

'A natural reaction to bad verse ... and the reason for my own abstinence in that direction.'

'Well, I must say I think you're wise,' she owned candidly. And then, with more than a hint of hesitation, 'But you ... I think you have been sending me roses, haven't you?'

Taking her fan from her, he flicked it open and plied it gently, his eyes never leaving her face.

'If I have ... and if you only *think* I have ... then it would seem a wasted exercise, would it not?'

Nell met the pale grey gaze with uncertainty and a frisson of excitement. Every day for the past week, a single tightly-budded, dark red rose had arrived, accompanied only by a small square of pasteboard bearing a pair of elaborately entwined initials.

'Very well, sir,' she said, deciding to employ her new skills. 'I am very sure they come from you. What I wanted to ask was – why?'

'Why?' He shrugged, whimsically. 'My dear Lady Elinor, I am but sending one perfect rose-bud to another. And I give to you the same pleasure I am receiving myself ... that of seeing each charming petal unfurl.' And watched, smiling, as she blushed in confusion.

*

Not too far away, Diana Franklin looked on with shrewd interest.

'I wonder if she means to have him?' she mused. 'He's extremely attractive – and the fact that he hasn't any money wouldn't matter to her, would it? I imagine she's rolling in riches already. You must ask her about him, Thea. Thanks, no doubt, to her precious brother, she hardly ever *speaks* to me these days.' Her mouth curled, showing sharp, pearly teeth. 'And that's something else Rockliffe and his trollop will be made to pay for. Nell was useful to me.'

Althea looked at her sister with frightened concern.

'Di, dearest, don't you think …?'

'No. I don't – and if you weren't so feeble-minded, neither would you.' Diana turned a withering cornflower gaze on her sister. 'And while we are about it, I wish you'd try standing on your own two feet for a change. I'm never going to get anywhere with you hanging on to my petticoats.'

A ballroom is no place to cry. Althea swallowed hard and stared down at her hands.

'I – I'm sorry. I d-don't mean to get in your way.'

'Then don't. And for heaven's sake, pull yourself together. Mr Ingram's coming towards us.'

Had he been asked, Jack would have been hard put to explain just what had drawn him across the floor to the Franklin twins. The one he had scarcely exchanged two words with - and the other he had formed an almost instantaneous dislike for. If Mistress Althea was as like her sister in disposition as she was in looks therefore, he was condemning himself to unnecessary irritation; and if not … well, if not, she *was* an uncommonly pretty girl.

He bowed, opened his mouth to speak and was forestalled by Diana.

'Why, Mr Ingram – how delightful. You find us but newly-arrived and quite deserted. Isn't that dreadful? And most unusual, too, I do assure you.'

'I am sure it is,' said Jack. 'I -- '

'Yes. In this last week since we met you – at Bedford House, was it not? – we have quite ceased to be the country cousins you must have thought us. We have met – oh, everyone! Have we not, Thea? Ah – the gavotte has finished at last. I thought it never would.' She turned a melting regard on him. 'I do so *love* to dance. Do not you, sir?'

And that, thought Jack, was less a hint than a twenty-gun salvo.

Smiling pleasantly, he said, 'I find it depends very much upon the company.'

'Oh yes. I do so agree with you.'

'Which is why,' he continued, grimly enjoying himself and letting his eyes wander to the other girl, 'I am hoping Mistress Althea will honour me.'

Althea turned scarlet. So, for different reasons, did Diana. Jack felt moderately pleased with himself and wished that Rock had been there to see it. He collected Althea's gaze and held out his hand. 'Well, Mistress? *Will* you honour me?'

His voice was gentle and the grey eyes kind. Resolutely avoiding her sister's gaze, she drew a long breath and said softly, 'Yes, sir. Thank you.' Then she put her hand shyly in his and allowed him to lead her out on to the floor, leaving Diana standing conspicuously alone.

*

Leaving Adeline to chaperone Nell to a small gathering of young people at the Delahaye residence in Conduit Street, Rockliffe set off for White's in a mood of gentle anticipation which was almost immediately justified.

'Rock, my loved one!' Mr Fox stopped dead at the sight of him, one hand laid dramatically over his heart. 'To what do we owe this immensely unexpected pleasure?'

'Must there be a reason?'

'It seems likely. We had begun to think marriage had changed you beyond recognition. Is that not so, March?'

'The notion had occurred to us,' agreed his lordship. 'But your visit, as ever, is timely. Your wife's uncle ... Richard Horton, is it? ... has been put up for membership of the Club.'

'Ah.' A faint smile bracketing his mouth, Rockliffe flicked open his snuff-box and presented it first to Mr Fox. 'May I ask, by whom?'

'By Ludovic Sterne,' replied Lord March, his tone cooling a little. 'I was given to understand that you would endorse the nomination and stand sponsor to the gentleman.'

'Were you indeed?' The Duke offered snuff to the Earl then snapped the lid shut and gazed at its enamelled panel with satisfied pleasure. 'Tell me ... are you acquainted with Mr Horton?'

'No,' said March. 'I don't, however, care to rely on any recommendation of Sterne's.'

'I see. And you, Charles?'

'I have met the gentleman,' replied Mr Fox languidly. 'I regret to say that I did not find him entertaining. Not, of course, that one can hold that against him. The same could be said for half of London. More than half.'

'You are too critical, Charles,' said his lordship. And then, to Rockliffe, 'Meanwhile, where does this leave Mr Horton? Do you wish him to be admitted to the Club?'

There was a long, enigmatic pause. Finally, the dark eyes rose and the Duke said blandly, 'No, my dear. I most certainly do not. And I would be obliged if you could ensure ... in whatever manner you see fit ... that Ludo Sterne is made aware of the fact.'

'So that he can tell Mr Horton?' enquired Mr Fox, evincing faint signs of interest.

'Just so. With life so full of disappointments, it seems only fair that he should know who to blame for this one, don't you think?'

'If you have a particular reason,' remarked March thoughtfully, 'I suspect we might be glad to be made privy to it.'

'Yes.' His Grace paused for a moment and then said, 'Have either of you ever played cards with Mr Horton?'

'I haven't,' replied the Earl. 'You, Charles?'

'No.'

'Then I would suggest,' said Rockliffe gently, 'that you never do.'

He settled down, by and by, to a game of picquet with Jack Ingram and won it by an unusually large margin.

'Am I,' asked Jack, examining the score with mock-gloom, 'playing particularly badly this evening – or have you been visited by divine inspiration?'

'A little of both. But I hope that you're not going to dwell on it. I had thought to ask you a trifling favour.'

Jack grinned at him.

'I must say, you pick your times. But – very well. Ask away. And I'll commit myself when I know what it is.'

'Dear Jack. Always so cautious.'

'Well, for all I know, you've challenged some poor fool and are about to ask me to be your second.'

'Perish the thought!'

'Good – because I wouldn't do it.'

'I think you may safely assume me to be aware of that fact.' Rockliffe smiled. 'I sometimes wonder, however, what exactly I've done to make you think me eternally bloodthirsty.'

'I don't think it,' said Jack frankly. 'What I *do* think is that you'd do it out of boredom. You used to be forever offering to fight Dominic.'

Laughter flared in the dark eyes.

'Ah. But that, beloved, is an entirely different matter. But we digress. I wished to ask you – since I must leave town for two or three days – if you would be good enough to keep an eye on Adeline and Nell. It shouldn't, I hope, prove too taxing.'

Mr Ingram stared at him incredulously.

'Not taxing? Looking after Nell? You must think I'm less than the full shilling!'

The Duke considered him for a moment. Then, 'I suppose you may have a point. Very well. Adeline will keep an eye on Nell and you may keep on Adeline. Is that better?'

'Much!' grinned Jack.

'And why,' demanded Harry Caversham, arriving in time to catch Rockliffe's last words, 'can't you keep an eye on Nell yourself?'

'Because,' came the patient reply, 'I have to go into the country.'

His lordship pulled up a chair and sat down, frowning. 'Is it urgent?'

'Yes.' Rockliffe paused and then said sweetly, 'I was not aware of any need to ask your permission.'

Harry had the grace to look mildly abashed.

'I beg your pardon. But the thing is, I'm getting dashed sick of seeing Nell with that Brierley fellow – and I should think you would be too!'

'Would you?' The Duke sipped his claret, apparently unperturbed. 'Now why should you think that?'

'Isn't it obvious? He's twice her age and has been hanging out for a rich wife for the last two seasons. I'd be damned if I'd let him get his hands on *my* sister.'

'So crude,' sighed his Grace. 'But you see, Harry, I have no intention of allowing him to ... get his hands on her. Indeed, I doubt he has any desire to do so; and if I should find that he *has* ... then it will be my sad duty to dissuade him.'

His lordship leaned back in his chair, chin on chest, and turned a sardonic blue gaze on Mr Ingram. He said, 'I must be missing something. Do *you* know why it's all so simple?'

'Trusts and trustees, I should imagine,' replied Jack. And then, glancing briefly at Rockliffe, 'Think about it, Harry. Nell's eighteen and I'd guess that her inheritance is tied up in the usual way until she's twenty-five.'

'Or,' countered Harry, 'until she marries.'

'Or until she marries with Rock's approval. There's a difference. Rock won't give his blessing to Brierley; and, if it's low water with Brierley now, he won't want to wait seven years for the tide to come in.' He looked back at the Duke. 'Am I right?'

'I couldn't have put it better myself,' drawled Rockliffe. 'And now, Harry, I really must ask what concern all this is of yours? Can it be that you've an eye to Nell yourself?'

Lord Harry came abruptly to his feet, looking distinctly and uncharacteristically irritable.

'You would think that, of course. But why shouldn't I have a care for a chit I've known since she was ten years old? Especially since it seems you're too damned busy to do it.' On which Parthian shot, he left them.

Grey eyes met black.

'Touchy, isn't he?' asked Jack, companionably. And then, 'I think you'd better prepare to welcome him into the family.'

'Probably.' Rockliffe shuffled the cards lazily. 'If, that is, Nell ever decides to look beyond the end of her nose. Will you deal – or shall I?'

*

On the following morning he entered Adeline's room to find her sitting up in bed, sipping her chocolate and sifting through a number of gilt-edged invitations. The dark brown hair cascaded around her shoulders and over a thin, blue silk nightgown, threaded interestingly with silver ribbon. Rockliffe's heart missed its accustomed beat and caused him to pause for an infinitesimal second before moving calmly on.

Adeline, meanwhile, narrowly avoided choking on her chocolate and felt herself blushing. It was not that he was any longer a stranger to her rooms – for, since the night of the Bedford House ball, he had made a habit of attending the final stages of her *toilette* and even, sometimes, of staying to talk with her while she discarded her jewels at night. It was, however, the first time he had caught her in bed ... and she felt decidedly disadvantaged by it.

'Good morning,' he said. And, as Jeanne discreetly removed herself, 'You look delightful.'

'Are you sure you don't mean untidy,' she asked, striving for her normal tone and sternly repressing a childish inclination to pull the covers up to her chin. She eyed his austere black coat and polished top-boots. 'You're up and dressed betimes. Are you going somewhere?'

'With reluctance, yes.' He crossed the room to sit on the side of her bed. 'A small matter of business necessitates a visit to the country. And suddenly I find I do not at all wish to go.'

Adeline didn't want him to go either but wasn't quite up to saying so. Instead, she kept her gaze resolutely fixed on his buttons and said casually, 'Will you be gone long?'

'Not long. Three days, perhaps. Dare I hope that you'll miss me just a little?'

His tone was light but his eyes, had she looked, told a different story. She said, 'But of course. Who will help me choose my jewels?'

'I'm sure there will be no shortage of volunteers ... though I'm rather hoping you'll decline them.' *'Particularly,'* he thought, *'in the case of my lord March, who is already more than half in love with you - which means that if you don't discourage him soon, I'll have to do it.'* He took possession of her hands and said, 'Why won't you look at me?'

Her breath snared and the aquamarine eyes flew to meet his.

'Ah ... that's better.' He smiled at her. 'At least I shall have a charming picture to carry with me.'

She said, 'You're ... you are particularly gallant this morning.'

'Yes. I'm glad you noticed that. It's because, you see, I was rather hoping that you might give me something.'

'Oh? What?'

'This.' And, entirely without haste, so that she could read his intention and thwart it if she wished, he gathered her into his arms.

The warmth of his hands seared her through the flimsy stuff of her night-gown and her head fell back, exposing the long, creamy column of her throat. He folded her close against him, sliding his fingers slowly into the mass of unbound hair to cradle her skull and letting his eyes caress her face. Their expression set Adeline's nerves alight and, as the moment stretched out on an invisible thread, she thought hazily, '*If he doesn't kiss me now, I'll drown.*' Then he did kiss her ... and she drowned anyway.

This time there were no interruptions and he was in no hurry. His mouth teased and tempted, soliciting a response that sent a tremor thought the pliant body in his arms and causing him to gradually deepen the kiss until she made a tiny, helpless sound and her arms slid round his neck, holding him even closer. Releasing her mouth and letting one hand glide unhurriedly down her back to discover the curve of her waist, he trailed his tongue lightly down her throat to kiss the place where a pulse was erratically beating ... and felt her hands tangle in his hair. Very briefly, he lifted his head to look at her and then, satisfied, captured her mouth again.

Long moments later, he drew back a little and, still holding her, absorbed the dilated blue-green eyes and the fact that her breathing was hopelessly disrupted. Controlling his own voice with an effort, he murmured, 'Well ... that was undoubtedly worth waiting for.'

Her whole body flooded with sensations she was now able to recognise for what they were, Adeline said huskily, 'Tracy ... ?'

'Yes, darling?'

Her heart was screaming, '*I love you, I love you, I love you. Don't go.*' Her head, ingrained with caution, made her reduce it to, 'Must you really go?'

Even this was more than he had dared hope for; and it was intensified by the fact that she was still toying with his hair – from which the riband seemed to have vanished - in a way he found curiously erotic. Summoning all his control, he reminded himself that it was broad daylight and her maid was in the next room. Moreover, the sooner his errand was completed, the better it would be for both of them. So with enormous reluctance, he said, 'I'm sorry ... but, yes. I really must. However, when I come back, do you think we might regard this as a beginning?'

Adeline drew a long breath. 'Yes,' she said. And managed not to add the word, '*Please.*' Instead, letting her hands slide away from him, she added, 'I have disordered your hair.'

'So you have – and may do so again any time you wish.' He kissed her hands and rose from her side. 'And now I'd better go – or it is quite likely, with you looking so inviting, that I'll forget it's a matter of some importance. If you need money, see Matthew. Problems of any other kind, should there be any, you may safely take to Jack. He knows I have to go away. And if Nell is difficult, tell her there will be dire retribution.' He smiled at her. 'I promise I won't linger. Will you be all right?'

'Yes,' said Adeline mechanically. 'Yes, of course.'

'Good.' He allowed himself the indulgence of fleetingly touching her cheek. '*Au revoir*, my dear.'

Then he left her for Oxfordshire ... and the home of Sir Roland Franklin.

The decision to go there was the right one. The timing of it was to prove disastrous.

FIFTEEN

Sir Roland accepted his arrival cautiously but without any undue surprise and led him to the privacy of the book-room. Then, when wine had been brought and the servant withdrew, he said simply, 'Thought you might come. Been half-expecting it.'

Banishing from his mind all images of a certain momentous evening in June, Rockliffe concentrated on the matter in hand.

'Have you? Why?'

Sir Rowland regarded him owlishly.

'It seemed to me you'd start asking yourself questions. Bound to, really. Adeline's your wife – but you don't know much about her.'

'About Adeline, I know everything I need to know,' came the cool reply. 'It is – as I suspect you are well aware – her mother who interests me.'

'Ah.' Sir Roland nodded several times, his face settling into lines of worry. 'You want to know about Joanna.'

'I do. The question is ... are you going to tell me?'

'Depends.'

'On what?'

'On whether you've already asked my wife. She doesn't want you told, you see – so it's better if she knows nothing about it. Thing is,' he said earnestly, 'Miriam can be a very difficult woman. Wouldn't like her to guess you'd found out from me.'

Rockliffe repressed a temptation to tell the baronet it was clearly time he got a grip on his own household and said, 'There is no reason why she should. I have not approached her and can safely promise not to do so. Neither have I told anyone of my visit here today.'

'Not even Adeline?'

'*Particularly* not Adeline. I need to learn everything I can in order to protect her as best I may. Then, if necessary, I can reveal those things she ought to know at a time when I judge her best able to cope with them. I trust that makes the position plain?'

'Very,' said Sir Roland. 'Agree with you. Always thought she should be told. Said so often.' He paused, thinking it over. Then, 'Better start by telling me what you know.'

Resting his elbows on the arms of the chair, his Grace laid his fingertips lightly together and eyed the other man across them. At length, he said, 'I *know* nothing. What I have is a collection of surmise and supposition which leads me to the conclusion that Joanna Kendrick did not die twenty-four years ago and is still, in fact, very much alive. Am I right?'

Roland drained his glass.

'Yes,' he said flatly. 'More or less.'

'Meaning?'

'She was alive six years ago.' He opened the bureau and rummaged about till he released the catch of a concealed drawer. Then, pulling out first a slim packet of letters, he produced a small box. 'Sent this for Adeline's eighteenth birthday. Trouble was, I couldn't give it to her.'

Rockliffe accepted the box and opened it to reveal a gold locket engraved with a tracery of flowers. Inside was a beautifully painted miniature that could have been Adeline herself. For a moment he was silent. Then, snapping the lid shut, he said, 'Could you not have lied a little more and called it a bequest?'

'No,' said Roland. He turned the letters over in his hands and then added baldly, 'Joanna wrote to me from time to time and I sent her news of Adeline. Miriam didn't know.'

His Grace expelled a long breath.

'I see. When did you last hear from her?'

'Told you. Six years ago. She was in Paris.'

'Lodging with Charles' inviting little widow,' thought the Duke. And said, 'I think it's time you told me the whole story.'

'Suppose I'd better.' Sir Roland fortified himself with another glass of canary. 'The Hortons were a respectable enough family but they'd connections with trade. Joanna and Miriam were supposed to mend that by marrying well. Problem was that Joanna fell in love. Younger son, no prospects and a Frenchie, to boot. Old man Horton wouldn't have it, of course. Gave the Frog his marching orders and sent Joanna to his sister in Hexham.'

'Where,' suggested Rockliffe, 'she met Tom Kendrick?'

'Yes. Wouldn't have anything to do with him at first so they told her the French fellow was married.' Roland took a gulp of his wine. 'Not true – but she believed it and married Tom. He idolised her – even more so after she had Adeline. Would have done anything for her. Shouldn't have taken her to London, though.'

'Let me guess.' The dark eyes were gently reflective. 'She met her French lover again?'

'That's it. Met him and ran off with him straight away. Just vanished – and Adeline less than three months old.'

'Quite. So you all joined ranks to bury the scandal by announcing that Joanna was dead. Was that not rather drastic?'

'Wasn't my idea,' replied Sir Roland, a shade irritably. 'Not my business, either. Only recently married to Miriam at the time. Old man Horton wanted it – Kendrick wanted it. I just did as I was told.'

'I see.' For a long time, Rockliffe was silent. Then he said, 'If Joanna is still alive, I need to find her. And to that end, I'd like her last known address in Paris.'

'Take it,' came the prompt reply. 'Take all the letters and the locket. Not my responsibility any more, thank God.'

'No,' agreed the Duke. He rose and pocketed the items he had been given. 'You have been most helpful. I'm grateful.'

'Pleasure. Just don't involve me, that's all.'

'I won't. There is, however, just one other question I'd like to ask. Has it at any time ever occurred to you that Adeline might not be Tom Kendrick's child?'

'Yes,' came the blunt reply. 'But it ain't likely. Joanna wouldn't have left her if she'd been Michel's.'

'Michel?' queried Rockliffe gently.

'The Frenchie. Michel du Plessis. It's all in the letters. Rather you than me – but I wish you luck all the same. Just hope Adeline don't get hurt by it. You looking after her?'

'I am doing my best.' His Grace paused, an odd smile lurking in his eyes. 'And will continue to do so. Always.'

*

In London, meanwhile, Adeline was living with a heady mixture of fear and delight and trying hard not to let it show. The fear was in finally accepting the fact that, against Tracy, she had no defences – the delight, in the ravishing possibilities to which this might lead. She didn't know what he felt for her and, for the first time, it occurred to her that perhaps *he* did not either. But that, when suddenly put beside what she should have seen long ago, was not so very important. He had made it plain from the first that he wanted her but she had made him wait because she had been so afraid of falling in love with him. And that, she now knew, had been pointless – for she loved him anyway and had done for weeks, with an intensity that was beyond anything she had ever imagined.

It was hard to think when all the time a golden bubble of sweet anticipation was steadily growing inside her. She went shopping with Nell and Cassie and came home with a swansdown-trimmed negligée – the transparency of which both excited and alarmed her and provoked the girls into a variety of unseemly remarks. Then, without quite knowing how it came about, she found herself accepting Isabel Vernon's invitation for Nell and herself to spend the following evening at Ranelagh.

'It will be a very small party,' explained Lady Isabel in her gentle way. 'Just Philip and myself and Harry and Jack, I thought. It's so pleasant, sometimes, to simply relax amongst friends.'

Lord Philip emerged at his wife's side looking faintly sheepish.

'I'm afraid your party has grown, my love. Charles Fox and March want to come.'

'Do they indeed?' asked Isabel, not without humour. 'Well, unless I can find two more ladies to balance the party, they can't.'

'One more,' grinned his lordship. 'Jack has already suggested – ever so casually! – that we include one of her Grace's cousins.'

'I wish,' said her Grace absently, 'that you would call me Adeline.' And then, 'Which cousin?'

'The quiet one. Althea, is it? Though personally I don't see how we can ask one without the other.'

'Why not? Since Diana would happily go without Thea, there's no reason why it shouldn't work the other way about,' responded Adeline. 'And, quite frankly, it would do Thea good.'

'Then that's settled,' said Isabel. 'We'll invite Mistress Althea to please Jack ... and I'll ask Lady Delahaye to spare us Cassandra.'

'To please Mr Fox?' grinned Adeline. 'Or Lord March?'

'Neither.' Isabel smiled mischievously back. 'They are both coming to flirt with you. I thought you realised.'

Naturally pleased at the prospect of visiting Ranelagh, Nell said less than might have been expected on the subject of Lord Harry's inclusion in the party and, instead, threw herself with gusto into the absorbing matter of what to wear. What she *thought* was therefore less apparent than usual ... and Adeline, caught up in her own private whirlpool, was too pre-occupied to enquire.

They were to travel to Chelsea in cavalcade – Harry having elected to join the Vernons and Jack to ride with Lord March and Mr Fox. Adeline, who had volunteered to bring Cassie and Thea but had no desire to meet her aunt or Diana, solved the problem by despatching Jeanne in the carriage to collect both young ladies. Then, her party complete and filled with varying degrees of *joie-de-vivre*, they set off for the pleasure gardens.

The girls, reflected Adeline idly, made a pretty trio. Nell had chosen a white ruffled gown and a domino of her favourite rose-pink; brown-haired Cassie wore topaz taffeta over primrose and Althea was pale but excited in lavender and blue. Since the only person who mattered would not be there to see it, Adeline spared little thought for her own pale apricot ball-gown and domino of cream watered-silk – but she supposed she looked well enough.

Certainly, on arrival at Ranelagh, it seemed that March and Mr Fox thought so for they both immediately offered their arms to her and showed every sign of allowing no one to proceed until one of them had ousted the other. It was, of course, all perfectly amicable and Adeline let them hone their wits for a moment before saying kindly, 'Don't squabble, gentlemen. I am not a bone to be picked.' And then, with an oblique, provoking smile, she offered her hand to Lord Harry.'

'Such style,' sighed Cassie. 'I wish *I* had it.'

Nell, her eyes dwelling with dawning resentment on his lordship's oblivious back, vouchsafed no answer. And Althea, smiling shyly into Jack's grey eyes, did not even hear. Cassie shrugged, accepted Mr Fox's arm with complete good-nature and left Nell to follow with Lord March.

The gardens were lit by a myriad of coloured lanterns, cunningly concealed amidst trees and shrubs. There were numerous tiny kiosks, grottos and bowers - ornamental ponds, fountains and cascades; and strains of music drifted out from the elegant pavilion where dancing was already in progress. Ignoring all of it, Harry Caversham laughingly informed Adeline that she was a minx.

'I don't know what Rock's about to leave you to your own devices this way. Where's he gone, anyway?'

'To the country. He didn't say where,' she replied tranquilly. And then, 'You've got a whole evening in which to make Nell see you in a new light. Do you think you can do it?'

'The question is – do I want to?' The blue eyes were seraphic but his voice was not. 'One gets tired, I find, of being repeatedly kicked. I think I'll further my acquaintance with Cassie.'

They supped in one of the booths in the Great Rotunda in an atmosphere of increasing conviviality. Nell wished that she had stayed at home. It wasn't that she minded Charles Fox and March flirting in that absurd way with Adeline … though by the time she'd been subjected to it throughout supper and for a full half hour afterwards, she was beginning to find it tedious. And of course it was entirely beneath her to resent the trouble everyone was taking to set Thea at her ease when she knew – who better? – that this was exactly what the poor girl needed. But she *did* think it was a bit much for Harry to ignore her in that rude way and for Cassie to encourage his nonsense quite so blatantly. Not, she told herself firmly, that she was in the least bit jealous of Cassie – who was, after all, her very dearest friend; but she *did* wish that someone would take some notice of *her* for a change … just so that she wouldn't feel so miserably left out.

Pride and a solid grounding in good manners pinned a smile on her face but beneath it lay a well of confusion. She ought not to mind Lord Harry's defection since she herself had ordered it. But somehow, now it no longer seemed that he'd been pursuing her with Rock's connivance, the triumph of successfully repudiating him had lost a lot of its savour. And the worst of it was that she did not know why.

'*Nell!*'

She dragged herself reluctantly from her thoughts to meet Isabel Vernon's mildly exasperated gaze.

'I'm sorry, Isabel. Did you say something?'

'Not above three times. Indeed, I'd not have persevered but for the fact that I'd like you to tell me if the gentleman in salmon brocade who is approaching us is Althea's uncle.'

'Probably,' replied Nell carelessly. And then, 'Yes. It is. Why do you ask?'

'Because I've let her slip away with Jack – and Cassie and Harry too, of course. There seemed no harm in it. But her uncle may enquire and it seems unfair to let Adeline bear the brunt.'

'Oh.' Depression lodged like a lead weight in Nell's chest. She said tightly, 'I wouldn't worry about it. I doubt he'll care a fig.'

Adeline, responding coolly to Mr Horton's overly-elaborate bow, was thinking much the same thing. It therefore came as a slight surprise when he said chidingly, 'You must forgive me, my dear, if I observe that your care of Althea leaves something to be desired. I have just seen her in the pavilion, dancing with Mr Ingram – and apparently unchaperoned. I do not, you will notice, count the presence of Mistress Delahaye.'

'Most understandable,' said a composed voice at his elbow. 'But – as Mistress Althea's hostess – I'm afraid that these strictures should more properly be addressed to me.'

Turning sharply, Mr Horton found himself meeting a pair of soft but surprisingly direct pansy-brown eyes.

'I hope you'll pardon my intrusion, Adeline,' continued Isabel pleasantly, 'but I couldn't help overhearing – so it seemed only right that I trouble you to present me.'

To the mild liking Adeline already felt for Isabel Vernon was added respect. She smiled, took up her cue and watched her uncle losing the initiative beneath her ladyship's gentle flow of apology.

'And now,' concluded Isabel at length, 'it might be best if I recovered my charges from the pavilion – if, that is, my husband has not already done so. March ... your arm, if you please.' And with the briefest of gleaming glances for Adeline, she walked away.

Mr Fox, who was not averse to making the most of Lord March's absence and did not, in any case, care for Mr Horton, drew Nell's hand through one arm and offered the other to Adeline.

'Though one cannot, of course, imagine dear Jack doing anything in the least clandestine,' he remarked languidly, 'doubtless we are all equally agog to find out.'

More interested in finding Cassie and Harry, Nell merely nodded.

Adeline, however, delayed to say sweetly, 'I trust that your mind is now sufficiently relieved, Uncle?'

'Not entirely. I believe I would be grateful for a moment of your time,' he replied. 'I daresay Mr Fox will be pleased to escort Lady Elinor to the pavilion in order to allow us a moment's privacy.'

'I doubt it,' observed Adeline dryly. 'And really – having just taken me to task for being an indifferent chaperone – I'm surprised at you for suggesting it.'

Something flickered in Richard Horton's eyes and his mouth tightened. Then the cat-like smile re-appeared and he said, 'You mistake me, my dear. I meant only that they precede us. Her ladyship need never be out of your sight.' He offered her his arm. 'Shall we?'

The old Adeline would simply have refused and cared nothing for the consequences. The new one was irritably aware that he had made it impossible for her to do so without being blatantly rude in front of Charles Fox. Then, as she hesitated, Nell said abruptly, 'It's all right, Adeline. Mr Fox will take me to Isabel and you can join us presently.' And without giving her startled escort time to demur, she hauled him off along the Azalea Walk.

'How delightful,' purred Mr Horton. 'Tact is such a rare quality in the young that I am quite *bouleversé*.'

Ignoring both this and his proffered arm, Adeline started to follow in Nell's wake, saying crisply, 'Come to the point. I don't intend to let you ruin my entire evening.'

'Don't you? That remains to be seen.' He fell into step with her and abandoned his smile. 'I asked a favour of you, Adeline – and you failed me.'

So it was that. She had suspected as much. The aquamarine eyes filled with sympathetic mockery and she said, 'So you haven't been elected to White's, after all? What a shame. But you only have yourself to blame, you know. Rockliffe doesn't like being fleeced at cards.'

The blood rushed to Mr Horton's head and, beneath the paint, his face burned.

'Are you suggesting that *I* have done so?'

'Yes. Did you think he wouldn't notice? If so, the experience should be a valuable lesson to you. And instead of bemoaning the fact that he probably saw to it that you were black-balled, you should be hoping that he hasn't also exposed you for the cheat you are.'

Richard Horton swung her round to face him.

'Hold your tongue and listen, my clever little bitch. Your high-and-mighty husband won't expose me. Of course he won't. And do you know why? It's because he has the misfortune to be married to my niece – and he won't have scandal attached to his family. He can't touch me, Adeline. He daren't.'

'I suspect you'll find,' came the calm retort, 'that he'll dare anything – when it suits him. The world isn't going to point a censorious finger at Rockliffe, Uncle. And, even if it did, he has more than enough character to carry it off.'

'Does he?' His hand dropped away from her and he was breathing rather fast. 'And what if someone … myself, for example … were to tell him that his wife is a bastard? What then, do you suppose?'

For a moment, Adeline simply stared at him. Then, with a shrug and a tiny, derisive laugh, she said, 'He'd probably say – as I do – that it's pot calling kettle. With the possible exception of Diana, you are the biggest bastard I know.'

His mouth curled unpleasantly.

'You misunderstand, my dear. I am not insulting you. I am stating a literal fact.'

Something in his expression reached her and her scalp prickled. The words still had no meaning but she found that she was standing very still, as though any movement might send her hurtling over the precipice. With careful detachment, she said, 'What, in plain language, are you trying to tell me?'

'Why, just that you are a by-blow, dear heart. A base-born, misbegotten, illegitimate so-called love-child. Your mother was a slut, Tom Kendrick was a cuckold and you – *Duchess* – are a true bastard in every sense of the word. Is that plain enough for you?'

The ugly words dropped like stones into her mind, drowning out the music and laughter of Ranelagh. Finally, she said distantly, 'I don't believe you. If it were so, Aunt Miriam would have told me years ago.'

'Would she? Think about it. Have you never wondered why none of us spoke of your mother – or why you were never taken to visit her grave? Of course you have. And now you have the answer – or part of it.' He paused, enjoying the moment. 'Now ... shall I tell you the rest, I wonder? Or shall I take my story straight to Rockliffe? How difficult it is to decide.'

Adeline's brain seemed paralysed. Something didn't make sense but she couldn't think what it was. She said, 'Don't trouble yourself. I'll ask my aunt.'

'By all means – if you think you can trust her to tell you the truth. She doesn't like you, Adeline. She never has. But now you're a duchess, she's rather anxious to secure your goodwill ... so for Diana's sake, she'll say exactly what appears to be necessary.' He smiled and smoothed a crease from his salmon-pink sleeve. 'Sleep on it, my dear. One should never be hasty. I'll give you twenty-four hours before I seek out Rockliffe. And that is generous of me ... for I should so enjoy humbling him.'

With difficulty, she said, 'The person who could do that hasn't been born yet.'

'You think so? Well, we shall see. And in the meantime, should you decide to send for me, I'd advise you to assemble sufficient resources to

… incline me in your favour.' He stepped back and made her a flourishing bow. 'The choice is yours, dear Adeline. I trust you'll use it wisely.'

And pivoting gracefully on his high, red heels, he strolled unhurriedly away down the gravel path.

Not unnaturally, the rest of the evening was a nightmarish blur in which only the effort of appearing normal when she re-joined the others made any real impression. And, once in the carriage, she was equally oblivious of Thea's gentle radiance, Nell's silence and the line of worry that was beginning to mark Cassie's usually placid brow. The truth, of course, was that by then her mind was on a treadmill … and, until she was quite alone, it was only sensible to leave it there.

'Richard would say anything. I don't believe it,' ran the refrain. And, in counterpoint to it, 'Richard would say anything – but it could be true.'

Cassie was set down in Conduit Street and Althea restored to South Street. Then they were back in St James' Square and Nell, with an unconvincing yawn, made straight for her bedchamber.

Adeline remained motionless in the hall for a moment, her hand on the smooth end-sweep of the banister. Jeanne would be in her room, waiting to help her undress. Someone else to be faced. She did not think she could bear it.

Numbness was turning to nausea and the house seemed suddenly stifling. Without stopping to think, she turned away from the staircase and swept across the marble floor to the salon … and from there into the small, moonlit garden.

'Richard would say anything. Richard would say anything. It could be true.'

It could be true. And that, it seemed, was as good a place to start as any. Adeline sat down on the stone parapet, drew a long steadying breath and forced herself to concentrate.

What, exactly, had he said? That she was a bastard.

Her hands started to shake and she gripped them together, deciding to by-pass this point for a while. Very well. He'd called her mother a slut. Would a man speak so of his own sister if it were not the truth? Richard might. But why? Well, that at least was easy. He took pleasure in hurting. She'd known that for years. More ... for, on this occasion, he planned to kill two birds with one stone by making a profit as well.

'*Assemble sufficient resources to incline me in your favour,*' he had said. In other words, 'Pay what I ask or I'll tell your husband instead.'

It was hard to examine the possibilities logically and stop her thoughts flying ahead to the only thing that really mattered – but she knew that she had to do it now or she never would. The trouble was that the little she knew pointed both ways at once. There were reasons why Richard might lie – but nothing that said he *was* lying; and, if there were recollections from the past that aligned with his tale, she could not remember them.

Stalemate then ... unless she gave him the satisfaction of asking him to finish what he'd begun. And show her proof of it. She shivered and pulled the silk domino more closely about her, thinking, '*I can't – I can't. I don't want to hear any more of it*.' But that was no solution – for if she didn't buy the poisoned dart, it would be aimed at Tracy. And that, of course, was something she couldn't – wouldn't – permit.

She rose and began restlessly circling the garden, her skirts sighing over the dew-wet grass. She thought of Tracy's face as it had been yesterday morning ... and the sweet, budding expectancy that had been growing inside her ever since.

'*Why now?*' her heart cried. '*Why now? It isn't fair!*'

Not fair? No. But then life often wasn't. She'd known that for years, too. And though this monstrous thing obviously had to be faced, there was still a strong chance that it wasn't true. So it would be stupid to wallow in self-pity or give way to panic. If she wanted to protect both Tracy and her own fragile promise of happiness, she would have to fight.

She stopped pacing and looked up at the first fingers of dawn striking the sky.

'It's already tomorrow,' she thought. 'Tracy may be home and it should have been the happiest day of my life. But I – God help me – *I have got to send for Richard*.'

SIXTEEN

Nell slept badly and arose with a headache. Adeline had not slept at all and it showed. The result, not surprisingly, was the nearest thing they'd ever had to a quarrel.

It began over breakfast when, tired of the silence, Nell said pettishly, 'The coffee's cold. Shall I ring for some more?'

'By all means – if you want it.'

'Don't you?'

'No. No, thank you.'

'Oh. Then I won't bother.' Nell toyed aimlessly with her knife for a moment and then tried again. 'I imagine Thea's going to find herself being scolded this morning – if that horrid uncle of hers told tales to Lady Franklin, that is.'

For the first time, the aquamarine gaze focused slowly on her face. Having already despatched a message to Mr Horton, Adeline's mind was busy with the problem of how to receive him without Nell being aware of it. She said, 'I think it unlikely that he'll trouble himself. Are you and Cassie going for your fittings at Phanie's today?'

'No,' replied Nell tersely. And then, with a creditable attempt at nonchalance, 'Do you suppose Ha– Lord Harry's really taken with Cassie? He ... he certainly appeared so last night.'

Adeline repressed a sigh and prepared, dutifully, to do her best for his lordship.

'Why not? They're both good-natured and fun-loving. I imagine they could deal very well together. And, of course, Harry's extremely eligible – not to mention, attractive.'

'Oh – extremely,' said Nell, past the pain in her chest. 'It's just a pity he's so rude, that's all.'

'*Is* he rude? I can't say I've ever noticed it.'

'No. I daresay you wouldn't. But last night he virtually ignored me for the entire evening. He didn't even ask me to dance.'

Adeline suddenly discovered that she had neither the energy nor the inclination to be tactful. She said flatly, 'Well, you can't be surprised by that, can you? As far as I can see, he's merely giving you your own again.'

Nell flushed and her eyes grew rather bright.

'What do you mean by that?'

'Isn't it obvious? You've made it plain to the world at large that you want nothing to do with him so I expect he's decided to leave you to stew in your own ill-temper and look elsewhere.'

'I'm *not* ill-tempered!'

'No. But I doubt if Harry knows that.'

'He's known me since I was ten!'

'So? Is that any reason for treating him with contempt?'

Nell surged impetuously to her feet.

'I don't! I *haven't*! Oh – you don't understand!'

'No,' agreed Adeline. 'I don't. But I do know one thing. If you're going to play dog-in-the-manger and allow it to come between you and Cassie, you'll soon find yourself with no friends left to you.'

'*Oh!*' Nell quivered with indignation. 'How can you suggest such a thing? It's not like that at all.'

'Isn't it?' Setting down her cup, Adeline prepared to leave the table. 'Good.'

'*Good*? Is that all you can say?'

'No. I could ask you why you dislike Harry when he's done nothing to deserve it – or tell you that it's high time you stopped encouraging the dubious attentions of Jasper Brierley. But I don't somehow think you're in the mood to listen.'

'I'm not in the mood to be lectured, if that's what you mean!'

'It isn't. But let it pass.' Adeline rose and shook out her blue taffeta skirts. 'I'm sorry, Nell. I can't sympathise with you because I don't blame Harry in the least. And now you'll have to excuse me. I've a lot to do today.'

For a moment after she had gone, Nell continued to stare at the closed door out of eyes stinging with tears. Then, brushing them angrily aside, she sped off to order the carriage. Half an hour later, she was up to her ears in an orgy of spending.

*

At much the same time, Adeline was informed of the arrival of Mr Horton. She had him shown to the library and then kept him waiting for ten tactical minutes before joining him.

'Good morning, Uncle. I won't say it's a pleasure to see you because we both know it isn't, don't we?'

Richard Horton turned slightly from the large portrait he had been studying. 'Your predecessor, I believe ... chosen, they say, from amongst the best blood in England. You do well to stand in her shoes, Adeline. But can you keep them?'

Her face remained completely expressionless.

'If you have a tale to tell, tell it. If not, leave.'

'All in good time, my dear. All in good time.' He settled himself in a chair and smiled cordially at her. 'First I should like to be assured that you have the means to ensure my co-operation.'

'He who pays the piper calls the tune,' she observed contemptuously. 'If you want your money, you'll first have to earn it.'

There was a pause. Then, 'I want five hundred guineas.'

She stared at him. '*What?*'

'And do not, I beg of you, waste time trying to barter with me. Five hundred or I go to Rockliffe. Take it or leave it.'

The size of his demand brought fright several steps nearer. She had placed four hundred in the drawer of the escritoire and it was all the money she had - for though Tracy was more than generous, she had already settled several accounts and would have to leave others unpaid until after quarter-day. She swallowed, pulled the purse from the drawer and threw it on the table beside him.

'I can't give you what I don't have. Four hundred – and be damned to you.'

The seconds ticked by in silence while he looked at her and debated the wisdom of pushing her at this stage. The cards had been unlucky of late and the remaining hundred would undoubtedly have been very useful. On the other hand, it would be a pity to kill the goose which he intended should lay him quite a number of golden eggs ... and if he frightened her too much, too soon, she might do the very last thing he wanted and tell Rockliffe.

With a faint sigh, he stretched out a languid hand for the purse and said, 'It's probably very foolish of me ... but I suppose I must give you the benefit of the doubt.'

'How kind of you!' said Adeline acidly. 'Your generosity will be your undoing, one of these days.'

'And your sharp tongue will be yours. If you wish to hear what I have to say, I suggest you sit down and listen.'

She sat, simultaneously thankful that he had not pressed her over the money and dreading what was to come. She said, 'Very well. I'm listening – and I'd be glad if you were brief.'

He inclined his head and smiled maliciously. Then, in silky tones and with his own particular interpretation, he embarked on the history of his sister, Joanna.

It did not take very long but, by the time he ceased speaking, Adeline discovered that every muscle and bone in her body was aching. For a long time she remained silent and then, in a voice that seemed to come from a long way off, she said, 'You ... you are saying that it – it's possible my mother is still alive.'

'Yes.'

'Have you any proof?'

'Again – yes.' He drew a folded sheet of paper from his pocket and handed it to her. 'This came into my possession on the death of my father. I always suspected I might find a use for it one day.'

Very slowly, Adeline opened out the page and stared at the few faded lines inscribed on it.

I am going with Michel. I'm sorry for Tom and the baby – but I have to go. I love him. This time you cannot stop me. Perhaps God will forgive you your lies. I never shall.

Joanna.

The blood seemed to congeal in her veins. Whatever else she had expected, it was not this. She said carefully, 'Did you never hear from her again?'

'No. But that was scarcely surprising. I was five years younger and scarcely knew her. Miriam was only a year younger but resented the fact that everyone – especially men – always preferred Joanna. Our parents, of course – as you can see from the letter – had already sunk themselves below reproach.' He smiled. 'So she may be alive – or she may not. We have no way of knowing.'

'I – I see.' Adeline swallowed and kept her hands pressed tightly together. 'Why was I never told?'

'Because Miriam did not trust your discretion,' he shrugged. 'And what purpose would it have served?'

'But I had a *right* to know! She was my *mother*!'

The cry was wrenched from her with a force that left her shaking. Her brain was racing round in circles and it took time to control her breathing. Richard waited with an air of gentle satisfaction until she said, 'My grandfather – did *he* know?'

'Old man Kendrick? No. Tom went back alone, positively swathed in black and said that Joanna had succumbed to a fever. As far as we were all aware, his father believed him.' He paused and then added sweetly, 'As for the gentleman in question being your grandfather ... that is, as I have already explained, open to doubt.'

As far as it was possible, Adeline completed the process of pulling herself together. There was an obvious flaw in what he'd said and it was important to expose it.

'Is it? I don't see why. This letter was written after my birth and before my mother disappeared. There is no reason to assume that my father wasn't Tom Kendrick.'

'None, dear heart – save that Joanna was besotted by du Plessis before her marriage and ran off with him not so long after it. Also, if she was clever enough to vanish without a trace, she was certainly clever enough to conduct a discreet liaison, don't you think?'

Sick with confusion and paper-white, Adeline forced herself to cling tenaciously to her point. 'It is – it may be a possibility – though I don't think so. If ... if I was not her husband's child, surely she would have taken me with her?'

He shrugged again. 'Who can say? Perhaps she wasn't sure herself; perhaps she wasn't cruel enough to deprive poor Tom of you as well; perhaps it wasn't so easy to disappear with a babe in arms. Sadly, we shall never know.'

'But it's all supposition. It is *not* – as you said last night – a fact.'

'Perhaps not. But the melancholy truth is that, given a shred of doubt, people are apt to believe the worst. That no-one can *prove* you illegitimate will be immaterial. All that will count, should this story become common knowledge, is that your birth is …questionable. And birth, dearest Adeline, matters.' He eyed her consideringly. 'Doors will be closed to you – and that will naturally affect Rockliffe. I would *so* enjoy watching him cope with that.'

Unaware that she did so, Adeline came to her feet and let the letter fall unheeded to the floor. She said, 'You are threatening to tell the world? Is that what all this is about?'

'Not quite, my dear. Not quite.' Still entirely at his ease, Richard bent to retrieve the letter and then rose to face her. 'I don't need to tell the world. Or not yet. For the moment, all I need do is tell Rockliffe. Think about it. I'm sure you'll soon work it out. And when you have, we can speak again.'

And without troubling to take his leave, he sauntered blithely from the room.

For a long time after he had gone, Adeline remained where she was, standing alone amidst the wreckage of her emotions. It seemed that her brief taste of security was over and her hopes of happiness no more than dust. In the space of twelve hours, Richard Horton had turned light into dark and sweet anticipation into dread. All she could think of now was that Tracy was coming home … and she did not know how she was going to face him.

*

Sir Jasper Brierley was just on the point of entering his favourite coffee-house when he espied Lady Elinor Wynstanton, accompanied only by her maid, emerging from Madame Tissot's exclusive hat-shop. It was, he decided, too fortuitous a chance to be missed; and when he observed the distinctly wistful droop to her ladyship's mouth, his eye brightened still further. So the child was feeling hard-done-by, was she? Better and better. She was all the more likely to soak up his blandishments.

For years, Sir Jasper had lived without visible means of support and on the brink of insolvency. He was actually quite good at it and even derived a certain satisfaction from fooling his creditors. Unfortunately, however, his debts were accumulating to the point where he might find himself forced to flee the country rather than face Newgate ... which was not a pretty prospect and one which, for some weeks now, had been spoiling his ability to sleep at night. The result was that he was reluctantly contemplating matrimony; and, with his customary sense of self-preservation, he had taken the precaution of making sure he had two strings to his bow.

One was the widow of a wealthy cloth merchant from Bermondsey; a cosy enough armful and already in possession of a fortune – but undeniably vulgar. The other was Lady Nell – with whom he had always known he would have to play a very far-sighted game indeed if he were not to spend the next seven years living on her expectations. It was a delicate situation all round ... and Sir Jasper found it stimulating.

Nell greeted him with unconcealed pleasure and said impulsively, 'Oh – you can't imagine how glad I am to see you! I've had a perfectly horrid morning and now, to cap it all, Madame has trimmed my new hat with quite the wrong shade of pink so I shan't be able to wear it this afternoon after all.'

'How provoking,' murmured Sir Jasper soothingly. He drew her hand through his arm and, leaving her maid to follow, began to stroll down Bond Street. 'But I suspect, you know, that it is something more than a mere hat that has dimmed those incomparable eyes.'

Nell looked up at him, coloured and then looked away again, once more on the verge of tears.

'You – you are very perceptive, sir,' she whispered. 'It's simply that I ... I passed a very uncomfortable evening last night at Ranelagh.'

'That is most understandable. Ranelagh is grown very tedious these days. Quite *passé*. Indeed, in my humble opinion, it is only fit for children and the *bourgeoisie* ... though I imagine it is still possible to enjoy it if one has the good fortune to be in the right company. But somehow, I sense that you were not.'

'No,' agreed Nell, a fraction more cheerfully. 'I wasn't.'

'Just so.' Sir Jasper gazed down at her with just a hint of regret in his smile. 'Do you know ... it is no doubt reprehensible of me and certainly out of the question ... but I should so much like to escort you to a Covent Garden masquerade. I think you would enjoy it very much.'

Nell's eyes grew round. 'But aren't they vastly improper affairs?'

'My dear Lady Elinor!' He laughed softly. 'They are all the rage amongst the ... how shall I put it? ... amongst the less *staid* persons of fashion. For naturally one retains one's mask at all times and so, even if the proceedings are a trifle less decorous than one would find in the Pantheon, what possible harm can come of it?'

'None,' said Nell thoughtfully. 'It sounds rather entertaining.'

'It is.' He allowed just the right degree of ruefulness to inform his voice. 'But it was wrong of me to mention it.'

'Why?'

'Because you would not, I fear, be permitted to attend such a function.'

Nell tilted her chin to a militant angle.

'I don't see why not. I'm not a child, after all. When Rock comes home, I'll speak to him about it. And I hope – when we *do* go – that I shall see *you* there.'

Sir Jasper – who knew it would be a cold day in hell before Rockliffe let his sister attend a Covent Garden romp – stopped walking and raised her hand to his lips.

'You must know by now that your slightest wish is my command. And, in this case, I wouldn't miss it for worlds.'

*

Adeline had not intended to attend Lady Linton's drum that evening and still had not the least wish to do so. However, since the idea of waiting at home for Tracy sent her nerves into spasm and it also seemed unwise, just at present, to send Nell under the chaperonage of Lady Delahaye, she was moved to change her mind. She therefore allowed Jeanne to dress her in her new lilac silk and, for the first time in her life, sought a remedy for her pallor in the rouge-pot. Then, in a mood of mutually observed civility, she and Nell set off for Clarges Street.

Under normal circumstances, Adeline would merely have considered the party a little dull. As it was, the strain of making light conversation over the turmoil in her mind rendered it one of the worst evenings of her life. She was still no closer to deciding what – if anything – to say to Tracy; and that, plus the shock of learning that her mother might not be dead after all and that her father might be a Frenchman called Michel du Plessis, seemed a load too heavy to bear. The only bright spot was that neither the Franklins nor Mr Horton were present.

Nell, for different reasons, was glad of that too and, throwing her heart and soul into appearing cheerful, she wasted no time in apologising to Cassie for her lacklustre behaviour of the previous evening.

'It's just that I didn't feel terribly well,' she lied breezily. 'I don't think the crab patties agreed with me.'

Cassie's brow cleared as if by magic.

'Oh – I'm so glad! I mean, I'm sorry you felt ill, of course … but I was rather afraid that I'd annoyed you in some way.'

'Annoyed me? Goodness, no! How could you possibly have done so?'

'Well … I wasn't sure, but I thought that perhaps it had something to do with Lord Harry,' confided Cassie truthfully. And then, laughing, 'I really should have known better, shouldn't I?'

'Yes,' agreed Nell brightly. 'Indeed you should.'

The evening was well-advanced by the time Harry Caversham arrived and caused Nell's heart to perform the hitherto unknown feat of leaping into her mouth. Her fingers tightened painfully on her fan and she stared across the room as though seeing him for the first time. Then he met her gaze and, quirking one mobile brow, continued to hold it. Nell smiled, blushed and found she had completely lost track of what Lady Linton was saying to her.

Seconds later he was at her side and begging his hostess's pardon for his lateness with all his usual audacious charm. Her ladyship, who was Isabel Vernon's mother and a creature of eccentric vagueness, listened for a while and then said kindly, 'Yes, Harry. I understand perfectly. But you really need some new excuses, you know. The ones you have are becoming threadbare through constant use.' And she drifted amiably away.

Harry and Nell were left looking at each other. Finally, he grinned and said laconically, 'Well? Do you think it's time we agreed a truce?'

'I – I didn't know we were at war.'

'Didn't you?' The blue eyes brimmed with laughter. 'Then perhaps we weren't. I don't suppose there's much point in my asking if you'd care to dance?'

And that, Nell suddenly realised, was generous of him. She swallowed and said, 'Yes. Yes, there is. And I'm sorry I've been behaving so rudely. The truth is that I thought that you and Rock had come to – to a s-sort of agreement. About me, that is. And I didn't want to be ... manipulated.'

She felt pardonably pleased with the last word. Harry looked mildly stunned.

'Are you saying,' he asked at length, 'that you suspected Rock of offering me your hand – or me of asking for it – without finding it necessary to consult you?'

Put like that, she realised how unlikely it sounded.

'Yes. But it isn't true, is it?'

'I should damned well say it's not! It's the most outrageous idea I ever heard. What do you take me for? Another Jasper Brierley?'

'That's not fair,' she said feebly. 'It's just that I've always known it would suit Rock to have me married. And then, when we were staying in Oxfordshire and he was so insistent about my being polite to you, it began to seem that he – that you – oh, *I* don't know! I can see now how stupid it was – but that's what I thought.'

Harry's expression relaxed and the familiar gleam crept back into his eyes.

'At least now you've seen your mistake – so I suppose that's something. And perhaps I can best set your mind completely at rest by categorically stating that, if and when I wish to be married, the lady concerned will be the first to know of it. Better?'

'Oh yes.' Even to her own ears, Nell's voice sounded hollow. 'Much better.'

'Good,' said Harry cheerfully. 'So now, at last, perhaps you and I can try being simple friends. What do you think?'

*

Simple friends. Driving home in the company of a silent Adeline, Nell wondered why those two words should be so curiously depressing. She was still wondering it when they entered Wynstanton House to be told that his Grace had returned; and then something in Adeline's face pierced her self-absorption and made her decide that, if something peculiar was brewing between her brother and his wife, she would prefer to be well out of the way.

Adeline responded mechanically to Nell's "goodnight" and then, as calmly as she was able, asked the butler where the Duke might be found.

'I believe, your Grace,' said that stately person expressionlessly, 'that his Grace has retired.'

'I see. Thank you, Symonds.' *And thank God, too*, she thought. *It will be easier tomorrow.*

Wearily, she climbed the stairs. Soft candlelight spilled over her as she paused in the doorway of her boudoir to brace herself for one final performance in front of Jeanne. Then, closing the door behind her, she moved on into the room ... and stopped as if she had walked into a wall.

Rockliffe sat by the hearth, watching her. His face was in shadow but she could see that he had discarded his coat and held an untouched glass of wine in one tapering, white hand. Adeline's throat closed with shock and her brain froze. She did not know how long she stood there, mutely staring. It could only have been seconds; it felt like an eternity.

'You look startled,' he said. 'Did you not guess that you would find me here?'

'I – no.' Her mouth was dry as dust and it hurt to breathe. 'Symonds said you had retired.'

'Without first seeing you? How could you think it?' His voice was warm ... half-teasing, half-not. He set down the glass and came smoothly to his feet. 'And it seemed unlikely that you would stay very late at the Lintons. In my experience, no one ever does.'

She managed a smile of sorts.

'It *was* a somewhat insipid party.'

'They usually are.' Leaving the fire, he moved unhurriedly towards her. 'Which is why I rather hoped you might have chosen not to go.'

'I – I had to.' Without thinking about it, Adeline turned away to her dressing-table and began stripping off rings and bracelets with shaking hands. 'Nell and Cassie had a small falling-out at Ranelagh last evening so it didn't seem a good idea to send Nell to the Linton's with Lady Delahaye as I'd originally intended.' Reaching up to unfasten the pearls around her neck, she caught sight of his face in the mirror and her fingers fumbled clumsily with the catch which wouldn't open. 'Of course, they've made it up now – so I could probably have stayed at home after all.'

He closed the space between them and, gently putting her hands aside, said, 'Let me help you. I took the liberty of telling Jeanne that you wouldn't need her. I hoped that you might make do with me, instead.' The pearls slid from her throat and he reached past her to place them on the table, his shirt-sleeve brushing her bare arm as he did so. 'I'm not, you may find, entirely inexperienced in the role ... and, if you were to sit down, I could demonstrate it by unpinning your hair.'

Her nerves snarled into knots. She said, 'I – no, thank you. I can manage. Did you have a pleasant journey? I'd half expected not to see you until tomorrow. I hope your business was successful?'

This was not the home-coming to which he had looked forward through every mile of the long drive back from Oxfordshire. Disappointment washed over him and he took a moment to conquer it. Then, when he finally spoke, it was not in answer to her questions, but to say thoughtfully, 'I returned as soon as I could. I believed, you see, that I had an incentive.'

There did not seem to be any satisfactory answer to that. She began removing pins from her hair with elaborate and time-consuming care.

'Adeline.' Frowning slightly, the dark magnetic gaze fixed on her reflection. 'What happened while I was away?'

'Happened? Why, nothing.' *My life has been ripped apart and I don't know how to mend it - or how to tell you.* 'We did a little shopping and went to Ranelagh, as I told you. Nothing at all extraordinary.

'I see,' he said. 'So nothing has occurred to upset or worry you?'

'Of course not. Why should you think that? It's only been three days, after all.'

'Quite. But you seem a trifle … nervous. And then there is the rouge.'

'The rouge? Oh – that!' She gave a tiny, careless shrug. 'It's this gown. I don't think lilac suits me. But there was no time to change so I tried to mend matters with artifice, for once. I don't think it worked, do you?'

What Rockliffe thought was that she looked under-slept and feverishly brittle – but that he was getting no closer to discovering why. Three days ago she'd melted in his arms as though there was nowhere else she wanted to be; now the barriers were back with a vengeance and she was further away than ever – retreating behind a wall of light, meaningless chatter. There had to be a reason for it, something she wasn't telling him; unless … but he wouldn't explore that possibility. Not yet. It hurt too much.

Setting his hands on her shoulders, he turned her gently to face him and said, 'These things matter, of course – but need we discuss them now? I have been waiting to greet you and have yet to do so.'

'Of course.' Adeline forced herself to remain still and knew not which temptation was the stronger – the one to hurl herself against him or the one to run away.

He could feel the tension running through her and her mouth remained coolly unresponsive under his. This time the disappointment he'd tried to put aside solidified like a stone and, repressing a pointless desire to tell her so, he made one last attempt to get her to talk to him.

'Adeline, I don't wish to be tiresome … but if something is wrong, I wish you would tell me. It's just possible, you know, that I might be able to help.'

'But nothing *is* wrong,' she replied brightly. 'Nothing at all. It's just that I'm very tired and – and therefore not the best of company just at present.'

His hands dropped away from her and he said, 'You are saying you would simply like me to go.'

'If – if you wouldn't mind. I think it might be best.'

The subtle change in his expression all but undid her and she turned abruptly back to the task of unpinning her hair. She had chosen her course almost by accident and it was even worse than she had feared. Three days ago she'd let him see that she wanted him; now she was pushing him away. She could only imagine how that must feel. But, at some point in the last ten minutes she'd somehow come to the muddled conclusion that she either had to tell him everything right now - or avoid any further intimacy until she could do so. Anything else didn't bear thinking about. And though the second was going to be hard, the first – at this stage – was downright impossible.

'*Oh God,*' she thought miserably. '*What can I do? I can't tell him. I can't cheat him by* not *telling him ... and I can't let Richard hurt him. What can I do? I am in a cage.*'

Rockliffe regarded her out of hooded eyes for a long moment and then made her a small, ironic bow. 'It seems we are faced with yet another instance of my lamentable timing, doesn't it?'

'Not at all. The fault is mine ... and I'm sorry.'

'Are you?' He walked away to pick up his coat. 'That's nice. But don't allow yourself to feel too guilty, my dear. It might lead you to do something else you will come to regret.'

The door closed behind him with a gentle click that might, as far as Adeline was concerned, have been the slamming of Hell's gate. An uncontrollable shudder tore through her body and, dropping slowly to her knees, she put her face in her hands and cried.

*

Rockliffe rarely drank to excess and never alone. That night, he went downstairs to the library and did both.

The first glass did little to numb the pain that was carving its way through his chest. He had come home prepared, at last, to say the words he'd never said to any woman in his life before – and she'd brushed him aside like a minor inconvenience. She had said there was nothing wrong – which, if it was true, left only one logical explanation; that her response to him on the morning he'd left for Oxfordshire had been a mistake she didn't intend to make again. He found he could just about live with the thought that she was still not ready to let him make love to her. What he *couldn't* live with, however, was being held at arm's length like a total bloody stranger. That had hurt more than he would have believed possible.

It took time, effort and a third glass of port before he was able to think with his brain instead of his emotions ... not a problem he was accustomed to ... and, when he did, a number of other things occurred to him.

She'd insisted there was nothing wrong. He hadn't believed her - but had wondered if that was just because he didn't want to. However, when she had first walked into the room and seen him, her expression had not been just startled – it had been stricken. As if she was afraid to face him. Why? What could have happened – what could she have done that was so terrible she couldn't tell him about it? Didn't she know there was nothing he wouldn't forgive her?

'Ah,' he thought wryly. '*Well, perhaps just one thing.*'

But he knew it wasn't that. She hadn't managed to keep him out of her bed all this time only to fall headlong into that of some other man in the space of three days.

And that brought him back to what had happened between them before he had left. Her response had been real. He was experienced enough to know when a woman wanted him ... experienced enough also to know that what Adeline had been feeling that morning had not been purely physical. All of which meant that the situation, though unfortunate, was not – could not be – irretrievable.

His mind recovered its tone and he left the fourth glass untouched.

Aside from the one thing she'd denied him, he'd tried everything he knew and it had not been enough. Perhaps it was time for a change of tactics.

SEVENTEEN

Nell, who – despite one niggling reservation – felt a good deal better after her talk with Lord Harry, arose refreshed and brimming with vigour. She sang on the way down the stairs and, finding her brother alone at the breakfast table, bade him a sunny "Good morning", prior to launching into her chosen theme. She was not, of course, to know that she had chosen a bad time – or even that the answer would have been the same had she chosen a good one. But Rockliffe, having heard her out in enigmatic silence, was in a mood of less than his usual tolerance and not disposed to mince his words.

'No, Nell,' he said flatly. 'I will not take you to a ridotto at Covent Garden. You had as well ask me to take you sight-seeing in Bedlam.'

'But *why*?'

'Because vulgarity amuses me no more than the misfortunes of the insane. And it would do you no good whatsoever to be seen in such a place.'

'But if one is masked, who is to know?' she objected. 'And Sir Jasper says that many fashionable people go there.'

'Does he indeed?' Rockliffe folded his arms and eyed her sardonically. 'But I, sadly, do not consider his judgement superior to my own – and, furthermore, I believe I have already desired you to terminate that friendship.'

'Well, yes. But -- '

'No more buts, if you please. They grow tedious. And that is the end of the matter.'

Nell stiffened. 'I think you might at least listen to me.'

'Do you? Then I suggest that you start doing as you would be done by. Ah.' This as the door opened on Adeline. 'Good morning, my dear.'

It was a moment before she replied. Since the night of their own ball, he had always left his hair unpowdered ... until today. Plainly, this was a message of some kind. 'Good morning.'

'I trust you slept well?'

She hadn't – but it would obviously not do to say so. 'Yes, thank you. And you?'

'More than I'd anticipated, shall we say. Coffee?'

The tone was bland enough but his meaning was unmistakeable. Adeline set her teeth, allowed him to fill her cup and wondered, bleakly, what else she had expected.

It was Nell who unwittingly broke the tension by saying baldly, 'I'm sorry about yesterday, Adeline. You were right, of course – I see that now. So I apologised to Cassie and – and made my peace with Ha– Lord Harry, too. I just thought you'd like to know.'

And, on this laconically uttered invitation to applause, she left the room.

The door closed behind her and Rockliffe returned to the piece of correspondence he'd been perusing when she first came in. This, too, was unusual. His manners were invariably impeccable and Adeline had never known him read at the table when anyone else was present. The sinking feeling in her chest intensified and she toyed aimlessly with a slice of bread-and-butter. Then, when she couldn't stand the silence any longer, she said, 'About last night ... '

The dark eyes rose to encompass her. 'Yes?'

'I – I'm sorry. I know I disappointed you.'

He refrained from saying that disappointment in no way covered it. In fact, he refrained from saying anything at all.

Adeline waited and, when he continued to regard her with an air of mild enquiry, said weakly, 'It ... truly, it was just that I was tired and out of sorts. This constant round of balls and parties with Nell ... I suppose I'm not quite accustomed to it yet.'

Finally, he laid down the letter he had been holding.

'If that is so, the solution would seem to be very simple. You once said, I believe, that if I ever suggested a quiet evening at home, you would listen. I'm suggesting it. Tonight, perhaps?'

'Oh.' She swallowed, belatedly recognising the pit into which her excuse had led her. 'It's the Cavendish House ball. We accepted Dolly's invitation weeks ago.'

'Of course. Tomorrow, then?'

'The Delahaye's masquerade. Nell and Cassie have talked of little else for weeks. And after that, the Vernon's rout --'

Rockliffe silenced her with a movement of one hand.

'Pray spare me a catalogue of all our social engagements for the rest of the season. I would also be obliged if you could stop insulting my intelligence.'

'I wasn't.'

'Of course you were. The situation is perfectly plain. You have no intention of allowing our relationship to progress. I think I may be said to be well aware of that fact. The only thing I *don't* know is – why.'

'Are you asking me?'

'Would there be any point?' He waited and then, when she did not reply, leaned back in his chair and said, 'Very well. Since you raised the subject, let us talk about last night – dispensing with any further excuses, if you don't mind. There are only two reasons to account for your behaviour. One is that the idea of lying with me is still ... insufficiently appealing; the other is that something happened while I was away – something you don't trust me enough to share with me. If one of them has to be true, I suppose I'd prefer the latter. Well?'

Adeline stared at him aghast. This was worse than she had anticipated and she didn't know what might make it better. She said, 'It's not either of them. I -- '

'Don't lie to me.' Suddenly his voice was clipped and incredibly cold. 'I think I deserve better than that.' He paused, letting silence take over again. Then, in something closer to his usual manner, he said, 'I have been patient. Indeed, I think you will own that I have shown commendable restraint – given the circumstances.'

'Yes.'

'Thank you. You may count on that restraint lasting a while longer yet. But I should point out that my patience is not inexhaustible. As you have always known, I did not marry you purely to chaperone Nell and grace my breakfast table. And as you must also have realised, I would prefer you to come to me because you wanted to ... rather than as a result of any coercion on my part or because of all this.' He waved a dismissive hand at the elegantly-appointed room. 'There comes a point, however, when that may have to change. I trust that makes the position reasonably plain?'

'Extremely plain.' Adeline reached towards her coffee cup, then, realising that her hand was shaking, withdrew it to the safety of her lap. 'Yes.'

'Good.' For the first time that morning, the merest glimmer of his usual expression entered his eyes. 'They say patience is a virtue and that virtue brings its own rewards. I am still hoping that may prove true. In the meantime, if you should decide to tell me what is worrying you, my door is always open.' He pushed back his chair and stood up. 'And now I am afraid you must excuse me. I have an appointment this morning.'

'Of course.'

'Ah.' This as he turned to go, 'Just one thing more. I feel I should, in all fairness, withdraw my embargo with regard to your various cavaliers attending your *toilette* ... since, for the foreseeable future at least, I will not be attending it myself.'

The door closed softly behind him. Adeline pressed the heels of her hands over her eyes and realised that she felt sick.

*

An hour later and equipped with all his customary *sangfroid*, Rockliffe received his man of law and laid before him the fruits of his visit to Sir Roland Franklin. Then, despite Mr Osborne's air of gathering gloom, he gently requested him to journey to Paris in search of Michel du Plessis.

'But your Grace – it is a near impossibility!' said the lawyer incredulously. 'The address is six years old. The gentleman may be anywhere by now. He may even be dead!'

'Or he may not. Look on the bright side, Mr Osborne. I am giving you the chance to explore France at my expense.'

Mr Osborne shuddered.

'You don't find the prospect alluring, I see,' remarked the Duke with the faintest suspicion of amusement. 'Have you something against foreign travel?'

'My French,' replied the lawyer, thinking miserably of sea-sickness, strange indigestible food and flea-infested inns, 'is not of the highest order.'

'But adequate, my dear fellow. I am sure that it is adequate. And the task is not as hopeless as you may think. We know from the letters that du Plessis was a military man, serving for a time under one Maréchal Rebec … and he, at least, should not be difficult to trace.' Rockliffe paused, fingering the miniature of Joanna. 'You may also take this. But I would ask you to treat it with great care as I hope, one day, to give it to my wife.'

'Does her Grace know?' asked Mr Osborne weakly.

'No. Put yourself in her position, if you can. After a lifetime of ignorance, what use do you suppose half a story would be to you?'

'Very little, your Grace.'

'None at all, Mr Osborne. And that is why you are going to France with all possible speed and, once there, to make what discoveries you can.' With a peculiar glinting smile that veiled the magisterial reality, Rockliffe handed over a substantial packet of papers. 'I think you will find everything you need. Money for the immediate future, a draft on my Paris bankers and a letter instructing Captain Lennox to put both himself and my yacht at your disposal. You will find the *Boreas* at Southampton. If you leave this morning, you may – weather permitting – sail on tomorrow's evening tide. Do you have any further questions?'

'No,' said the little man unhappily. 'That is – no, your Grace.'

'Then I will wish you Godspeed, Mr Osborne. Good luck – and good hunting.'

*

That evening Rockliffe did not, as he had said, attend Adeline's *toilette* and, when she joined him downstairs with Nell, he merely kissed her hand lightly and complimented her on choosing the sapphires to set off her silver-grey brocade gown. Despite the misery in her heart, Adeline's bones melted at the sight of him and she knew a desperate longing to touch the immaculately powdered head, bending over her hand. As always, he looked magnificent and, as always, she was dazzled by it.

Since the Cavendish House ball was regarded as one of the highlights of the social season, the rooms were already crowded and Adeline looked nervously about her for the willowy figure of her uncle. Mercifully, she did not see it and soon, finding herself accosted by Thea, she discovered why.

'Oh – Adeline!' Althea's eyes were wide with excitement. 'You'll never guess what Andy's done!'

'Andy?' queried Adeline, not really attending.

'Andrew – our brother, Andrew. He's run off with Lizzie Pickering!'

This got through. 'He's *what*?'

'Run off with Lizzie. Mama is furious. She's sent Uncle Richard home to make Papa do something about it. Only I should think it's too late by now, wouldn't you?'

'Very probably,' agreed Adeline, weak with relief. 'I take it your papa didn't come and break the news himself?'

'No. He just sent a letter. I don't think he minds very much. He likes Lizzie. I used to think Mama liked her, too – but it seems not. I suppose that's why Andrew thought they'd better elope. It's awfully sudden, though. I hadn't the least notion of them caring for each other. None of us had. And, of course, Di is as mad as fire about it.'

It was probably the longest speech Althea had ever made in her life. Adeline smiled encouragingly and said, 'Why is that?'

'Well, she *says* it's because Lizzie is a Nobody,' came the confiding reply. 'But I think it's really because she never thought to see Lizzie married before her. Is that horrid?'

'No. Just perceptive. And where is Diana this evening?'

'At home in a temper. Mama said she wasn't fit to come.'

'Oh? Well, I'm sure Mama knows best,' responded Adeline with a glimmer of her usual irony. 'And, in the meantime, you are free to enjoy yourself ... speaking of which, I suspect that here is Mr Ingram on his way to claim you.'

Althea blushed and, so softly that even Adeline failed to hear her, said 'Oh. I do hope so.'

On the other side of the room, Rockliffe was engaging Charles Fox in lazy conversation whilst watching Nell flirt her way through a gavotte with Harry Caversham.

'Do you expect them to make a match of it?' enquired Mr Fox, following his gaze.

'I expect nothing. I merely await events,' responded the Duke placidly. 'And just now I am waiting – in vain, it would seem – to hear the gossip of the last three days.'

'There's little enough to tell, my dear – would that there were! But let me see. Brackenbury's wife has given him yet another girl ... Marcus Sheringham has retired to his estates to escape the duns and – ah yes! Mistress Diana Franklin is said to have been overheard remarking that your delightful wife ... er ... entrapped you into marriage.'

His Grace's expression remained completely unchanged.

'Indeed? And what, dear Charles, do you make of that, I wonder?'

'Nothing – save that the young lady is in a fair way to making herself ridiculous,' replied Mr Fox calmly. He flicked open his snuff-box and added languidly, 'I doubt – were the town not so damned dull these days – that I'd have mentioned it at all.'

'I rejoice to hear it,' said Rockliffe. And then, raising his quizzing-glass, 'You know, Charles ... that is a very pretty box.'

'Yes. I thought you'd like it.'

'You were right. Unless I am mistaken ... one of Mr Wedgewood's pieces?'

'Specially commissioned,' nodded Mr Fox. 'Are you sorry that you didn't think of it?'

'Do you know, I believe I am.' The Duke allowed his gaze to travel meditatively to his friend's coat. 'But if I had ... you may be sure that I would never have allowed it near that particular shade of green. Garish, Charles – definitely garish.'

At the end of the gavotte, Harry smiled cloudlessly down on Nell and informed her that he had seldom enjoyed a dance more. She dimpled back at him and waited archly for him to beg her to partner him again. He didn't. Instead, he escorted her cheerfully back to Adeline and then went off to claim his dance with Cassie. He did not even seem disposed to linger.

Nell's eyes followed him thoughtfully for a moment and then a martial gleam dawned. Two, she decided sagely, could play at that game. Amongst the knot of gentlemen clustered about Adeline were a number of her own admirers. She resolved to dance with them all ... and began by bestowing her hand upon young Mr Petworth with such warmth that he was quite overcome.

She kept a discreet eye on Lord Harry. After Cassie, he progressed to Althea and then Adeline. Then, sickeningly, he danced with Cassie again. Nell's heart plummeted inexplicably, causing her attention to wander briefly ... which was how she came to accept Sir Jasper Brierley's hand for the minuet.

Not, of course, that she'd meant to ignore him. But, after what Rock had said that morning and now that she was feeling so much better about Harry, she had resolved to gradually end her flirtation with him. It was likely, in any case, that she'd had the best out of it – and it would be silly to wait until *he* tired of *her*. But here he was being as charming and entertaining as ever – and so understanding that she found herself confiding Rock's total rejection of the Ridotto Scheme ... which only went to show how one thing had a habit of leading to another.

She went home in a fever of indecision which, characteristically, could have only one result. By morning, she had persuaded herself that it really was too famous an escapade to be missed – yet perfectly harmless so long as she was careful.

'And I *will* be careful,' she thought. 'So careful no one need ever know. And then I'll be good again.'

*

A week later when Rockliffe had left for a hand of picquet at White's with Jack, Adeline was informed by her maid that Lady Elinor had a sick headache and begged to be excused from attending Lady Crewe's assembly. Not having previously supposed that Nell knew what a headache *was*, Adeline was surprised and not a little concerned to find the sufferer lying down on her bed with the curtains drawn and a cologne-soaked handkerchief adorning her brow.

'I'm sorry,' whispered Nell bravely, 'but I really don't think I can go.'

'Don't apologise. Just lie still and I'll have Jeanne make up a tisane for you. In fact, I've a good mind to do it myself. It won't disappoint me in the least to miss tonight's assembly.'

'Oh no! You mustn't think of it,' said Nell. 'I – I should feel so guilty. And Isabel promised to take us up in her carriage, didn't she?'

'Yes. But Isabel will understand. And I don't care to leave you. You are extremely pale.'

'I know – I mean, I daresay I am. But all I want is to be left alone ... and if I have a tisane, I shall sleep, you know. Do go, Adeline. I'd feel so much better if you did.'

Adeline hesitated and then allowed herself to be persuaded. But an indeterminate prickle of unease persisted at the back of her mind – and this, had she known it, was entirely justified. For as soon as she had left the house, Nell leapt from her bed, washed the white hair-powder from her face and began furnishing her maid with a *feu-de-joie* of instructions.

Lady Crewe's assembly was every bit as tedious and crowded as Adeline had feared. She suppressed a yawn, tried to appear fascinated by what Mr Walpole was saying and let her mind drift wistfully to Tracy. Unless they had a shared engagement, she found she saw very little of him these days ... and, when she did, he was pleasant but rather distant. She found that she missed him ... and wondered if he intended that she should. But it couldn't last. She knew that. Sooner or later they would find themselves back where they had been on the night of his return – and the question facing her would be the same. The only difference might be that her chances of responding as she would wish would be greater if only her evil uncle would leave her alone.

An hour later she was just wondering if Isabel would mind her taking a chair and going home when Harry Caversham put in his usual belated appearance and found his way to her side.

She said resignedly, 'You really are dreadful, you know. Don't you *ever* arrive at a respectable time?'

'It's not much after eleven,' he grinned. 'And no one minds. It's expected of me. As a matter of fact, I wasn't planning to come at all –

only the devil's in the cards and Rock happened to mention that you were here so I thought I'd look in.'

For the first time in a week, Adeline laughed.

'You're well-served, then. Nell's at home with a headache.'

'*What*?' Harry's head jerked round and his tone caused at least five other guests to halt in their tracks. 'You're saying Nell cried off because of a headache?'

'Yes.'

'And you *believed* her?'

'Yes,' said Adeline again, this time with mild irritation. And then, differently, 'Oh.'

'Oh,' agreed Harry sardonically. 'Nell never had a headache in her life.'

'Well, I thought that myself. Only she looked so -- '

'Forget how she looked,' he cut in ruthlessly, already steering her across the room. 'Come on and be quick about it. For what you wouldn't know but Rock ought to have told you is that Nell's done this before. And if she's at home, I'm a Dutchman.'

*

'You're no Dutchman,' said Adeline bitterly, returning breathlessly to the salon after visiting Nell's room. 'Her maid doesn't know where she is but I think I do. She's taken a domino.'

'Oh Christ,' groaned Harry. 'Vauxhall? Ranelagh?'

'Covent Garden,' came the flat response. 'She's been teasing Tracy to take her but he refused.'

Harry shut his eyes for a moment.

'The stupid little fool,' he breathed. And then, 'All right. I'll go and fetch her. Try not to worry. It's not your fault. But it will be interesting, won't it, to see which bastard has taken her there?'

And he was gone.

*

Covent Garden was a riot of light and noise and colour which Nell had at first enjoyed. Now she sat very still and straight and watched the proceedings outside the box degenerate from harmless vulgarity into something that, to her sheltered eyes, seemed almost bacchanalian.

The food she had eaten lay like cement in her stomach and she wanted more than anything to be able to go home.

In the seat beside her, his arm resting negligently across the back of her chair, Sir Jasper considered how best to make sure she was seen and recognised. For, if her reputation were sufficiently damaged, it was just possible that Rockliffe would bestow her hand on the only man likely to ask for it – namely, himself. It was a long-shot. And the tricky part was to arrange matters so that he did not end up facing the Duke over a yard of steel – particularly as his Grace was known to possess more than average skill in that area.

Sighing a little, he removed his arm and said cajolingly, 'My dear – will you not come and dance?'

'I'd rather not, if you don't mind. Indeed, I'd quite l-like to go home now.'

'Would you? Then of course you shall. But – as a reward – just one dance before we leave?'

The relief was so great that she gave in without a second thought. Sir Jasper's smile grew. His goal was within sight ... for less than four yards from the parapet of their box, he could see two admirable witnesses. One was Viscount Ansford, that lisping, peevish gossip; and the other was Rockliffe's former mistress, Carlotta Felucci. All he had to do was to ensure that Nell lost her mask.

He manoeuvred her towards Carlotta and the Viscount and then, at the optimum moment, allowed his buttoned cuff to catch in her curls.

'Ah – how clumsy of me! But if you will be still, I'll have you free in a trice.'

It seemed only sensible to do as he said. And then, as she waited, several things happened at once.

Her mask dropped neatly from her face; a familiar voice, unfamiliarly furious, said, 'I might have known it!'; and Sir Jasper lurched inexplicably backwards to collide with the pink-clad Viscount before ending in a heap on the floor.

'And that,' said Lord Harry, coolly adjusting his sleeve, 'ought to be the end of *that*.'

Nell stared at him. 'Harry?'

'Who else?' The blue gaze was perfectly inimical. 'Unless you want to be utterly ruined, you'd better replace your mask so that we can leave. I've several things to say to you – and, for once in your life, you're going to listen.'

By the time the carriage drew up outside Wynstanton House, Nell was sobbing heartbrokenly into her handkerchief. Ignoring this, his lordship hauled her inside and, meeting Adeline in the hall, said, 'I think I've said everything necessary. The best thing now might be for her to go to bed so that you and I can discuss how best to minimise the damage. Though why anyone should bother to help such stupid, ill-conditioned brat is entirely beyond me.'

It was the last straw. Nell fled to her chamber.

'Well done,' said Adeline. 'You seem to have made an impression at last. Come in and let me pour you a glass of wine.'

'Brandy would be better.'

'Then brandy it shall be.' She moved to the side-board and said calmly, 'Do you love her?'

'Unfortunately – yes. But that is strictly confidential.'

'Naturally.' She handed him the glass. 'And you'll marry her?'

'Perhaps. If she ever grows up.' He frowned into the amber liquid. 'It was Jasper Brierley, of course. I hit him.'

'That must have been enjoyable.'

'It was.' He looked up unsmilingly. 'It should also help remind Lord Ansford to keep his mouth shut – though, of course, I can't guarantee it.' A pause, and then, 'The thing is, Adeline – with your permission, I'd like to try keeping this from Rock.'

Her heart sank. More secrets. Everything in her recoiled from the thought and she said protestingly, 'We can't. It wouldn't be right. She's his *sister*. And, anyway, he'd find out.'

'Not necessarily – and it's a risk I'd like to take. If the worst happens, I'll take the blame and you can say you knew nothing about it.'

'Why *why*, Harry?'

'Because if he's told, I suspect he'll send her to Lucilla. And that would do more harm than good.' Setting down his glass, he reached out to clasp her hand. 'I know it's a lot to ask but – if not for Nell's sake – do you think you could please do it for mine?'

She looked back at him, a prey to conflicting emotions. Finally she said reluctantly, 'I can't pretend to like it ... but I suppose you may have a point. Tracy isn't ... he isn't in the best of moods right now and Nell's folly isn't likely to improve that.'

He gave a long, slow sigh of relief.

'Thank you. And if there's ever anything I can do for you, don't hesitate to ask,' he said, taking her hands. 'Those aren't just empty words, my dear. I mean it. If you ever want an adopted brother, I'm your man.' And, leaning towards her, he kissed her cheek.

The door opened and Rockliffe came in.

For a moment, there was utter silence. Then, 'Dear me,' drawled his Grace. 'I had no notion that you were visiting us this evening, Harry. Never say that I am interrupting something?'

'No.' Harry released Adeline's hands and looked at the Duke with no hint of discomposure. 'And you know better than to suppose it. I brought Adeline back from Lady Crewe's and was just bidding her goodnight.'

'I had thought,' remarked Rockliffe, his gaze dwelling reflectively on his wife, 'that you and Nell were sharing Isabel Vernon's carriage this evening. My lamentable memory, no doubt.'

'Not at all.' Adeline could feel her colour rising but managed to keep her voice level. 'Nell had a – she'd twisted her ankle so she couldn't go ... and then the ball was so very dull that I decided to leave early.'

'And Harry was most fortuitously on hand to escort you.'

'Yes.'

'I see.' The dark eyes took in Adeline's blush and the half-full glass of brandy before smiling at his lordship with deceptive blandness. 'It seems that I am in your debt.'

'By no means. The boot's on the other foot, in fact,' replied Harry, trying hard to banish his sudden sense of unease. 'I seem to recall losing some three hundred guineas to you at basset earlier this evening.'

'Ah yes. So you did.' Rockliffe continued to smile but the glint in his eyes was far from reassuring. 'One can't have everything, after all. And lucky at cards, unlucky in love - isn't that what they say? So no doubt the reverse also holds true.'

EIGHTEEN

In all his thirty-six years, the Duke of Rockliffe had never before had reason to suppose himself a fool – but he was beginning to do so now. Common sense told him that there was nothing save friendship between Adeline and Harry; and yet finding them together had filled him with a distressingly primitive desire to throw Harry bodily from the house and then put an end, once and for all, to the four-month-old charade between himself and Adeline. The first of these impulses faded fast enough; the second didn't … and, during the course of the white night that followed, seemed only to grow stronger. And that wasn't merely worrying – it was a problem.

He had never been a possessive lover nor known what it was to be jealous and each of his *affaires* had been conducted with the lightest of touches. But that was gone now – destroyed by the bitter-sweet smile of a woman who might never care for him the way he cared for her and to whom he had promised more patience.

Patience? When he had just discovered himself prey to the same lack of control he'd always deplored in others? Rockliffe stared up into the darkness and swore gently. There was only one way that offered any guarantee and it was the very last thing he wanted. Damn.

Damn, damn, damn.

He debated the matter carefully before finally reaching a decision that, in the end, was mostly based on the possibility that, this time, she might just miss him.

'I am afraid,' he announced calmly over breakfast, 'that I have to go to Paris.'

They were alone – Nell, not surprisingly, having failed to put in an appearance. Neither did Rockliffe miss her. All his attention was given to the upsurge of hope produced by the stricken look in Adeline's eyes.

'Paris?' she echoed faintly. 'Why Paris?'

'A trifling matter of business concerning a property I have there,' he replied smoothly. 'I should not be away much more than a week. Two, at most.'

Exactly as he had intended, Adeline recognised the lie and was scalded by it. She forgot her first sickening jolt of fear that this sudden decision of his had some connection with her mother and knew only that a black band of pain was settling round her heart. She swallowed and, assuming a mask of cool indifference, said carelessly, 'I see. And will you be leaving today?'

'It seems likely – unless, that is, you have some objection.' *Ask me not to go. Be as oblique as you like ... but ask me not to go.* 'Have you?'

'None at all. How should I?' *What would be the point? You're only going in order to get away from me - and I can hardly blame you for that.* 'I shall be perfectly all right. So there is no need to delay – or, equally, to return any sooner than you wish.'

The dark eyes regarded her with an expression that defied interpretation and it was a long time before he spoke. He wondered if she had any idea how many ways she had of hurting him. Finally, in a voice as soft as silk, he said, 'Dear Adeline ... always so beautifully direct. But now that you have pointed out that my presence is entirely dispensable, I need have no qualms. You offer me *carte blanche*; and I, beloved, shall be delighted to accept it.'

And with the slightest and most elegant of bows, he was gone.

*

It was early afternoon before Nell came cautiously downstairs and, when she did, she was still too woebegone to notice Adeline's strained pallor.

'Wh-where's Rock?' she asked nervously.

'Gone to Paris,' came the flat reply. 'And if you're wondering whether or not he knows, the answer is that he doesn't. A fact for which you have Harry to thank.'

Nell sank weakly into the nearest chair and started to cry again.

Adeline stared at her for a moment and then said irritably, 'Oh – for God's sake, stop it! What good does it do? You've risked your reputation, involved me in a web of deceit and utterly infuriated Harry –

and for what? A stupid, childish prank of the kind you ought to have out-grown years ago.'

'I know,' sobbed Nell. 'I know and I'm so s-sorry. It was a horrid evening anyway and I d-don't know why I agreed to go in the first p-place. Rock was right about everything.'

'He usually is. You should know that by now. But it's no use repining. The best you can hope for is that it doesn't become common knowledge ... and for that, once again, you'll have to rely on Harry.' Adeline paused and took a long look at her young sister-in-law. 'You don't deserve Harry, you know. He's probably the best friend you'll ever have – and a better one than you seem to realise.'

This made Nell dissolve afresh.

'He – he'll never forgive me. I know he won't. I d-didn't know could *be* so angry.'

'No? Well it's always seemed to me that there's a lot you've never noticed about him,' responded Adeline, coming wearily to her feet. 'And I still don't know what on earth you saw in Jasper Brierley.'

Nell shuddered and then brightened a little.

'Harry knocked him down,' she said wonderingly. 'That was rather splendid of him, wasn't it?'

'Yes. And it will be even more splendid if he doesn't end up fighting a duel as a result of it.'

'Oh!' For once in her life, Nell was struck by reality rather than romance. The dark eyes became perfectly stark and she said oddly, 'I didn't think of that.'

'No.' Adeline gazed astringently back at her. 'That's your trouble, Nell. You never think at all.'

*

The whispers started three days later and Harry, with his ear firmly to the ground, was the first one to hear them.

'It's not Ansford's doing,' he said grimly to Adeline. 'He was so frightened I'd blame it on him that he was on my doorstep at virtually the crack of dawn to swear his innocence. He says – and I believe him – that we have Carlotta Felucci to thank.'

'Who?' she asked blankly.

'Carlotta Felucci,' He met her eyes squarely but with faint discomfort. 'She's a singer. She was also, once upon a time, Rock's mistress.'

'Oh.' Behind her stiff taffeta bodice, Adeline's insides lurched unpleasantly and she had to work quite hard at not letting it show in her face. Of course he'd had mistresses – probably quite a number of them. What had she expected? How else had he learned how to make a woman want him with no more than a look or make her bones melt with a single kiss? She said colourlessly, 'That would explain it, I suppose. But what do we do now? Brazen it out?'

'Yes. There's not much else we can do. And if we do it well enough and are really lucky,' said his lordship sourly, 'we may even get away with it. Enough, at any rate, for the gossip to die down before Rock gets back from Paris.' He paused, frowning a little. 'What's he gone there for, anyway? Not that I'm not glad of it – because I am. But why Paris?'

'Why not?' came the would-be flippant reply.

Harry's frown deepened and the blue eyes expressed concern.

'Have you two quarrelled?'

'Something like that.'

'Want to tell me about it?'

'Yes. But I don't think I will, if you don't mind.' She summoned a bleak smile. 'The faults are all mine, Harry. And even if they weren't I don't talk about my husband to anyone. Not even you.'

*

The business of brazening out Nell's indiscretion was made a little easier by the fact that Sir Jasper Brierley had taken to the heather in Bermondsey and was therefore not available for comment. But the whispers and sideways glances were still unpleasant enough to teach Nell the full extent of her folly and, after attending a ball where she spent quite half the evening sitting conspicuously at Adeline's side, she was ready to die of mortification.

As was to be expected, the main task of denial fell to Harry and he handled it with an adroit blend of incredulity and amusement that served to convince the gentlemen at least. Then - unasked and unasking - Isabel Vernon, Serena Delahaye and Dolly Cavendish also set about squashing the rumours ... and gradually the scandal began to lose its bite and subside.

Worn out with having to hold her head high and simulate ignorance, Nell waited humbly for Harry to thaw – and, in doing so, made a startling discovery. It was, quite simply, that no one else's opinion mattered a jot and she would not care that the entire world refused to speak to her if only Harry would smile. But he didn't smile ... or not at her. Instead, he preserved a chilly front, danced with her only out of duty and then went away to flirt outrageously with Diana Franklin.

Diana, whose season had somehow failed to live up to expectation, was enjoying every moment of Nell's discomfiture. It almost made up for the shock of learning that plain, freckled Lizzie had not only reached the altar ahead of her but would henceforth take precedence over her in her own home. Horrid fears had begun to assail Diana of late; fears of returning unbetrothed to Oxfordshire. It didn't seem possible that it should be so ... but she had so far received not one offer of marriage and, among her *côterie* of admirers, the best prospect was now Lord Harry Caversham – a bitter blow when she had hoped, at the very least, for an Earl. She could not understand what she was doing wrong. She was beautiful, everyone said so – and she knew exactly how to drive a man to distraction. So how was it that the flirtatious banter and odd snatched kiss never led to a proposal?

The result of all this – not to mention Lady Franklin's increasing impatience – was that she tried extra hard to captivate Lord Harry whilst joining gleefully in the gossip about Nell. She introduced the topic at every opportunity, added several small gems to the general speculation and was finally unable to prevent herself crowing. It was her misfortune that she did it within earshot of Adeline and Harry.

'They're doing their best to hush it up, of course – but I don't think many people are fooled. Poor Nell's been noticeably lacking in partners recently, hasn't she? One could almost feel sorry for her – except that, being the sister of a Duke, she plainly thinks she can get away with anything.'

Her Grace the Duchess of Rockliffe was wrenched temporarily free of her own private hell and, eyes darkening, prepared to descend on her cousin.

'No.' Harry's hand closed lightly on her elbow. 'No. Leave it to me, will you?'

Adeline looked at him and was surprised by the concentrated implacability of his expression. 'Why?'

'Because I'm already dealing with her in my own way. All you need to do is sit back and watch,' he said. And strolled away to bow extravagantly over Diana's hand before leading her into the dance.

Slowly, an incredible suspicion took shape in Adeline's mind. It rather looked as though Harry Caversham – who everyone agreed had the sunniest and most open of natures – was deliberately setting out to raise false hopes in Mistress Di's egotistical breast for the twin purposes of teaching her a well-deserved lesson whilst simultaneously making Nell jealous.

'*Simple, yet masterly*,' thought Adeline appreciatively. '*I hope it works*.'

'I hear you are once more a grass widow, my dear,' said a feline voice beside her. 'You must have been careless indeed if Rockliffe has tired of you so soon.'

Adeline froze and felt the all-too-familiar churning start again in her stomach. Finally, she said distantly, 'You're back. What a shame. I was rather hoping you'd break your neck whilst riding *ventre à terre* after Andrew and Lizzie. How are they, by the way? Suitably sundered?'

'Hardly. It was much too late for that.'

'Good.' If only she could keep him talking, perhaps he wouldn't say anything else to terrify her. 'Lizzie has character and Andrew does well for himself. Left alone, I imagine she might be the making of him.'

'Very possibly.' Richard Horton spread his chicken-skin fan and plied it with apparent languor. His mood, however, was decidedly grim – having recently come to the conclusion that his little ways at the card table were gradually becoming common knowledge. He had no hesitation in blaming Rockliffe for this and even less in deciding that Rockliffe's wife should be the one to pay for it. 'I did not, however, join you to discuss Andrew ... but to inform you that I stand in somewhat urgent need of five hundred guineas.'

She stared at him for a moment and then managed a seemingly careless shrug. 'Why tell me?'

'Because you are going to provide them for me.'

'You think so?'

'I know so.' He smiled at her over the fan but his eyes were hard. 'Otherwise I am afraid ... I am very much afraid that I shall have to seek an interview with your husband. He wouldn't, I feel sure, wish the world to know what a sorry *mésalliance* he has made. And, on top of this scandal involving his sister and Jasper Brierley, it really would be altogether too much – don't you agree?'

*

Two days later she paid him and, although she knew that she was sinking deeper and deeper into the quagmire, she also knew that she had no choice. Aside from the business of her mother, Richard was now also threatening to tell Tracy about Nell's indiscretion. And, if that happened, Harry and Nell would be in as much as trouble as she herself was.

This time she'd been forced to get the money from his Grace's secretary and, though Matthew hadn't demurred, his surprise had been so obvious that she'd found herself stammering an excuse about unfortunate losses at cards and thinking that, not for anything, could she bring herself to do this again. And that was when she had the idea.

The following evening saw her in the select establishment of one Maria Denby where gambling of all kinds was the order of the day. It was all quite respectable – even fashionable – and she met several people that she knew. What she hadn't anticipated and could have done without was to see Jack Ingram walk in just as she sat down to play basset.

His brows lifted a little at the sight of her but he greeted her pleasantly enough and then took a seat at the same table. Adeline could have screamed with vexation. She had done reasonably well at *ecarté* and was hoping to multiply her winnings – but Jack's presence seemed to destroy both her concentration and whatever luck she'd had.

At the end of an hour she was back where she had started and, at the end of two, fifty guineas worse off. The risk of going on was too great. Smiling as though it didn't signify a scrap, she signed a vowel and rose from the table. Jack followed her.

'Come on,' he said comfortably. 'I'll take you home. And then, if you like, you can tell me all about it.'

'All about what?' asked Adeline coolly when they were settled in the carriage. 'There's no harm, surely, in my taking the fancy to play a hand of cards?'

'None – if that were solely the case. The harm comes when you do it because you need to win.'

Her breath leaked slowly into her blue satin bodice.

'Good heavens! What makes you suppose that?'

The grey eyes took on a rueful gleam but his smile was kind. 'I'm no gamester, Adeline. Rock would probably tell you that I haven't the right instinct for it. But I'm not exactly green either ... and I know the difference between playing for pleasure and playing for profit.' He paused and then said delicately, 'I don't wish to pry ... but I presume you've some debt or expenditure which you feel Rock wouldn't approve of?'

'And if I have?' she asked impassively.

'I'd advise you to tell him, my dear. He isn't easily shocked, you know – and not in the least prone to condemn.'

A small, wry smile touched her mouth.

'Do you think I don't know that?'

'Then why not try trusting him? To speak plainly, it's what he would want. And I doubt there's much that he couldn't – or wouldn't – put right for you.'

To her utter horror, Adeline felt tears stinging her eyes. She said baldly, 'Leave it, Jack. I don't need to hear it – and it's no help, believe me.'

There was a long silence. Then, 'It's as bad as that?'

'Worse,' came the bitter reply. 'But I've no intention of telling you about it. Nor – knowing I've not even confided in Tracy – would you expect me to. Would you?'

'No.' Concern deepened as he took in the hollows beneath the exquisite cheekbones and the strain in her eyes. 'No. But if whatever it is gets beyond you ... if you ever need help ... I hope you'll know where to come.'

'I will. Thank you.' Her throat constricted again and, resolutely banishing the subject, she said, 'I've been meaning to congratulate you on what you've achieved with my cousin, Althea. You have the distinction of being the first gentleman ever to value her for herself and not be taken in by Diana's glitter instead. It's done her so much good – and does you much credit.'

The hint of colour that stained Mr Ingram's cheek was mercifully lost in the darkness.

'Mistress Diana,' he remarked obliquely but with a certain grimness, 'is acquiring a somewhat tarnished reputation. It would be a pity if Thea – who is worth a hundred of her sister – should be tarred with the same brush.'

'Quite. But I don't think she will be. There are surprisingly few people who still can't tell them apart ... and Thea appears to be well-liked.' She eyed him reflectively for a moment and then said lightly, 'No. I think the only problem Thea will have to face is a very understandable reluctance on the part of any suitors she may have to relate themselves to her family. But I'm sure a man who loved her wouldn't let that stand in his way ... aren't you?'

It was a neat little trap but not quite neat enough and it took Jack no more than a few seconds to come up with the answer.

'Well, you should know,' he grinned. 'It didn't deter Rock, after all. And that ought to be a shining enough example for anyone.'

*

At the end of a fortnight, there was still no sign of Rockliffe and Adeline existed in a limbo of depressing imaginings concerned with what – or who – could be detaining him. Aside from that, life went on pretty much as usual. Richard Horton, having pocketed his five hundred guineas, left her more or less alone; Nell, her indiscretion eclipsed when Lord Maybury married his cook, was accepted back into the fold but remained unduly quiet and submissive; and Harry continued to flirt with

Diana. Jack Ingram, meanwhile, went on cultivating Althea but still found time – so it seemed to Adeline – to keep a watchful eye on herself.

Then she attended Lady Marchant's *soirée* and was back on a knife-edge again. Across the room, expensively if unbecomingly clad in pink silk with wreaths of roses, Cecily Garfield was talking hard and fast to Cassie Delahaye.

'Oh God,' sighed Adeline wearily. 'That's all I need.'

Nell followed her gaze and grimaced.

'Don't worry. She won't say anything. And even if she does, Cassie wouldn't believe it. You know how she admires you.'

'Cassie,' came the arid response, 'is the least of my worries. If Cecily decides to tell the world what she's convinced happened at that thrice-damned ball – or that, prior to it, I was no more than a sort of upper servant – there's nothing we can to do stop her. And if *she* starts to talk, Diana will join in. She won't be able to resist.'

A shadow crossed Nell's face but she looked searching around the room and said, 'I don't think the Franklins are here – I don't see any of them. If they're not, all we have to do for now is silence Cecily.'

Adeline's brows rose sardonically. '*All?*'

'Yes.' Nell's grin held a glimmer of her old mischief. 'I can see Lewis. I should have thought that, between us, we ought to be able to charm him into telling his sister to hold her tongue – shouldn't you?'

It was not, as it happened, very difficult for Mr Garfield had some very natural misgivings about facing a lady to whom he'd once made a dishonourable proposal and who had since become a duchess. It was a relief, therefore, to have Adeline offer her hand with complete cordiality and behave as though she was genuinely pleased to renew his acquaintance. Perhaps he had been worrying unnecessarily and she really *had* misunderstood him, after all. Looking at her now, his only regret was that he hadn't had the same foresight as Rockliffe ... for there was no doubt that she had more style and presence than any other woman in the room.

He found himself asking both of them to dance. Nell dimpled roguishly and Adeline gave him a breathtakingly dazzling smile. They both accepted. Then, with such delicate artistry that he scarcely even noticed it, they came to the point. Whilst in Oxfordshire, dear Cecily had been led into certain misconceptions. It was by no means her fault but it would be better for all concerned if she could be ... encouraged to recognise her error.

'Of course,' agreed Mr Garfield, fathoms deep in dark-fringed pools of aquamarine. 'I always thought it a prodigious unlikely story and will be happy to drop a word in Cecy's ear. Your Grace need not give the matter another thought.'

'I knew,' said Adeline charmingly, 'that I might rely on you. Did I not say, Nell, that one might place absolute faith in Mr Garfield's powers of perception?'

'Those,' vowed Nell gravely, 'were your very words.'

Mr Garfield puffed out his chest.

'Your Grace is too kind. I am overwhelmed.'

Her Grace finished binding her spell.

'I shall be holding a reception when Rockliffe returns from Paris – just a small, intimate affair, you understand – and shall send you a card. In the meantime, I hope you will call at Wynstanton House ... and bring dear Cecily, of course.'

And that, she thought cynically, ought to be a big enough carrot to stop dear Cecily's mouth permanently.

It was, however, belated. Even as she spoke, Cecily was reiterating her tale to Mistress Delahaye in the hope, this time, of convincing her.

'It's true,' she finished stridently. 'Rockliffe *had* to marry her. He didn't have any choice. Her gown was torn and he was kissing her. I saw it myself.'

'I still don't believe it,' said Cassie stoutly. 'It sounds to me like utter nonsense.'

'Of course it's nonsense,' said a light, musical voice behind her. 'And I'm delighted that you recognise the fact.'

With a gasp of pleased surprise, Cassie whirled round to meet a remote violet gaze set beneath slender brows, arched like bird's wings.

'It's Cassandra, isn't it?' continued the lady smoothly. 'And ... your friend?'

'Cecily, my lady,' replied Cassie thankfully. 'Cecily Garfield.'

The beautiful eyes moved to where Cecily was standing with her mouth open, staring.

'Well, Mistress Garfield ... allow me to point out that if you are wise you will not repeat this foolishness about Rockliffe and his duchess. No one will believe you, you see – and therefore you will only make yourself ridiculous.'

'I know what I saw,' said Cecily doggedly. 'And if you don't believe me, you can ask Mr Richard Horton.'

'My dear, I don't need to ask anyone. I know his Grace – and that is more than enough.'

'But I - '

'Cecy!' Lewis, arriving with Adeline on his arm, felt his muscles go into spasm at the thought that his sister might already have ruined everything – and apparently done so in front of the Marchioness of Amberley. 'Come with me. I've something important to say to you.'

'Why?' Cecily's eyes travelled unrecognisingly over Adeline and then back again. 'I was just - '

'Then don't!' Her brother was too harassed to be polite. 'Just do as I ask. Now!' And he hauled her away.

'Nasty, lying creature!' muttered Cassie crossly. 'Honestly, Adeline – you won't believe what she said about you. It makes my blood boil just to think of it.'

'Thank you, Cassie. You're a comfort,' smiled Adeline. And then, looking at the silent figure in amethyst taffeta, 'But won't you present me?'

'Oh!' Cassie looked faintly stunned. 'But don't you know each other?'

'No.' It was the lady who spoke and, though her voice did not vary at all, the pansy eyes held an odd gleam. 'No, we don't. But I should like, if you don't mind, to introduce myself.'

Cassie blinked and then laughed.

'By all means! I ought to be listening to March's verses, anyway.' And she whisked herself off.

Adeline was left staring at the most beautiful woman she had ever seen and who, at length, said simply, 'I know who you are, of course. Truth to tell, I'd probably not have come to London at all just at present except that it seemed so odd not knowing Rock's wife that I was determined to meet you at last.' She paused and gave a smile of delicious sweetness. 'I'm the Marchioness of Amberley, you know. But I'm rather hoping you'll see fit to call me Rosalind.'

*

Thinking about it afterwards, it seemed to Adeline that nothing anyone had said had in any way prepared her for Rosalind Ballantyne. True, the unexpected gift of the gold pin for her wedding had betokened warmth and Nell had spoken of her with considerable affection ... then, eventually, they had told her about the blindness. But that was all. Nothing to warn her of that shining beauty – or the grace and charm and wit that went with it; or even the sheer, unadulterated friendliness.

It was, of course, impossible not to like her – and equally impossible not to feel suddenly and hopelessly outclassed. It was also tempting to encourage Nell to talk ... for that way she could discover if Tracy had ever aspired to Rosalind's hand himself. But that was stupid; stupid and dangerous. What *ought* to concern her was why he was so long in coming home – and it did. The thought could not help but occur that, following their last conversation, he might have decided to seek consolation elsewhere ... and even, by now, have found a replacement for Carlotta Felucci. It was a possibility that began to haunt her nights; for if he *had* done so, she had only herself to blame.

NINETEEN

As it happened, Adeline need not have worried. Rockliffe had neither the time nor the inclination to set up a mistress and would probably have started for home after ten days, had he not – by the merest chance - stumbled upon the very information that Mr Osborne had been so diligently and unsuccessfully seeking.

Mr Osborne, as it turned out when the Duke finally ran him to earth, had drawn a series of blanks and was rapidly losing heart. He had found three gentlemen to whom the name du Plessis was vaguely familiar but no one who appeared to actually *know* the man ... and the Maréchal Rebec, du Plessis' one-time commander, was currently serving in the Americas.

This piece of information, combined with the lamentable stews at the Coq D'Or, brought on a severe attack of colic followed by a fresh spurt of effort. France, in Mr Osborne's book, was quite bad enough; nothing ... not even his noble employer ... could induce him to sail half-way round the world to a land peopled by savages and at war with his own countrymen.

To his relief, however, the Duke showed no sign of suggesting this but merely sent him to find out if Joanna Kendrick – or possibly Joanna du Plessis – was known at the Embassy. Mr Osborne departed with alacrity only to return with lagging feet and nothing to report. His Grace sighed and desired Mr Osborne to widen his acquaintance with the French army. Mr Osborne also sighed – and then consoled himself with the thought that, tedious as this would undoubtedly be, the choice between America and dismissal was worse.

Rockliffe, meanwhile, visited a few old friends and accepted more invitations than he could possibly hope to attend whilst attempting not to miss his wife. He also began making the occasional reference to the business that had brought him to Paris – namely, his hope of tracing and acquiring the rare and particularly fine ivory snuff-box recently sold in London to one Michel du Plessis. Fortunately, his collector's passion was widely enough known for this to cause nothing more than mild amusement; and, if there should be anyone in a position to question it ... well, it followed that that person must also be in a position to lead him to du Plessis.

He was not surprised, however, when the name fell repeatedly on stony ground for it had always been unlikely that Joanna had eloped with a gentleman from the upper *échelon* of French society. After more than a week of casting his bread uselessly upon the water, Rockliffe came to the depressing conclusion that – unless he found out something in the next day or two – he might as well go home and leave the matter to Mr Osborne. And he would undoubtedly have done so had not the Vicomte de Charentin persuaded him to share his box at the Comédie Française ... and one thing had, unexpectedly, led to another.

'It's a revival of Molière's *La Malade Imaginaire*,' said the Vicomte, as though expecting premature applause. 'You shouldn't miss it.'

Rockliffe raised his brows and remarked that, since *The Hypochondriac* had been written some hundred years ago and he had already seen it twice, he felt quite able to do so.

'But *L'Inconnu* will be playing! He always takes the lead when the company does Molière – and the house is invariably packed. Share my box this afternoon and you will see.'

'*L'Inconnu*. Really?'

'Really!' The Vicomte stopped and then, sighing, 'You haven't heard of him, have you?'

'No. But since he styles himself The Unknown, that's hardly surprising, is it?'

'In Paris, he is famous – and also a mystery. It's said that when he leaves the stage, he vanishes. If he were not such a remarkable actor, one would laugh at such an obvious ploy ... but since he *is*, one goes to watch him.'

And so it was that Rockliffe found himself in an off-stage box in the Comédie Française's temporary home in the Tuileries. As Charentin had said, the house was indeed full to over-flowing. It was also exceedingly noisy – a fact which his Grace didn't expect to change a great deal when the play started. He was wrong. As soon as the curtain opened on

Argan sitting at a table adding up his apothecary's bills, the audience fell utterly silent.

'Three and two make five, and five makes ten and ten makes twenty. Item; on the twenty-fourth, a little emollient clyster to mollify, moisten and refresh his worship's bowels – thirty sous. Thirty sous for a clyster? In your other bills you charged but twenty; and twenty sous, in the language of an apothecary, is only ten sous – so there they are. Ten sous.'

The first laugh came, one of many. Argan polished his pince-nez, fussed busily with his papers and, timing it to perfection, resumed.

Rockliffe was surprised. The fellow was good. More than that – he was different from the common run of his profession because he was utterly believable. He actually *was* an old man mumbling over his counters and coins and bills ... and he was holding the house spellbound.

'So then. In this month I have taken one, two, three ......six, seven, eight purges and one, two, three ... ten, eleven, twelve clysters; and last month there were twelve purges and twenty clysters.' He paused, shaking his head. '*I don't wonder that I am not so well this month as last.*'

During the first interval, Rockliffe asked if The Unknown had a name and was told that, if he did, no one knew it. During the second, he reflected that if there were actors of this calibre on the English stage, he might attend the play more often.

And then, in the third act, something odd happened. Whether it was caused by a certain turn of the head or a particular inflection in the fellow's voice, Rockliffe couldn't be sure ... but he suddenly had the peculiar feeling that *L'Inconnu* wasn't unknown at all; and, consequently found himself caught less in the performance than in mentally eradicating Argan's old-fashioned wig, false eyebrows and pince-nez. It wasn't easy. In fact, it was downright impossible. It was also probably pointless – since it was highly unlikely that an actor performing at the Comédie Française could, in reality, be a man who'd fled England some eight years ago in the wake of a particularly nasty scandal. Rockliffe was just about to dismiss the notion when, unexpectedly, *L'Inconnu's* eyes met his; and, just for a fleeting second – and only because he was watching so closely – his Grace saw recognition in them.

'Dear me,' he thought wryly. 'How very interesting.'

When the performance concluded in a storm of applause, Rockliffe rose and informed the Vicomte that he would like to meet *L'Inconnu*. Laughing, the Vicomte replied that so would half of Paris but no one had managed it yet.

'But go ahead and try, my friend. You won't find him – that I guarantee. My advice would be to try the Maison Belcourt – some of the players go there and you might find someone who'll talk to you. Though I personally doubt it.'

The Maison Belcourt, being both a gaming-house and a place where the better class of prostitutes hawked their wares, was not a place Rockliffe would normally have visited but on this occasion he made an exception. He did not, as it turned out, discover anything about *L'Inconnu*. On the other hand, if he hadn't gone there, he would probably never have run into the Vidame d'Aurillac who - newly released from the Bastille - strolled in just as the Duke was thinking of leaving.

The Vidame had been clapped up for duelling – which was not unusual and released in less than a month – which was. And he and Rockliffe were old friends.

It was a pleasing encounter and, with so much to be told on both sides, they had broached the third bottle – mostly thanks to the Vidame – before his Grace found himself once more recounting the excuse of the snuff-box – more, this time, for the sake of continuity than in the hope of striking a chord.

Then it happened. The Vidame began to laugh gently and said, 'Really, my friend, you are so very *English* are you not? You leave your ravishing bride to search for a snuff-box – no, no! Do not interrupt. I am very sure you wouldn't have married her if she was not entirely exquisite. And this, doubtless, is why you haven't brought her with you.'

'You think I feared to have her fall victim to your fatal charm, Raoul?' enquired Rockliffe lazily.

'Naturally! But I forgive you. It is very understandable. I even forgive you for not visiting me in my miserable cell – for you are about to be extremely sorry that you didn't.'

'Am I?'

'But yes!' D'Aurillac grinned wickedly. 'For if you had, you might even now be cradling in your hand the ... what was it? ... ah yes. The rare antique ivory box you say you came here to find.'

Heavy lids veiled the dark eyes and there was a long silence. Then his Grace said softly, 'Raoul ... are you telling me you know where to find Michel du Plessis?'

'How could I not? He is my tenant. But I have to say, my friend, that I can't imagine him leaving France – let alone travelling to London and buying snuff-boxes of any age or rarity.'

'Ah.' Rockliffe stared meditatively into his glass. 'But life is full of surprises, is it not?'

'And mysteries,' nodded the Vidame with cheerful cynicism. 'But tonight, for you, I will break the habit of a lifetime and not ask awkward questions – much though I would like to.' He paused. And then, 'Very well. You will find Michel du Plessis at a small farm just outside Nevers – and I hope your business with him prospers. All I ask in return is that, next time you come to Paris, you will bring your lovely duchess.'

*

Early next morning, Rockliffe set off alone on horseback along the valley of the Loire and, two days later, reached the small town of Nevers where he obtained directions to du Plessis' farm. He could not help wondering what – or, more particularly, who – he would find there. It had not seemed politic to ask the Vidame about du Plessis' wife. Last night Raoul had been disposed towards discretion; today ... who knew?

The farmhouse was a pretty place, well-kept and prosperous-looking. But it was the tiny garden – still, despite the lateness of the season, a riot of colour – that took Rockliffe's eye for it struck him as somehow untypical. Then the door opened ... and all thought was temporarily suspended.

There was no doubting who she was. The line of brow and cheek and jaw – the wide mouth and long, slender neck – even the grace of her step, were all heart-stoppingly familiar. Caught unprepared, the Duke remained where he was and simply stared. Then, mercifully, she came closer and the differences became visible; the dark brown hair was lightly frosted with silver ... and her eyes, not aquamarine but blue, were lucent with a serenity Adeline had never possessed.

She reached the end of the path and looked up at him, the narrow brows expressing faint surprise.

'Can I help you, *monsieur*? You are looking for my husband, perhaps?'

The voice was different too, thank God. Rockliffe pulled himself together, smiled and came collectedly from the saddle.

'No, *madame*. I think ... indeed, I am very sure ... that it is you I came to see.'

'I?' She looked doubtfully at the elegance of his person. 'But I don't think - '

'No. We have never met. And my name – which is Wynstanton – will probably mean nothing to you.' He paused briefly and switched from French to English. 'I am the Duke of Rockliffe, *madame*. And though I have strong reasons for coming here to find you, I do not think there is anything in them that need distress you.'

Some of the colour left her face and she laid one hand on the gate, as if for support. Then, still in French, she said stiffly, 'I cannot imagine what an English Duke might want with – with the wife of a French farmer.'

'Can you not?'

She shook her head emphatically. 'No.'

His Grace hesitated and then said gently, 'There really *is* no cause for alarm ... Joanna.'

'Oh God.' Her hand closed hard on the gate and this time she answered him in English. 'You know who I am. How? Why are you here?'

'Primarily, I suppose, to make your acquaintance.'

'I don't understand why you should - ' She stopped and drew a long, bracing breath. 'Very well. You'd better come inside and tell me what it is you want.'

The parlour into which she led him was as neat as a pin and comfortable. Rockliffe took the seat she indicated and, coming directly to the point, said simply, 'You left a daughter behind you in England. She is now my wife.'

Joanna sank abruptly down on a cushioned settle.

'*Adeline?*' she said weakly. 'You've married my Adeline?'

'Just so.'

She stared at the tall, suave and exceptionally good-looking man who claimed to be her son-in-law and said helplessly, 'But you ... you said you were a Duke.'

'And so I am.' A tiny gleam disturbed the gravity of his expression. 'And 'your Adeline' is now my duchess. You would be proud, I think, to see how well it suits her.'

'I'm sorry. I can't ... it's difficult to take in.' Her hands twisted restlessly in her lap and at length she said, 'They told her I was dead.'

'Yes.'

'They told her I was dead ... and, even when I knew, I let it go on. It seemed better that way. I couldn't take her from Tom, you see – and it wasn't right to leave her handicapped for life by my disgrace.' She paused and looked him full in the face, her expression anguished. 'It was never that I didn't want her – but how can she ever understand that? Now that she's discovered the truth, she must hate me.'

'As yet, *madame*, she knows nothing.'

Her eyes widened. 'Then how did you find out?'

'Let us say that – thanks to a series of small coincidences – I guessed.' He smiled at her. 'It is a facility that I have. And, having guessed, Sir Roland was ... persuaded ... to confide in me.'

'But you – you haven't told Adeline?'

'No. It seemed preferable to wait until I could offer a complete story ... and there is still, I regret to say, just one very delicate question I must ask you.'

'Of course.' Her hands were at rest now but her tone was wry. 'You want to know if Adeline is Tom Kendrick's child, do you not? But before I answer it, *I* want to know if it matters.'

'To me – not in the slightest; to Adeline – quite a lot, I should imagine. And she will ask, you see.'

Her shoulders relaxed and she seemed to sigh.

'Forgive me asking … but do you love her?'

'Yes. Very much.'

'And she? Does she love you?'

'I don't know,' Rockliffe replied truthfully. 'Obviously, I'd like to think so but – after almost five months of marriage – I still can't be sure.'

The blue eyes dwelled on him thoughtfully and it was a long time before she spoke. Then, with a smile of unexpected warmth, she said, 'Adeline is as legitimate as you are, your Grace. Had she not been Tom's child, I could never have left her.'

'Thank you. I had suspected as much.'

'I'm glad to hear it.' She came smoothly to her feet. 'I think it's high time I fetched some wine. And then, as you wish, you may tell me all about it.'

His desire to do exactly that surprised him and he gave way to it without hesitation. Joanna cried a little when he described Adeline's life in the Franklin household; she shook her head over his account of the night of the ball when he'd proposed; and she listened in thoughtful silence when he spoke – somewhat less smoothly – of the difficulties within his marriage.

At the end of it all, she said angrily, 'They have damaged her, haven't they – Miriam and Richard and the rest of them?'

'I think so. Yes.'

'You say she's reserved and distant – that, at times, she retreats to a place where even you can't reach her. And that's why. I could *kill* Miriam.'

'I'm not too fond of her myself,' agreed Rockliffe.

'She's not your sister.'

'No. But I have one almost equally unlikeable.'

A tiny laugh escaped her at that. She said, 'Aside from the obvious, I'm beginning to feel that Adeline is very fortunate.'

'I am delighted that you think so.' His smile, this time, was a trifle crooked. 'I shall be even more delighted when I can be sure Adeline thinks so, too.'

Joanna thought for a moment and then said slowly, 'Forgive my asking ... but have you actually told her that you love her?'

'Not in so many words, no.'

'Then perhaps you should. I imagine they are words she has not heard for a very long time – if ever.'

'That thought had occurred to me.'

'Then why haven't you remedied it?'

'Because I couldn't be certain she was ready to hear it.' Rockliffe paused and then, shrugging slightly, added, 'And because I've never said those words to any woman before. Nor even wanted to.'

Joanna reflected that, if the little she had seen of him was any true indication, it was difficult to understand how her daughter – or indeed, any woman – could have lived with this man for five months and not be totally *bouleversé*. But, as she rose to refill his glass, she said merely, 'This hasn't been easy for you, has it?'

'Not particularly. But I daresay it's done me no harm to become a little less sure of myself. And my feelings aren't the issue here.'

'Aren't they?'

'No. My chief concern at the moment is that something happened a few weeks ago to undo everything I thought I'd achieved. And she won't tell me what it is.'

There was a long silence and then Joanna said, 'Is my brother Richard in London?'

'Yes. Why?'

'Be wary of him. He was a sly, sadistic child who enjoyed trapping birds and drowning kittens. He's weak – but flawed. And it wouldn't surprise me if he tried to do you – or Adeline – a mischief of some kind just for the fun of it. I'm not saying that he *is* the cause of your problem – merely that you shouldn't discount him.'

'That is interesting advice. I'll bear it in mind.'

The afternoon sped by as they talked ... and when Michel du Plessis came in with the limp that had made him quit the army, Rockliffe saw that the love for which Joanna Kendrick had left her husband and child still glowed like a beacon.

'You don't judge us,' remarked Michel after a time.

'No. That would be impertinent. And what right have I?' the Duke replied. And found himself accepting an invitation to stay the night.

It was not until the following morning when he was preparing to leave that Joanna, from within Michel's sheltering arm, voiced the question that must have been in her mind all along.

'When you go back – will you tell her?'

'Yes – though perhaps not immediately. If I am to minimise the shock, I'll need to choose the moment carefully.'

'Of course. But when you *do* tell her ... if she should feel disposed to come ... will you bring her here?' she asked diffidently. 'I should so very much like to see her.'

Rockliffe took her hand and, with a swift uncluttered smile, said, 'I know. And you may be sure that, if she wishes it, I shall bring her to you. In the meantime, there is no need at all for any anxiety. I assure you that I am to be trusted.'

'Yes.' Joanna smiled back at him. 'Yes. I know that you are.'

*

After an absence of three weeks and having stopped off in Paris to collect Mr Osborne, send both the Vidame d'Aurillac and Monsieur and Madame du Plessis a dozen bottles of Sancerre wine and, finally, purchase an extremely pretty aquamarine and diamond ring from a shop on the Rue St Honoré, the Duke walked into his house at around eight in the evening and asked for his wife.

'Her Grace and Lady Elinor,' came the grandiloquent reply, 'are dining with the Marquis and Marchioness of Amberley in Hanover Square. A small family party, as I understand it, your Grace.'

'And I away? How very uncivil of them,' drawled Rockliffe. 'They might have waited. Do you not think they might have waited, Robert?'

Robert Symonds was not deceived but it was beneath his dignity to smile.

'Lord Amberley,' he announced, 'has been in town for a week, your Grace.'

'Only a week? A bagatelle, Robert. I am cut to the quick. And I do not think ... I really do not think that they can be allowed to perpetrate this atrocity.' Rockliffe paused and with laughter in his eyes, contemplated his immaculate travelling-dress of sapphire broadcloth. 'The only question is – will they let me in or shall I be turned ignominiously away?'

The faintest of tremors afflicted Symonds' expression. In all his time in the Duke's service, he had never known his noble employer go out incorrectly attired.

'Your Grace could change?' he ventured to suggest.

'I could,' agreed his Grace with reflective devilry. 'But for a small family party, I do not think I will. And it would be a shame, would it not, to spoil the effect?'

In Hanover Square, the Marquis of Amberley's butler welcomed the latecomer without so much as a blink and informed him that the company had but now sat down to dine.

'As well as her Grace and Lady Elinor, it is only Lord Philip and Lady Isabel with Mr Ingram and Lord Harry, your Grace. Not a large party. And my lord Amberley will be delighted to see you, I'm sure.'

'Thank you, Barrow. You relieve my mind.'

'Not at all, your Grace. Does your Grace wish to be announced?'

'An interesting question.' Rockliffe appeared to consider it. 'But no. I think not. I believe I am inclined to ... make an entrance ... if you will be so good as to humour me.'

Then, smiling a little, he opened the door and went in.

Harry was the first to see him. He said resignedly, 'I might have known it! You smelled the pheasant.' And thus heralded a melée of bantering welcome.

Adeline stopped breathing and narrowly avoided choking over a morsel of turbot. She was so glad to see him she could have cried and an epic blush stained her skin. Mercifully, everyone's attention was on her husband as he bowed extravagantly over Rosalind's hand. Or so she thought. Lord Amberley, seeing her breath catch and the way the light suddenly flared in her eyes, smiled to himself before turning his gaze on his friend.

'Rosalind, my love ... you look radiant,' Rockliffe was saying. 'Motherhood must suit you. Dare I hope you will also be charitable enough to forgive me for ruining your party?'

'It's possible,' she retorted. And then, lightly touching his cuff, 'I thought so. You certainly wasted no time, did you? I hope Adeline is suitably flattered.'

Fortunately, since Adeline was still incapable of speech, Jack filled the gap by saying easily, 'I daresay she would be – except that, like us, she suspects he is merely eager for his dinner.'

'Damned Jack-in-the-Box,' grinned the Marquis, signing a footman to lay another place. 'He only does these things for effect.'

Rockliffe, by this time, had reached his wife's side and was melting her bones with the lazy glinting smile that was so peculiarly his own. He said, 'I am maligned. And why does everyone talk about me as if I weren't here?'

'Probably,' responded Adeline creditably, 'out of habit.'

'Do I detect a note of displeasure over the length of my absence? How charming!'

'Is it?'

'But of course. Only think of the fun you can have encouraging me to make it up to you.' And, possessing himself of her hand, he placed a warm, lingering kiss in her palm.

Laughter became the key to the evening. Only Nell, nervous lest Rockliffe discover her misdemeanour, stayed unhappily on the fringe until Harry took pity on her and said quietly, 'Stop worrying. It's all in the past and Rock won't eat you. In fact, just to make sure he doesn't, I thought I might have a word with him myself.'

The great dark eyes regarded him wonderingly.

'Would you really? That's kind of you. I – I don't know why you should bother to help me, though.'

'Don't you?' he asked dryly. And then, 'No. Come to think of it, you probably don't. I haven't been very kind recently, have I?'

'N-no. But I deserved that.'

'True – but that's not the reason. I don't suppose it occurred to you that, under the circumstances, a defence that was too obviously partisan would be seen as no defence at all?'

It took Nell a moment to work this out. Then, a faint glow touching her cheeks, she said, 'Oh – I see. You wanted everyone to think you didn't c-care about me in the least.'

'You could put it that way.'

'How clever of you. And is that why you were ... flirting with Diana?'

'Oh no.' An unholy gleam lit the seraphic blue eyes. 'That was for a different purpose altogether.'

Later, while Rockliffe was above stairs admiring his friend's son and heir, Isabel took the opportunity to say softly to Adeline, 'I take it Rock doesn't know about Nell's little escapade?'

'No. You're going to suggest I tell him before someone else does – and you're right. Unfortunately, it's not that simple.'

Isabel looked at her for a moment and then sighed.

'Don't tell me. The fell hand of Harry. Has he *any* idea what he's asking of you?'

'Oh yes. And when the thunderbolt strikes, I've his full permission to disclaim all knowledge. But since I can't do that, I suppose I'd better have a stern word with him. Why is nothing straightforward any more?'

But his lordship, when she approached him, proved to be surprisingly amenable.

'I've been thinking that myself,' he said. 'If Rock hears about it elsewhere – and he's more or less bound to – we really *will* be in the soup. So would you rather I told him?'

'No. But if you want to take your share of the blame, you can come and do it when I've finished. Shall we say tomorrow morning?'

'I'll be there. Are you going to warn Nell or am I?'

'You are.' Adeline smiled sardonically. 'You've begun to figure as a cross between Sir Galahad and the Oracle ... so it would be a pity not to put it to some good use, wouldn't it?'

Upstairs in the nursery, having promised to stand sponsor to Amberley's son, Rockliffe said, 'Rosalind looks very well and is clearly happy. A weight off your mind, I imagine?'

Leading the way out of the room and away from the ears of the nursery-maid, the Marquis said, 'Yes. I've written to the German doctor I told you of – so perhaps, in a few months, depending on his reply... well, we'll see.' He paused. 'Meanwhile, how are things with you?'

Rockliffe shrugged slightly. 'If you are asking about my marriage ... it's not exactly what I either hoped for or expected. But I persevere.'

Amberley opened his mouth to say, *'But she's besotted with you!'* and then thought better of it, realising that, since Rock must know that, the problem – if there was one – had to be something else. He said lightly, 'Including your wedding, this is only the second time I've met her – but I like what I've seen. And Jack and Harry both seem exceptionally fond of her.'

'Yes. They do, don't they?' drawled his Grace. Then, pointedly changing the subject, he said, 'You may recall a conversation we had quite some time ago about the mysterious whereabouts of Francis Devereux.'

'Vaguely,' agreed his lordship, somewhat taken aback. And then, 'Are you saying you've found him?'

'Possibly. I could, of course, be completely wrong ... but I rather think he's currently treading the boards at the Comédie Française under the fanciful stage-name of *L'Inconnu*.' And, smiling a little, 'If it *is* him, he's actually surprisingly good.'

*

The short journey home found Nell decidedly subdued and, in the darkness of the carriage, she slid her hand surreptitiously into Adeline's for comfort. Then, escaping to her chamber, she spent a large part of the night wondering whether Harry's words offered any basis for hope.

Finally left alone with his wife, Rockliffe smiled and said lightly, 'If I promise to do nothing alarming, would you agree to drink a glass of wine with me?'

Adeline gazed back at him and was invaded by a sudden recklessness.

'It has to be said that – to some of us – everything you do is alarming. But just this once, I'll take my chance.'

He opened the door the salon and stood back to let her pass.

'Am I supposed to applaud your courage?'

'No. Just watch out for my elbows.'

He was still laughing as he poured the wine. Then, handing her a glass of Burgundy, he said, 'So what else have I missed – apart from the unheralded descent of Dominic and Rosalind?'

'The equally unheralded descent of Lewis and Cecily. Which reminds me. I have to plan a reception.'

'For Lewis and Cecily?'

'Who else? It's quite simple. I pave Cecily's way in society and she keeps quiet about what happened in Oxfordshire.'

'I see. Very resourceful.' He contemplated her over the rim of his glass. 'And how does dear Lewis like all this?'

'Lewis,' came the demure reply, 'is not a problem.'

'And will not, I trust, become one,' returned Rockliffe blandly.

The new, temporarily audacious Adeline merely shook her head and smiled provocatively. Then she said, 'Paris was obviously entertaining. I trust your business prospered?'

'Eventually, yes.' His mouth curled in a slow smile. 'And no. I neither extended my absence in order to worry you nor took … unhusbandly advantage … of my liberty.'

The narrow brows soared. 'Didn't you? Why on earth not?'

'In the first instance,' replied Rockliffe gently, 'because I was quite legitimately detained; and in the second … because of all the women who came my way, not one compared favourably with my wife.'

He paused and watched her cloak of levity disintegrate. Then he said, 'And if that is alarming, I apologise. But you did ask for it, didn't you?'

TWENTY

Rising betimes on the following morning, his Grace was conscious of a strong sense of optimistic well-being. He breakfasted alone, allowed his secretary to bring various matters to his attention and then began sifting through the heap of correspondence engendered by his three-week absence. Half an hour later and with every trace of lazy contentment effectively wiped from his face, he strode from the room and virtually collided with Adeline who had been on the point of entering.

'How fortunate,' he said with unusual crispness. 'I was just about to come in search of you.'

'And I you,' she smiled. Then, uncertainly, 'Is something wrong?'

'Why yes, my dear. I rather think it is.' Rockliffe ushered her grimly into the library and closed the door. 'I should like to know why – when Nell sees fit to make herself the talk of the town - *you* do not see fit to inform me of it.'

Adeline's heart sank.

'Oh,' she said feebly. 'I suppose it's no good saying I was just about to do so?'

'Were you?'

'Yes.'

'Then no doubt you had an excellent reason for not telling me last night.'

'Well, yes – I thought so.' She met his gaze with wry candour. 'I felt that there was no purpose to be served by immediately ruining your home-coming – and that therefore this morning would do. Obviously I was mistaken. Do you mind if I ask who told you?'

'Who but Lucilla?' His tone was caustic but his mouth had relaxed a little and, handing the letter out to her, he said, 'Read it for yourself.'

Adeline skimmed swiftly through the tightly-scripted page and learned that Lucilla had been apprised of Nell's disgrace by her friend, Maria Fitzroy. The details, moreover, appeared to be depressingly accurate. Sighing, she looked up at the Duke and said, 'It's difficult to tell from this which Lucilla enjoys most; blaming you – or criticising Nell.'

'Quite. But it's an ill wind, they say, that blows nobody any good.' He paused. 'It is true?'

'I'm afraid so.' She braced herself and then continued simply, 'Nell attended a public ridotto with Sir Jasper Brierley and was brought home by Harry – who not only gave her a thundering scold, by the way, but also tried to break Sir Jasper's jaw into the bargain. Unfortunately, she was seen and there was some gossip. The only consolation I can offer is that it's over now – and no real harm was done, so far as one can tell.'

'That,' observed Rockliffe, 'remains to be seen. But enlighten me. How did Nell manage this feat? And how come Harry was the one to put an end to it?'

'She told me she had a headache – and I was stupid enough to believe her,' came the bitter reply. 'I let her persuade me to leave her and go to the Crewe's ball with Isabel as planned. Then Harry came ... and of course I told him. It was sheer luck that he knows Nell well enough to guess that she was up to no good. We came back here, found her missing and put two and two together.'

There was a long silence when she finished speaking and Rockliffe's expression, though it defied interpretation, made her distinctly uneasy. Finally, when he showed no sign of answering her, she said defensively, 'Harry was a great help, you know. And Nell is truly sorry.'

'I daresay she is. It is, after all, the usual result of being found out.' His voice was smooth as silk. 'Correct me if I am wrong ... but did not the Crewe assembly take place the night before I left for Paris?'

Adeline's breath leaked away.

'Damn,' she thought weakly. *'That's torn it. Now he'll never believe I meant to explain that as well.'*

'Yes,' she said flatly.

'I thought so. The occasion is distinguished in my memory as the one on which I found Harry here with you ... on the point, I believe he said, of bidding you goodnight.'

'Yes. He – he'd just brought Nell home.'

'So I gather. And yet, so far from telling me what had occurred, the two of you seem to have actively chosen to keep it from me.' The dark eyes examined her coolly. 'Unless, of course, I am missing something?'

'No. No – you're not missing anything. Harry had hopes of hushing the thing up and he thought that, if you knew, you'd send Nell to Lucilla. So he asked me not to tell you.'

'And you agreed.'

'At the time, yes. I suppose I thought that there was no point in worrying you needlessly.'

'My dear! Such touching concern for my welfare!' he exclaimed sardonically. 'I only wish I could appreciate it. Sadly, however, I find myself unable to be grateful to you for first conspiring with Harry to deceive me and then allowing me to leave for Paris ignorant of the fact that my sister might at any moment be facing social ruin. Quite apart from the damage you might have done Nell by denying her my support, it makes me wonder what exactly you think I am – and whether you take *all* your troubles to Harry.' He paused, his mouth curling in something that wasn't a smile. 'The only thing I know for certain is that you don't confide them to me.'

Adeline stared at him and discovered that she felt rather sick. She said with difficulty, 'What troubles? I don't know what you mean.'

'Don't you, my sweet? Then let me remind you. I'll admit that – but for this business over Nell – I wouldn't have remarked on it. But perhaps you'd like to explain why you found yourself so ill-provided-for that it was necessary to ask Matthew to advance you five hundred guineas?'

She stood very still while a raging, black desolation filled every corner of her soul. It was, of course, her cue to tell him everything ... and she'd actually hoped that, this time, she'd bring herself to do it. But the timing was inescapably wrong. She could not do it ... and, if not now, probably not ever.

Despair tinged her gaze with acid and put an edge in her voice.

'Can't you guess? I lost it at cards. And if I'd realised it was so important, I'd naturally have made my confession the instant I laid eyes on you. But you will doubtless be relieved to learn that the rest of my bills are paid – and that I can, if you wish it, account for every penny you've given me.'

'You know perfectly well that I don't give a tinker's curse what you do with your allowance,' snapped Rockliffe, his temper beginning to rise in earnest. 'I do, however, very much resent being relegated to the edges of your life and given no more of your confidence than you'd accord a stranger. You never ask for my help, you won't accept my affection – you don't even appear to care for my company. In fact, it's beginning to seem that the only things you *do* want from me are my title and my money. And *that*, my dear, is something I never thought to hear myself say.'

Silence, inimical and catastrophic, yawned about them while stricken aquamarine eyes met shuttered black ones.

Somewhere at the back of her mind, Adeline was aware that she ought to say something ... but did not know what.

Rockliffe recognised that he had hurt her but repressed the urge to apologise.

'You don't deny it, I see,' he said, at length.

She drew a long painful breath and managed the merest suggestion of a shrug.

'Where's the point? Simply telling you that you're wrong isn't going to do anything to convince you, is it?'

His anger ebbing, Rockliffe stared back at her and – just as he had done five months ago in Lady Franklin's garden – tried to decide whether he most wanted to shake her or kiss her. Then, in the distance, he heard the pealing of the door-bell.

'Hell,' he sighed, 'and damnation. I am in no mood for morning callers.'

'It's Harry.'

'*What?*' Suddenly the dark gaze was no longer hooded.

'Harry,' Adeline repeated, concentrating hard on keeping her voice steady. 'He seemed to feel he ought to explain things to you himself, so I -- '

'Are you telling me,' interrupted Rockliffe with dangerous calm, 'that you even discussed with Harry when and what I should be told?'

Her throat closed up and she nodded mutely.

'I see. Then you'd better go and give him a detailed account of our conversation, hadn't you?'

Adeline swallowed hard. 'Tracy ... I -- '

'No. Don't say any more. I think I've heard enough. And though I can't pretend that this morning hasn't been a revelation to me ... you can rest assured that you've made yourself perfectly clear.'

'But – please – won't you see Harry for a moment?'

'I think not.' Sheer temper flared suddenly in his eyes. '*You* see Harry. After all, why break a habit? *I* am going to see Nell.'

*

Under the circumstances and all things considered, Adeline would also have preferred not to see Harry ... but since the alternatives were either to leave him kicking his heels in the red salon or tell Symonds to evict him, it did not appear that she had much choice in the matter. Neither, as it turned out, was his lordship's attitude particularly helpful.

'*Won't see me?*' he exclaimed when she had finished. 'I never heard anything so bloody silly in my life! Oh – I beg your pardon, Adeline ... but it is, isn't it? What good does he think that will do?'

Adeline sat down and leaned her brow against one slender palm.

'Leave it, Harry. Tracy won't see you – and even if he did, there's nothing you can say that would make it any better. He's right and we're not - and there's an end of it. So the best thing you can do is just go away.'

'Damned if I will!' Harry also sat down and crossed one satin-clad leg over the other. 'I want to know what he's saying to Nell - and I'll sit here all day if necessary.'

'Oh don't be so stupid!' Lifting her head, she stared at him in exasperation. 'Can't you see that you're only making everything worse?'

Harry blinked and then appeared to regain his sense of proportion. He said meditatively, 'You must have made a shocking poor job of it. Not that I'm surprised. I always thought making a *completely* clean breast of it was a bad idea.'

'Very likely. And now you've said that, will you please leave?'

'I suppose I'll have to.' He rose, strolled towards the door and then turned back as if struck by a sudden thought, 'My God! You don't suppose he's *jealous*, do you? Because if he is, it's the most -- '

'*Go!*' Adeline surged to her feet, goaded beyond endurance. 'Just go away! Or I swear I'll not be responsible!'

Harry opened his mouth and then reluctantly closed it again. Knowing a last word but having the sense not to say it, he went.

*

While Rockliffe was asking his sister to explain her stupidity and Adeline was trying to get rid of Lord Harry, Jack Ingram paid a formal call on Lady Franklin and received gracious permission to pay his addresses to Mistress Althea.

Since, in typical fashion, Jack had done the thing properly and made sure that her ladyship was expecting him, his request came as no surprise; and, because it did not, Lady Franklin had taken the sensible precaution of sending Diana to be fitted for the new gown she'd insisted on ordering for the Queensberry Ball. Thus it was that Althea – robed in pink tiffany and hovering between doubt and delight – found herself summoned in due course to the parlour. And there, under her mama's eagle eye, Mr Ingram took her hand and, with the sweetest of smiles, asked if he might keep it.

Thea blushed but did not avoid his eyes.

'Oh *yes*, sir – if you please. Th-that is to say, I would be very happy.'

'And I,' vowed Jack, raising her fingers to his lips, 'consider myself undeservedly fortunate.'

'Very prettily said,' approved Lady Franklin. And then, 'I daresay you would like to be alone with your treasure ... and I am not so insensitive as to stand in your way – for I am sure I may rely on your sense of propriety, sir.'

'Certainly, your ladyship.'

'Very well, then. I will leave you.' She sighed sentimentally and patted Althea's cheek. 'No more than ten minutes, mind! It would never do for Mr Ingram to think I do not know what is proper.'

Mr Ingram watched her go and repressed a sigh of relief only to have Althea do it for him. He laughed and, capturing both of her hands, said, 'Yes. It *is* pleasant to be left alone, isn't it?'

She nodded shyly and her eyes held such a glow of wonderment that Jack's amusement faded and his fingers tightened on hers.

'I love you, you know,' he said simply. 'The only reason I've not said so before is that I was determined to demonstrate my respect by doing everything correctly. But that doesn't mean I don't care – for I do. Very much.'

Blushing even harder, Althea's gaze fluttered down to his cream silk vest.

'S-so do I.'

'Do you?' asked Jack with careful restraint. 'Oh – I know you *like* me. But that's not enough for marriage. And ... I hope you haven't accepted me because your mama wished you to do so.'

'No – of course not!' The blue eyes flew back to meet his. 'How could you think it? Surely you know that I ... that I ...'

'That you what?'

'That I've b-been in love with you for weeks,' finished Thea bravely. 'Only I never thought you'd want to marry me.'

'No?' Joy transformed Mr Ingram's pleasant but usually unremarkable countenance. 'Then why did you suppose I've been dancing attendance on you quite so assiduously? I've scarcely set foot in my club for a month. Oh Thea – my little love!'

Finding herself swept almost literally off her feet into an embrace that deprived her of breath, Althea did the only thing possible. She flung her arms round his neck and kissed him back.

*

Half an hour after Jack had taken his leave, Diana bounced in upon her mother and sister with an armful of parcels.

'What a morning I've had! I've worn myself to the bone searching for just the right shade of ribbons to replace those on my satin-straw and *still* haven't found them. But I did see the most delicious bonnet in Madame Tissot's and couldn't resist buying it; and I got a new pair of shoes so they can be dyed to match my new gown.' Sitting down with her booty scattered around her feet, she looked pettishly at her mother and added, 'But I do wish you'd permitted me to go to Phanie, as I asked. Her gowns are by far the most stylish – and no one who is anyone goes to that stupid Miss Wood.'

'As I have pointed out on numerous occasions,' replied her ladyship repressively, 'our resources are limited. It is a case of one gown from Phanie or three from Miss Wood. Now Diana – I wish you will cease fidgeting for there is something I must tell you'

'Oh?' Engaged in trying on her new shoes, Diana sounded less than interested. 'What?'

'Mr Ingram has this morning asked for Thea's hand and I have given my consent to it. In short, they are betrothed.'

Diana's head jerked up. '*What*? I don't believe it!'

'Then you had better try. It will be announced in the *Morning Chronicle* the day after tomorrow.'

Uniquely, Diana was dumbstruck for several seconds. Then, two bright spots of colour burning in her cheeks, she said fiercely, '*No*! I won't have it, do you hear? I won't have it!'

'You have nothing to say in the matter.'

'I don't care.' Diana came abruptly to her feet and, finding she had on only one shoe, wrenched it off and sent it hurtling across the room. 'I won't have Thea betrothed before me. *I won't*!'

'On present showing,' replied her mother acidly, 'if we wait for you, we'll wait forever.'

'That's not fair. I *will* get a husband – you see if I don't!'

'And who, precisely, did you have in mind? You let Rockliffe slip through your fingers and, since coming to London, have signally failed to attract any gentleman of consequence.' Lady Franklin's gaze was icy. 'Althea, on the other hand, has succeeded in making a very satisfactory match. Not brilliant, perhaps – but certainly more than respectable. And I have no intention whatsoever of allowing you to spoil it, Diana.'

'Then put a stop to it,' snapped Diana, mercilessly shredding her handkerchief. 'They can be betrothed later – at the end of the season, perhaps. I don't care. But I don't want it announced yet. It *shouldn't* be announced yet. Mine ought to come first.'

'But why does it matter?' asked Althea timidly.

'It doesn't,' said Lady Franklin. 'And it will be a relief to me to see at least *one* of my daughters creditably established.'

'You call this creditable?' Diana's voice started to rise. 'If I couldn't do better than a mere Honourable, I'd as soon cut my throat.'

'Di – dearest!' begged Althea. 'We all know you can do better than me. Of course we do. And there's no hurry now, is there? For, if you wish to wait for exactly the right offer, you will be able to come and stay with Jack and me. And I'm sure you'll find a husband in no time.'

Had it been uttered by anyone else, the implications of this speech might have been dubious. As it was, Althea meant well; it was not her fault that, to her twin, it was the last straw.

'How dare you?' spat Diana. 'How *dare* you patronise me, you mealy-mouthed little bore? Do you think I need your help – or the help of that dull, pompous fellow you've managed to catch?'

'He's *not* dull!' Stung, Althea leapt to her feet in defence of her Jack. 'He's a dear, kind man and I love him!'

'Fiddlesticks! You're just grateful. And so you should be. But *I* wouldn't have had him if he'd been the last man on earth. And I could have, you know. Just like that.'

'No, Di. You couldn't.' For the first time in her life, Althea faced her sister without fear. 'The truth is that Jack doesn't like you very much and never has. So it's probably just as well that you won't want our help ... because I daresay he'd rather not have you in his house.'

And, so saying, she walked calmly to the door and went out.

For perhaps a minute there was utter silence. Then, rising to fix her erstwhile favourite with a basilisk stare, Lady Franklin said flatly, 'You asked for that. If you've shown this side of your nature to the gentlemen, it's no wonder you've received no offers. Your temper is quite deplorable. And, if you're not careful, it will be your undoing one of these days.'

Then, following in Althea's wake, she too left the room.

There is no point in having hysterics without an audience and the scream Diana had been preparing died in her throat. Staring unseeingly down at the litter of shopping, she thought numbly, '*Thea is betrothed.*

Poor, timid Thea who's always been my shadow – is betrothed. How Cecy Garfield will laugh!' It was not to be borne. Something would have to be done ... and there was only one possibility. Very slowly, she sat down and began assessing her chances of bringing Harry Caversham to the point.

*

Rockliffe dined at White's that evening and then, meeting the Marquis of Amberley, moved on with him to the Cocoa-Tree where, as luck would have it, they were presently joined by Mr Ingram and Lord Harry.

'Well!' exclaimed Harry with dry humour. 'Am I allowed to sit down – or had I best take myself off to the other room?'

'That,' replied his Grace, 'rather depends on what you want to talk about.'

'Oh – I'll be dumb, never fear. Though it would be a damned sight easier if I knew exactly what's eating you.'

'What is all this?' asked Lord Amberley, laughing. 'Do you know, Jack?'

'It looks,' observed Mr Ingram, 'rather like a quarrel.'

'Lord, no! Nothing of the sort,' said Harry, seating himself. 'You have to *talk* to each other for that.'

'I thought you were to be dumb?' enquired Rockliffe sweetly. And then, 'I suppose you've been to the Portland's ball?'

'Yes.' Having discovered from Nell that, though his Grace had been uncommonly angry, he had not spoken of banishment, Harry felt safe in offering a little provocation. 'I thought Adeline was in quite her best looks – didn't you, Jack?'

Faintly startled, Jack busied himself pouring wine and wisely said nothing.

'Indeed?' The Duke's gaze continued to rest on his lordship while his hand toyed idly with a pack of cards. 'Then I am surprised you did not choose to remain ... in order to escort her home.'

Amberley's brows rose. *'My God!'* he thought. *'If that's what's in the wind, Harry had better be very careful.'*

Harry, belatedly recognising the expression in the dark, heavy-lidded eyes, thought so too. Changing tack, he said, 'And spend another hour tripping over Diana Franklin every time I turn round? No thank you! The girl's like a confounded bloodhound.'

Jack looked up. 'Serves you right for encouraging her.'

'Oh – that. It was only a flirtation, you know. And I never expected to wake up one morning and find her attached to my shirt-tails. I felt dashed ridiculous this evening. Anyone would think she didn't have other fish to fry.'

'Perhaps she hasn't,' grinned Amberley. 'Or none so eligible.'

Harry laughed. 'Thank you.'

'I happen to know,' said Jack, who had been patiently waiting for the right opening, 'that something has occurred to ... upset Mistress Di.'

'Oh?' asked Harry. 'What?'

'I believe I can guess.' Rockliffe gave his peculiar glinting smile. 'My felicitations, Jack.'

Mr Ingram coloured faintly and then laughed.

'Damn you, Rock! May a man not even announce his own betrothal?'

'*Betrothal*?' Harry sat up straight. 'You sly dog, Jack! Never say you've done it at last?'

'Yes. I have. And thought to surprise you all.'

'Surprise Dominic,' advised the Duke. 'He's as much in the dark as you could possibly wish.'

'More,' complained the Marquis. 'Who is she, Jack?'

'Althea Franklin,' smiled Mr Ingram. 'The gentlest and most beautiful girl I ever saw in my life. And also – as Harry is itching to tell you – the bloodhound's twin sister.'

TWENTY-ONE

The rift between the Duke and Duchess of Rockliffe showed no sign of mending ... mainly because, with no solid ground to rely on, neither of them knew where to begin. He was wary of inviting another rebuff; she was devoured by guilt at her other, more significant deceit. And the result was a chilly state of impersonal courtesy that excoriated them both and, in time, gravely concerned their friends.

At a saner level beneath his involuntary jealousy, Rockliffe was well aware where Harry's heart lay and, although this did not help him in his dealings with Adeline, it did make it possible for him to tacitly heal the breach with his lordship.

'But he made damned sure I wouldn't dare ask any awkward questions,' confided Harry later to Nell. 'Gave me the sort of smile you usually see over a yard of steel and advised me – ever so gently, mind – not to meddle. Then he showed me his newest snuff-box.'

Nell nodded, frowning a little.

'Adeline won't discuss it either. She simply looks straight through one and says something cutting.'

'Don't I know it! But though I daresay the root of it is that they're both too stiff-necked to make the first move, it don't make me feel any better. For, whichever way you look at it, it's my fault.'

'No, it isn't,' denied Nell firmly. 'It's mine.'

He looked down at her for a moment and then, smiling, took her hand companionably in his.

'All right. Ours, then. But I still wish Rock would let one of us near him.'

*

As it happened, he was not alone in this wish and the next person to try was the one best equipped to succeed.

'What's wrong, Rock?' asked the Marquis of Amberley simply one evening over a hand of picquet. 'You can't keep us all at arm's length forever. And if you get any more tense, you'll snap.'

'I shall certainly snap if I have to endure any more of this kind of thing – however well-intentioned it may be,' came the caustic response. 'It's becoming extremely tedious.'

'Well, there's a simple way to avoid further repetitions, isn't there?'

'For whose good? Yours or mine?'

'Oh for God's sake! Do you have to be so bloody difficult? I'm trying to help!'

'I'm aware of it. I'd prefer that you didn't.'

'You think after all the years we've known each other I'm just going to leave it?'

'Now that *would* be helpful.'

The Marquis eyed him implacably. 'What is it? A quarrel you can't mend?'

'First Jack and now you,' sighed his Grace. 'Why does everyone think me so quarrelsome?'

Laying his cards face down, Amberley leaned back in his chair and fixed his friend with a direct grey-green stare.

'It's no use playing off your airs with me, Rock. I'm wise to them.'

'You are also,' returned the Duke, 'annoyingly persistent.'

'That too.' There was a pause. Then, 'It *is* Adeline, isn't it?'

'And tactless – and intrusive – and cocksure.'

'*Isn't it?*'

'*All right!*' Releasing a sharp breath of pure irritation, Rockliffe flung down his cards. 'All right. It's Adeline. Are you satisfied now?'

'No. Talk to me.'

'Why? For the good of my soul? I really don't need this, Dominic.'

'Yes, you do. You need it very much.' Amberley met the inimical gaze unwaveringly. 'What's the problem? *Is* it just a quarrel? Or have you begun to wonder – now that you have her – whether you were not a little hasty in leaping into wedlock?'

Quite slowly, the dark eyes filled with bitter amusement and then the Duke said mockingly, 'Dear me ... how very banal of you, my loved one. I'm disappointed.'

'I take it I'm wrong, then?'

'You are. Indeed, I may truthfully say that you were never more so.'

The derisive quality of Rockliffe's irony was not lost upon the Marquis. He considered it for a moment and then, eyes widening with incredulous realisation, he said, 'Oh Christ. Are you telling me that, despite marrying her for just that reason, you've still not -- '

Rockliffe stood up with a force which almost overset his chair.

'No. You may not have noticed ... but I have been endeavouring – for the last ten excruciating minutes – to tell you nothing at all.'

And he walked out.

*

In her turn and with rather more success, Adeline fended off a similar approach from the Marquis's wife. Then, entirely without pleasure and purely in order to occupy her mind, she set about planning her promised party. That it would be narrowly preceded by the most glittering event of the season bothered her not at all for she was neither aiming to compete with nor eagerly anticipating the Duchess of Queensberry's ball. To her, it was just another interminable function at which she and Tracy would have to maintain the polite fiction of not being strangers. And, but for Nell, she would not even have ordered a new gown.

'Wear your blue silk?' echoed that lady aghast. 'You can't! Everyone's seen it!'

'So?'

Nell opened her mouth, closed it again and took a long, calming breath.

'You don't understand, Adeline. This isn't any ordinary ball. People sell their souls for an invitation. And those who get one don't go in a gown they've worn at least three times before.'

Adeline eyed her sardonically.

'That must be a boon to the mantua-makers. Or does her Grace claim a percentage?'

'That,' said Nell severely, 'is not funny. Now ... will you please stop arguing and come with me to Phanie's? Or do you want Rock to be ashamed of you?'

And that, of course, was not only unanswerable but also responsible for Adeline choosing to buy the exquisite but criminally expensive peacock shot-silk.

*

For almost a week, nothing much changed.

Congratulations poured in upon Jack and Althea; Diana fermented with jealous rage even before she'd been forced to put up with Cecily Garfield's spurious sympathy; and Harry, finding himself suddenly under hot pursuit, took to lurking in lonely antechambers – as often as not, with Nell. Rockliffe, meanwhile, remained scrupulously polite to Adeline in public and equally scrupulous in avoiding her at home ... and Adeline, drowning in an ever-deepening well of misery, tried to comfort herself with the view that matters could not possibly get any worse.

Then several things happened at once.

It was the evening of Lady Lacey's rout-party and, for Adeline at least, the auspices were bad from the moment she came downstairs to find that she had misjudged her timing and arrived before Nell. His Grace, formidable in bronze watered-silk with gold lacing, accorded her the most elaborate of bows and then proceeded to conduct a leisurely head-to-foot appraisal.

Adeline set her teeth, aware that he was being deliberately provoking. Finally, he said languidly, 'You look charming, my dear – as always. And you are wearing the aquamarine set, I see. How delightful! They remind me so irresistibly of our wedding-night, you know ... and, if it was not plainly a silly question, I am almost tempted to ask what they remind *you* of.' He smiled blandly and then, looking past her, 'Ah – Nell. At last. Perhaps now we can go?'

After such a beginning, Adeline's expectations for the evening ahead were naturally low – but not, as it transpired, low enough. At the very first opportunity, Richard Horton materialised at her side and purringly demanded another five hundred guineas.

Adeline's skin turned clammily cold and there was a distant roaring in her ears. Willing herself not to faint, she said baldly, 'No. I can't go on with this.'

'As I see it, you're in too deep to do anything else,' came the smooth reply. 'And with your noble husband somewhat less than attentive these days, I'd say it was a little late to confess all and throw yourself on his mercy – wouldn't you? Then again ... if you daren't tell him yourself, you can't afford to have *me* do so, can you?'

She stared at him, racked with nausea. And then, unevenly, 'You think you have it all worked out.'

'And have I not?' He smiled again, reading the answer in her face. 'Five hundred, Adeline ... in time for the Queensberry ball, shall we say?'

She continued to gaze defeatedly at him until, from somewhere inside her, she found enough energy to say, 'If – if I agree to give you the money, it will be for the last time. And I want my mother's letter.'

Richard laughed softly.

'All in good time. Bring me the money ... and then we'll see.' Upon which he strolled unconcernedly away.

From a position just out of earshot yet close enough to study Adeline's face, Jack Ingram watched with increasing grimness. Then, crossing to her side and registering the helpless blankness of her expression, he said quietly, 'Come with me. You look ready to collapse – and you can't do it here.'

Unresistingly, she let him lead her to a curtained alcove and press her gently down on a small sofa. With growing concern, Jack thought she resembled nothing so much as a glassy-eyed doll. He said, 'Adeline, my dear – what is it? What did he say to you?'

'He wants five hundred guineas,' came the courteous, mechanical response. And then, as if the mere effort of speaking had jerked her from the lethargy, the blankness vanished and, drawing a ragged breath, she said, 'Oh God. Forget I said it.'

The grey eyes narrowed and it was a moment before he replied. Then he said reasonably, 'Did I not suspect that it's not the first time, I might perhaps try. As it is, I don't think I can.' He paused briefly. 'This is it, isn't it? The reason you tried to win money at cards rather than ask Rock for it?'

She gripped her hands tightly together to prevent them from shaking and bent her head over them, saying nothing.

'Adeline ... you can't go on dealing with this yourself. You need help.' Again, Jack waited in vain for a reply and finally, when none was forthcoming, 'What exactly is Horton threatening you with?'

A tremor ran through her and very slowly she raised her head to look bleakly back at him.

'The skeleton in the family cupboard,' she said, 'Only, ironically enough, the whole problem is that there isn't one.'

Jack blinked and sat down beside her.

'I think you'd better start at the beginning. And, before you refuse, allow me to remind you that I've some right to know. I'm about to become part of the family myself, remember?'

Adeline stared at him and gave a tiny, sobbing laugh.

'Oh God. Althea. You're marrying Althea.'

'Yes. I am. And if her uncle is the ugly customer I'm beginning to think he is, I'd rather like to know about it,' he returned flatly. 'So tell me. And then we'll see what can be done.'

Her defences were broken and she was at her wits' end. Also, there was undeniable justice in what he'd said. Clinically and without elaboration, she told him.

There was a long silence when she had finished speaking and at length she steeled herself to look into his face. He was frowning a little but more with concentration than shock. Then he said calmly, 'Yes. I can see why all this has frightened you into playing your uncle's game ... but I doubt it's as bad as you think.' He gave her a faint, encouraging smile. 'And two things are crystal clear. You must stop paying Horton to keep quiet ... and you've got to tell Rock. You should have done so in the first place you know.'

'Yes. I do know.' Her voice was low and bitter. 'But when it first started I never guessed that Richard would come back again and again. As for Tracy, I had the wild idea that I could protect him ... and then later, when I realised I couldn't, I didn't know how to explain it all to him – or to prevent the kind of scandal he didn't deserve to be part of. Also ... to be truthful ... I suppose I was afraid it would kill any – any affection he might have for me.'

'My dear – you underestimate him.'

'No. Never that. But you don't understand, Jack. Tracy's reasons for marrying me were not ... not what you might suppose. And, as a result, our marriage is ... precarious.' She looked at him out of stark aquamarine eyes. 'So many secrets spinning out of each other until one is trapped. But I never meant it to happen. I just thought that, since *one* of us must silence Richard, it had better be me.'

'Yes. I believe I can understand that. But it was a mistake, Adeline. If you'd told Rock in the first place, it would never have got to this stage. He may give the impression of indolence but I assure you that it's only skin-deep ... and he'd have annihilated Horton between breakfast and lunch.' Jack took her hands in a comforting clasp. 'So this is where it stops. You must see that. Tell Rock the truth; now – tonight.'

'I can't. Not just yet. We're ... we're barely speaking to each other as it is and I don't think either of us could cope with this as well.' She hesitated and then said, doggedly, 'I have to buy time – and make one last attempt to make Richard let go.'

'You'll never do it. Once a leech, always a leech,' he said flatly. And then, sighing, 'All right. I must be mad – because I think you're making a colossal error of judgement – but, if you're truly set on this, you'd better let me handle it.'

This shook her. '*You?*'

'Yes. But only on one condition,' came the firm reply. 'That, on the morning after the Queensberry ball and no matter *what* the circumstances, you tell Rock everything. Agreed?'

'Yes.' She managed a crooked smile. 'I promise. And thank you.'

'Don't thank me – just do what I ask. Because if you don't, *I* will. I can't say I'm comfortable going behind his back in this way and -- '

'Do you think I am?'

'No.' He grinned ruefully. 'But he'll forgive you quicker than he'll forgive me.'

'Not necessarily,' murmured Adeline miserably.

'Of course he will. Once he knows how frightened and upset you've been, how can he not?' said Jack, rising. 'I'll see your uncle as soon as I'm able and do what I can. In the meantime, stop worrying and try to mend matters with Rock. I don't know what the two of you have quarrelled about and I don't *want* to know – but the sooner you make it up, the better for all of us.' He grinned suddenly. 'You may not have realised it, but you're not the only sufferer. It's making him extremely touchy and putting a nasty edge on his tongue.'

'Dear me,' drawled a soft, mocking voice, 'Who *can* you mean, I wonder?'

The pit of Adeline's stomach fell away and she flushed hotly. Framed in the doorway, one white hand holding back the heavy curtain, Rockliffe regarded her with lethal urbanity.

'You,' replied Mr Ingram calmly. 'You know perfectly well we're all tired of walking on broken glass – and I thought Adeline might be able to help. The only trouble is, she's as stubborn as you are.'

'I see.' The Duke let fall the curtain and advanced slowly. 'How busy you all are about my concerns. It is beginning to weary me. And you must, surely, have other interests?'

'We have. But --'

'Then pray attend to them. I find I object … rather strongly … to both curiosity and interference. And – much though I may regret it – I am quite willing to press the point, if necessary.' He paused, meeting Jack's gaze with cold amusement. 'I'm sure you understand me.'

'Oh for God's sake, stop being so damned ridiculous,' came the irritable and largely unexcited retort. 'I've told you before – it'll be a cold day in hell before I let you provoke me into crossing swords with you. And particularly over something like this.'

Against all expectation, a glimmer of humour dawned in the veiled gaze.

'Still craven, Jack?'

'No. Still sensible.'

'Ah. And do you consider it sensible to closet yourself away with my wife for a full fifteen minutes?' asked his Grace sweetly. 'For, if so, I believe I must acquaint you with your mistake.'

*

In another quiet corner, Harry Caversham was reprehensibly instructing Nell in the art of throwing dice.

'Beginner's luck!' he taunted when she won for the third time. 'No doubt you're sorry now that you wouldn't name a stake.'

Flushed with pleasure, Nell nodded and said, 'That's easily mended, though. What do you want to play for?'

'Anything you like. A flower from your corsage?'

'Done!' She cast the dice enthusiastically, causing one of the small ivory cubes to bounce towards the edge of the table. '*Oh!*'

Seeing it about to fall, she dived forward to catch it ... only to find herself almost nose to nose with Harry as he did the same. And then, without warning, the inevitable happened. The laughter faded from the blue eyes, leaving an expression that set her nerves tingling; and, as if it were the most natural thing in the world, they moved slowly into each other's arms.

Aeons of time later, Harry said hazily, 'Are you going to marry me, you witch?'

And Nell, with a tiny gurgle of delicious laughter said, 'Yes. I suppose I'd better, hadn't I?'

'Minx.' He indulged in the absorbing pastime of feathering her neck with kisses. Then, 'Of course, you know what this means, don't you?'

'Yes,' said Nell, finding it difficult to speak. 'What?'

'I'm going to have to call on Rock. Again.' His shoulders shook a little. 'Only *this* time he'll be so glad to see me, he'll probably fall on my neck.'

*

If, on the following morning, Rockliffe did not actually fulfil this prophecy, he was at least pleased enough to send down for a bottle of the best Chambertin. And when Nell – who, since seeing Harry arrive, had been prowling excitedly around Adeline upstairs – decided she could wait no longer and put her head round the library door, he did not even object to the damage her raptures inflicted on his coat.

Once Adeline had also joined them and toasts had been drunk, his Grace said blandly, 'It seems, my dear, that you will have to revise your plans a little.'

'What plans?' asked Adeline. And then, 'Oh. You mean our party.'

'Just so. I think your small reception had better become a dress-ball in honour of the betrothal. Will that suit you, Nell?'

'Yes, please!' she beamed, one hand tucked into Harry's. 'Only ... do we have to wait till then before letting it be known?'

'Do you think you can?'

'No,' grinned his lordship.

'No. I thought not.' Rockliffe smiled faintly. 'I shall therefore have a notice inserted in the *Morning Chronicle* ... the day after tomorrow, I think.'

'The Queensberry ball,' said Nell promptly. 'Wonderful!'

'Quite. You shouldn't have too much difficulty keeping your secret till then ... and I see no reason why we should not steal some of the duchess's thunder.'

Adeline's mind wandered again. It began to seem that there was nothing left which did *not* hinge upon the Queensberry ball – and she was getting sick of the very sound of it. Nervily, she wondered how soon she could expect to hear from Jack or whether it would be more sensible to just send him a message telling him to stay out of it. During the course of a sleepless night and with her wits functioning properly again, it had become abundantly clear that, in involving Jack rather than her husband, she was making exactly the same mistake she'd made with Harry and Nell. And if Tracy had been angry before, this time he was likely to be incandescent.

She became aware that Harry was taking his leave, escorted by a radiant Nell. Suddenly and alarmingly alone with Rockliffe, Adeline kept her eyes fixed on her hands – half-expecting some sarcastic remark about the previous evening.

It did not come. Instead, sounding rather tired, he said, 'This can't go on, Adeline. We need to get past it ... but I don't know what I can do. I'm not blaming you – I'm aware of just how many of the faults are mine – but you don't leave me with many options.'

'I know.' Slowly, she looked up at him, for once not bothering to veil her expression. 'I know ... and I'm sorry. But, like you, I don't know how to mend it.'

He absorbed the unhappiness in her eyes and thought, *I could mend it. I could mend it right now... but you won't let me. And if you push me away again, we'll be worse off than we are now because I don't think I could stand it.* He said, 'Then perhaps you should take a little time to think about what you want. And then, when you are ready, we can talk.'

She nodded and then, as if the words were being torn from her, 'But it isn't your fault. None of it is. You never did anything to deserve ….' She stopped, trying to steady her voice. 'I hate this as much as you do.'

'Well, that's a start, I suppose.' Rockliffe's mouth curled in something not quite a smile. 'Perhaps we can build on that. And, in the meantime, I'll try to be less ... difficult.' He walked to the door and then, turning back, said so softly that she almost did not hear it, 'I miss you.'

And left her grimly holding back the tears she wouldn't shed – along with the terrible urge to run after him and tell him everything. Instead, she fled up to her room and started writing a note to Jack, only to realise that – after paying Phanie for that extravagant gown, she had no way of finding five hundred guineas before tomorrow.

*

It was not until the following afternoon that Mr Ingram finally found Mr Horton at home – and, by then, he had paid no less than three calls in South Street, where he'd been forced to make laborious conversation with Althea's mother and sister. Consequently, when he was at last alone with his quarry, he was too intent on accomplishing his task to notice that one of the doors of the parlour had been left very slightly ajar.

'I'll come straight to the point,' he said crisply. 'I'm here on behalf of the Duchess of Rockliffe. I imagine you know why?'

Mr Horton's eyes narrowed a fraction and then he said smoothly, 'I am not at all sure that I do. Suppose you tell me.'

'As you wish. You told Adeline that her mother did not die but, in fact, eloped with her lover. You showed her a letter confirming this and further suggested that her own birth was ... questionable. You then demanded money from her under the threat of making these things known – first to the Duke and then to the world.' Jack paused, smiling grimly. 'I have come to inform you that the game is over.'

There was a long silence. Then Richard said, 'And just what leads you to suppose that you can stop it?'

'The draft I have in my pocket for five hundred guineas – which you won't get without first handing me your sister's letter and also writing a few lines of your own, indicating your family's solid belief in her Grace's legitimacy,' came the cool reply. 'It all depends on how much you need the money. But I think we both know the answer to that, don't we? I imagine you've had some difficulty finding suitable partners at the card table recently.'

'Damnable lies.' Mr Horton lost a little of his polish and his smile vanished. 'However, you can't be surprised that - thanks to whoever began them - the price of what you want is far in excess of a paltry five hundred.'

'You may think so. But the buyer sets the price.'

'I doubt if the Duke would agree with you. I'm sure he would consider the purity of the Wynstanton name to be worth ... shall we say two thousand?'

'You can say it, by all means,' Jack retorted easily. 'But the truth is he's more likely to spit you on the end of his sword. And if it wasn't for Adeline and Thea, I'd be more than happy to let him.'

'If Rockliffe knew,' said Richard, 'you wouldn't be here. So it seems I still hold an ace or two.'

'Not for long. You have roughly thirty-six hours in which to either accept my offer or risk being filleted.' Jack smiled again and added conversationally, 'He's quite good, you know.'

Mr Horton did know and it was the very reason he had hoped to continue threatening his niece. He was not particularly well-acquainted with Rockliffe but he had a feeling that he was not the man to submit tamely to being squeezed – and that therefore, once he knew what was afoot, the game would indeed be up. Richard did not consider himself a fool and he was perfectly well aware that there was little point in proceeding once his bluff was called – for Rockliffe's credit with the world was great enough to withstand a twenty-year-old scandal. His own – and that of his family, on the other hand – was not; and it was he and Miriam and Diana who would suffer most from disclosure. Adeline, luckily, had been too shaken too realise that ... but Rockliffe would see it immediately. And Mr Horton had no desire to measure blades with one who was generally held to be an expert.

He smiled and said composedly, 'Very well. I take your point. But the price of what you want is still two thousand.'

Jack thought quickly, debating the odds and reluctantly coming to the conclusion that time was not on his side. He said, 'A thousand. And that's my last word. Take it or leave it.'

'I'll take it,' came the unruffled reply. 'Naturally. And you can tell Adeline that I hope she spends the rest of her life wondering. Because unless she finds Joanna, she'll never know.'

'Hold your tongue and write,' snapped Jack. 'Or I may forget you are Thea's uncle and lay hands on you myself.'

Mr Horton's eyes sneered but he had no intention of risking his person. Pulling Joanna's letter from his pocket, he tossed it on the table. Then, crossing languidly to the bureau, he sat down and began to write at Mr Ingram's brisk dictation.

Silent and unseen behind the partly open door, Diana flexed her cramped muscles and smiled to herself. It had been a surprisingly interesting half-hour and what she had learned was undoubtedly valuable. The only question now, was how best to use it.

*

On learning that Nell and Adeline had resolved upon a quiet evening at home in order to conserve their energies for the morrow, Rockliffe stated his intention of dining at White's and left the house. He drank a couple of glasses of wine, played a hand of cards with Charles Fox and ate a meal he didn't enjoy. And all the time, his mind was on Adeline.

'*I hate this as much as you do,*' she'd said. And it was evident in the bleak, almost despairing look in her eyes and the emerging shadows beneath them, lying stark against the flat pallor of her face. He thought, *Am I responsible for that? Because if I am ... or if, as I suspect, something is frightening her – why am I not* doing *something about it instead of making it worse?*

The business with Harry and Nell had made him angry – and justifiably so. But he ought to have been able to put it behind him before now - and the fact that he'd come back from Paris with a ring in his pocket and the hope that, this time, he would be able to tell Adeline that he loved her, was no excuse. It was becoming obvious that neither of them could stand much more of this ... and if he didn't do something about it soon, there would be nothing left to salvage.

Which left him with what? The only thing he hadn't tried yet because he'd hoped he wouldn't need to. Unfortunately, it was also the only thing that he could be fairly sure would work. Pushing aside his wine glass, he rose from the table, bade Mr Fox a pleasant, if brief, goodnight ... and went home to seduce his wife.

*

Back in St James' Square, Adeline had spent two hours trying to listen to Nell's prattle without fidgeting unduly. Then, as the clock struck ten, salvation appeared in the unlikely guise of the butler.

'Mr Ingram has called, your Grace,' announced Symonds with the merest hint of disapproval. 'Do you wish me to admit him?'

'Why not?' Adeline came smartly to her feet. 'Show him in.'

Nell's brows rose but she waited for the butler to withdraw before saying, 'Now what on earth can Jack want at this hour?'

'It – it's a family matter,' responded Adeline desperately. 'And private.'

'I see.' The dark eyes examined her speculatively for a moment and then Nell also rose. 'Then it's fortunate that I was about to retire, isn't it? But you'd best take care what you're about, Adeline. Rock's behaving very oddly these days.' And on this worldly-wise, if cryptic note, she walked out of the room.

Thirty seconds later, Jack entered it and said, by way of greeting, 'What's the matter with Nell? She just passed me without so much as a word - but smiling most peculiarly.'

'She's being discreet,' said Adeline. 'Forget Nell. Just sit down and tell me. Have you seen Richard?'

'Yes.' He drew two papers from his pocket and handed them to her. 'And you can stop worrying. It's over.'

Adeline scanned both sheets and then sat down rather abruptly.

'Thank God – thank God. But *how*, Jack? How did you do it?'

So he told her and, by the time he had finished, she did not know if she was laughing or crying.

'I don't know what to say. I'd begun to think I'd never be free of him – never. And now you tell me it's over and even the *relief* is more than I can bear.' She fought for control for a moment and then, rising, held out her hands to him. 'I'll pay you back as soon as I can, of course ... but I doubt I'll ever be able to thank you sufficiently. You – you can't know what it means to me.'

Smiling into the over-bright eyes, he took her hands into a comforting clasp and said, 'Oh I think I do. And you've no need to thank me. I'm happy to have been of service – and, also, I'm grateful. But for you I'd not have known precisely what a blackguard Richard Horton is ... and that's important.' He grimaced ruefully. 'The sooner I have Thea safe, the better. It seems to me that house is a veritable vipers' nest.'

'It is. And Thea has never belonged there.'

'I know it. And neither, my dear, did you.'

Her mouth curled and she gave a small, husky laugh.

'There's a difference. *I* could hold my own.'

'And can you still?' He released her hands and grinned quizzically. 'With Rock, for example?'

'No. But that's an entirely different matter.'

'Yes.' He paused and then said, 'You love him very much, don't you?'

'Yes. Very much. And now, thanks to you, I can tell him.' Placing her hands on his shoulders, she reached up to kiss his cheek. 'So thank you with all my heart.'

'This,' remarked his Grace of Rockliffe icily from the doorway, 'is becoming a habit – and one, moreover, which does not commend itself to me. No – pray don't trouble to explain.' This as Jack would have spoken. 'I have absolutely no desire to tax your powers of invention for a second time. And really ... one way and another ... I believe I have heard enough.'

He turned on his heel and was gone.

'Hell!' breathed Mr Ingram.

'And damnation,' agreed Adeline, the colour draining from her face. 'Go home, Jack. There's nothing to be done tonight and it would be a mistake to try. But as soon as this wretched ball is over tomorrow, I'll put everything right. I promise.'

'Forgive my asking,' he said wryly, 'but do you think you can?'

'I don't know. I hope so – for you, at any rate.' She met his gaze with bitter candour. 'As for myself … well, we'll see. I'll tell Tracy everything and hope he listens. If I'm lucky, he may even understand – though I suppose I shouldn't count on it. For the last two months, I've been dogged by nothing less than total disaster.'

TWENTY-TWO

There was no denying, thought Adeline, as she examined herself critically in the glass, that the shimmering, shot-silk gown was a triumph. The blue of a peacock's throat, it changed to violet when she moved ... and the bodice was trimmed only with entwined ribbons of those two shades. The sweeping neckline clung to the points of her shoulders, the narrow sleeves ended at the elbow in a clever overlay of silk petals and the slyly whispering skirt was drawn back over a petticoat that echoed the dress but in reverse ... violet to peacock. The only difficulty was in deciding which of her jewels would best compliment the shifting, vibrant shade. Tracy, of course, would have known instantly ... but he hadn't attended her *toilette* for so long that it was stupid to hope he might do so now. Especially after last night.

Sighing, she told Jeanne to bring her the Wynstanton diamonds. She had never worn them before but the occasion seemed to warrant full armour and, after what had happened last time, she couldn't bring herself to wear the aquamarine set.

By the time Nell sailed into the room, she was ready ... diamonds at her throat and on her wrists, and her hair piled in loose curls with feathers fastened by a diamond clip nestling behind her left ear. Nell stopped dead and stared.

'Oh!' she breathed. 'Adeline, you look beautiful. That gown is ... *amazing*.'

'Thank you – and yes. It is, isn't it?' She smiled and absorbed the glory of Nell's gold net over white satin. 'You look rather splendid yourself. Harry will be dazzled.'

'That was the idea,' confided Nell. 'He's here, by the way. I asked Symonds to let me know the instant he arrived. I didn't want to go down before he came, you see.'

'Naturally not. If you can't make a Grand Entrance tonight, when can you?'

'That's what I thought.' She dimpled mischievously. 'So let's go and do it together – and see if we can't render *both* of our gentlemen speechless.'

'That,' observed Adeline dryly, 'will be the day. But I suppose it's worth a try.'

Descending to the turn of the stair, they paused to look down on the hall below where his lordship was engaging Rockliffe in desultory conversation. By prior consultation with Nell, Harry wore a coat of dull gold brocade and had chosen, for this one special evening, to leave his fair head unpowdered. He had never looked more handsome and Nell glowed with pride. Adeline, however, had eyes only for her husband … elegantly saturnine in silver-laced black with the Order of the Garter displayed upon his chest and diamonds winking on his fingers and in his cravat. As always, his hair was confined at the nape in long sable ribbons – to which, tonight, was added a narrow diamond clasp; and as had been his habit again in recent weeks, it was thickly powdered. Adeline sighed.

Then the night-dark eyes were upon her, causing the now familiar dissolving of her bones and he said with only a hint of mockery, 'Behold, Harry. We are meant, I believe, to be dumbstruck.'

Fortunately, Harry was - and while he was gallantly presenting Nell with a corsage of yellow roses, Adeline took the opportunity to say as quickly and quietly as she could, 'Tracy – I know you're annoyed but -- '

Annoyed? he thought. *Darling, you have no idea!* But said blandly, 'Now why should you suppose that?'

'You know why. And you can say whatever you like to me later. But don't … please don't let it spoil Nell's evening.'

'I doubt very much if anything can spoil Nell's evening,' he drawled. 'On the other hand, if you insist on slipping away to kiss my friends, it may very well spoil mine.' He surveyed her appraisingly and then offered his arm. 'You look exquisite, by the way. The diamonds suit you. Shall we go?'

To which, of course, there was no answer whatsoever.

Queensberry House was already bidding fair to become crowded when they arrived and Harry and Nell were instantly besieged by well-wishers and affectionate teasing.

'I do think you might have *told* me,' said Cassie Delahaye in mock-dudgeon. 'It was quite monstrous of you to leave me to read it in the *Morning Chronicle*. Indeed, if I wasn't so very pleased for you both, I'd probably not speak to you at all.'

'Well, I did want to tell you,' owned Nell, 'but Harry said that if I once began, there'd be no stopping me – and he was right, of course!' She paused and looked doubtfully at her friend. 'Are you *sure* you're not just a little cross with me?'

'You mean,' grinned Cassie, 'am I jealous? Yes – absolutely *green*. But only on account of your luck, you silly creature. Harry's a darling ... but I never had an eye to him myself. And much good it would have done me if I had – for it was always plain as anything that you and he belonged together.'

Having congratulated Harry and left him talking to Rosalind, the Marquis of Amberley directed a thoughtful gaze at his Grace and said, 'Well, Rock? Are you pleased?'

'I believe so,' came the languid reply. 'I had thought better of Harry's intelligence, of course ... but there's no accounting for taste, I suppose. And, oddly enough, he appears well able to cope with her.'

'That must be a comfort to you. But it's a good match - and universally popular by the look of things.' He paused. 'At the risk of receiving another rebuff, am I allowed to ask if you and Adeline have ... resolved your difficulties?'

Rockliffe looked at him. 'You can ask. I'm no more inclined to talk about my marriage now than I was a week ago. I do, however, apologise for my lack of manners.'

'Oh – well, that's all right then!' retorted the Marquis with rare sarcasm. And then, sighing, 'I sometimes despair of you, Rock. But if *you're* not going to dance with your wife, I trust you won't mind if *I* do.'

'By all means – if you can prise her away from March and promise to keep her out of secluded alcoves.'

'*What?*'

'Nothing.'

His lordship's brows rose.

'If I didn't know better, I'd think you were jealous.'

'No. This is something else,' said Rockliffe thoughtfully, as he watched the minuet draw to a close. Then, as if reaching a decision, he muttered something under his breath that, to Amberley, sounded suspiciously like 'Buggrit!' and strode purposefully across the floor, leaving the Marquis to stroll behind him, laughing.

'March, my dear fellow – you won't mind if I steal my wife for a moment?' his Grace said pleasantly, taking a firm grip on Adeline's arm. 'No. I thought not. Adeline – a brief word with you, if I may?' And he drew her inexorably out on to the chilly, deserted terrace.

Completely startled, she said, 'Tracy? What -- ?'

Then his arms were round her and his mouth stifled both words and thought. She had wondered if he would ever kiss her again ... and, if he did, whether it would produce the same dizzying response. It did more. Fire rushed through every fibre of her body and stars exploded around her. She gasped ... and he deepened the kiss until he felt her clinging weakly to him. Then, slowly, he released her.

'I thought,' he said, as if nothing had happened, 'that if you wanted to kiss someone this evening, it might as well be me.' Completely disorientated and beyond speech, Adeline allowed him to lead her back into the ballroom. 'Dominic is waiting to dance with you. Hopefully, it is now safe for him to do so.' And, placing her hand on Amberley's velvet sleeve, he strolled unhurriedly away.

The Marquis looked down into dazed aquamarine eyes with some amusement and said, 'What was that all about?'

She shook her head as if to clear it. 'I don't know. He ...'

'He what?'

Adeline swallowed, summoned a smile and said, 'Nothing.'

In another room and exquisitely gowned in blue, Diana Franklin found her path suddenly blocked by Mistress Garfield.

'Di – *dearest*! How lovely you look.'

Diana smiled and let her gaze travel over Cecily's expensive but grossly over-trimmed pink satin.

'Thank you. I'd say the same to you, if I could – but you know I've always held that pink makes you look sallow.'

Cecily's undistinguished eyes narrowed a little but she continued to smile.

'How irritable you are this evening. But one can hardly wonder at it, of course. You must be feeling dreadfully low. I only wish I knew what to say to cheer you up – but it's rather difficult. You really aren't having much luck lately, are you?'

Diana stared at her freezingly.

'I haven't the faintest idea what you're talking about – and, to be honest, I don't care. Excuse me.'

'Wait! Do you *really* not know?'

'Know what?'

A gleam of avid pleasure informed Cecily's sharp features.

'But, my *dear* ... about Harry Caversham and Nell. Haven't you heard? They're betrothed.'

Quite slowly, the blood drained away from Diana's skin leaving her patchily pale. She said distantly, 'I don't believe it.'

'Well, it's true, I assure you. The notice was in the newspaper this morning. I can't understand how it was that you didn't see it. And they're in the ballroom this very minute, receiving everyone's felicitations.'

Diana discovered that she felt rather sick.

'If you're making this up,' she said viciously, 'I swear I'll make you sorry for it.'

'Don't be stupid, Di. Where would be the point of making it up?' Cecily paused to savour the moment. 'I'm just sorry I had to be the one to tell you. It must be a horrid shock – particularly when we all know you had such hopes of attaching Harry yourself – *oh!*' This as Diana pushed her violently aside in order to blaze a trail towards the ballroom.

It took no more than a few seconds' observation to convince Diana that Cecily had spoken the truth ... but much longer than that for her brain to start functioning again. She looked at Nell in her gold and white gown, leaning laughingly on Harry's arm whilst replying to words thrown at her by Philip Vernon and Mr Fox ... and then at the expression of tender amusement in his lordship's blue eyes as he smiled down upon her. For a time, the picture had no more meaning than a scene in a play; and then, deep down inside her, something began to stir.

Harry had cheated her. He'd flirted with her and deliberately led her to suppose that his intentions towards her were serious. But they hadn't been. He'd probably always intended to have Nell ... and she, Diana, had been his dupe. It was not something she was prepared to tolerate.

Of its own volition, Diana's gaze moved on to encompass her twin, moving lightly through the gavotte with Jack Ingram. Thea had been different of late ... less admiring and a good deal more assertive. It wasn't satisfactory – and neither was the improvement in her looks. Thea was becoming just a little too pleased with herself; and the cause of it was that dull, ordinary man who'd not only been stupid enough to prefer Thea to herself but also dared take her in open dislike. He ought to be made to regret that, thought Diana clinically; and then, looking on Althea's transparent happiness, 'They both *should*.'

Adeline danced by with the Marquis of Amberley ... and the cornflower eyes followed her stonily. Who would have thought that her dowdy cousin could have acquired such style? But so it was. From the curling, peacock-dyed feathers in her luxuriant hair, to the high jewelled heels of her shoes, Adeline was the epitome of seemingly effortless elegance. Her gown – almost devoid of trimming but of such cut and so daring a shade that it made every other woman in the room look insipid – could only have come from the master-hand of Phanie and must have cost upwards of three hundred guineas. And the diamonds sparkling on her wrists and around that slender white throat caused Diana's hands to clench savagely on her fan. She would have sold her soul for those diamonds ...and, but for Adeline, she would almost certainly have had them.

At this point it was no more than a logical progression to let her glance seek out Rockliffe; and, though she had not anticipated the hot tide of feeling that surged through her when she found him, she was not surprised by it. She had known for a long time that he was her evil genius and somehow responsible for all the ills that had befallen her.

She looked at him now, standing slightly apart in his magnificent black and silver and doing nothing to court attention, yet in some way commanding it. He was, without question, the most attractive man in the room ... tall, perfectly-proportioned and, above all, *masculine*. And those dark, enigmatic eyes ... that just now were resting so intently on – whom? Diana interrupted her train of thought to find out – and then stiffened as the knife twisted unexpectedly in her stomach.

Adeline. He was watching Adeline ... and watching her, moreover, as though no one else existed. The blood began to seethe in Diana's veins. She thought, *'So that's the way of it, is it? What a fool he is ... what fools they all are! But I could change that. I wonder how his Grace will like to learn that his precious duchess is on such intimate terms with his good friend Jack that she tells him all her dirty secrets? I wonder how he'll feel if he hears that he's probably married a* bastard?'

A little smile curved her mouth and her eyes gleamed with malice. A sense of power flowed through her, as exhilarating as wine; and, with a step as light as it was predatory, she bore down on Rockliffe.

His gaze was still on Adeline and his mood, one of determination. In recent weeks, he had somehow lost sight of the fact that there was an explosion of sparks whenever they came together. Last night he'd gone home intending to seduce her but had let Jack's unexpected presence deflect him. Tonight, he would make no such mistake. Tonight, come hell or high water, he intended to turn the sparks into a full-blown conflagration; and then ... then he might finally find out if he had her heart as well.

'Good evening, your Grace. Are you admiring your wife – or keeping an eye on her? I'm sure you could be forgiven for either one.'

Rockliffe looked down into the jewel-hard eyes and took his time about replying. Under normal circumstances, he would have nipped this overture firmly in the bud. Just now, however, his particular devil was stirring ... and Mistress Di was as good a target as any.

He said gently, 'And why is that?'

'I should have thought that was obvious,' she shrugged. And then, as though changing the subject, 'Nell looks happy. One can only hope it lasts.'

'But you, of course, doubt that it will.'

'Don't you? You must know that Harry only - ' She broke off artistically. 'Well, let's just say he is a desperate flirt.'

His Grace smiled.

'I am not sure of my cue. Do I observe that it is a case of pot calling kettle – or simply remark that it takes one to know one?'

Something flickered in the blue eyes and then was gone.

'Oh - that! That was nothing.'

'No,' agreed the Duke. 'So Harry has said.'

'Has he? Well, well.' Her voice thickened with spite. 'And has he also said that there's nothing between himself and Adeline? Because if there isn't, I'd not wager a groat that there soon won't be. Why else is he marrying Nell?'

Rockliffe appeared to be in rapt contemplation of his snuff-box.

'You are the one who appears to have all the answers. You tell me.'

'To make it easier for him to be close to Adeline, of course. I should have thought you were bright enough to have worked that one out for yourself.'

'Did you? Then you did me an injustice, my dear.' His tone was like honeyed silk but his eyes, when he looked at her, held an expression of icy contempt. 'You see ... unlike yours, my mind is not filled with sordid imaginings.'

Diana's mouth contorted, showing small sharp teeth.

'The truth hurts, doesn't it? But go on deluding yourself, if you like. It's nothing to me. I'm just sorry for you all ... you and Nell and my poor sister. Yes – particularly for Thea.'

'Desolate as I am to be obliged to contradict you,' came the blighting reply, 'it has to be said that you have never been sorry for anyone in your life. *Particularly* your sister. Your problem, at this precise moment, is that you are jealous.'

'*Jealous*? Not I! Why should I be?'

'I should have thought,' he mocked, 'that the reason was obvious. Despite your undeniable beauty, you are being forced to watch others succeeding where you have failed. In short, Mistress, you are just beginning to suspect that you may be unmarriageable ... and you still don't know why.'

'It's a lie!' she spat breathlessly. 'I'm not unmarriageable – I'm just choosier than some. *I* won't make do with other people's leavings.'

'It's unlikely that you will ever be given the chance.' The lean mouth curled in a hard, derisory smile. 'It is plain that you have accosted me for the purpose of saying something I should probably much prefer not to hear ... and, in a moment, I shall permit you to do so. But first you must allow me the satisfaction of informing you that you are undoubtedly the most vain, selfish, and unprincipled brat it has ever been my misfortune to meet ... and the man who is foolish enough to marry you will have my profoundest sympathy.'

For almost a minute, Diana's fury threatened to choke her. Something was boiling inside her and the closing strains of the gavotte seemed to come from a long way off. The sticks of her fan snapped in her hands as she fought for control of her lungs. Then she said unevenly, 'Save your sympathy for yourself, your Grace. By the time you've heard what I have to say, I doubt you'll have any to spare.'

'By the time I hear what you have to say,' drawled Rockliffe, flicking open his silver snuff-box, 'I am likely to have expired from pure boredom.'

The bubbling cauldron inside her brain reached its zenith and was propelled, by the sheer unconcern of his manner, into violent explosion. Freed of its last feeble constraint, her self-control snapped and she hissed, '*Bastard!*' Then, her voice starting to rise, 'You're a bastard – and that's funny, if you only knew why! But you don't, do you? Shall I tell you? Or shall I just tell you to ask your dear friend Jack? *He* knows. She told him. *She told him*, do you hear? But she didn't tell you, did she? It's so funny – I vow I could die laughing!'

The gavotte had finished and, in the area around them, people were already staring; so Rockliffe refrained from saying that he rather wished she would and, instead, snapping shut the lid of his snuff-box, said coldly, 'You are distraught. Were it not that I am all too well aware what could come of it, I might offer to listen to you in private. As it is, I can only suggest that you strive for a little self-discipline and abandon this … charade … until you are calmer.'

'Oh no!' She backed off a little way, wild-eyed and laughing. 'You won't stop me like that – no, nor frighten me with your clever little threats, either! I'm going to tell you something interesting about my sweet, irresistible cousin and there's nothing you or anyone can do to stop me!'

The silence was spreading and a space was beginning to yawn about them. Behind Diana, the dance-floor had all but emptied and, strewn in little knots along its edges, the cream of London society was gradually congealing in blank astonishment.

Inwardly cursing himself for letting it get this far, the Duke said softly, 'You have overlooked one small thing. I can deprive your drama of point by refusing to listen.' And, turning his back on her, he started to walk away.

'Go, then!' she jeered shrilly. And, with a bright, sweeping glance, 'There's audience enough to suit my purposes – and they say, don't they, that the husband is always the last to know? So go, your Grace. Then you can be the last to find out that your slut of a wife's a bastard!'

Rockliffe stopped as if turned to stone. Then, very slowly, he turned round. Throughout the whole of the Duchess of Queensberry's vast, magnificent ballroom the silence was so acute that he could hear the whispering wind-song of the great crystal chandeliers. His gaze took in Althea, clinging to Jack's arm and looking ready to faint … Harry, half-baffled and half-murderous … Lady Franklin, belatedly moving like a sleep-walker towards her ungovernable child. And, finally, Adeline … standing at the far end of the room beside Isabel Vernon, her face paper-white and her wide, horrified eyes staring straight into his.

'Well?' demanded Diana. 'Are you deaf – or is it that, just for once, you've nothing to say?'

'I say that it is a damnable lie,' replied Rockliffe, in a tone calculated to cut to the bone. 'My wife is as well-born as you are – and a hundred times better bred.'

'Diana!' Lady Franklin had arrived at last. 'You are quite hysterical and making a complete exhibition of yourself. Now stop this foolishness at once and come -- '

'*Foolishness*?' The force with which the girl threw off her mother's restraining hand sent her ladyship staggering backwards. 'You ought to have told him. If you'd told him, he wouldn't have married her. I'll never forgive you for that – never!'

Despite all his months of care, Rockliffe could see the ground opening up in front of him and, in a final bid to avert catastrophe, he said curtly, 'Lady Franklin – take your daughter home. Now.'

'What do you think I'm trying to do?' Her voice shook and she looked ill. 'Richard ... I need my brother, Richard.'

'Oh yes. Don't we all?' Diana laughed harshly. 'Or no – I was forgetting. Adeline doesn't, does she?' She paused, looking round again. 'But where is she? Where *is* my poor fatherless cousin? I'd hate for her to miss all the fun.'

'I'm here.' Sheathed in a curious frozen detachment, Adeline stepped forward into no-man's land. 'Say what you have to say and let us be done with it.'

'*Dominic*!' The word cracked like a pistol shot and Rockliffe's eyes flew to command those of his friend. 'For God's sake --'

'Yes.' The Marquis was already on the move.

'No.' It was Adeline who spoke. 'No. It's too late, don't you see? She's said too much already and, short of physical restraint, she's going to finish it. So it's only fair that I hear it.'

'Of course it is,' nodded Diana. 'And you'll want to see his face, won't you? The noble Duke who only married you because you appeared compromised. You were clever there, Adeline ... and he fell for it, didn't he? He fell neatly into your little trap and married you. So now you want to know how he'll look when he finds out that his mama-in-law – my late lamented Aunt Joanna – isn't really dead at all ... but actually living in some cosy love-nest with her paramour!'

If the hush had been deathly before, it was now positively electric. Rockliffe let it seep into every sinew and fibre and then, without taking his eyes from Adeline, said calmly, 'But I knew that. I could even tell you where the ... love-nest ... is.'

He saw the uncontrollable shudder that ripped through her and his soul wept. In every other respect, however, the effect of his words was exactly what he'd hoped. A collective murmur of shock echoed around the room and Diana's jaw dropped.

He had never felt less like smiling but he did it anyway and said smoothly, 'I'm sorry if I have disappointed you. But if you have engineered this unpleasantly vulgar scene for no better purpose than to exhume a scandal that is already more than twenty years old, you have wasted your time. For, as anyone who knows me could have told you, I am rarely left in the dark – about anything.'

This time there was a ripple of uncertain laughter. He was winning – but it was small consolation when Adeline was staring at him out of stark, lightless eyes as though she had never seen him before. He tried to communicate courage to her and held out his hand, inviting her to cross the floor to his side ... but then, swift as a hawk, Diana struck again.

'So you know. But you didn't find out from *her*, did you?'

'Does it matter?' A spasm of utter distaste crossed the Duke's face. 'I think you've edified us enough.'

'More than enough.' Leaving Althea leaning on Cassie Delahaye, Jack stepped into the fray. 'And if no one else is willing to put a stop to this, *I* will!'

'Ah!' Eyes blazing, Diana wheeled round to face him. 'You want to prevent me telling them all you're Adeline's lover!'

A gasp ran round the room and Jack halted mid-stride, looking decidedly sick. He said, 'That is both untrue and completely ridiculous. I'm betrothed to your sister.'

'So you are. Poor, simple Thea. She's not hard to deceive, is she? But *I* know better. And if Adeline's *not* your mistress, how come she tells you things she won't tell her husband? Why,' she finished, on a rising crescendo of triumph, 'did she send *you* to pay off my uncle?'

The heavy lids flew wide and Rockliffe impaled Diana on a hard, dark stare.

'*What did you say?*'

'You heard. She sent Jack to buy my uncle off. I heard it all.'

Seconds ticked by in silence and then the whispering started. Rockliffe and Adeline remained remote as statues, their eyes locked together; Althea began to cry; and Mr Ingram, with murder in his face, resumed his advance on Diana.

'No, Jack.' His Grace turned at last and, though his voice was smooth as ever, the pure rage in his eyes sufficed to kill the whispers and make Mr Ingram halt in his tracks. 'We have arrived – albeit somewhat laboriously – at the point where Mistress Diana finally begins to interest me. Indeed, I sense that it may well prove to be the crux of the matter.' He paused to sweep the room with a glance of stinging mockery. 'And when our friends have borne with us so patiently, it would be uncharitable to deny them the climax, don't you think?'

Jack, who understood only too well that he was being punished, compressed his lips and said nothing.

'Just so,' agreed Rockliffe, sardonically. The dark eyes drifted inimically to Adeline, dragging her painfully from her frail carapace of ice and driving her to cover her mouth with one shaking hand before stumbling blindly from the room. Dispassionately, he watched her go – followed quickly by Isabel and Rosalind; and then, seemingly satisfied, he strolled urbanely into the centre of the stage.

'Very well, Mistress. You have our undivided attention. But first I think we should complete the cast of our little comedy. Where, I wonder, is your uncle?'

'Skulking by the card-room door,' volunteered Harry Caversham grimly. 'And about to make a run for it.'

Rather pale beneath his paint, Richard Horton hesitated and found his arm being drawn in an iron grip through that of the Marquis of Amberley, who said cordially, 'You mustn't think of leaving us now. The performance might founder completely.'

Without quite knowing how it happened, Mr Horton found himself effectively marooned in the magic circle inhabited by his niece and the Duke. He stared at Diana, willing her to hold her tongue and then recognised, sickeningly, that she was completely beyond reason.

Beginning to sweat, he looked at Rockliffe – and wished he hadn't. All around were silent, watching eyes, none of them friendly. He tugged at his cravat and said chokingly, 'She – she's mad! My niece is mad – you must see that!'

'Yes,' agreed Rockliffe expressionlessly. 'I do see it. Indeed, I think the whole room does. However ... let us hear what else she has to say.' He turned a cold, inviting smile on Diana. 'We had reached the point where you were telling us that my wife sent Mr Ingram to buy your uncle off. Why was that?'

Diana's chin lifted and she held out her blue silk skirts as if to curtsy. Then, with a slow secret smile, she said, 'Because he threatened to tell everybody she was a bastard. She wouldn't have wanted you to know that, would she? So she paid him to keep quiet. Oh - and Uncle Richard had a letter from her mother. She wanted it back. But she must have got tired of paying him ... so Jack came and gave him a thousand guineas for the letter and on condition that he kept quiet and didn't ask for more money.'

There was a long airless pause. Then, 'I see,' said the Duke. 'Jack?'

'Yes.' Mr Ingram spoke curtly. 'It's true.'

'And do you know when this piece of gutter-debris started blackmailing Adeline?'

'Not exactly. It – I think it began when you went away that first time.'

'Thank you. That's all I need to know. For the moment.' Eyes glinting with incipient danger but his step as languid as ever, Rockliffe advanced on Mr Horton. 'Your sister, Joanna, described you as sly, sadistic and weak. To that we can add that you are a vicious, cheating liar of the kind any decent person would spit on.' He paused and then added coldly, 'Although you are not aware of it, you have caused me a considerable amount of trouble ... but it's possible I could have supported that. What I will *not* tolerate, however, is that you have gone out of your way to frighten and distress my wife with your threats and completely unfounded allegations.'

'Here it comes,' murmured Harry cheerfully in Nell's ear. 'He's going to challenge him.'

Mr Horton thought so too.

'I won't fight!' he said wildly. 'You'd kill me – I know you would. So say what you like – but I won't fight, I tell you!'

A slow, unpleasant smile bracketed his Grace's mouth.

'You won't be given the opportunity. A duel is an affair of honour between gentlemen,' he said, deliberately unlocking each lethal syllable. 'Neither of those qualities apply to you. And, rather than have it touch filth of your sort, I would as soon drop my sword in a midden.'

Upon which, Tracy Giles Wynstanton, fourth Duke of Rockliffe, astounded the noble company and delighted his friends by doing the unthinkable. Without any warning whatsoever, he smashed his fist into Horton's face.

The crack of bone sounded loud in the silence and Horton went down as if pole-axed, sliding across the polished floor, spewing blood and teeth. And the room erupted into a buzz of shocked chatter over which rose the eldritch descant of Diana's wild, hysterical laughter.

Seeing the Duke advancing on him, Mr Horton tried to drag himself away only to be stopped by the Marquis of Amberley's foot. Dropping on one knee, Rockliffe gripped the man's throat in one long-fingered hand and squeezed hard enough for him to cough up more blood. Then, so softly that only Amberley and his quarry could hear, he said, 'If you come near Adeline again, I promise that it will be the last thing you ever do. And now I suggest you take your hell-born niece, get out of my sight – and, if you're wise, *stay* out of it.'

Leaving Mr Horton to his own devices, Rockliffe ripped the bloodstained ruffles from his wrists and said, 'Dominic ... I doubt there's anything that can make this any better – but do what you can. I have to go.' And tossing the contaminated lace down with a gesture of complete disgust, he walked the length of the ballroom, its guests falling back to create a path for him ... and then was gone.

TWENTY-THREE

Driven from the ballroom by Rockliffe's hostile eyes, Adeline had succumbed, finally, to panic.

It was plain that he had known for some weeks about her mother – but not that she had known too and been paying Richard Horton so keep it from him. What that was likely to mean to him, she was as yet too emotionally battered to evaluate. All she was aware of was that she couldn't face him yet ... not until she'd had time to think.

She had reached the hall before she realised that Isabel and Rosalind were with her.

She said raggedly, 'I can't go home ... I have to get away.'

'You can't,' objected Isabel, shocked.

'Yes she can. It might be for the best,' said Rosalind decisively. 'She needs time and – after whatever's going on in there is over – so will Rock.' Concentration creased her brow and then she went on rapidly, 'She'll need a head start in case he follows. Isabel – let her take your carriage so she needn't go back to St James' Square. I'll take you home to Jermyn Street as soon as she's on her way. Adeline – I don't want to know where you're going but you should tell Isabel. Rock will come to me first and, apart from the fact that I don't *want* to lie to him, he'll know if I do. Once he gets to you, Isabel, it won't matter and you can tell him the truth. I'll wait here for you. Now go – *go!*'

Somehow, Adeline found herself outside, stripping off her necklace and bracelets with stiff, clumsy fingers while the carriage was brought round. Then, thanking Isabel with a swift kiss whilst piling the Wynstanton diamonds into her hands, she told the coachman to take her to Sittingbourne.

Throughout the journey her mind went round in circles, playing and re-playing the whole nightmarish scene in Queensberry House ... and always stopping in the same place. The moment when Tracy, realising the full extent of her deception, had looked at her with cold condemning eyes ... and she had known that there was nothing she could say now that would undo the damage.

She arrived at Wynstanton Priors an hour or so after dawn, directed the Vernon's coachman to the Rose in Sittingbourne and told him to lay whatever expenses he incurred to his Grace of Rockliffe's account. Then, avoiding the house, she walked down into the deserted park.

When he came she had been alone at the lakeside for an hour, gazing unseeingly across its glassy surface. The air was still and laden with bird-song and the early mist lay heavy on the water. Then the peace was shattered by the sound of hoof-beats and the bird-song became a flurry of beating wings as he rode into the clearing behind her.

Very slowly, Adeline turned to face him. For a moment, he sat motionless, staring down at her from eyes which, though no longer inimical, held a look that sent alarm feathering down her spine.

He watched her clutch the thin evening cloak about her, saw that her hair was falling down her back and the bottom of the peacock gown sodden from contact with the wet grass. And then, with a courtesy they both knew meant nothing, he said, 'I hope I haven't kept you waiting?'

'I – no.' She discovered that her mouth was tinder-dry and tried to moisten it. 'How could you? I – I didn't know you would come.'

He smiled then, but not in any way she found either comforting or even recognisable.

'No?'

'No.' She said it quickly and immediately knew it for a lie. Of course he would come. Taken all in all, how could he not? She had known he would come; what she had *not* known, and still did not, was why.

'You thought, having gone home to find my wife missing, I might have simply shrugged and sat down by the fire with a book and a night-cap?' he asked. 'Really?'

She swallowed. 'No.'

'No.' He dismounted and, without bothering to tether his horse, closed the space between them. The black brocade coat he had worn to the ball was mantled with dust and the right sleeve seemed to be partially adrift. The Garter had gone from his chest, as had the lace at his wrists, while the buckled shoes had been replaced, somewhat incongruously, by top-boots. And traces of last night's powder still clung to hair which appeared to have been at some stage hurriedly brushed and re-tied but was now hopelessly windswept.

Adeline absorbed these signs of swift and relentless pursuit with misgiving but continued to avoid his gaze, preferring to watch his horse canter away in the direction of the stables. Then her hand was taken in a too-firm clasp and he started to lead her away from the lake towards the house.

She said abruptly, 'I didn't mean you to follow me. I didn't think you'd want to.'

Rockliffe did not reply. The crippling weight of fear that had accompanied him all the way from London, followed by the unimaginable relief of finding her safe were transforming themselves, inevitably, into over-whelming anger; and it was choking him.

Keeping pace with him only through lack of choice, Adeline tried again.

'I'm sorry. I just c-couldn't stay in London.'

'So I gathered.' He stopped walking and swung her round to face him. 'You'll have to forgive the lack of subtlety – but it's been a very long night. I understood why you left Queensberry House – I was even glad of it. I did, however, expect you find you at home. Instead, I found no sign of you whatsoever and no one with any idea where you were. So I went to Hanover Square where Rosalind took a damned sight longer than necessary to admit that she didn't know where you'd gone but that Isabel Vernon might. Are you beginning to get the general idea? Do you even care?' His hands tightened on her shoulders and he went on, his voice hard and rapid, 'So; off to Jermyn Street where I had to kick my heels for twenty minutes while Isabel made herself presentable enough to come back downstairs ... and finally I learned that she'd lent you her carriage so that you could come here. Alone, through the night – without a thought for what you'd do if the coach lost a wheel or there were footpads on the road. And you didn't think I'd follow you? *Christ!*'

'I'm sorry. I – it didn't occur to me that you'd be worried. I thought ... I thought you m-might be relieved.'

'You didn't think full stop. If you had, we wouldn't be having this conversation at all – never mind having it in the bloody park.' He paused and drew a steadying breath. 'So far, I've lost my temper, my finesse and a particularly fine snuff-box. I've bruised my knuckles, winded my favourite mare and missed my breakfast. But what I have *not* done is to ride forty miles in a guise I can only describe as lamentable, merely for the pleasure of your conversation. Let's go.'

She met his eyes then and instantly regretted it as something in them made it impossible to look away. Through the maelstrom of her nerves, she summoned enough breath to say shakily, 'We need to talk first.'

'Why? So you can give me more evasions and platitudes and excuses? So you can find yet another way of saying no? I think not.'

Adeline realised then that he was a hairsbreadth away from losing his temper. She had seen him angry perhaps twice - and never for more than a minute or two; and though she had perhaps guessed that, beneath the suave exterior, lay something volcanic, she had never seen him lose control of it even for an instant. She said, 'I'm not saying no. If you'll -- '

'Well that will make a change. Or perhaps you're just not saying it yet.'

'-- listen to me for a minute -- '

'Adeline.' There was a white shade around his mouth and he looked very tired. 'I should perhaps explain that this isn't a suggestion or even an invitation – though I'm sure we'd both prefer it to retain the appearance of one. This time – with or without your consent - I'm going to do what I should have done months ago. And I think we both know by now that – whatever you may *say* – consent isn't going to be a problem.'

Her heart thudded against her ribs and her knees turned to jelly as he started walking again.

'I won't say no. I promise. But I need to tell you something before - ' She stopped, stumbling over her skirt as he towed her onwards. 'Tracy – please! Just wait a moment! Oh God – why are you *doing* this?'

'Why?' He stopped so suddenly she nearly fell. '*Why?*' he repeated bitterly, his hands gripping her arms while his gaze scorched her face.

'Because, damn it, it's the only thing I haven't already tried – and the only thing I have left.'

His hands fell away from her and he stepped back ... but not before Adeline saw and finally recognised the look in his eyes. Not temper – or not *just* that – but sickening, soul-searing hurt; a hurt so deep and, to her, so unexpected, that it sliced through her like a knife and caused her to drop nervelessly to her knees on the wet grass.

Through the raw ache in her throat, she said, 'Tracy – don't. I'm so sorry.'

'Am I supposed to be grateful for that? Well, let's think, shall we? I've done my utmost to give you the security I thought you needed and I've crucified myself being patient and not making demands of you. Oh – I know I said I married you for your body but even on our wedding-night I suspected that wasn't all I wanted. I thought that, if I could only wait, one day you might --' He broke off as if to steady himself, then went on. 'That one day you might want me, too. And you did, I think. Only by then, I'd committed the ultimate folly. I fell in love with you. I didn't say it, of course. Partly because I've never said it to any woman before – but mostly because I wanted some small sign that, when I did, you wouldn't react as if I'd merely offered you a second cup of coffee. But though I may not have put it into words, I tried to show you in every way I could. I loved you so much that that nothing else mattered. I'd have given you whatever you wanted – done anything you asked of me. Only you didn't ask me, did you? You confided in anyone *but* me. First Harry – which I could have forgiven; and then Jack – which I can't. As for allowing Horton to blackmail you rather than tell me the truth – do you think I couldn't or wouldn't have dealt with him? I don't think I'm a fool but I'll never understand why you found it so impossible to trust me.'

The tears that Adeline had refused to shed for herself came now in a steady, silent stream. She said huskily, 'I *didn't*. It was never that.'

He gave a short, abrasive laugh.

'That's a lie. If you'd trusted me, your hell-spawned cousin wouldn't have been able to stand in the middle Queensberry House telling – not just me, but half of London – that you'd been paying Richard Horton not to tell me you were illegitimate ... and that, when it all got too much for you, you took your troubles to Jack.' He stared at her over folded arms, breathing rather hard. 'To that, of course, we can add the not insignificant fact that, as soon as the whole sorry tale came to light, you did your damnedest to put yourself out of harm's way. And that, my sweet disappointment, hurt more than all the rest. But since you so obviously had expectations of me, it seemed churlish not to fulfil them – and so here I am.' Reaching down, he pulled her to her feet and added, 'Tears aren't going to solve anything ... but something else might.'

Her last thought as his head blotted out the light was that he did not understand; and then his mouth came down on hers with a savagery that scalded them both. For perhaps half a minute, all the hurtful rejections and suppressed longings of the past months flooded through Rockliffe in a conduit of untrammelled violence; and then it was gone as he suddenly realised that she wasn't even trying to resist him. She was simply crying – so silently that the only indication of it was the taste of salt on her mouth and in his. Somewhere in a corner of his mind was the thought that this was the first time he'd ever seen her shed a tear. Slowly, very slowly, he raised his head to look at her and then, his hands dropping to his sides, he said distantly, 'My apologies. That was ... unnecessary. Do you think we might go back to the house? They should have lit some fires by now and you're cold.'

And that, after everything that had gone before, completely over-set her. Without stopping to think, she said baldly, 'I love you.'

The shock of it drove the blood from his skin. There was a pause while he fought for control and then he said raggedly, 'Congratulations. I really didn't see *that* one coming.'

She wasn't surprised that he didn't believe her. She hadn't, after all, made a particularly convincing job of telling him. His response, however, was alarming. She took a step towards him and opened her mouth to speak, only to stop dead as he flung up his hand.

'No. Don't come any nearer.' His voice was clipped now and completely impervious and his eyes resembled discs of obsidian. 'Let us cling to the charitable assumption that you made that perfectly witless remark out of a desire to repair my shattered equilibrium. Very well. It didn't quite work but I thank you for the kind thought.' He bowed with exquisite grace. 'I am going inside. You can join me or not – as you wish.'

His careful courtesy left her stricken and dumb so that she could do nothing but watch as he walked away from her towards the house. Then, finally, she realised that it was time to assert herself - that if she didn't do it now, there might never be another opportunity. Gathering up her skirts in both hands, she ran after him and grabbed his sleeve.

'You can listen to me here or in the house – I don't care which – but you *are* going to listen!'

He shook off her hand and continued walking. 'In due course, perhaps. But not now.'

'Why not? I've listened to you ... and I'll go on listening for as long as you've anything left to say to me. Don't I get a turn? I said I love you – and I do. That's not so terrible, is it?'

'Leave it, Adeline. The veneer is somewhat fragile and may crack at any moment. If you are wise, you'll stop this while you still can.'

'But I don't want to stop it. I want you to let me explain. Is that so unreasonable?'

They had reached the house. Rockliffe laid his hand on the door-latch and then, closing his eyes for a moment, drew a long bracing breath. Finally he said, 'Very well. But first I intend to wash and change – and, since that gown is soaked, I suggest you do the same. I also require coffee. Then, if I must, I'll listen.'

*

Inside the house, he ascertained that fires had been lit upstairs, requested hot water for washing and asked for coffee to be brought up to her Grace's sitting-room. Then, as he and Adeline climbed the stairs, he said, 'If you want to talk in private – and I presume you do – your boudoir is the best place. So don't read too much into it.' And he vanished into his room.

Adeline's fingers having inexplicably become thumbs, she had to wait for the girl with the hot water before she could get out of the ruined peacock gown. Then, telling the maid to find her something - anything - clean to wear, she washed her face and hands and tried to get a brush through her hair. It was only then that she saw the gown that the maid had laid out for her; the same pale blue dimity she'd worn on their first morning here in the summer ... the day she'd gone downstairs to find Tracy with his hair unpowdered and he'd swept her outside to see The Trojan. The day she'd first realised that she loved him. For a moment, Adeline stood quite still, forcing back a wave of misery and telling herself that it was only a dress. Then, unwilling to waste any more time, she put it on and, fastening her hair loosely back in a ribbon, returned to the sitting-room. It was empty. She sat down by the coffee-pot, wishing that her hands would stop shaking and that she knew what she was going to say.

Had she but known it, she need not have hurried. Aware that he needed to regain at least a semblance of composure, Rockliffe was taking his time. He threw his coat at the bed with a force that sent it slithering off the other side to the floor. Then, stripping off the rest of his clothing, he washed away the dust of the road, shaved without managing to cut his throat and rinsed the last traces of powder from his hair. And throughout it all, he tried to make sense of just one thing; why his immediate reaction to Adeline's declaration had been disbelief. He thought of half a dozen reasons, none of which satisfied him. Finally, his mind calmer but no clearer, he pulled on clean clothes and, having no further excuse to linger, walked through the door to the boudoir.

Adeline looked across at him, taking in the snowy-fresh shirt and the damp ebony hair, and forgot to breathe. Then, waiting until he sat down, she poured coffee and said 'They've sent up some breakfast if you'd -- '

'No.' The thought of food made him nauseous. 'Thank you.'

'No. I couldn't either.'

He took the cup she offered him. 'Then perhaps we could get this over with. I'd like to sleep for a couple of hours before I start back.'

'*What?*'

'It's necessary. I can't reduce the harm from here.' He paused, drank the now-tepid coffee and grimaced. 'So. What did you want to say to me?'

There was only one thought in her head so she voiced it. 'Don't go.'

'I need to speak to Dominic and ... yes, to Charles Fox, I think. His ear is perpetually to the ground,' said Rockliffe thoughtfully, as if he hadn't heard her. 'And I'll put in an appearance at White's. That should silence a few tongues.'

'Don't go,' she said again, this time more urgently. 'Please don't.'

He looked at her for a moment and then sighed.

'Adeline – I'm here because I had to satisfy myself that you were safe. *You're* here, as I understand it, because you wanted ...' He stopped briefly, then resumed a little less smoothly, 'You're here because you wanted to be away from me for a time. So my returning to town --'

'No. I *don't* want that,' she interrupted, trying to quell the unreasoning panic that was taking hold of her. 'Last night, perhaps. But not now. Not any more. Please don't go. I c-couldn't bear it.'

Rockliffe frowned a little.

'It would be helpful,' he said dryly, 'if you could make up your mind. However. This is getting us nowhere. You wanted to talk – so talk. And, afterwards, we'll see. Say what you wish. I'm listening.'

She collected his gaze and held it. Then, summoning all her courage, 'I I -- '

'You love me. Yes, so you said. I suggest, however, that you work up to that gradually. What else?'

Not without difficulty, Adeline found a shred of her old astringency.

'Tracy – you're entitled to make this difficult. I accept that. But if you want me to be brief, you can't interrupt every second or third word.'

A flicker of something more like his usual expression passed through his eyes and then was gone. He said, 'I stand corrected. Please ... do go on.'

She drew a deep breath and said, 'I should begin by pointing out that I don't expect anything I say to mend matters. After last night, I know that nothing can. But I can't leave you thinking that I don't care for you – or trust you – or want you. Because I do. And that's why I didn't tell you about Richard. I thought, rather naively as it turns out, that I could deal with him myself.'

'But you didn't deal with him yourself, did you? You told Jack.'

She shook her head. 'No – or not in the way you mean it. He found out by chance about a week ago. He – he happened to be watching me when Richard was demanding yet more money; and he persuaded me to tell him *why* because he's marrying Althea.'

It occurred to Rockliffe then that, if *he* had been watching instead of keeping her at a distance, the story might have been different. He said, 'Go on.'

'Perhaps I had better start at the beginning?'

His face was inscrutable. 'I think you had.'

She nodded and said, 'It began when you went away that first time --'

'To consult with Sir Roland.'

Her eyes widened. 'Oh. Is that how you found out about ... about my mother?'

'It is how I confirmed my suspicions. But that's beside the point, just now. Go on.'

'Well ... you may remember how we parted that morning.'

'Vividly. Is it important?'

'Yes.' The merest hint of colour stained her cheeks. 'I didn't want you to leave. I nearly asked you not to ... but I wasn't quite brave enough.'

'Asking me to stay required courage? Why? You asked quickly enough just now.'

'That day was different. Because ... because that wouldn't have been all I was asking.' She looked down at her hands. 'I think you must have known that.'

Less to make it hard for her than to see what she would say, Rockliffe said negligently, 'Remind me.'

He watched her breath catch and her colour deepen. Then, to her credit, she looked him in the face and said, 'I wanted you to make love to me – you have no idea how much I wanted it. And if you had, I would have told you then that I ... how I felt about you. I should say that it never occurred to me – not then, nor at any time since – that you m-might love me. I couldn't help hoping that one day ... but mostly I couldn't see why you would.' She paused and made a small dismissive gesture. 'Anyway. I didn't ask and you left. But it didn't matter because I thought ... I thought that when you came back ... only then we went to Ranelagh and Richard said I was a bastard and demanded five hundred guineas. And that was how it started.'

'Did you believe him?'

'Not entirely – but I couldn't be sure he was lying. He showed me the letter my mother had written when she eloped. So I paid him and hoped that was the end of it. Then I tried to come to terms – not just with what he'd said – but what it meant.' Her hands clenched in her lap and she bent her head again. 'I thought about all the things you'd put up with already because of our marriage; the gossip, the disapproval of your sister and the acquisition of my unsavoury relatives. I knew I ought to tell you about Richard – I even *wanted* to. But it didn't seem right to burden you with anything else. More importantly, I had to find a way to stop your name being dragged in the mud because of me.' She managed a wry smile. 'I wanted to protect you because I loved you. It might have been foolish of me – that's how it was. I suppose I thought that what you didn't know couldn't hurt you.'

His eyes narrowed a little and he said, 'A singularly naïve notion. And no doubt you also thought that keeping me in the dark and at arm's length wouldn't hurt me either?'

She flinched. 'I didn't realise that it could. If I'd known, perhaps I might have behaved differently. I don't know. But, at the time, I just felt that letting you make love to me without knowing whether what Richard said was true or not, would be the worst kind of deceit.'

Seconds ticked by in silence and finally Rockliffe said, 'Very well. Bizarre though I find it, I believe I have followed your reasoning thus far.' He paused. Then, 'Why did you run?'

Adeline hesitated and then, reluctantly, told the truth.

'When Diana said I'd sent Jack to my uncle, you looked at me as though ... as though --'

'I know how I looked. It was designed to get you out of Queensberry House before things got even uglier than they already were. However, if I'd known it would send you headlong into Kent, I might have thought better of it. Was that the only reason?'

'Not quite. I couldn't face anyone.'

'Not even me?'

'Especially not you. How could I? Thanks to my stupidity and Diana's talent for eavesdropping – at least, I assume that's how she found out - you're now the subject of a particularly sordid scandal. And it's irreparable. So saying that I'm sorry hardly seems enough, does it? And if nothing else has killed any feeling you might have had for me, this can't fail to have done so.'

Rockliffe looked back at her for a moment and then, rising, walked away to stare out of the window. He said quietly, 'You've never understood me at all, have you? The things you feared never existed and I came here with the intention of proving it to you ... though I would undoubtedly have regretted doing it in anger.' He paused and then, apparently at random, asked, 'Earlier, in the park - why were you crying?'

The unexpectedness of it unnerved her.

'For you,' she said faintly. 'I didn't know, until today, that I'd hurt you so much ... and I couldn't bear it. I still can't.'

Something shifted in his chest and he turned slowly. 'And that's the only reason?'

'Yes. Why do you doubt it?' Adeline stood up, facing him across the room. 'Do you still think I'm – what did you say? – repairing your shattered equilibrium? Or do you believe, as you remarked some time ago, that I'm just intent on hanging on to your rank and your money?'

'No. I don't think either of those things. And, for the second of them, I apologise.'

'Don't. It's just - if you *did* think that - there would be nothing left to say.' She could feel tears threatening and resolutely swallowed them. 'Eight years ago, I was dazzled by you – and I still am. Only now it isn't only your looks and charm; it's your innate kindness and courtesy and endless consideration ... things that never failed even when I didn't deserve them.' She hesitated and then said, 'And at this moment, I only want two things from you; belief ... and the possibility of forgiveness.'

'Ah.' The merest hint of a rueful smile lit his eyes. 'Despite anything I may have said to the contrary, there is virtually nothing you could do that I would find unforgivable – and certainly not this. No. The only forgiveness you need is your own.'

'I can't,' she said, unevenly. 'I *can't* forgive myself. And I don't know how you can either.'

'Don't you?'

'After all this? No.'

'Then perhaps some of what I said earlier escaped you.' The smile touched the corners of his mouth. 'Leaving that aside for the moment, let us move on to the thing you want me to believe … and which, I suspect, I may now be ready to hear.'

Adeline hesitated, seeing the smile but afraid, as yet, to rely on it. Holding his gaze with her own, she said, 'That I love you. So much that I don't know how to tell you.' She paused and then added simply, 'You stop my breath. You always have.'

Rockliffe's heart slammed against his ribs. This was more, so very much more, than he had ever hoped for. He looked at her, reading the longing and uncertainty in the wide, blue-green eyes; and, holding out his hand to her, he said gently, 'Do you think you might consider coming over here and repeating that?'

Still she hesitated, unable to believe he could mean it. 'What are you saying?'

'I'm saying I'd like you to banish last night from your mind. It doesn't matter. What *does* matter is that you have said something I was afraid I might never hear – and that, finally, I believe it. So I'd like … I would really like to hold you and hear you say it again.'

The tears she had been holding back were suddenly sparkling on her lashes.

'Tracy …'

In three swift strides he was across the room to fold her in his arms.

'Don't, darling. It's all right. I meant what I said before. I love you.'

Adeline's fingers clutched his shirt and she pressed her face against his shoulder, feeling his heart beating under her hand. She said painfully, 'I don't understand – after everything - how you can.'

'Hush. The faults were as much mine as yours. Nothing outside this room matters.'

'It does. Of course it does. That's why you want to go back to town.'

'It was – but not any more. I'm not leaving you now. Don't cry.'

Relief washed over her. She said, 'I love you so very much. How could I not?'

'I can think of a few reasons,' he murmured. 'Most recently, the way I behaved earlier. I've waited for what has seemed a very long time to tell you that I loved you ... and then to hurl the words at you in temper ... well, for that, I can only apologise.'

'Please don't. There's no need. You had every right --'

'No I didn't. No right at all and only the vestige of an excuse - in that I had been more frightened than ever in my life before that I wouldn't find you safe. Or, worse, not at all.' Drawing her down to sit on the sofa, he dropped on one knee before her so that he could look into her face and, holding both of her hands, said with a smile, 'I offered to do this once before, if you remember. You should have let me.'

Adeline shook her head and tried to pull him towards her.

'No. Not yet. Look at me.' And, when the lucent, dark-fringed eyes locked with his, he said, 'I once told Rosalind I was looking for a duchess. It wasn't true. What I wanted was a wife who would occupy every corner of my heart and set my blood on fire; a woman I could make the very core of my being and who I hoped might feel the same about me. When you and I married, very little of that existed between us and yet I had an unreasoning instinct that, one day, it would. This, finally, is that day. I love you and want you more than I dreamed was possible ... and nothing will ever hurt you again while I have breath in my body.' He paused, the dark eyes still looking deep into hers. 'And now it's your turn to believe. Do you?'

She nodded and, freeing one of her hands in order to lay it gently against his cheek, said, 'Yes. But I'd like ... I'd really like you to hold me and say it again.'

Laughter stirred in his eyes and he said, 'What – *all* of it?'

But he rose to sit beside her and settled her within the shelter of his arm. He felt her coil even closer, her face against his throat and her hand reaching for his free one. His fingers tangled with hers and his thumb brushed lightly and rhythmically over the inside of her wrist. Peace settled over them.

For a time, he said nothing, content to simply hold her while the tensions of the last hours subsided a little and a new tenderness welled up in him. But finally he said carefully, 'You haven't asked ... but you may wish to know that what I said last night in the ballroom was true. You are not illegitimate. You should also know that it wouldn't make the slightest difference to me if you were.'

She lifted her head to look up at him. 'You've met my mother?'

'Yes.' His eyes travelled to her mouth and then back again before temptation got the better of him. 'And, in due course, I'll tell you about that. But not quite yet.'

'No. I don't want to think any more ... I just want to be with you.'

That gave temptation an unfair advantage. Turning her slightly and releasing her hand in order to cup her face, Rockliffe bent his head and kissed her. Gently, lightly, his mouth caressed rather than demanded ... and was immediately rewarded as Adeline's arms went round him and her body curved into his.

By the time he finally released her to look into her face, the blue-green eyes were filled with something that sent his hunger for her soaring. But still he forced himself to say, 'You must be exhausted. Do you think you could sleep for a while?'

'Perhaps.' She paused, seeming to consider it. 'Perhaps. But not alone.'

Unsure exactly what she was suggesting - but suspecting that, if she meant it literally, it might present him with certain difficulties, Rockliffe said cautiously, 'We could try that, if you wish.'

'I do. I don't want to be apart from you just now.' Adeline leaned back against his shoulder and sought his hand again. 'And then, of course, I'll need help with my laces.'

And that was when he knew. A slight tremor of laughter ran through him and he said, 'Ah. I should perhaps point out that, by the time I've finished helping you out of your clothes, sleep might not be an option.'

'No?' Slipping out of his arms, she rose and drew him to his feet. Then, smiling a little shyly but with no hint of uncertainty, 'Then we'll sleep later. Afterwards.'

He looked at her for a long moment, his expression already making her blood run faster. He said, 'Adeline ... forget, if you can, what I might want. Is this what *you* want?'

'Yes. Oh – yes,' she replied on something between a sob and a laugh. 'Please.'

Rockliffe loosed the breath he was not aware he had been holding and, with an almost imperceptible shake of his head, murmured wickedly, 'You might consider saving that word until later.'

Lifting his hand, he gently pulled the ribbon from her hair to let it fall from his fingers ... and waited, smiling, while she reached up and mirrored his gesture. Then, entirely without haste, he gathered her into his arms and let his mouth find hers.

Having wanted her so much for so long, he had always known that – when the time came – control might be an issue. He had also always known that, regardless of that, he wanted to make the pleasure last as long as was possible ... primarily for Adeline, but also for himself. So now, holding her lightly in the circle of one arm and letting his other hand slide up into her hair, he teased her mouth with tantalising slowness until he felt her go weak; and then, releasing her mouth, he forged a lazy trail of small kisses along her jaw to the place where her pulse was hammering. She made a tiny, involuntary sound and her arms tightened about him.

Still with the same unhurried ease, Rockliffe moulded her against his body and sought her mouth again, this time letting the kiss gradually deepen and intensify. Adeline drew an unsteady breath and plunged her fingers into his hair. Quite deliberately, he broke the kiss to say with a smile, 'Today is ours – and tonight, too; and I am in no hurry.' And kissed her again.

Sparks were exploding in Adeline's veins and her bones seemed to be dissolving. Everything outside the circle of his arms ceased to exist and she couldn't tell if it was his heart she could feel beating or her own. She did not know when his fingers found and unfastened the laces of her gown – was only aware that he had done so when it slithered down to pool on the floor at her feet and his mouth travelled down to sear the skin of her shoulder. Her head fell back, offering him the creamy column of her throat ... and, slowly, sensuously, he took it.

Some exquisite minutes later, her stays and petticoats followed the gown. Then, for the first time, Rockliffe let his hands explore the slender line of her back and the curve of her waist and hips though the thin linen shift. Shaken by pulses and her breathing hopelessly disrupted, Adeline gasped and, releasing his hair, slid her hands inside his shirt. For the space of a heartbeat, he remained perfectly still and then, having re-established his control over the desire that was roaring through him like a rip-tide, he pulled the shirt off and cast it aside.

'*Oh*,' said Adeline helplessly, as she discovered the smooth warmth of his chest. 'Tracy ... I ... I want you so much.'

That produced a sudden urge to hurry but he forced it back and, with a dark, gleaming smile, said, 'And you shall have me, my darling – but not, quite, yet.' And, sweeping her up in his arms, he carried her through the door to his own room.

Even then, though his hands continued their leisurely exploration, he did not immediately remove her shift. He even, from time to time, paused to simply hold her face in his hands and smile at her. And when, at long last, he slid the shift from her shoulders, his eyes feasted on her with an expression which made her tremble and sent heat flooding through her body as he said unevenly, 'Oh yes. *Definitely* worth waiting for.'

Without taking his eyes from hers, he lifted her into his bed and discarded the rest of his clothes in a way which suggested that she was welcome to look if she wished.

So she looked and felt her breath leak away. She had known that, beneath the elegant clothes, lay a well-proportioned body. The reality, however, was beyond anything she could have imagined. Almost unaware that she did so, she murmured the only word that seemed appropriate ... but did not see, as startled laughter flared in his eyes, that he had heard her.

Laughter which vanished as he drew her into his arms and flesh met flesh.

Adeline's breath caught and she traced the muscles of his shoulders and back while her mouth burned kisses against his throat. Leaving her free to explore his body as she wished, Rockliffe allowed his own caresses to become gradually more intimate, his mouth following his hands until every inch of her skin was on fire as he led her through the labyrinth of desire towards the well of delight that was its core. There was no uncertainty in her and no reticence. Instead, she offered herself willingly and without reservation, enabling him to relish every catch in her breath, every gasp of pleasure and every tiny tremor which ran through her. Her response was so open ... so indescribably sweet, that it almost undid him. And when she was beyond everything except sobbing two incoherent words, one of which was his name ... when he knew that, like himself, she was very close to the edge ... he imprisoned her hands in one of his own and, using the other to brush the hair from her face, said raggedly, 'Slowly now, darling. Look at me.'

Then, releasing her hands but continuing to hold her gaze, he moved slowly and with infinite care into the molten, silk of her body. Her eyes told him when he hurt her ...and, moments later, revealed surprised wonder at feeling him fill her. He waited. And finally, just when his control was starting to falter, the shift in her expression let him know that she was ready for more. Rockliffe kissed her ... and gave it, sending her spiralling back to the edge; and, when he knew she was there, he abandoned the restraints he had placed on himself so that they might make the fall together.

'Heart of my heart, I love you.'

Later, quite a lot later, with her head pillowed on his shoulder and her breathing slowly returning to normal, she said huskily, 'I didn't know. I never guessed it could be like that. Is it always so – so -- ?'

'No. Nor even close.' Rockliffe felt a tear drip on to his chest and, though he thought he understood, still looked into her face to make sure. Then, satisfied, he said plaintively, 'Adeline ... if you're going to cry every time I make love to you, I think my self-esteem could be seriously damaged.'

A tiny uncertain laugh rippled through her.

'You know it's not ... I'm not ...' She stopped and stifled a yawn. 'I don't know what I am. I can't think.'

'Good.' He dropped a light kiss on her hair. 'Go to sleep.'

Her fingers sought his hand. 'You won't go away?'

'No. I won't go away. Go to sleep.'

Adeline fell asleep very quickly. Rockliffe, his brain resuming its function rather quicker than he would have liked, lay awake for some time before sleep finally over-came him. And then knew nothing for several hours.

He awoke to find Adeline propped on one elbow, her hair straying wildly around her shoulders and her eyes devouring his face. Smiling a little, he said, 'Good morning. How long have you been staring at me?'

'Not long. Not long enough.'

'Of course.' Laughter - mocking, tantalising and real - lit his eyes as he sat up and pulled her to him. 'I've been called many things. But *beautiful*? Seriously?'

Adeline flushed a little. 'I didn't think you'd heard. You weren't meant to. But if you really want to know, then yes ... seriously.'

'I don't know whether to be flattered ... or worried.' Beneath the sheet, his hand was investigating the silky skin of her thigh. 'But I'm glad you weren't ... disappointed.'

'Yes. I'm sure that must have been a relief,' she retorted, making him laugh again. She lay quietly for a moment, her body already in turmoil from the as yet unfamiliar delight of having him naked beside her; and then she said hesitantly, 'Tracy ... what will we do about the scandal?'

'Allow it to burn itself out. Don't worry about it. It will do so soon enough – or something else will come along to eclipse it. And I imagine your part is already paling into insignificance beside Diana's remarkable descent into social ruin and palpable insanity.'

'What do you think they'll do about her?'

'Lock her in the attic?' His fingers moved lazily on to the curve of waist and hip. 'I really don't care.'

'And Richard?'

'Ah. Yes. Him.' His hand stilled and his voice acquired a certain grimness. 'He won't bother you again. He knows what will happen if he does.'

Adeline angled her head to look into his face. She said, 'What did you do?'

Rockliffe sighed. 'I think I broke his jaw. I certainly relieved him of a couple of teeth.'

Startled into laughter, she sat up. 'You *hit* him? In the middle of Queensberry House?'

'I hit him – in the middle of Queensberry House,' he agreed, pulling her back beside him in order to continue beguiling her. 'Crude, of course ... but oddly satisfying. Harry was most impressed. But then, Harry would be.'

The levity was back in his voice and his fingers were trailing enticingly up her rib-cage. Not without difficulty, Adeline pursued a sudden thought.

'Oh God – *Nell*! What have you done about Nell?'

'Left her with Dominic and Rosalind – where she'll stay until you and I return from our honeymoon.'

'I don't wish to cavil,' she murmured unevenly, 'but isn't it a little late for that?'

'Not at all. I want you to myself for a time. And how else are we to escape Lucilla?' His knuckles brushed her breast with exquisite lightness making her breath catch. 'I thought Paris ought to be far enough.'

Giving up the unequal struggle, Adeline turned towards him and slid her hands slowly up into his hair. 'Anywhere you like.'

'Paris, then,' The dark eyes looked deep into hers. 'And from there, as and when it pleases you, to a small farm that I know of in the region of Nevers where a certain very charming lady is waiting to meet you.' He paused for one lingering kiss before stretching down to retrieve his maltreated coat from the floor. 'Meanwhile, speaking of Paris ... I bought something for you there that I've been carrying with me ever since, waiting for the perfect moment. And having you in my arms like this ... with a look in your eyes that stops my heart ... I can't imagine a moment more perfect than this one.' And he slid the ring on to her finger beside her wedding-band.

Tears misted her eyes, less at the beauty of the betrothal ring than the thought which, at that particular time, had prompted him to buy it. She said, 'I don't ... I don't know what to say to you.'

'You could say *'Thank you, Tracy – I'll wear it always*.' Or you could simply kiss me. Or better still,' he murmured with a disturbingly wicked smile as his hand slid enticingly down her body, 'you could do both.'

So she did.

Author's Note

As a point of interest regarding Rock's Christian name ... are two possible derivations of the male form of Tracy. One is from Norman French, meaning 'of the domaine of Thracius'; the other is Irish-Gaelic, meaning 'warlike'.

The female form of the name did not become popular until 1940 with the advent of Tracy Samantha Lord in *The Philadelphia Story*.

Stella Riley

Printed in Poland
by Amazon Fulfillment
Poland Sp. z o.o., Wrocław